William Frederick Deacon

The Adventures of a Bashful Irishman

William Frederick Deacon

The Adventures of a Bashful Irishman

ISBN/EAN: 9783337122331

Printed in Europe, USA, Canada, Australia, Japan

Cover: Foto ©Andreas Hilbeck / pixelio.de

More available books at **www.hansebooks.com**

THE ADVENTURES

OF A

BASHFUL IRISHMAN.

"All men have their foibles: mine is too much modesty."
GOODNATURED MAN.

𝔑𝔢𝔴 𝔈𝔡𝔦𝔱𝔦𝔬𝔫.

LONDON:
ROUTLEDGE, WARNE, AND ROUTLEDGE,
FARRINGDON STREET.
1862.

ADVENTURES

OF

A BASHFUL IRISHMAN.

BOOK THE FIRST.

THE ADVENTURER.

CHAPTER I.

INTRODUCTORY AND APOLOGETIC.

I AM the most unfortunate of men. Some people have been ruined by their candour, and some by their cunning —this man by his parsimony, and that by his extravagance ; but I am the victim of—modesty ! The O'Blarneys of Connemara (the very prefix O is symbolical of *mauvaise honte*) were always a bashful race ; would that they had degenerated into impudence in my person ! But, alas ! I could never look a bailiff in the face without crimsoning like a peony, nor pass a sheriff's officer without instinctively averting my head. I am a living evidence that there is a certain something in the climate of Erin peculiarly favourable to the growth of modesty. In a word, I am the personification of a blush !

The censorious reader—but for him I write not—will doubtless attribute my misfortunes to anything rather than my bashfulness. He will say, perhaps, that my autobiography is throughout an illustration of rare impudence and roguery : he, however, who is blessed with philosophic discernment—who knows the exact relations between

1

cause and effect, and how to trace the one up to the other through all the various ramifications that lie between—will see at once that every calamity which it has been my lot to endure may, directly or indirectly, be traced to its first great cause—modesty !

But to the point. In the following autobiographical sketch, which, I should premise, is the mere transcript of a fragmentary journal that I have for years amused myself by keeping, I have held it as the first of duties to adhere religiously to truth. So scrupulous have I been in this respect, that I have not even spared myself, but exposed my occasional little irregularities of conduct—for who among the best of us is perfect ?—with a minuteness and sincerity which I trust will be duly appreciated. Of my enemies, too, and of the frequent unpleasant incidents to which their machinations gave rise, I have everywhere spoken with a calmness and apathy which the lapse of nearly fourteen years has engendered in a disposition once more sensitive than an aspen leaf. Had I chosen to resign fact for fiction, I might easily have manufactured a more acceptable work ; but my conscience would not allow of such an unworthy compromise : hence my narrative contains no extraordinary nor pathetic adventures ; it has neither continuous interest nor artfully-elaborated plot ; but abounds in "passages that lead to nothing," and characters, or rather shadows of character, that come and go without a why or wherefore, like the phantoms that flitted before the eyes of Macbeth in the cavern of Hecate. But thus is it with human nature. To few is granted the opportunity of making intimate and enduring connexions ; by far the majority of us are like travellers at an inn, who, before they have had time to become acquainted with each other's habits, manners, modes of thought, action and so forth, are compelled to hurry away north, south, east, and west, never perhaps to re-assemble.

CHAPTER II.

THE YOUNG IDEA TAUGHT HOW TO SHOOT.

My name is O'Blarney. I was born beside a hedge, under an umbrella, during a shower, about a stone's throw from my father's farm-house, in the immediate vicinity of Galway. The night previous to my introduction into this vale of tears was marked by a singular occurrence. My mother, a plump philanthropist of forty, dreamed that she was delivered of a *rope*, a circumstance which the gossips in the neighbourhood one and all agreed was ominous of a rather unpleasant event in my career.

My father was a middle-aged farmer, in the usual indifferent circumstances. In his notions of business this gentleman was a staunch advocate of the free-trade system, and, from his vicinity to the sea-coast, he had frequent opportunities of reducing his favourite theory to practice. He was not, however, one of your vulgar, showy tradesmen, who make a boast of their profits, and carry on business, as if from ostentation, beneath the glaring eye of day ; far otherwise. He was quiet, diffident, and reserved in his nature, shy in alluding to his gains, and allowed night only to be the witness of his more important occupations.

Such being the twofold nature of his vocation—that is to say, being a farmer by day and a smuggler by night—it must be manifest that he had little or no time to throw away on my education, and I, accordingly, shot up from infancy to boyhood as wild and undisciplined as a Connemara colt.

The history of all childhood is pretty nearly the same ; I shall therefore pass it by, and come at once to the period when I attained my seventeenth year. At this epoch I was placed in the shop of a certain village doctor, by name Killquick, a waggish, good-humoured little fellow, who was famous throughout the district for the invention of divers specifics, by the help of which he wrought the most surprising cures. As the doctor in his personal appearance passed the verge of the extraordinary, and approached to the miraculous, I must pause to give a sketch of him. He had the head of a giant fixed upon the shoulders of a dwarf. His eyes were of a gooseberry colour; his nose was gathered up in a bunch in the middle, just as if Dame Nature in a frolicsome mood had tied it in a double knot; his teeth were tusks in shape and size; he had a split in his upper lip, which enabled him to give a full and perfect development to the broadest grin that ever threw a stranger into hysterics; his mouth was not so much a mouth as a huge gash scored at random across his face; and he had two big red ears, which projected from each side of his head like the lamp-lights of a mail-coach.

Next to the doctor, the greatest curiosity in the county was the doctor's horse; which, having long been the subject of its master's experiments, had been physicked into a most promising state of atrophy. The very leanest hackney coach-horse that ever crawled would have blushed to be seen in company with such a prodigy of attenuation. It was just the sort of animal you would expect to see grazing on the Great Zaara. Of course the doctor was proud of such an evidence of his medical skill, and it was as rich a treat as eyes could behold, to see him mounted on its back, swaying to and fro like a scarecrow in a steady wind, while every little ragged urchin for miles round would take flight at his approach, if only to look were to be physicked.

Under this original my genius for pharmacy (which at a subsequent period, as the reader will find, I turned to excellent account in South Wales) developed itself with such signal precocity that the doctor spoke of me everywhere among his patients as the most promising pupil he ever had; and even went so far as to intrust me with the secret of his recipes, at which, in process of time, I fully equalled, if not surpassed him. Moreover he imbued me with my first notions of the drama : for, strange to tell, he imagined he had a gift that way ; and whenever a new company made its appearance at Galway, he always took me with him to witness their performances. His favourite character was Hamlet, which, he contended, should be played in a strait waistcoat, as furnishing a lively and original comment on the peculiarities of the character.

It is a pity that such a versatile genius should die and "leave the world no copy ;" but doctors, like the rest of mankind, are mortal—more especially when they are in the habit of taking their own physic—and accordingly it came to pass that my excellent master quitted his patients in this world, to rejoin those who crowded the other, in consequence of having, in a moment of forgetfulness, drunk a hearty draught of one of his own elixirs.

From his hands I was transferred to those of Father O'Flannaghan—a round, rosy, comfortable ecclesiastic of the old school, who, at my mother's express instigation, invited me to take up my abode with him. This was a change in my condition, if not for the more agreeable, at least for the more edifying ; for the ghostly father was clever, and even learned ; possessed a decent miscellaneous library ; taught me arithmetic, together with a smattering of English, French, and Latin, as also how to manufacture whisky-punch. I owe to this worthy man my first fit of inebriety. The debt is not considerable, certainly ; but, in recapitulating past civilities, it is but justice to acknowledge it.

Unlike the generality of Catholic priests, Father O'Flannaghan had seen much of the world, and, as is usually the case with such men, piqued himself not a little on his discernment of character. He early prophesied my rise in life, from having marked the attention with which I listened to his remarks, and the facility with which I adapted myself to his habits. The respect of youth is the most effective compliment that can be paid to age. Worldly natures are peculiarly alive to this flattery.

They imagine it the outpouring of artlessness and sincerity, which experience has taught them it is al lbut vain to expect from those of their own age and standing. Many a shrewd, experienced veteran have I seen, whom Machiavel himself would have failed to hoodwink, become the dupe of unsuspected boyhood.

Father O'Flannaghan felt my deference to his opinions as a compliment in its fullest acceptation, and showed that he felt it, by the way in which he repaid me with exhortation. " Ever bear in mind, Terence," he was often in the habit of saying, " that the world is large enough for us all, and that, in order to succeed, it is only necessary that we desire it.   True, society is a sea full of rocks and breakers ; still, he who trims his sails according to wind and weather will be pretty sure to navigate it with safety. Most men, however, quit the port in the ' Shippe of Fools' —that is to say, start on their voyage in what they call a spirit of truth and independence.   Now these, though plausible, are silly terms, and mean neither more nor less than that they are resolved to set up their own judgment in opposition to that of the world.   You, I should hope, will be guilty of no such presumption. Clever as you may deem yourself, the world is cleverer still ; so take my advice — yield to it, flatter it, fall in with its humours, and adopt its prejudices, till you have made it your friend for life.   A man who quarrels with society, O Terence ! is like a schoolboy, who hopes to spite his master by going without his own dinner.

"The great object of existence is the acquisition of power. Gain this conscientiously if you can ; but, at all events, gain it—for the world respects you solely for your influence ; it has neither leisure nor inclination to canvass the means by which you gained it.   Remember, also, that man is the natural prey of man, and that, if you refrain from turning your friend to a rational and profitable account, you will do him no service, but yourself much injury, for some other less fastidious individual will be sure to step into your position.   But, whatever you do, be it with friend or foe, always do it in what Englishmen call ' a business-like fashion,' for the word ' business' has a talismanic virtue, and, like charity, covereth a multitude of rogueries.

"Moreover, in your intercourse with society, be careful to reserve your smiles for those above, and your frowns for those beneath you. If, however, you cannot reconcile it to your innate sense of virtue to be perpetually flattering your superiors, you can easily make up matters with your conscience, by telling truths by wholesale to your inferiors. There is one more point which I cannot too strongly impress upon your attention. Never forget that you were born and bred a Catholic. Without religion, O my child! vain are the hopes of man! *Dixi :* I have done."

Such, with few or no variations, was the usual substance of Father O'Flannaghan's rather questionable admonitions, which, by being frequently repeated in terms of kindness and good-humour, produced a strong but imperceptible impression on my mind—indeed, I may almost say, moulded my entire habits of thought and action.

I continued with this good man up to the period of my twenty-first birthday, when he was unexpectedly summoned to take his seat in paradise, beside St. Peter ; and I returned to my father's roof, wiser, certainly more self-confident, and more ambitious, but quite as poor as when I quitted it. About this period, too, another visitation befell me in the death of my mother, who was accidentally killed by her own brother, in one of those pugnacious moods with which the best of Irishmen are at times afflicted. It is soothing to reflect that the worthy lady died in excellent spirits, and that, on the Sunday following her wake, one-half the parish appeared at chapel with their heads bound up.

CHAPTER III.

EARLY DEVELOPMENT OF CHARACTER.

PASSING over a host of unimportant incidents, I approach the period of my first love. My first love! What a world of ineptitude and insanity is comprised in these two words! How many wits have they set a wool-gathering! How many, qualified for Bedlam! The object of my attachment was the only daughter of the seneschal of the manor. She was a graceful, sprightly young creature, a piquant mixture of the coquette and the prude; with an eye blacker than a Berkshire sloe; hair soft and dusky as twilight; a mouth small, flexible, expressive, and in the angles of which an arch smile perpetually nestled; a bust formed on the purest classic model; and a figure tall, slim, yet just sufficiently plump and rounded to convey the idea of perfect health and symmetry.

I had been in the habit of encountering Miss Mahoney in the course of my daily strolls about the neighbourhood, and, though I cannot take it on myself to assert that she made me the object of any *very* marked scrutiny, yet a thousand casual acts of attention made me fancy that I was not altogether indifferent to her.

When once this flattering notion had fixed itself in my thoughts, it is astonishing how, chamelion-like, it contrived to feed and thrive on air. There is nothing like idleness to nourish the sentimentalities and conceits of youth. Once or twice Miss Mahoney called at Father O'Flannaghan's cottage—I could not choose but remember the visit, for my revered preceptor happened to be seriously indisposed at the time—and on these occasions she never failed to intreat me to watch over her father's friend and confessor, for her sake. Once, too, as I was guiding a remarkably handsome young English officer towards Galway, whither his regiment had been lately ordered, Miss Mahoney passed us on horseback, when I instantly detected a blush on her countenance. These, together with a multitude of other trivial circumstances, which I cannot stop to explain or analyse, brought home to my mind the delightful assurance that I was not unbeloved by the finest girl in all the west of Ireland.

We moved, to be sure, in different circles ; but what of that ? Love is an arrant leveller, whose pride it is to over-throw all the obstacles which circumstance and situation may oppose to his progress.

Irishmen are proverbially sanguine, and from the first moment of my encounter with Miss Mahoney I felt per-suaded that fate had destined us for each other. This idea haunted me incessantly. I became shadowy and transparent, affected the moonlight, and sought for sym-pathy in the stars. If I went out for a ramble, it was to steal a glance at Miss Mahoney. If I smiled, it was on Miss Mahoney. If I prayed, it was for Miss Mahoney. If I rhymed, it was on Miss Mahoney. If I swore, it was by Miss Mahoney. If I dreamed, it was of Miss Mahoney.

My father was the first to perceive my altered mood. We were seated together, one raw night, beside a turf-fire, when roused by a sigh, which involuntarily escaped me, he laid down his jug, and, looking at me with a serio-comic air, said, " Terence, jewel, what ails you ?"

For the life of me I could not answer.

" By the powers, the boy's bewitched !" rejoined my father.

" Right, sir, I am bewitched."

" Aisy, lad, and tell me all about it ; sure, then, it's myself will see you righted—at least, so there's no law in the case."

There was a plausibility about this that at once gained my attention ; for I could not but remember that my father had himself, in early life, been a martyr to the tender passion, as he proved to demonstration by the forcible abduction of two farmers' daughters, one of whom was an heiress. For these sprightly sallies he had fallen under

the serious displeasure of the law, against which he had
ever since entertained a strong, and, under the circumstances, not, I think, an ill-founded prejudice.   From such
a man, therefore, I felt I had every right to look for sympathy ; so after a moment's hesitation, when he had twice
repeated his question, I burst out with, " Father, I'm in
love !"

I thought he would have gone off in a fit at this confession.   " Father, I'm in love," he said, mimicking the
touching sadness of my voice and countenance.   " Ha, ha,
ha ! was ever such a thing heard of !   And pray, Terence,
who are you in love with ?"

When I mentioned the lady's name, my father's laughter
broke out with more violence than ever.   " Oh, murder !"
he exclaimed, digging the tears out of his eyes with his
knuckles, " this *lad* 'll be the death of me !"

" Then, sir," I suddenly replied, " since you turn my
sufferings into ridicule, and give me not an atom of en-
couragement, I shall go and hang myself."

" And what good 'll that do—hey, Terence ?"

The question was a striking one, and reconciled me at
once to existence.   Nevertheless, despairing of receiving
any further serviceable suggestions from a man who was
fast hastening to pass the boundary-line of sobriety, I
resolutely refused to answer any more of his cavalier in-
terrogatories, but wrapping myself up, as with a mantle,
in the silence of a lofty indignation, quitted the room,
and retired up the ladder to bed.

CHAPTER IV.

LOVE'S LABOUR LOST.

THE next day the conversation of the preceding night
was resumed.   But, singularly enough, my father's notions
had in the interim undergone a total change.   Instead of
ridiculing my presumption, or giving up my case as hope-

less, he now advised me to persevere, and even went
the length of urging me to indite what he called "a fine,
flourishing" love-letter to Miss Mahoney, to which I added
a postscript, stating that the individual to whom the note
referred would himself wait for a reply the next day in a
certain sequestered lane, whose geographical position I
took care to lay down with all the accuracy of a Guthrie.

Well, the letter, penned, folded, and addressed, was
consigned to my father's custody, who forthwith set out
to deliver it into the hands, if possible, of the lady herself,
while I spent the interval of his absence in conjuring up,
like Alnaschar, a thousand flattering anticipations. Within
the hour the old man returned. He had delivered my
missive, he said, with an arch smile, to a footman at the
hall-door, and, after waiting full ten minutes for a reply,
was informed by the servant, at the express command of
his mistress, that none was needed.

Silence gives consent. This, I believe, is a generally
admitted axiom. I, at least, was not willing to suppose
otherwise, and so persuaded myself that I had but to make
my appearance, in decent trim, at the appointed place of
rendezvous, to be received as my merits deserved.

Decent trim! The phrase was an awkward one, and
replete with discouraging reminiscences. I was, in truth,
most delicately situated in this respect. My coat, like
the "Giaour," was "a fragment ;" and my hat, like Charles
the Tenth, had lost its crown. In the more secluded
Irish villages, among the humbler class of farmers, pos-
sessions such as these are either acquired by inheritance,
or left by will as legacies. No man dreams of purchasing
them on his own account ; he would as soon think of setting up a carriage. I was not an exception to the general
rule, consequently my ancestral wardrobe was in a condition better calculated to extort reverence than admiration ; and nothing but the ingenuity and perseverance
of my father, who assisted me in the arduous endeavour
to render it again fit for service, enabled me at length to
work out my ideas of decent trim.

It was a delightful morning, when, like my celebrated countryman Sterne, I set out on my "sentimental journey." The birds were singing on every hedge they could find to sing on ; the wild colts were running races on the moor ; the spirit of universal happiness lay soft and sunny upon the earth.

As I tripped onward, I felt the gladsome spirit of the hour pervade my every thought. The breeze that blew freshly about my brow ; the grass with its cool, cheerful green, brought brighter out by the sunshine ; the streamlet chattering beside my path, like some young companion who prattles out of the exuberance of animal spirits ; in a word, all sweet sounds, and sights, and refreshing influences of earth and heaven seemed to have entered into a benevolent conspiracy to elevate me to the very pinnacle of buoyant self-confidence.

On I went, through fields and across moorlands, till I caught the first glimpse of the appointed lane ; when, halting beside a stile, close under the shadow of an elm, I began to frame an address worthy of myself and Miss Mahoney. I felt that I had but to speak to conquer.

Thus absorbed in seductive reverie, I came within sight of the place of rendezvous. On reaching the nearer end, I again halted, and cast a hurried glance around me, to ascertain if aught in the shape of female form were moving behind or before me. But all was still and breathless. Presently I heard a rustling in the hedge close behind me. I listened—the branches parted with a crash—but instead of the laughing, sylphide figure I expected to see bound through the aperture, an old cow stared me full in the face !

At length my disappointment bade fair to be terminated. The sound of footsteps came quickly up a narrow bend of the lane, and in a few minutes three men, in whose faces I was not slow to recognise more mischief than sentiment, advanced towards me. The foremost of the squad—and my heart sank as I made the discovery—was a favourite English groom of Mr. Mahoney. "What," said I, "can this advent import? Nothing surely but disappointment. Yet why should it be so? I cannot have been mistaken in my anticipations. Those smiles, that look, can they have—? No, no—it must not, cannot be. Courage, then; all will yet be well;" and, thus re-assured, I boldly resolved to await the result of circumstances.

" Terence," said the vile Saxon, "is this your letter ?" holding forth the very note on which I had so much prided myself.

" Yes," I replied, in a tone of becoming confidence.

" And you hope to receive an answer from my young lady in person ?"

" Undoubtedly."

" Truly, a very modest confession."

" Sir," said I, "it is not with you that I want to speak ; when I need your counsel, I will not fail to ask it."

The wretch turned to his fellows with a sneer. I caught the malign expression, and, overcome by a vision of the stocks and horse-pond, prepared for instant flight. But the man was not to be thus baulked. He had evidently anticipated some such manœuvre ; and before I had time to enter into satisfactory explanations made a sign to his satellites, who, with an alacrity which I shall never think of without disgust, seized me by the legs and arms, and trotted off with me towards a neighbouring field, where a mob of Mr. Mahoney's tenantry were anxiously expecting my arrival.

On seeing me approach, the whole assembly burst out into uproarious laughter, and in an incredibly short space of time adjusted a blanket, threw me like a sack of potatoes right into the middle, and sent me, head over heels, high up into the astonished sky.

I forbear to enumerate the reluctant somersets I threw ; I shrink from details of the height to which I rose, or the depth to which I fell : suffice it to say, that at one moment I was as near to heaven as a doctor's patient, and the next as far removed from it as a lawyer.

f'or at least half-an-hour I kept rising and sinking in
this very indecorous fashion—now impersonating the sublime and now the pathos—at the expiration of which
time I was set once more on my legs, and complimented
on my brisk evolutions, amid the cheers of some hundred
plebeians. What a termination to "Love's young dream!"

Overcome with shame, disgust, and offended delicacy, I
was just preparing to sneak from the field, when whom
should I encounter but—my father! The old man said
nothing ; but when he winked his eye, and laid his fore-
finger beside his nose, at the same time casting a sly glance
at the blanket, I thought I should have gone distracted.
To be thus outraged by a mob and jeered by a parent—
to have one's earliest and holiest sensibilities thus blighted,
as it were, in the bud—flesh and blood could not endure
the shock ; so, like a maniac, I rushed from the scene of
action, nor once halted till many long miles lay between
me and the scene of my humiliation.

CHAPTER V

THINGS AT THE WORST ARE SURE TO MEND.

AFTER three hours' incessant walking, during which
my fertile fancy had shaped out a thousand plans for the
future—for, resolved never to return home, I already
looked on myself as a citizen of the world, who must
henceforth be the artificer of his own fortune—I was compelled from sheer exhaustion to come to a halt ; so seating
myself on a hillock a few yards from the high-road, I
reviewed, as dispassionately as the state of my ribs would
allow, the events of the last few hours.

"Had I possessed but ordinary assurance," I said, "I
should not have been thus situated. What had I to do
with sneaking like a vagrant about lanes waiting for
stolen interviews with young ladies? I should have
known better what was due to the dignity of manhood

—have gone boldly up to the hall—pleaded my cause in person—and trusted to my stars for the result. Instead of which I have proved myself an arrant spooney! Is it wonderful, then, that I am treated with contempt? Is not a blanketing the legitimate inheritance of such a ninny? O fool! fool! this confounded modesty will be thy ruin!"

Turning from this by no means agreeable reverie, I next proceeded seriously to discuss the plan of my future proceedings. And now the advice of Father O'Flannaghan recurred to me with healing effect. "Yes," I exclaimed, "I will indeed adhere scrupulously to thy admonitions, thou kindest and most apostolic of sages! I will neither despond nor become desperate, for the world is wide enough for us all, and Fortune is rarely coy to those who know how to contend for her favours. If one thing fail, I will try another. I have talents, I have—thanks to thy tuition —something of education; and Nature, if she has cursed me with shame-facedness, has, it is to be hoped, blessed me with sufficient energy to neutralise it. *En avant,* then, be my motto."

By this time the day was wearing on, and as my afflictions, though severe, had not wholly deprived me of appetite, I made all possible haste towards the nearest wayside inn. My speed was unincumbered with bag and baggage, for my whole wardrobe was on my back, and my whole stock in cash consisted of two shillings and a few stray tenpennies.

By twilight I reached a little town, or rather village, and entering a small social inn, over whose door frowned a fierce likeness of Brien Boroihme, called for the landlord, and ordered supper in that tone of authority which implies the possession of the ways and means.

The man hastened to obey my summons, and in a few minutes returned into what he was pleased to style the coffee-room, with some cheese by no means improved by age, hot potatoes, a loaf of home-made bread, and, what I feel justified in asserting was, very passable whisky.

The sharp edge of appetite was soon blunted on these viands, to which a bowl of whisky-punch lent the finest possible relish, and rendered me a while insensible to all anxieties.

In the course of the evening the room gradually filled ; and just when my spirits had attained an enviable point of elevation, and I was ripe for any frolic, a random remark in abuse of certain of Mr. Martin's electioneering agents at Galway, let fall by an individual who was drinking with some others at a table at the far end of the room, gave rise to a tart rejoinder from one of his companions, to which he as tartly replied ; and with such effect, that he drew down on himself the notice of some half-dozen others, who, though they evidently knew nothing of the merits of the case, yet could not witness these first virgin blossoms of a row without doing their best to bring them to maturity.

A crowd, therefore, was soon gathered about the disputants ; the strife of tongues began to wax loud and louder, till at length a blow, aimed at the author of the fray by one of the aggrieved Martinites, brought on as pretty and promiscuous a fight as could be desired. It was indeed a lovely "scrimmage." No one dreamed of siding either with this party or with that ; impartiality being the order of the day, all you were expected to do was to pitch into your next neighbour, and get as much fun out of him as possible.

Was I idle all this time ? No ! It was not in human —certainly not in Irish—nature to resist the temptation. In a wonderfully short space of time, therefore, I found myself in the very thick of the battle, anchored alongside the individual whose wild rattle had originated it. Scarcely had I taken up this position, when such a terrific blow was aimed at my neighbour's head as must infallibly have demolished him, if I had not intercepted it by dexterously interposing the leg of a broken stool with which I had armed myself.

On seeing this, he turned round, and giving me a look,

as much as to say, "I am too busy now, but will thank you when it is all over," set to work again, in concert with myself, with such well-directed energy, while the others were all hammering away at random, that when the landlord rushed in to separate the combatants, we were the only two who were not lavishly embellished with black eyes, and other such pugilistic illustrations.

After a cleverly-sustained affair of about half-an-hour, peace was restored. Some quitted the coffee-room for the purpose of anointing their wounds; others resumed their places in high glee at the entertainment they had just received; while the stranger whom I had so opportunely befriended, after squeezing me by the hand a dozen times, took his seat beside me, and insisted on drinking to our better acquaintance.

Something there was about this individual which at once conciliated my good-will. He was smart and flippant in speech; frank and cordial, with a dash of independence and assumption, in his manner; which, combined with a certain knowing air, half-comic, half-disconsolate, betokened the reckless adventurer whose entrance into a coffee-room is the signal for the landlord to take away the silver spoons.

In the course of conversation with the stranger, after he had explained to me the origin of the late quarrel, we slided imperceptibly into that most attractive of all topics, the state of our mutual affairs. My story was soon told, though not without repeated interruptions from the laughter of my companion, who inquired, when I had brought it to a close, what I intended to be my next plan of proceeding.

"I know not," was my reply; "my wits are completely at sea on the subject. Possibly I may enlist as a soldier."

"And serve your first campaign against the White boys in a Connemara or Tipperary bog, with an equal chanc of being shot, smothered, hanged, or carded! Why, my good fellow, your project is as green as the Green Isle itself. Think again."

2

"Well, then, I have been considering also whether I should not make the best of my way to Dublin, and endeavour to procure a situation with some chemist or apothecary. I have had some little experience in that line."

"Killed your man, no doubt. What say you to offering your services to some of the farmers hereabouts? This is just the right time, you know."

"Sir!" said I indignantly, "I was born for nobler objects than to walk at the plough-tail behind two bullocks."

"Ambitious! 'Gad, I like your spirit."

"Yes, Father O'Flannaghan used often to say, that if I played my cards well, I should rise in the world. 'The lad is not without genius,' was his frequent remark to my father."

"Genius! Curse the phrase! I never hear it, but I think of a bailiff. Nothing flourishes that has the slightest connexion with it. Look at me—I should have been a rich man by this time, if it had not been for my genius."

"Yet Father O'Flannaghan used to say that genius, properly—"

"Hang Father O'Flannaghan! He knew nothing about the matter. Will genius fill your purse when it is empty—will it go bail for you—will it even pay your bill to-night? But let us drop the subject. Are you fond of the stage?"

"Very. In fact, I believe I have a turn that way; for when living with Dr. Killquick, I was a constant visitor at the theatre."

"Indeed! Then, perhaps, I may be able to do something for you. I am an actor myself."

"Is it possible?" said I, in a most deferential manner; "yet, now I come to look more closely into your features, I do think I saw you play Hamlet one night at Galway —at least I remember a performer being hissed off the stage in that character."

"Sir, you have a very absurd way of expressing yourself. I never played Hamlet at Galway, and never mean to do so. The people there are wholly incapable of appreciating a man of mind in such a part."

I was convinced by this I was right, though I discreetly kept my opinion to myself, while the Thespian proceeded as follows :—

"Yes, sir, I am not only an actor of experience, but, unfortunately, also of just sufficient genius to—"

"Excite the jealousy of your brother actors."

"Egad, you have hit it. The last corps to which I attached myself was the one now playing at Limerick, where I was a deserved favourite ! "

"How, then, came you to leave it ? "

"Leave it ? It was impossible to stay. Why, sir, would you believe it, notwithstanding the houses I drew as Dennis Brulgruddery, the manager, jealous of my genius, put another man into the part ; and, not content with this, actually stuck his name in large red letters at the top of the play-bill, while he printed mine in the very smallest type at the bottom — just above *Vivat Rex !* Scandalous ! Wasn't it ?"

"Yes ; but what brings you to this out-of-the-way place ?"

" I have been assisting at a friend's benefit at Galway, and am now on my way to join the company at Mollymoreen. Were you to take my advice—by the bye, just hand me over the whisky, talking always makes me thirsty —you would do the same. Talk of pleasure ! The actor is the only man who really knows what it means. At one moment, flush of wealth ; at another, without a sixpence ; this night, figuring in a gorgeous theatre ; the next, in a homely barn ; now, sipping champagne with squires ; and now, swipes with vagrants ; hanging loose on the skirts of society, a very Arab in independence— there is no condition in life so replete with all the elements of change and, consequently of interest, as that of the actor. True, he has his cares ; but how slight—how very slight must these be, when a glass of such punch as this can put them all to flight! No, no; despite my own ill-luck, your stroller is the happiest dog in existence."

"You don't say so!" said I, catching the infection of his convivial enthusiasm.

"Indeed, but I do, though. Conceive the ecstacy of a first appearance! The crowded house—the glittering lights—the inspiring music—the stare of approving critics from the pit—the fond gaze of beauty from the boxes—and then, as the first wave of your plumage is caught from the side-wings, the profound, universal hush, so sudden, so intense, that were a god but to blow his nose, there would be an instant cry from all parts of the house of 'Throw him over'—conceive all this, I say, and allow, with me, that the actor's life is the only one to which the name of pleasure can really apply!"

My fancy was fired with this description! In idea I was already a Garrick! My companion marked my emotion. "You would make a capital actor!" he continued; "but I will not press the question further at present. I see you're affected; probably by to-morrow you will be inclined to entertain a favourable opinion of my project. Meantime, let us replenish. Come, I'll give you a toast—'Success to the stage.' 'All the world's a stage,' as the divine Billy says. Not bad, hey?"

A fresh bowl was the result of this sally, over which we sat carousing till long past midnight; when, our fuel being exhausted, the candles low in the sockets, and the landlord imperative, we retired to our dormitories.

The next morning I awoke with a desperate headache, which was still further increased by the amount of the bill sent in by the landlord; who, deceived, naturally enough, by my appearance, had charged me at a most exorbitant rate. This comes of looking like a gentleman!

Rabelais has well observed, that the hour of reckoning is the most melancholy in the whole twenty-four. I found it so; and was ruminating sadly on my destitute state, when my new friend came to my assistance.

"I can guess your thoughts," said he; "whenever a

man puts on a long face, it is always for want of money."

"You have guessed right. I am seriously troubled just now on that score."

"No wonder! all scores are troublesome. But be of good cheer, man, I will pay the reckoning. Nay, no apologies; I happen to be tolerably well off at present, so can afford to do a good turn. Besides, I have taken a fancy to you."

"But, my dear sir—"

"Not a word, Hal, an' thou lovest me. Remember, I am now in your debt, for you last night saved me from a broken head. If, however, your pride dislikes the idea of obligation to a stranger, you have it in your power to appease your conscience by accepting an engagement at Mollymoreen. I am sure I shall be able to get you one; for our company is sadly in want of a novelty."

Needs must when the devil drives; so, dismissing all further solicitude from my mind, I allowed my friend to discharge the entire reckoning; which novel task performed, we set forward on our journey, under the refreshing influence of a slow drizzle, which threatened to keep us company the whole way to Mollymoreen.

CHAPTER VI.

STROLLING AND ITS CONSEQUENCES.

Contrary, I believe, to nine out of ten theatrical aspirants, I commenced my campaign under very flattering auspices. Thanks to the dramatic predilections of Doctor Killquick, and the licence allowed me in my studies by Father O'Flannaghan, I had been in the habit, during my unbewhiskered juvenility, of devouring a vast variety of plays; so that when I entered on my stage career, what with these and the additional advantages of a few preliminary lessons from my new acquaintance, it was not altogether a novelty to me.

My first appearance was in Romeo. The citizens of Mollymoreen are a remarkably discriminating race, for they at once pereceived my worth ; and the editor of the leading journal there, in his theatrical critique, published the day after my début, put forth the following striking and pertinent remarks :—" Last night, a Mr. Terence Felix O'Blarney made his first appearance here as Romeo, in the immortal bard's well-known play of that name. Barring a slight brogue, this young aspirant possesses every qualification for the part.   He has excellent lungs ; is exceedingly vigorous in his movements ; and stands nearly, if not quite, six feet in his shoes.   His dress was singularly picturesque, and he was received with enthusiasm by a most respectable and fashionable audience. We understand he appears to-morrow night as Harlequin. Judging from his Romeo, we should conceive he would play this very difficult part to admiration.   Both characters have many points in common ; both are young, active, in love, and fond of leaping, and condemned by unpropitious destiny to experience the most startling vicissitudes.   We wish Mr. O'Blarney all the success that his genius so richly merits."

This able criticism brought me into instant notice at Mollymoreen.   Indeed, such and so sudden was my reputation among them, that before my first month had expired, I was promoted on the manager's books from 15s. to £1 5s. per week, with the offer of a free benefit at the close of the season.

My second and third appearances were as Hamlet and Harlequin, both which trying characters I personated the same evening.   Public opinion was seriously divided on this occasion.   The more intellectual among the community preferred my Hamlet ; the more mercurial, my Harlequin.   If, on so delicate a topic, it may be permitted me to volunteer an opinion, I should say that my Hamlet was the triumph of mind, my Harlequin of muscle.   I state this with the less hesitation, because the world long entertained a notion that I myself gave the preference to my Harlequin ; whereas it was ever my fixed opinion that no parallel could possibly be instituted between the two characters. As well might the fervent passion of a Shakspeare be compared to the sparkling vivacity of a Sheridan.

In consequence of my flattering reception at Molly-moreen, I was invited to play the leading parts at every theatre and barn in that civilised quarter of Ireland. This desultory mode of life introduced me to many odd characters, and engaged me in many odd adventures, some of a tragic, others of a comic character. One in particular, of the latter class, I well recollect, as it took place under circumstances of marked singularity.

The manager had announced for representation a melo-drame, in which, among other attractions, was to be introduced a view of the Lakes of Killarney, painted expressly for the occasion. The announcement took pro-digiously, and on the appointed night the barn was crowded to suffocation. So far, all was well ; but, un-luckily, just at the moment when we were preparing to draw up the curtain, we discovered that our scene-painter, in revenge for some real or fancied affront offered him by the manager, had inoculated the entire landscape with charcoal ; and, not content with this lively sample of independence, had actually eloped, and, accompanied by the treasurer, carried off with him the night's proceeds.

Here was a dilemma! What, in Heaven's name, was to be done ? This question we kept perpetually asking each other ; but, alas ! not one of us all could answer it.

Meantime the audience became clamorous for the cur-tain to draw up. Oaths, squalls, shouts of laughter, and threats of vengeance pealed in all directions, and even the orchestra—notwithstanding it consisted of two cracked fiddles and a hurdy-gurdy—failed to allay the storm.

In this predicament, our manager proposed an appeal to the audience. But here, again, a difficulty presented itself. Who was to be the spokesman ? Each declined the honour in favour of the other, until at length—no better scheme presenting itself—it was resolved, *nem. con.*, that we should all of us attempt our escape out of a window at the rear of the stage.

The manager was the first to make the experiment, and being of a thin, spare habit, succeeded to his heart's content. The rest followed in rotation, until it came to the manager's wife's turn, who was an immensely fat woman, with a singular exuberance of *bustle*, and consequently stuck fast in the window, with her neck and shoulders out, but the rest of her person hanging suspended over the stage. In this grotesque position, she kicked, shoved, and strove to wriggle herself through the aperture : but in vain—her obesity put a veto on all hopes of emancipation. I think I never saw a tighter fit !

At this critical juncture I was the only one left upon the stage. There was evidently no chance of escape ; so, as a last resource—for the audience had by this time become furious—I summoned the orchestra, bade them strike up " St. Patrick's Day," and then, slowly drawing aside the curtain, advanced in front of the stage, made a profound obeisance, and, pointing to the fat dame who hung wriggling from the window, exclaimed aloud, " Ladies and gentlemen, behold a view of the Lakes of Killarney !"

Whether the likeness struck them or not, I cannot say ; but never was any appeal more successful. The audience literally shouted with laughter, nor was peace restored till they had testified the excess of their satisfaction by a general fight, in the bustle of which I effected my escape. How the manager's wife effected hers, I know not—possibly she is sticking in the window to this hour.

For nearly two seasons I continued in Mollymoreen, the delight of all eyes. My portrait, or something like a portrait, was exhibited at every print-shop ; my witticisms repeated at every table ; my attitudes were the envy of the men, my countenance the admiration of the women.

Among the number of those to whom my convivial abilities especially recommended themselves was a rich, retired old hunks of a tradesman, by name O'Brien. This man had a niece, who, though perhaps not much of a beauty, and still less of a chicken in point of age, inasmuch as she was full four years my senior, was yet—a circumstance of first-rate moment to one of my way of thinking—the acknowledged heiress of all her uncle's property.

It was chiefly through this lady's manœuvres that I first got a footing in the old man's house; for she had seen me in most of my favourite characters, and, being smitten with the faculties of the actor, was prepared by a natural transition to extend her predilection to the man.

When a woman is once determined on a point, there is little doubt that she will in the long run accomplish it. Convinced that I was the only man who would, could, should, or ought to make her happy, Catharine soon contrived to give me a hint of the nature of her feelings towards me. In vain did her uncle, who found means to gain possession of her secret, protest, intreat, threaten; in vain forbid me his house; in vain talk of disinheriting his niece; in vain point out to her the madness of marrying a fellow whose sole stock in trade was his assurance; —the young lady's spirit was up, and she vowed, with a saucy toss of the head, that she would marry the man of her choice, and him alone.

I, of course, reciprocated these sentiments, but frequent and various were the hazards I encountered in my efforts to impress them on the heart of Catharine. Once, while waiting for her at midnight by the garden-gate, I was mistaken by her uncle for a robber, and very nearly brought down at a long shot; on another occasion, I was saluted with the contents of a slop-pail from a garret-window; and in a third instance, I was kept cooling my heels a full hour beneath the moonlight, till my teeth chattered like a pair of castanets. Making love by midnight, when the thermometer is below zero, is harder work than most people seem to have any idea of.

But perseverance does wonders, and by the assistance of the friend who had first introduced me to the stage, I contrived to obtain—first one secret interview—then a second—then a third—then a fourth, fifth, and sixth—until at length it became but too clear that nothing was left but an elopement.

Mr. O'Brien was panic-stricken when the intelligence of this impending event first reached his ears. By way of preventive he had instant recourse to locks, bolts, and bars ; but finding that even these expedients failed, he made a virtue of necessity, and finally consented to our union.

CHAPTER VII.

ECLIPSE OF THE HONEYMOON.

WITHIN a week from the day when the nuptial-knot was tied, Mrs. O'Blarney and myself started off for the Continent. Old O'Brien, who, notwithstanding his munificence to Catharine, was very contracted and tradesman-like in his notions, was almost paralysed at the grandeur of our intentions, and would fain have kept us under his own eye in Ireland ; but the lady was bent on seeing the world, and would listen neither to advice nor remonstrance.

Our first stay of any duration was in Paris. I had long heard that this city was famous for the Fine Arts, and truly I never met with such finished specimens of *cookery*. As for my wife, she was in ecstacies. Paris was lor a time her El Dorado—her fairy-land.

After a stay just long enough to beget ennui, we quitted the French capital for Frankfort, whence we made a hasty tour through some of the minor German principalities. The magnificence of a few of these quite astounded me. Think of his Serene Highness the Prince of Saxe Schweighausen, with upwards of sixty quarterings on his arms, being absolute lord and master of a territory containing nearly ten thousand inhabitants, yielding a clear revenue of almost nine hundred pounds *rer* annum, and supporting an army of some twelve dozen private soldiers, exclusive of six field-officers, and a band worthy to vie with the orchestra of one of our minor theatres.

To this most puissant sovereign I had the honour of being publicly presented at court. To be sure, the exhibition cost me half-a-crown in fees. But what of that? Royalty is not, like Punch, an every-day show. Besides, his Highness was, without exception, the fattest man I had ever seen, and in England it would have cost me a shilling to see a prize ox.

We found the metropolis of this mighty monarch's kingdom in a grievous state of excitement. An Italian singer—at that time quite the rage on the Continent—had engaged to give a series of vocal performances at Schweighausen, but, just at the very moment when the royal family and *noblesse* were all anxious expectation, the fair *cantatrice* split upon terms, and declared off. Here was a shock to the *grand monarque!* Never had such an affront been put upon himself or his principality! It became quite a national affair. A cabinet council was instantly summoned, which, after some hours' deliberation, despatched a courier, with sealed despatches, to the contumelious vocalist; while, from the hurryings to and fro of the dames of honour, and the grave, mysterious looks of the courtiers, you would have sworn a revolution was impending. How the affair ended I know not, as I did not stay to see; but I heard, subsequently, that the cabinet, deeming it beneath the national dignity to reinforce the army and proclaim war against a woman, wisely came to her terms, which were so exorbitant that they crippled the exchequer for months afterward.

From Schweighausen, we ascended the Rhine, where, for the first and last time in my life, I witnessed the perfection of river-scenery. I have no very acute apprehension of the picturesque; but I shall never forget this voyage. Imagine a stream, now expanding into a lake, and now contracting into a canal, with a thousand laughing rivulets leaping into it on either side, as if delighted to enhance its beauty and share in its renown—now dark with the shadows of overhanging cliffs, and now reflecting images of sunny pastoral loveliness—here, a grey solitary fragment of a castle, still breathing the spirit of its old grandeur, starting up like a spectre before your eyes ; and there, a graceful modern chateau, apt haunt of love and beauty—in one place a luxuriant slope flush of vineyards, and crowned with romantic terraces ; in another, a village hanging, as it were, self-poised in air, above the regions of the clouds, while, ever as the magic stream wafts you onward, island, mountain, city, town, and monastery, appear and disappear like dreams ! Oh ! never was so unequalled an assemblage of all that is sublime and beautiful in nature or art. Well may the Germans be proud of their legendary river. A fairer stream never graced the plains of Arcadia, or wandered through the groves of Eden.

Our next visit was to Switzerland. My wife's romance was here more on the alert than even on the waters of the Rhine. We peeped at a glacier—explored a waterfall —climbed half an Alp or so—and stared at Mont Blanc through an opera-glass. One day while, for want of something better to do, we were floating lazily over the un-wrinkled bosom of the Leman, we came alongside a slim young Englishman, of a sallow, romantic cast of counte-nance, who was fast asleep in his boat, close under the immortal rocks of Meillerie. Just as our vessel passed, a book dropped from his hand into the water. We took it up. It was Rousseau's " Eloise !" Enviable enthusiasm !

Having gazed our fill on the Helvetian rocks, lakes, and mountains, we once more set out on our wanderings, and, in the course of a reasonable period, with a facility quite humiliating to all amateurs of the wild and the wonderful, arrived in safety at Naples.

Of all the continental cities, commend me to this. It is the Eden of Ausonia—an enchanted region, where all is song and sunshine, love, romance, and festivity. Still, even here, one thing is wanting to complete felicity ; and this one want I but too soon began to experience. What with our visits to Paris, Frankfort, Switzerland, and the other *et ceteras* incidental to such an expensive and desultory mode of life, I found, after a fortnight's residence on the Strada Chiaja, that my wife's fortune was daily oozing out of my possession ; so, in order to supply the deficiency, I was compelled to have recourse to gaming.

For a long time I concealed this propensity from Mrs. O'Blarney. But what can escape the lynx eye of curiosity? It so happened that she was one day smitten with a sudden fancy to make a purchase of some tempting *bijouterie ;* when, on applying to me, she found that I was wholly unable to accommodate her.

In the course of the evening a mutual explanation took place, when I candidly told Catharine that, unless she assigned over to me the annuity which the suspicions of her uncle had settled on her, I should infallibly become a ruined man. To my astonishment she refused, adding that in future nothing should prevent her doing that justice to herself which I had so scandalously neglected. The remark was cutting, and, under the circumstances, ungenerous ; though its severity was somewhat blunted by the promise which my wife shortly after made me, of writing to Mr. O'Brien a statement of our embarrassments, with a request that he would render us prompt pecuniary assistance. To this note I attached a postscript, inclosing a Neapolitan physician's receipt for the gout.

By the earliest post—for the old man prided himself on his punctuality—an answer was returned to our application. But, alas! its import was anything but flattering. The writer began by observing that he could not think of advancing money to people so little acquainted with its value ; that he had always anticipated this would be the result of Catharine's ill-advised marriage, which she might do him the justice to remember he had resolutely opposed from the first ; that he thought, under the circumstances, the best thing we could both do would be to retrench our household expenditure, and, in the bosom of a strict and cheap seclusion, strive to regain that composure of which, it was but too evident, we both stood in need. The letter concluded by thanking me for my receipt for the gout, which, however, the churlish old fox asserted, whether intended to do so or not, had made him infinitely worse than he was before he had recourse to it.

This reply decided my fate. Poverty having come in at the door, timid Love, as a matter of course, was prepared to make his exit by the window. Henceforth I met with nothing but reproaches from my wife. For some weeks, however, I bore her altered conduct with submissiveness. When I espied a frown on her brow, I strove with words of endearment to avert the thunder-cloud; I reminded her of the days of our courtship, when she was my Juliet and I was her Romeo; but, alas! at the very moment when her heart was softening, the slightest allusion to the annuity would bring back all her unpoetic notions of self-interest.

Day by day, hour by hour, Mrs. O'Blarney's ill-humour increased. If one moment she was comparatively serene, the next she blew a hurricane. Having been a spoiled child from her very cradle, she had little or no command of her temper. To soften her was difficult—to subdue, impossible. As well might I have attempted to check Niagara with a bulrush.

Such was my domestic position, when one disastrous evening, after I had earnestly supplicated my wife to accommodate me, if only by way of loan, with the usual half-yearly allowance which she had just received from her uncle, in order that I might disembarrass myself of certain pecuniary obligations, and be enabled to turn over a new leaf, the impetuous lady not only refused my petition, but pointed her refusal by some scornful allusions to what she called my general profligacy.

Stung to the quick by her manner, I threatened to take leave of her for ever; on which she replied—

"Oh, do pray go! I desire nothing better; the very

sight of you is odious to me. Would to Heaven I had never met with such a monster!"

"Monster, forsooth! you must have been looking in your glass lately, my dear, which has made the monstrous familiar to you."

The cool way in which I said this had quite an electrical effect on my wife, who forthwith proceeded to pour on me such a torrent of abuse that at last my patience wholly gave way, and, springing down stairs, I was out of sight in an instant.

On reaching the street, I kept wandering up and down, cursing my evil destiny, and endeavouring to shape out some plans for the future, till, finding that I could settle down to nothing, I dismissed all further reflection, and bent my steps towards one of the public *cafés*.

Here I remained for upwards of half an hour, and, by way of calming down my ruffled spirits, swallowed bumper after bumper of the very headiest wine I could lay my hands on. With a brain thus heated by excitement, and, of course, craving still further stimulus, I strolled into the San Carlos, where, after looking about me for some time, and being challenged to try my luck at a game of hazard, I threw down a piece of gold—was successful—threw down a second, a third—then trebled and quadrupled my stakes, till at length, after an hour's play, without the slightest effort of skill, I came away the winner of upwards of a hundred pounds.

Such a run of good luck completely upset what little judgment I ever possessed. I felt my heart warm again to my wife; and, immediately on quitting the gaming-table, flew homeward, fully resolved, in the wild glee of the moment, to make her the *amende honorable*, though I must confess, at the same time, that I was in that feverish, unsettled state of mind when a sneer, or even a frown, is sufficient to turn the scale, and upset all one's best resolutions.

"So you have come back!" said my wife, misconstruing the motives of my return; "and in a pretty condition you have returned !" for my flushed countenance was too marked to escape her notice.

" For God's sake, Catharine, be quiet, or else—"

" Don't think to frighten me, sir ; I care nothing for the threats of a man I despise. You have insulted me too grossly to be forgiven, and now, by way of atonement, you come back in a state of intoxication. Shame on you ! I wonder you can **dare** to look me in the face !"

" Catharine," said I, with an effort at calmness, " listen to me, and for the last time. I have come back, believe me or not, as you please, solely for the purpose of making reparation for—"

" Reparation ! Is it by your drunkenness you hope to make reparation ?"

" Perhaps so, perhaps not. However, be this as it may, my return is now prompted by the best of motives."

" Oh, yes," replied my wife, with a sneer, " I know the motives well. I can see through them, sir."

" Hear me out !" said I, in a voice of thunder.

" I won't."

" Insulting termagant !"

" Drunken brute !"

" Spiteful, unforgiving old—"

The word " old " touched my wife in the sorest point. " Spiteful " she might have passed over ; " unforgiving " she might have smiled at ; but "old"—there was too much truth in the phrase to be readily digested ; so, despairing in the frenzy of the moment of finding words adequate to her feelings, she actually flew for assistance to the footstool—discharged it without ceremony at my head—and then, as I rushed a second time from the house, flew after me, crying at the very top of her voice, "Aye, go ! do go ! I dare you to go ! Brute ! monster ! barbarian ! *Old* indeed !"

This last insult was not to be borne ; and when I reflected on the motives that had drawn me home again— that I had sought my wife in a frank, conciliatory spirit, and, instead of being met by answering courtesy, had been treated worse than a dog—I became (an unusual thing with me) quite beside myself with passion, and before I was well aware of my proximity found myself standing close beside the quay.

Night was now drawing on, and it so happened that a felucca, taking advantage of a favouring wind, was just about to set sail for Marseilles. The opportunity was irresistible. Judgment, discretion, principle—all, all obeyed the headlong impulse of the moment; and with my wife's taunts still ringing in my ears, the footstool still whistling about my head, and a busy devil at my elbow goading me on to ruin, I sought out the captain of the vessel—caught him just as he was stepping into a boat, and concluded with him for a conveyance to Marseilles.

An instant after, and I was on board. The signal was made for sailing; the vessel shot merrily through the waters, and I was far advanced on my voyage across the bay ere I called to mind my deserted wife! Infatuated man! But remorse was then of no avail. It was too late to return. Besides, had it even been possible, I felt convinced I could never have mustered assurance enough again to face the woman whom I could not but feel I had wronged. My very modesty rose in arms against me. *Et tu Brute!*

After a brief voyage the felucca reached Marseilles, where I waited just one day to make some necessary purchases, and then set off for England.

CHAPTER VIII.

THE MODERN BABYLON.

BEHOLD me now in London—in that Titanic metropolis which is the envy and wonder of Europe; the heavings of whose mighty heart thrill to the uttermost regions of earth; whose merchant-flag is familiar with every wave, and streams in every port; which is the prolific

3

foster-parent of all arts, all professions, and all trades; encouraging alike the adept and the quack, the honest man and the knave, and combining exhaustless wealth with abject penury, the most refined civilisation with the grossest barbarism—behold me in this paradox of a metropolis, placed in the very thick of its crowd, yet oppressed with feelings of the most forlorn solitude. Oh, there is no sense of desolation so complete as that experienced by a friendless stranger on his first introduction to London! Talk of an Arabian desert! It is smiling, animated, encouraging, in comparison.

To meet a frown on every brow, a sneer on every lip; to be distrusted as an adventurer, and with the purest intentions to be perpetually misconstrued; to supplicate where there are few or none to pity; to die of a broken heart in the midst of rejoicing, of famine in the midst of plenty; and then, as if the cup of wretchedness were not drained to the dregs, to be carried out of a workhouse on four rough boards, flung like a dog into his hole, with just a prayer or two mumbled coldly and hurriedly above one's remains, as if they were scarce worth salvation: this it is to be poor and friendless in London.

To be the idol of every circle; to drivel like a fool, yet to be pronounced a sage; to be "a gentleman," when it is manifest you are his antipodes; to see woman's eye light up at your approach, and the fat porter at the great man's gate bustle forward at the hazard of his neck to usher you into the great man's presence; to be the "Sir Oracle" of *ton*, and the hero of a fashionable novel; to be painted by Lawrence, and engraved by Finden; and when put to death by a licensed physician, to be followed to your long home by some dozen agonised acquaintances, while the parson prays his best above your gilt coffin, and a splendid mausoleum records your worth to all posterity: this it is to be wealthy and well connected in London.

O London! thou art the rich man's heaven, but the poor man's hell!

O London! which art the cradle and the grave of hope,

how many aspiring pilgrims, some destined to achieve celebrity, but more to die neglected and broken-hearted, are at this moment, while I write, bending their steps towards thee ! What acts, too, of folly, madness, and guilt, are at the same instant of time in course of preparation within thy circuit ! Yet, if sin profane thy name, the virtues, sure, redeem it by their presence. Lo ! thou canst boast humility in lawn sleeves ; meek charity making public announcement of her benefactions ; modesty gazing at some half-denuded dancer through an opera-glass ; and patriotism defending the pension-list from a back seat on the treasury-bench !

O London ! who can listen to thy eternal whirl and roar—who can gaze on thy palaces, thy temples, thy solemn grey cathedrals, or pause on the stately fabrics that span thy famous stream, scarce seen for the forests of masts which crowd and blacken above its bosom to an extent no eye can traverse—who can pace the wondrous range of thy streets and squares, stretching away, as if to infinity, in showy splendour or sombre grandeur—who can "read, mark, learn, and inwardly digest" all this, and not feel every petty personal consciousness of self swallowed up in an overpowering sense of astonishment and admiration !

Yet, O vain, ambitious, paradoxical London, lay not the flattering unction to thy soul, that because thou art great, thou art necessarily immortal. Already the seeds of decay are at thy heart. Thou art dying by inches of a plethora. Thou art swollen and bloated with a dropsy, though thy massive shoulders and wondrous breadth of chest might seem to promise a lengthened life. Dream not, then, of immortality, but fall to thy studies, and learn wisdom from the past. Think of Rome, *now* the "Niobe of nations," but *once* queen-regent of the universe ! What she is, thou must one day be. The time shall come when thy gorgeous edifices shall fall, like hers, in ruins to earth ; when the grass shall grow in thy streets ; when the owl shall hoot from thy roofless palaces, and the adder crawl into sunshine from among thy mouldering fanes; when Silence and Solitude, twin mourners, shall sit with folded arms and weeping eyes beside thy grave; and the pilgrim from some far-off land, as he wanders through a scene of desolation, shall say, " And was this London!"

I have given thee good advice, London, scarce hoping that thou wilt follow it; and thus having discharged my duty as a patriot and a moralist, I descend from my stilts and resume the language of common life.

CHAPTER IX.

THE IRISHMAN IN LONDON.

THE first few mornings after my arrival were spent in a survey of the various public buildings in and about the metropolis—I remember in particular being much struck with Newgate—while my evenings were devoted to the theatres, and wound up by a social glass at one or other of the taverns in which the vestal vicinity of Covent Garden abounds.

With respect to a profession, my first serious views were of course directed to the stage, and accordingly, when I had devoted quite sufficient time to the gentleman-like occupation of doing nothing, I presented myself early one morning at the stage-door of Drury Lane Theatre; inquired of a servant in attendance whether the great lessee were within; and if so, whether he could honour me with an audience.

The man glanced at the modest, humble expression of my countenance; I understood the hint, and knew the manager was out.

The next day I called and met with the like success— the great man was busy, and could not be disturbed. The third day he was at rehearsal; the fourth, he was reading a new piece in the green-room; the fifth, he was negotiating an amicable arrangement with the hind-legs of an elephant, both of which had struck for an advance of wages; but on the sixth, as he had only two small melodramatists with him, he condescended to favour me with an audience.

On entering his august presence, I opened the proceedings by a few brief allusions to my astonishing success in Ireland, but saw at once, from the expression of his face, and the shrug of his broad, fat shoulders, that I had not the slightest chance. Indeed he hinted as much before I had well finished my exordium, and then, starting off from the subject, began to bewail his hard fate in being compelled to sacrifice health, time, and inclination on the altar of public interest; spoke of the important calls on his attention that daily beset him, from individuals of the highest rank and influence in the kingdom, and that, consequently, I might deem myself fortunate in the opportunity of seeing him but for ten minutes; rang the bell, and brought round him a whole host of theatrical subalterns, to each of whom he issued his mandates, with all the air of a despot; and then cast a sidelong glance at me, to see whether I were duly impressed with a sense of his temporal grandeur.

But I neither fainted nor went off in hysterics, but, perfectly unruffled, as though I were talking to a mere unit like myself, said, "I presume, then, sir, you decline my services?"

"Unquestionably, my good fellow;" then, as if he had committed himself by too much familiarity, he added, with a formal bend of the head, "You may retire, young man; we have business of importance to transact with our worthy friends here just now." And so ended my first and last interview with the manager of a London theatre!

My next speculation was in periodical literature. But here, too, I was as unsuccessful as with the stage. All the editors of all the current magazines seemed to have conspired to drive me frantic with disappointment. Grave as well as gay, prose as well as verse, every tale, essay, criticism, and epigram I contributed, met with precisely the same treatment. This, however, was to have been expected, for what author who dates from a first-floor front, with a French dancing-master constantly practising on a violin over his head, and a great healthy vagabond crying "Sprats!" every hour of the day under his window, can hope to write anything worth reading?

Luckily, about this time I was in the frequent habit of meeting with the late Colonel ——, at a tavern in the neighbourhood of Covent Garden. This well-known old *roué*, whose brain was a perfect granary of fashionable anecdote, and who had been closely connected with royalty in its most convivial and confidential moments, was never so happy, or so much in his element, as when he could procure a respectful listener; and as I suited him admirably in this respect—never yawning, never looking incredulous, and, above all, never laughing in the wrong place —he took a prodigious fancy to me, and entertained me with lots of sly, quaint, piquant anecdotes, in which I could not but fancy I perceived the germs of more than one fashionable novel.

Following up this bright idea, I took care to glean all the various stores of gossip the old man possessed; after which I proceeded to clothe them from the wardrobe of my own invention; super-added a plot full of delicate entanglements; an impassioned love-intrigue or two; an "intensely" interesting heroine, who, like the Paphian Venus, wore her zone loosened; and a brisk Bond-street Adonis, more accomplished than a Crichton, but more profligate than a Rochester. This done, behold—a fashionable novel!

So far, so good. My next endeavour was to secure the assistance of some stirring, influential publisher. In this I succeeded beyond my hopes (chiefly in consequence of my Carlton House anecdotage); and, in the course of a few weeks, had the satisfaction of seeing my "Bon Ton" duly advertised among the forthcoming novelties of the season, as "A tale of real life, by an author of the highest distinction."

No sooner had the work appeared than public attention was still further attracted towards it, by a series
of mysterious paragraphs in the papers, indirectly
ascribing it to the eloquent and sprightly pen of his
Royal Highness the Duke of ——; and, that nothing
might be wanting to confirm its celebrity, a fresh string
of advertisements was issued, with the following extracts
from the literary journals of the day attached to them by
way of rider :—

"Bon Ton" is a tale of first-rate ability; the author is the Scott of
fashionable life.—*London Museum.*

A most talented tale, full of point, wit, and sarcasm. The writer forcibly
reminds us of Sheridan.—*Weekly Lit. Miscellany.*

We have been favoured with an early copy of this work (which is yet *un-
published*), and may conscientiously say of the author that he is quite a prose
Byron.—*Town and Country Magazine.*

Transcendent! astonishing! superlative!—*Star.*

It is truly refreshing, in this age of cant and humbug, to meet with a
novel like "Bon Ton," penned in the good old spirit of Smollett and Fielding.
—*Weekly Repository.*

The puns of this exceedingly facetious novelist are worthy of Mr. Rogers,
the eminent banker.—*John Bull.*

From these discriminating criticisms, it will naturally
be concluded that "Bon Ton" created quite a sensation
in the world of fashion and literature. But no, nothing
of the sort. Notwithstanding I attired my hero in laven-
der-coloured slippers; made him sarcastic on port wine;
intolerant of those abandoned miscreants who eat fish
with a knife and fork; learned on all gastronomic matters;
and profoundly ignorant of the locality of Russell-square
—notwithstanding all this, "Bon Ton" fell as stillborn
from the press as if no royal duke had been conjectured
to be its author!

Having thus failed in *fact*, I thought—for the *cacoethes
scribendi* was still strong on me—I would next have recourse to *fiction*. Nothing venture, nothing gain; so I
set about a History of Italy, with which my residence at
Naples had of course made me familiarly acquainted.
Strange to tell, my book, even though filled with elaborate
descriptions of Rome—a city which nothing but an acci-

dent prevented me from visiting, met with as discouraging
a reception as "Bon Ton"—nay, I may even add, a worse,
for on bargaining for a portmanteau a few months afterward
in Long Acre, I found it lined with one of my most impassioned apostrophes to the glory of ancient Rome!

This was vexatious, but it was not my only grievance.
Misfortunes never drizzle upon a man's head.   They
always pour down on him in torrents.   The landlady—

> O sound of fear!
> Unpleasing to an author's ear—

at whose house I boarded, having long suspected my condition, now began to look after me with that restless
curiosity which a discreet father exhibits towards an only
son who has evinced a predilection for the sea.   At first
the good dame's inquisitiveness was confined within the
pale of politeness ; but at length, as my arrears with her
increased, she exchanged the oblique glance for the direct
frown, and daily vented her spleen in coarse allusions to
my appetite.

My situation was now become really critical.   My
money was nearly all expended, and my entire wardrobe
was on my back.   This last was the "unkindest cut of
all," for any one acquainted with London life knows that
a good coat is half the secret of success.   Boys dress well
from vanity ; men from policy.

Such was my condition, when one day, while seated at
a coffee-shop, I chanced to read in the *Times* journal some
proposals for the establishment of a new literary institution in the metropolis.   Quick as lightning the idea
crossed my brain that I might possibly obtain one of the
lectureships ; so, without a moment's delay, I despatched
a long, elaborate letter to Brougham, who was mentioned
as being one of the warmest patrons of the institution,
in which, after enumerating my intellectual qualifications,
I proposed myself as a lecturer on whatever branch of
knowledge he might feel inclined to suggest.   I added
that, though I did not object to teach mathematics, meta-

physics, chemistry, moral philosophy, jurisprudence, the fine arts, elocution, music, or even dancing, yet that my researches lay chiefly in the Belles Lettres.

Within the week I received an answer to this application, in which, after complimenting me in the most flattering terms on my modesty, the illustrious statesman declined my services, on the very natural plea that they would excite universal envy.

Well, this avenue to fortune closed, a variety of others suggested themselves. First I thought of a merchant's counting-house; but this idea was no sooner suggested than it was laid aside, for where and how was I to procure the requisite certificate of character, ability, and so forth?

Next I bethought me of the law. This, while it lasted, was an agreeable illusion enough, fraught with imposing images of the bench, the woolsack, and the king's conscience. But when I came to look at the question in a worldly, common-sense spirit, more especially when I reflected that without impudence a lawyer is as sounding brass or a tinkling cymbal, I felt with a sigh that the defects of nature were insuperable.

At last a grand idea struck me. I resolved to try the press. I had often heard and read of those sprightly adventurers who contrive to earn a subsistence by picking up, or, in case of need, inventing accidents, &c., for the newspapers; so I presented myself at a dull period at the *Planet* newspaper office, with an affecting report of a young lady who had swallowed a teacupful of arsenic and water, under the influence of derangement brought on by the "diabolical" conduct of a young Guardsman who had seduced her.

This paragraph being well timed, was much approved; became the subject of an indignant leading article in many of the ensuing Sunday journals, "on the demoralised condition of the higher classes," and went the round of the provincial press under the title of "Shocking Suicide."

My next literary perpetration was a Hatton-garden

police report, wherein I detailed the particulars of a pugilistic encounter between two Irish hodmen in a style of
the most rampant vivacity. About this time, too, I contributed about a foot and a half of good jokes weekly to
the *Looker-on*, for which the editor, who was himself a
wag of the first water, and liked, as he said, to encourage
genius, remunerated me at a very handsome rate. But
my chief reliance was on the *Planet* newspaper, on which,
by adroit flattery of the proprietor—an odd little fellow,
with a style of writing "peculiarly his own"—I contrived
to gain so strong a hold, that after a month's probation, I
was declared to be master of my business, and placed on
the establishment as a sort of flying reporter of all work.

In this capacity I exhibited powers of invention that
would have done honour to a Scotch novelist. Scarcely a
day passed but a Mrs. Tomkins and her only daughter fell
from a one-horse chaise in Tavistock or Brunswick squares;
or a Mr. Sibthorpe, a stout gentleman of sixty, with a
wig and six children, broke his leg by stumbling over a
bit of orange-peel which some urchin had inconsiderately
flung upon the pavement. My phenomena were equally
creditable to my fancy. The *Planet* abounded in accounts
of extraordinary gooseberries, which measured four inches
round the waist; of Irish potatoes, on which could be
clearly traced the words "Daniel O'Connell;" of three
children born *impromptu* at a birth; of goats without
beards; cows with five legs; and donkeys with horns like
my Lord ——.

Not unfrequently, when "extra hands" were wanted, I
made my appearance in the gallery in the House of Com-
mons—infinitely to the annoyance of the practised and
well-educated gentlemen who attended there—not one of
whom, however, came near me, whether in eloquence of
style, originality of metaphor, or vivacity of logic. They
stuck to fact, I expatiated in the airy regions of fiction.

But ingratitude is the vice of public men in England.
I had actually not distinguished myself above a dozen
times in the gallery, when I was summoned to the bar,

for a breach of privilege contained in a report of one of Sir William Wiseacre's orations; reprimanded by the Speaker in a style that brought the blood of a hundred ancestors into my cheeks; and then formally dismissed from the *Planet* establishment. In justification of his complaint, Sir William urged that he was not in the House at the time I attributed to him the speech in question, and that nothing but the unparalleled impudence of the forgery should have— But I need say no more. Men of bashful temperament will at once appreciate the motives for my silence.

I should have mentioned, that while engaged on the *Planet*, I had, in order to fill up my leisure time, been in the habit of occasionally advertising as a private teacher of the classics, arithmetic, &c., to which advertisements I had hitherto received no satisfactory replies. It chanced, however, that a few days previous to my dismissal from the gallery, a letter dated Walworth was brought to me by the twopenny post, wherein the writer stated, that having seen A. B.'s advertisement, and being in want of a tutor for his son, he would feel obliged if said A. B. would "step up," when, if terms and so forth were approved, the parties might " do business" together.

The quaint, dry wording of this missive gave me no great hopes of success. However, it did not become me to be fastidious; so, flinging distrust to the winds, I made the best of my way to the place pointed out in the address.

The writer, Mr. Stephen Spinks, a cheesemonger, was at home when I called, busily engaged with some customers behind the counter. On learning the purport of my visit, he made no more ado, but came at once to the point with me; while, at the same time, in order that business might not be neglected, he despatched matters with his customers. " So, Mr. What-d'ye-call-um," he began, "you're the A. B., I s'pose, as is to teach my Dick classics. Clever boy, Dick, sharp as a needle; has got 'Omer at his fingers' ends; do your heart good to hear him;" then turning to his shop-lad, " I say, Jack, why don't you serve that 'ere gentleman? he's been waiting these five minutes.—So, as I was saying, sir, Dick's as sharp as— A pound of Stilton, ma'am ? We never sells it by the pound; very sorry, ma'am, very sorry indeed, but 'twouldn't pay.—And so, Mr. What-d'ye-call-um, you see my boy Dick— Jack, I say, Jack, don't forget to send them two Cheshires up to Mrs. Jenkins, and, d'ye hear, mind and take the bill along with 'em; she's one as requires looking arter.—Excuse my bluntness, Mr. What-d'ye-call-um, I'm a plain John Bull.—Heyday, Mrs. Jackson, what, you here too! Well, and how goes the world with you? and how's your good man, and how's the little uns? I'm sorry to say my Polly's ill abed of the measles. —Beg your pardon, Mr. ——, for keeping you waiting; but business must be minded, you know."

I intreated him not to apologise, as my time was his, and then proceeded to seat myself leisurely in a remote corner of the shop, while the sly fox kept watching every movement of my hands, with the same keenness and pertinacity with which a tom-cat watches a mouse.

In a few minutes, having got rid of all his customers, he whipped off his apron, and led the way into a back room, whither I followed. There was no need of ceremony; we plunged, therefore, without a moment's delay, into the thick of the business. I proposed my terms; he proposed his: but there being, even on this preliminary point, a material pecuniary difference between us. Mr. Spinks, moreover, with the wary shrewdness of the tradesman, persisting in putting a variety of frivolous and vexatious questions to me touching the vouchers I was prepared to furnish him with, as to talent, respectability, and so forth, I at once broke off the negotiation, and stalked from his presence in the same sullen dignity in which Ajax turned from Ulysses in the shades.

I retraced my steps over Waterloo-bridge, towards my lodgings, not exactly *au désespoir*, but still in a state of mind far from enviable. Absorbed in the reflection that

I was the helpless victim of ill-luck, I seated myself moodily on one of the buttresses of the bridge, casting ever and anon a glance on the water, much to the horror of an old lady who was taking the air on the opposite side, and no doubt mistook me for an interesting martyr to unrequited love, when suddenly I heard my name pronounced, and, looking up, saw Patrick Donovan, a brother colleague on the *Planet* establishment, a smart, active fellow, who had always shown a disposition to cultivate my acquaintance.

On the present occasion he was all sympathy; and, as we strolled up and down the bridge together, he said, "You are unlucky, O'Blarney, but *nil desperandum*—as we used to say at Trinity College. What think you of editing a Sunday newspaper?"

"I am willing to try my hand at it, provided the principles of the journal are such as I can conscientiously advocate."

"Oh, if you come to talk of conscience, I have done with you! Your case is hopeless."

"Donovan," said I, with solemnity, "would you deprive me of the only luxury I have left?"

"Yes, for the very reason that it is a luxury. When a gentleman is in difficulties, what are the first things he retrenches? Why, his luxuries, to be sure. Conscience, forsooth! A pretty wall you are building to knock your head against. How can you ever expect to get on with such a stumbling-block in your way? Pray, get rid of it as soon as possible, or assign it over to your tailor or attorney; they stand more in need of it than you do."

"I am convinced; let me hear your proposals."

"You must know, then, that, in conjunction with a pushing young bookseller, I have just purchased the copyright of the *Squib* journal; but, as neither of us has sufficient leisure to do it justice, we are on the look-out for some one who will devote his chief time and attention to it. Under these circumstances I offer you the editorship; but, as there is not a moment to be lost, you must decide at once."

" I agree to your proposals."

" And you will throw overboard all romantic notions of —you understand me ?"

" Nature will at times prevail ; but I will do my best to weed out the delicate infirmity."

" Spoken like a very Canning ! You shall commence operations next week."

The bargain was accordingly struck, and within a fortnight from the period of my dismissal from the *Planet* establishment I was installed editor of a certain flashy, sporting Sunday journal, of no great literary or political character, I must confess, but which, nevertheless, happened to be just then remarkable for its extensive circulation.

This situation necessarily brought me into contact with many of the more puffing and mushroom class of booksellers, by whose means I was introduced to divers small literary characters, artists, actors, &c.; until at length, notwithstanding my diffidence, I began to feel that I was something more than a mere cipher in the republic of letters.

CHAPTER X.

THE LITERARY CONVERSAZIONE.

ONE day, when I was seated in the editor's room at the office, manufacturing a sly, mysterious paragraph respecting the elopement of Lady A—— with a Sir Bore Brocas, a note was put into my hands from the bibliopole who was Donovan's co-partner in the journal, containing an invitation to a literary conversazione, a weekly series of which he had projected during the publishing season.

Such a temptation was irresistible ; and at the appointed hour I twinkled among other literary luminaries at his domicile.

The room was crowded ; and among the invited was Donovan, who, taking compassion on my ignorance of

persons, volunteered to act as my cicerone. Pointing to
an ancient gentleman in spectacles, "In early life," said
he, "that man had the ill-luck to have his favourite
tragedy damned before the third act; since which time
his sole consolation has consisted in lamenting the decay
of the dramatic art, and witnessing the first representation
of every new tragedy, in the hope that it may experience
the fate of his own."

"Is that a dramatist, too, by his side?" I inquired.

"Oh, no; that is a well-known Platonic philosopher,
who reads Greek as fluently as English; has translated
all the sophists, from Plato to Proclus; insists that the
dark ages commenced from the death of Iamblichus; and
that the mythology of Greece and Rome is the only true
religion. He married his cook because her face reminded
him of Pomona, as depicted on an old medal. But mark
that tall, spare man, who has just shaken hands with our
host."

"I see him. Who is he? What's his name?"

"Dr. Ferdinand Fingerfee, the celebrated quack. His
system is a peculiar one. He holds that ill-health is
nothing more than the introduction of mephitic vapours
through the pores of the skin into the diaphragm, and
proposes, by a process of tanning, to render the hide air-
proof. The bills of mortality have increased surprisingly
since his system came into fashion."

"I presume that is one of his patients he is conversing
with."

"What! and in such plump condition! No, that is a
small poet, a cross between the classic and Della Crusca
schools. Suppose we join him?"

Accordingly we took our places beside the bard, who
was seated alone on a sofa; when to Donovan's inquiries
whether he had perused the last new poem, Mr. Singsong
replied in the affirmative, adding that it was of a superior
character.

"Yet the public think otherwise," rejoined Donovan.

"The public!" said Singsong, with a look of supreme

disdain; "and who cares what the public think? Rely on it, sir, no man of real genius ever yet published a successful poem. Where were ever more signal failures than Paradise Lost, the Excursion, Endymion, and Prometheus Unbound! Poetic popularity is a sort of thing I neither covet nor understand."

"You have reason to congratulate yourself in this respect," replied Donovan archly, "for yours is no mob popularity. Indeed, I *did* hear that your last volume failed so egregiously as not even to defray the expenses of publication."

"Failed! I know not what you call failure. Never was there a work more highly spoken of by the critics, or more warmly received by those who know how to appreciate taste and feeling. Failed, indeed! Why, certainly it is neither in fashion at Wapping, nor an oracle in St. Giles'; but the public generally have stamped it with their approbation. Failed, forsooth! If you mean this by way of joke, Mr. Donovan, trust me it is an uncommonly dull one."

"Have you heard the news, gentlemen, the news—the news?" said a squat, pompous little man, whom Donovan introduced to me as the editor of a minor monthly periodical.

"News! what news?" asked all of us in a breath.

"What! have you not heard of the change that we—"

"Oh, yes," said Donovan, "I have often heard (who has not?) of *We*. *We*, though dating from a back garret, has helped to write the country into a war before now. *We* told Byron he was no poet, and Cowper that he was a mere fanatic. But what of this Mr. *We* ?"

"Why, I thought, of course, you knew that *We* have commenced a new series of our Magazine."

"Astonishing," replied Donovan, with mock gravity; "no wonder all Europe is ringing with the intelligence."

"And, what is better still," continued the editor, wholly engrossed with his subject, "we have procured the assistance of the very ablest contributor of the day.

A wonderful fellow! Quite an universal genius! Ah! yonder's the very man. I must go and speak with him ;" and away he went to join his idol.

When he was gone, " That man," said Donovan, pointing after him, " has no conception of intellect, except as connected with a magazine. He dates from month to month, and is one of that numerous class of witlings who contrive to mount up in the literary world by no merit of their own, but solely by clinging to the skirts of some clever fellow who is on the ascent. As every substance has its shadow, so every literary lion has his literary jackall, who imitates his style, spreads his fame, echoes his good sayings, and, in return, is honoured with his patronage."

" What do you think of Wilson as a lion ?" I inquired.

" As a poetic landscape-painter," replied Singsong, " Wilson is unrivalled. What a fairy-land has he made of Windermere and its little bay ! I wonder the elfs and sylphs of the lake-country have never yet got up a public meeting by moonlight, under the shadow of Helvellyn (the spirit of Lodore in the chair), and presented him with the freedom of the lakes in a handsome snuff-box, made of Queen Mab's agate-stone ! But not only is Wilson a poet, he is remarkable also for a rich fantastic vein of humour, which—"

" Your mention of humour," said Donovan, " brings to my recollection two books which I lately *abstracted* from a friend's library, who is rather particular in these matters—"

" God bless me !" rejoined Singsong, " I have lately missed several volumes myself. Have you—"

" Sir, your inference is most disrespectful ; the books I allude to are ' Elia' and 'Melincourt.' What Wilson is to the lakes, Lamb is to London. Then who feels a snug, social rubber like him ? I should detest whist, if it were not for dear, delightful Mrs. Battle, whose gentle shade seems mildly to expostulate with me on my heterodoxy. As for ' Melincourt,' its Island of Cimmerian Gloom is an allegory worthy of ' Rabelais.'"

4

" You speak of 'Rabelais.' I am just fresh from an acquaintance with that elastic rogue Panurge, and cannot, for the life of me, help thinking that he is the original of Falstaff."

" That's an odd crotchet ; but go on. I love a bouncing absurdity."

" The two characters," continued Singsong, " have so much in common—such peculiar ingenuity in lying—such endless jokes on, and fantastic extenuations of their physical defects—such rich, quaint, ever-welling humour, glossing over, and even lending a grace to their preposterous cowardice—such amusing profligacy—such outrageous faculties of buffoonery—such readiness at contrivance—such incredible powers of face and bluster—to say nothing of a hundred other traits, equally far-fetched, yet congenial, that the resemblance could scarcely have been the mere result of a lucky chance. Falstaff is Panurge plumped out. Panurge is Falstaff fallen away. Panurge with Pantagruel plays the same game as Falstaff with Prince Hal. Panurge in the storm at sea is the counterpart of Falstaff at Shrewsbury. Both hold discretion to be the better part of valour ; both have no other idea of life than as a tipsy jest ; both are self-catechists on honour ; both have their Doll Tear-sheet ; both the same accommodating theory of debt. Again—"

"But how came Shakspeare acquainted with 'Rabelais?'" asked Donovan.

" How ? Why, when Shakspeare wrote, Rabelais was the one great name on the Continent ; and as Lord Bacon had already made him the theme of panegyric, and two of his most prominent characters were our Lord Chancellor Moore and Luther, the founder of our Protestant revolution, his fame could scarcely have been a stranger to Englishmen ; certainly, not to such an active, inquisitive spirit as Shakspeare, who passed much of his time in the better educated circles of the court. Now, our swan of Avon, we all know, was never very scrupulous about the means by which he gained plots and characters for his plays—as he has proved by his profuse pilferings from the old Italian novels; and I think it far from improbable that he had met with some garbled translation of 'Rabelais,' and, finding the dramatic capabilities of Panurge, had dressed up the rogue afresh, made him, by way of contrast, a miracle of obesity, and baptised him Falstaff."

"Yet, as rogues, both Falstaff and Panurge must hide their heads before the Spanish swindlers, whose genius was so abundant that it ran over at their fingers' ends. What think you of that prodigy of petty larceny, Don Raphael, who, when complimented on his uncommon faculties of appropriation, replied, 'Upon my word, signor, I would *almost* as lief be an honest man as a rogue!' Match me the sublime indifference of this, if you can!"

"Donovan," said I, sick to death of this conversation, "we wax prosy; Mr. Singsong, I must quit you, or I shall drop fast asleep;" and so saying, I passed on to a group who were standing at a table covered with prints, magazines, &c.

"This is finely executed," said mine host, pointing my attention to an engraving from a design by Haydon.

"It is far better than the original," replied a royal academician. "Haydon is at best but a vigorous dauber."

"Indeed!" said the bibliopole. "Yet he ranks high as an artist."

"Only among ignoramuses; the Academy thinks nothing of him."

"Is he not superior to Northcote?" I inquired.

"To Northcote!" rejoined the painter, with a sneer; and then, with a look that he thought would at once annihilate me, "Sir, that eminent artist has been an R.A. upwards of thirty years."

But I survived the shock, and added, "You will at least allow that Martin is a fine painter."

"Humph! he is no academician."

A sharp answer was just about to escape me, when Donovan recalled me to his side. "Singsong and Matter-of-fact, the Utilitarian," said he, "are, as usual, declaring

war to the knife against each other.　Let us join them :
I love a row."

"And so, Mr. Matter-of-fact," said the bard, as we
resumed our seats on the sofa, "you have really no faith
in the poetical temperament ?"

"Not an atom.　What you call inspiration is, in nine
cases out of ten, mere indigestion.　You are a sad, selfish
set, you poets ; and in the perverted ingenuity with which
you persuade mankind to be miserable, you stand out in
humiliating contrast to us Utilitarians, whose first principle it is to do our best to leave the world wiser and
happier than we found it."

"Wiser, certainly, if the essence of all wisdom consists
in a knowledge that two and two make four ; happier,
also, if the mechanical and the commonplace are the sole
requisites for felicity.　But, till you can persuade the
world of this, you and yours must be content to rank
among those learned philosophers whom Panurge speaks
of as sowing fields with gunpowder, in the hope that the
seed might sprout up into cannon-balls.　Humanity is no
spinning-jenny, Mr. Matter-of-fact.　There is such a thing
as passion."

"I know there is : I see it by your face."

"And yet you talk, write, and act as if human nature
were a mere machine !"

"Not so ; but we would make every effort of mind
tend to expound some principle, illustrate some truth,
answer some great purpose of utility."

"And so it does, when rightly estimated ; but yours is
a purblind, tradesman-like notion of the useful.　You
would take measure of humanity like a tailor, as if it
consisted but of one individual, and that one was a
political economist.　You would shatter to atoms the
golden images of poetry, deface its armorial bearings, and
set up, instead, the brazen calf of Utilitarianism.　There
is a want of scope, elevation, and tolerance in your philosophy.　Are you then, and such as you, to come forward
at this time of day, and gravely tell us that humanity

hitherto has been all a mistake—that its thoughts and interests have all taken a wrong direction, and that you are the Deucalions destined to regenerate it? You talk of the fictions of the poets—"

"Meaning thereby to deduce their genealogy from the Devil. He was the father of lies, and, of course, the first poet. Rant as you please, Mr. Singsong; facts are the only things worth a wise man's consideration."

"Agreed; and you will find more in one page of Shakspeare than in all the volumes McCulloch ever penned."

"McCulloch! why, he is full of facts."

"Nevertheless, match me, in all Shakspeare, a fiction equal in wild extravagance to your idol's theory of Absenteeism."

"What do you think of our Greatest-Happiness-Principle?"

"Think? why, that it is invaluable; and not the less so for being as old as the hills. It is the groundwork of the Socratic philosophy—the staple of the Sermon on the Mount."

"'This is a mere frantic assumption," said Matter-of-fact, in a passion; "and I now see more clearly than ever the necessity of adopting the suggestion of a friend of mine, namely, to establish a society for the suppression of poetry. Now, don't alarm yourself, Mr. Singsong; my project will not interfere with your interests. I propose only to suppress poetry, not prose run mad."

"Ah, my dear sir, I am not now to learn for the first time that, if you had your will, you would plant Parnassus with hemp and tobacco, turn the temple of the Muses into a cotton-mill, and carry a railroad right through the heart of fairy-land."

"God help me! the man's a lunatic!" exclaimed Matter-of-fact, casting a look of bewilderment at the poet.

"Lunatic!" said the bibliopole, who, attracted by the noise of the dispute, now joined us. "I suppose, sir, you are alluding to poor Cribb, the dramatist. His is a hard case, poor fellow ; but, I'm happy to say, a subscription is being got up for him, to which, I doubt not, each of you will gladly—"

The mention of the word "subscription" had an electrical effect on the company, and induced universal locomotion. One person just remembered that he had a call to make on his way home ; another, that he had promised to join a party at Drury Lane ; and a third, that he had got a proof-sheet to revise before the morning. Finding this to be the case, I also took the opportunity of slipping away, and amused myself for some hours afterward at my lodgings with noting down memoranda of the night's proceedings in my journal, which, however, under any circumstances, would have been vividly impressed upon my mind, from the singular fact of my losing neither my hat nor my umbrella ! They were not even exchanged !

CHAPTER XI.

A FASHIONABLE PATRON OF THE FINE ARTS.

IT is fortunate for young politicians that there happens to be such a place as Ireland. To me, at least, the sister isle has always proved a fortunate theme for speculation, and Catholic Emancipation in particular a perfect godsend ; for, during the whole period of my connexion with Donovan, while I was warmly advocating this question in his journal, I was as warmly opposing it in another. I am aware it will be said by those who are incapable of the more enlarged sentiments of humanity, that, by thus writing on both sides of the question, I was influenced by a base love of lucre ; but I scorn the ungenerous insinuation. My sole motive for such conduct originated in a conviction that the only way for a man to accomplish hirself as a politician is by discussing the white as well as the black of every question. Great truths are best struck out by collision.

As, for want of some fresher subject, I was busy at the office one Saturday morning, cudgelling my brains for a smart, terse "leader" on Ireland, in which the Liberator, as usual, should figure by way of episode, my thoughts were suddenly called off by the entrance of the office-clerk with a card for a private view of the British Gallery. There being not a moment to be lost, and the Fine Arts constituting one of the most material, indeed favourite, branches of my avocation, I gladly dismissed the great Liberator in a sentence, and posted off full speed to Pall Mall.

I know of no rarer intellectual treat than a fine collection of paintings. If only by way of contrast to one's usual occupations, it is worth a visit. At one moment you are trudging along the busy, crowded, every-day world of the Strand; the next, you are standing in the exalted presence of genius, amid comparative stillness and desertion, gazing on some blue Sicilian sky with Claude, drinking in the spirit of some fresh sea-breeze with Vandervelde; feasting on the luxury of some lovely woman's black eye with Reynolds; looking, till your very flesh creeps again, far down into the horrid depths of some sunless glen, while a grim, swarthy brigand lurks, half seen, among the woods, with Salvator Rosa; feeling what love is with Titian, and chivalry with Vandyke; now smitten with the coquettish Spanish gipsy girls of Murillo; and now ready to pour forth your whole soul in adoration of the Madonnas of Correggio or Carlo Dolce! Five minutes make all the difference in a case like this. It suffices to transport you from the world of business and commonplace into the seventh heaven of the imagination!

On my arrival at the British Gallery, I found a small sprinkling of critics and artists, together with a few really munificent, and a few would-be, patrons of the Fine Arts. The whole together scarcely exceeded twenty; and among them, I was particularly struck with a thin, tall, smirking, elderly personage, who kept hopping from painting to painting, as Beau Didapper might have been supposed to

do.   A more swift-footed amateur I never beheld.   The
finest skies of Claude failed to rivet his attention for
more than a few seconds.   Five minutes even of a Rubens
would have bored him to death.

"Hey, Barnet!" said this airy whirligig, as the keeper
accompanied him most deferentially in all his movements,
"what's this? what's this?—very pretty, fine colouring
—looks like a Claude."

"That, General, is a Rembrandt."

"Well, well—no matter—all the same—fine Titian
this!"

"I beg pardon, General, it's a—"

"Velasquez—so I see."

"I rather think, General, it's a—"

"You're right, so it is—so it is.   Clever artist, that
Paul Potter.   Hey, Barnet?"

"Very, General."

"Barnet, Barnet, what's this, No. 168?   Warm sky
—fine perspective!"

The keeper hastened to point out the number in his
catalogue ; but, before he could turn over two or three
leaves, the velocipede was off again to a distant part of
the room, Mr. Barnet moving after him as swiftly as his
years would permit.

Again the harlequin attacked him.   "Hey, Barnet,
whom have we got here ?   No. 325.   Very pretty—very
pretty—very pretty indeed !   Charming face ! sweet figure !
What a bust !"

"That is the celebrated—"

"So I thought ; and 327 is her husband, I suppose.
Sticks close to her side—hey, Barnet?" and the General
laughed blandly at this bright surmise.

In this mercurial style he pirouetted through the gallery, till, having finished his gallopade, and accomplished
his survey of about four hundred paintings in something
less than half-an-hour, he whirled out of the room, and
was off like a shot in his cab !

"Ah," thought I, as I stared after him in an ecstacy of

astonishment and admiration, " what a blessing it is to have a quick apprehension of the sublime and beautiful in art !"

CHAPTER XII.

PHILOSOPHICAL REFLECTIONS ON A HORSEWHIPPING— A CASE OF LIBEL.

" THE course of true love never did run smooth ;" and the same remark applies with equal force to the course of a public journalist.   One day, when I was seated at my desk reading a report of a grand Tory dinner given to Mr. Canning at Liverpool, the office-boy knocked at my door, with information that two gentlemen were below who were desirous of speaking with the editor on business of importance, which admitted of no delay.

Before I had time to consider what answer should be given to this pressing application, the strangers entered *sans cérémonie*, and, walking straight up to my desk, the taller of the two, a perfect elephant of a man, drew the preceding Sunday's publication from his pocket, and, pointing with a smile to a particular paragraph, asked if I was the author of that brilliant squib.

I am rarely thrown off my guard ; but on this occasion my vanity got the better of my discretion, and, contrary to all etiquette, I at once avowed the authorship, expressing at the same time my gratification that it had afforded them amusement.

" So much amusement," said the tallest of the two, " that my friend here and myself have come in person to offer our express acknowledgments."

" Yes, sir," added his companion, " the paragraph in question is one that cannot be too promptly acknowledged. It is a base, unwarrantable calumny on a lady with whom we have the honour to be acquainted."

" Calumny !" said I ; " believe me, gentlemen, you are wholly in error.   The paragraph contains nothing of the sort; it is a mere harmless *jeu d'esprit,* penned hastily in a moment of overpowering sprightliness."

"And do you presume to call this sprightliness?" interrupted the giant, slowly reading over the article, and laying a malignant emphasis on each word; "I tell you, sir, it is an infamous falsehood, such as no gentleman would have dared to circulate. However, I did not come here to talk, but to act;" and so saying, he drew forth a horsewhip from beneath his cloak, and half-strangling me with one hand, so as to render me utterly incapable of defence, laid it across my shoulders with the other.

There is a natural dislike in man to have his nose pulled, and the same disinclination extends, I have generally observed, to a horsewhipping. It will not appear surprising, therefore, that, partaking of the common prejudice of humanity, I indignantly resisted this encroachment on the liberty of the subject. "Sir," said I, "this ruffian personality is not to be endured, and if there be law or—"

"Personality, my good sir!" said the fellow who had planted himself before the door, "we have no wish to be personal; our quarrel is with the public editor, not the private individual. I trust we have too nice a sense of propriety not to discriminate between the two characters."

This was adding insult to injury, and being followed up by a brisk application of the other ruffian's boot to my rearward Adam as he let go his hold, after having nearly throttled me, wound me up to such a pitch of desperation, that, making a sudden rush to the door, I knocked down the sophistical scoundrel who guarded it, and was off like lightning to Donovan's lodgings.

There is nothing like passion to give wings to a man's speed; it would make a mercury of a Dutchman. Hardly had I lost sight of the office, when, behold! I was at Donovan's door. My appearance struck him with astonishment. My lips quivered, my legs trembled, my clothes exhibited samples of every crossing from Fleet-street to the Strand.

"So," said I, "a pretty condition you have reduced me to, Mr. Donovan! But you shall give me satisfaction, sir, instant satisfaction—no ruffian shall horsewhip me with impunity."

"Horsewhip? Nonsense—you must be joking, surely."

"Sir, it is no joke to me, whatever it may be to you. I tell you I have been insulted, bullied, and horsewhipped into the bargain, and all in consequence of that confounded paragraph about Lady A——, and her reported *liaison* with—"

"Sir Bore Brocas. I remember it perfectly; and so, for this harmless squib, you have actually, you say, been horsewhipped? Upon my word, O'Blarney, this is a monstrous lucky affair. It will give quite a lift to the paper. And then the damages!"

"Indeed!" said I, with a most bitter smile; "but you forget my shoulders, Mr. Donovan."

"Don't mention it; 'tis a mere trifle, not worth thinking about."

"Trifle, sir!"

"To be sure; what is a horsewhipping compared with the *éclat* it will give our paper? 'Tis a mere nothing when one's used to it. But," continued Donovan, seeing that, so far from being convinced, I began to manifest increased passion, "let us discuss the matter coolly and rationally, not like romantic boys, but like men of the world;" and, throwing himself back in his arm-chair, with an easy impudence that made me smile notwithstanding my rage, commenced as follows :—"There are two lights in which a horsewhipping may be regarded—first, as an affair of honour; secondly, as an affair of business. Your raw stripling, who is all for the heroics, views it only in the first light, and retrieves his 'honour' by being shot through the head; but your more shrewd worldling, having wit enough to view it in the other, obtains satisfaction by making his aggressor pay down a handsome per centage for his experiment. Now, I contend that all assaults, whether dorsal, humeral, or nasal, should be re-

garded in this light, and revenged in this spirit only.
For why should not a man make his shoulders as available
a property as his brains ?   Why let the slightest portion
of corporeal capital lie idle ?   It is an affront to an all-
wise Providence to do so, especially in your case, whose
Atlantean shoulders were manifestly built for the purposes of assault.   Be resigned, then, O'Blarney, ever bearing
in mind this consolatory axiom, that, after all, a horsewhipping is nothing more than a dispute taking a practical
instead of a theoretical turn.   Besides, consider, assaults
usually carry damages ; and that made on you being of a
highly-inflammatory character, ten to one it conjures a
cool five hundred out of Sir Bore's pocket into yours.
Now, with this sum you can make the grand tour !
Really, my friend, all things considered, I look on this
affair as quite a god-send, and am so far from condoling
with you that I beg leave to offer you my sincerest congratulations.   Of course, you'll prosecute ?"

"That's as may happen ; at present I can think of nothing but the intolerable pain in my shoulder-blades."

"Nonsense.   You must—you shall prosecute.   How is
the affair to get wind else ?   Consider, your ' honour,' as
you call it, is at stake."

"My honour, Mr. Donovan !   Why, sir, my very
seat of honour is at stake !   Would you believe it, the
ruffian—"

"You need not go on, I can guess what is to come ;
there are no half-measures in affairs of this sort ; so the
' ruffian' having done his business in a workman-like style,
it is now your turn to do yours.   Let me see.   In the
first place, you must enter an action of assault and battery
against Sir Bore Brocas ; secondly—"

At this stage of the conversation, a lad entered the
room with a most suspicious, lawyer-like note, which he
said had been left for the proprietor and editor of the
Squib journal, and which, as the bearer had declared it to
contain matters of importance, the clerk had ordered him
to forward to Donovan's lodgings.

Donovan opened the note, but before he had perused three lines his countenance visibly lengthened.

I watched the change, and, delighted with an opportunity of repaying banter with banter—for I had been more annoyed by his irony than I chose to confess—said, "Heyday ! what's the matter now ? Is there a second horsewhipping in the wind ?"

"Don't talk so like a fool," replied Donovan sulkily; "this is no time for joking."

"So I thought when you were favouring me just now with your facetious essay."

"Zounds ! O'Blarney, you're enough to drive one mad ! Here is a notice of action for a libel contained in our paper of Sunday fortnight. However, it's your business, not mine. It is monstrous that the innocent should suffer for the guilty."

"Capital ! So you are to monopolise all the profits of the paper, and I the horsewhippings and libels !"

"Why, are not you the editor ?"

"And you the proprietor ?"

"Granted ; but when I engaged you, it was far from my intention to stand godfather to your libels. No, no, sir, you must come forward and acknowledge your own paternity. I will have no order of affiliation made on me. How, in the name of common-sense, could you be fool enough to meddle with the private character of a cabinet minister ?"

"And how could you be fool enough to allow the paragraph to be inserted ?"

"Well, well, this recrimination is childish ; what's done can't be undone ; therefore our mutual safety is what we must now look to. I despise that sort of chivalrous spirit which would induce one man to go to jail for another ; at the same time, mark me, I would not wish to do anything unjust or—"

"Ahem ! I clearly understand you, sir."

After some further conversation of this nature, which terminated, as might have been anticipated, in a quarrel

—for I could not but see that Donovan meditated throwing all the *onus* of the libel on my already sufficiently afflicted shoulders—I left him with the fixed but secret determination of resigning my editorial functions, and never again venturing my person near the office.

This resolution was no sooner formed than executed. I instantly removed from my old lodgings, kept my new place of abode a more than Eleusinian mystery, and never once, for a whole fortnight, ventured out, except, like a bat or a burglar, by night.

Meantime the myrmidons of the law were not inactive, and within a very brief period from my resignation of the editorship the morning papers made me acquainted with the fact that Patrick Donovan, having been found guilty of a libel on a distinguished member of his Majesty's Government, was to be brought up the ensuing term for judgment.

About the same time, through the influence of a respectable news-agent, who alone was in my confidence, the editorship of a country journal, entitled the *Humbug Flying Reporter,* was offered me, for which town I forthwith took my departure, with the avowed intention of henceforth cutting all connexion with a metropolis where my industry and abilities had met with so unworthy a recompense.

It was on a chilly, foggy April evening that I took my seat inside the Humbug Mercury. My prospects were gloomy, my spirits still more so. Gradually, however, this despondency wore away, and gave place to livelier sensations. A night's journey in a stage-coach is an excellent recipe for the blues. A thousand little incidents are perpetually at work to call off the attention from self. There is the casual and often divertingly characteristic chit-chat ; the whimsical settling-down of the more practised insiders into a snug nook for a nap ; the cheering sound of the guard's horn, as the horses clatter along the stones of some provincial town ; the snatch of supper at the appointed inn, with the bright fireside and the blazing candles; then, again, the abrupt departure, with the "Good-night" of my landlord, and the "All right" of the regenerated coachman—these, and divers other minutiæ, though trifling enough, you will say, have at least a tendency to divert the mind, and so far re-assured me that, by the time I reached Humbug, I had wholly regained my serenity, notwithstanding I had for fourteen hours been wedged fast between two elderly ladies, one of whom took Scotch snuff, and the other talked incessantly of her son Tom.

BOOK THE SECOND.

THE POLITICIAN.

CHAPTER I.

A PROVINCIAL GREAT MAN.

WITHIN a walking distance of the borough of Humbu dwelt Miles Snodgrass, Esq., who was rich, consequently respectable, and possessed of considerable local influence. As the artificer of his own fortune, Mr. Snodgrass held himself in no slight estimation. His father had for years been the town-clerk; but dying suddenly when Miles was yet a boy, left him heir to little but his virtues and his wardrobe. The lad, however, being tractable, bustling, and gifted with what the experienced in such matters call "an eye to business," was taken notice of by the parochial authorities, who contrived to get him bound apprentice to an old friend of his father, a wealthy linen-draper of Humbug, in which capacity he rendered himself so gene-rally useful, that at the expiration of his servitude his master, finding he could not do without him, took the young man into partnership, and, in process of time, as he himself waxed old and indolent, invested him with the entire superintendence of the concern.

Years rolled on, and each successive one found Miles Snodgrass rising into gradual importance in the neigh-bourhood. By the death of his patron he became sole proprietor of the concern, which enabled him to enlarge the sphere of his ambition, and espouse the wealthy daughter of a retired butcher and alderman of the borough.

But his good luck did not stop here. Some men are born with a silver spoon in their mouths, and Miles Snodgrass was one of these lucky few. A successful specu-lation in cottons rendered him, shortly after his marriage, so wholly independent of trade as to justify him in with-drawing his name from the concern, and becoming what is called a "*sleeping* partner."

It is from this period that his standing in society may be dated. At the urgent intercession of his eldest daughter, who was now fast advancing to womanhood, he exchanged his snug private house in the main street for a spacious mansion, about half a mile from the borough ; emblazoned the armorial bearings of the Snodgrasses on the panels of his carriage ; suddenly discovered that his family was of ancient extraction ; and once, in a moment of enthusiasm, was heard to talk of his ancestors.

The town viewed these symptoms of unequivocal gen-tility with more than ordinary interest. The corporation, in particular, were delighted with such a handsome additament to their fraternity, and rioted in anticipation of the glorious feastings that would ensue, when Miles Snodgrass, Esq., should be metamorphosed into his worship the mayor.

Nor were they disappointed. After passing through all the initiatory phases, our worthy burgess, who had for many years been expanding into the requisite circum-ference, became mayor of the borough of Humbug. His inaugural dinner surpassed all expectation, and was rendered unusually popular by the death of two attorneys from apoplexy.

I have as yet said nothing on the subject of his worship's politics. Being more than ordinarily fortunate, he was, of course, loyal in proportion ; and having invested a con-siderable portion of his property in the five per cents., made a point of getting up Pitt dinners, together with all sorts of clubs, meetings, and addresses that might tend to strengthen the public securities, and evince his attachment to the ruling powers. His hostility to the Radicals was equally exemplary ; while the stocks, the cart's-tail, and black-hole bore testimony to his vigour as a magistrate.

Such services did not pass unnoticed. A cabinet minister happening, during his mayoralty, to be on a visit in the neighbourhood, a grand public dinner, at which his worship presided, was given to the great man, who after the customary loyal toasts, &c., not only proposed the health of the Mayor of Humbug, but even held him forth to the company as a shining public character, whose patriotism was as sterling as his eloquence, and with whom it was an honour to be acquainted.

This compliment—particularly the touch about his eloquence, on which he prided himself—was very nearly the death of Mr. Snodgrass. He did not get safely over it for six months. He talked of it by day, he dreamed of it by night ; looked about him with a consequential air ; affected reserve and mystery, as if vast ideas were fermenting in his brain ; until at length he reasoned himself into the conviction that he was *bonâ fide* a great man.

But there is a tide in the affairs of men ; and his worship's having been some years at its full flood, was now beginning to ebb. Notwithstanding the publicly proclaimed friendship of the cabinet minister, time rolled on and found him an unrewarded country magistrate. Though, on the occasion of a memorable Tory meeting at Humbug, he had gone the extreme length of declaring his perfect readiness to die in the last ditch in defence of the glorious Constitution, still he had been refused the only place he ever solicited from Government. This was a hard case, but he bethought himself of the proverbial ingratitude of public men, and for a time was reconciled to his lot. An event at length occurred which deranged the whole economy of his politics. Owing to the popular clamour, the minister of the day found himself compelled to reduce the five per cents. ; and Mr. Snodgrass, who, as I observed before,

5

had invested largely in these funds, experienced in consequence a considerable reduction of income. Heavens and earth! what was his indignation when the appalling tidings first reached him. He threatened, he raved, he talked of Tory madness and ministerial ingratitude—hinted that he had been mistaken in his prejudice against the Whigs —and brought himself to think even of the Radicals without horror! There is no affront so deeply resented or so long remembered as that offered to the pocket, and Mr. Snodgrass was proverbially sensitive on this point.

It was about this critical period, when he had withdrawn in disgust from public life, that I made my first appearance at Humbug. As the editor of the only Liberal journal—my contemporary was a red-hot Tory—it was, of course, requisite that I should cultivate connexion as much as possible. I instituted, therefore, minute inquiries into the character, politics, wealth, patronage, and so forth, of every leading family in the district, and soon became acquainted with all the circumstances relative to Mr. Snodgrass which I have just narrated.

Fortunately for my prospects of notoriety, the Liberal member died a few months after my arrival in Humbug, and it became a matter of pressing necessity to put another of similar principles in nomination.

I was among the first applied to on this subject—such influence had my bustling activity already procured me —and to the committee who paid me the honour of an official visit I ventured, after numerous candidates had been proposed and rejected, to suggest the name of Miles Snodgrass.

The committee, as I expected, were thunder-struck at the suggestion.

" Why, he is a Tory !" said one.

" A mere imbecile !" exclaimed a second.

" His very name would damn the cause !" hinted a third.

"Gentlemen," I observed, "believe me, you are all in error on this point. True, Mr. Snodgrass is a Tory ; but

why? Because his principles have hitherto squared with his interests. Of late, however, he has sustained grievous pecuniary inconvenience, and is just now, as I have every reason to believe, in that state of vacillation which it requires only an expert tactician to turn to account. Habit would still incline him to Toryism ; but wounded vanity, disappointed ambition, diminished means, urge him forward in an opposite direction.

"You say he is unpopular. That may be, but he is at least a favourite with our corporation, the majority of whom are likely enough to wink at his tergiversation, from the reverential reminiscences they entertain of his past dinners, and the avidity with which they look forward to future ones. Gentlemen, a politician, no matter whether Whig or Tory, who baits with a good dinner, is pretty sure to hook an alderman !

"Besides, let us bear in mind that from Mr. Snodgrass' nomination we derive these two positive advantages : in the first place, if he come over to our party, yet fail in his election, he is, from that moment, muzzled for life ; secondly, if he succeed, he will plead our cause with all the energy of which he is capable ; for, as neglected poets turn to raving critics, so disappointed Tories invariably make the stiffest Liberals. Of the exact amount of his imbecillity I am no judge, further than that he *is* an alderman, and *has been* a mayor. Trust me, however, it is not always the wisest man that makes the best patriot."

The committee were so struck with the sagacity—I quote their own appropriate expressions—of these suggestions, that, after one or two more discussions, they all came round to my way of thinking ; decided that Mr. Snodgrass should be invited to stand on the Whig, or, as we adroitly phrased it, the Independent, interest ; and waving the usual forms of going up in a body—as it was supposed that more could be done with Mr. Snodgrass in a confidential *tête-à-tête*—that I should wait on him singly with the intelligence, and exert all my powers of rhetoric to induce him to accede to the nomination.

CHAPTER II.

HOW TO TURN ONE'S COAT BECOMINGLY.

PURSUANT to the directions of the committee, I paid a visit in form to the worthy alderman.   I found him alone at breakfast, in what he called his study, hidden behind a double sheet of the *Times;* above him, over the mantel-piece, hung an autograph letter, framed and glazed, from the lord-lieutenant of the county, complimenting him on the zeal and ability he had displayed on some particular occasion, in his capacity of magistrate ; and directly opposite, his own portrait, a superb full-length, as mayor of the borough of Humbug.

From the circumstance of his being rich, I was prepared also to find Mr. Snodgrass genteel and handsome. Nor was I disappointed.   It is astonishing what a superiority, in point of appearance, a rich man possesses over a poor one.   I hate poor men.   In this respect I am quite a magistrate.

For the rest, the alderman was just such a man as may be met with in the Strand or on 'Change any hour in the day; a shrewd, active, hot-tempered John Bull ; about fifty years of age ; self-conceited, but far from proud ; frugal, and, perhaps, penurious, except where his vanity was concerned, when he could be as lavish of his money as a spendthrift.

On taking my seat, after the usual preliminaries, &c., I opened on the purport of my visit, which being duly explained, I drew forth the requisition from my pocket, placed it in the alderman's hands, and watched attentively each change of his countenance, as, adjusting his spectacles, he ran over the list of signatures, and muttered a few words on each :—"Giles Markland ; good, an old colleague of mine on the bench.   James Portsoken; hah ! a connexion, by marriage, of Mrs. S.—did a deal of business some years since in the soap line.   Anthony Catchflat ;

hem ! an attorney in the *Gazette* last year, but honest, I believe, notwithstanding. John—Charles—Battiscomb" —the alderman lingered over these words with evident satisfaction—"well, now, this really is most flattering. If there be one man in all Humbug I esteem more than another, Alderman Battiscomb is that man. A more respectable individual never breathed. They do say, indeed, he's worth half a million." In this manner Mr. Snodgrass kept commenting on the different signatures, till, having gone through the list, he placed it on the table, and said with a sigh, "The requisition, Mr.— I beg pardon, but I really forget your name."

"O'Blarney."

"Well, Mr. O'Blarney, the requisition which you have done me the honour to be the bearer of is, I need scarcely say, most flattering to my feelings, and could I but accept the handsome offer of the committee, I would do so most gladly ; but, sir, there are grave considerations in the way, which—"

"I know to what you allude, sir, but I flatter myself I can adduce reasons that will convince you that, as a public man, you are perfectly unfettered."

The alderman shook his head. "It is impossible, sir ; I am too old to rat."

"Nor would the committee dare to hope such a thing. In fact, sir, it is the conviction that such a phrase cannot, by any possibility, apply to you, that brings me here to-day."

"Not apply—not apply ? Indeed, how so ? Explain yourself."

"Why, sir, it must be evident to all men of the slightest discernment, that a public character so well known and so generally esteemed as yourself, and one, too, who has so much at stake, would never dream of altering his line of policy, except from the pressing dictates—"

"Humph !" interrupted Mr. Snodgrass, with a disappointed air ; "very correct, no doubt ; but fine words butter no parsnips. As a man of honour, and holding the

station I do in the borough, I am compromised beyond
all hope of escape.   Am I not pledged to Tory principles?"

"Certainly ; but not to Tory tergiversation.''

"No ; *that* I should set my face against, as I did against
the reduction of the five per cents.—a most scandalous
business, which I shall never forgive, were I to live a
thousand years."

"You say you are compromised," said I, bringing him
back to the point, "to Tory principles, but not to Tory
tergiversation.   Be it so.   But suppose that Government
is going to do with other great questions what it has
already done with the five per cents., will you tell me that
in such a case you will be still compromised ?   Believe
me, Mr. Snodgrass, I am supposing no extreme case.
The emergency has already arisen.   The whole system of
Tory policy is at this moment on the eve of important
changes, so loud is the discontent of the country, and so
influential the Independent party, whether in or out of
Parliament."

This staggered the alderman, who, I could clearly perceive, held his opinions more from habit than conviction.
After a short pause, I resumed as follows :—"Taking all
the peculiarities of your position into consideration, I
cannot see how, with any consistency, you can longer support the ministers.   They are of opinion that the five per
cents. should be reduced.   You hold that such reduction
is a breach of faith with the national creditor."

"But you forget, that question is settled now."

"True ; and being so settled in the teeth of all their
former professions, what security can you have for the
future good faith of ministers?"

"Ahem !   There is some sense in what you say ; but
remember, that on every other question I hold the same
sentiments as Government."

"So you think ; but who is to know what those sentiments are ?   Between ourselves, sir, I have it on the very
best authority—for it is surprising how soon these things
get wind—that many of the leading Tory land-owners,

whose members have hitherto supported Government, are now beginning to think that they will be safer under a more liberal one."

The alderman here fell into a profound fit of musing. I did not disturb his reverie, for I saw that it was at work in a right channel. Unwilling, however, that his vacillation should be noticed, he observed, in an indifferent tone, " Your last piece of intelligence, I must own, surprises me ; for, notwithstanding your arguments, and really there is a good deal in them, I cannot see how those who have hitherto acted with the Tories can now consistently support the Whigs."

" For two excellent reasons. First, because the necessities of the day demand a change of measures ; secondly, because the Whigs, equally with the Tories, are pledged to the support of the great landed and moneyed interests."

" Right," said the alderman, with suitable pomp of manner ; " property must have its influence—vested interests must be supported. Let who will be minister, *we must* have this protection."

" Can you doubt it ? The two parties, whatever they may once have done, now differ only on minor points."

" Indeed ! What say you to reform ? Your Whigs, or Independents, as you please to call them, are pledged to that at least ; and, really, to be candid with you, a late abominable transaction has convinced me, too, that some sort of snug, quiet, temperate reform is necessary. Little did I think I should ever live to entertain such a notion ! But I will encourage no wild Whig theories. I'm a plain, practical man, and always look to facts."

" Wild Whig theories ! Ah, Mr. Snodgrass, if the Whigs have their faults, the Tories have them a thousand times worse. Consider only the indifference, not to say the ingratitude, with which ministers have passed you over. Why, even that glorious testimony to your public worth which I see hanging above my head has brought with it nought but barren honour ; while others, even in this very neighbourhood, have been loaded with ministerial bounty."

" Yes, there was Spraggs the barrister, who got that very living for his eldest son which Lord Leatherhead has promised me for Tom a dozen times."

" What ! a Spraggs preferred to a Snodgrass ? Impossible !"

" Fact."

" Monstrous !   Were I situated as you are, sir, I would at once show ministers that I was not a fool to be trifled with—a worm to be trodden on with impunity."

" You are warm, sir," said Mr. Snodgrass, with a bland smile ; " and though your feelings do you credit, still, as I have long since forgiven what, between ourselves, I cannot but look on as a slight—"

" A slight !   A breach of common honesty, you should say."

" Well, well, my young friend, be it as you please ; only do pray be calm.   You see how composed I am.   With regard to the question before us, I have merely to say— and I beg you to assure the committee that I say so with deep regret—that, under existing circumstances, I must decline their handsome offer.   A man of my station, Mr. O'Blarney, cannot chop and change as if he were a mere nobody !   I have a character to support, sir."

" Since this is the case, then, Mr. Snodgrass," I replied, rising to take leave, " there is no more to be said.   Yet I could have wished it had been otherwise, if only by way of answer to those gentlemen whom, no later than yesterday, I myself heard declare in the town-hall, that no matter what tergiversations ministers might be guilty of, Miles Snodgrass would still stick by them, for he had neither the sense to think, nor the spirit to act for himself."

This seasonable taunt changed the whole nature of the alderman's position.   With a loud voice, and flashing eye, he exclaimed, " Ah ! what's that you say ?   Sit down, sir, sit down ; you are so hasty—so precipitate."

Resuming my seat, I repeated slowly and emphatically every word I had just uttered, with the addition of such inflammatory phrases as might make the fitting impression on Mr. Snodgrass' mind. My sneers had just the effect I calculated on; for, before I had half finished, he started from his seat, rudely interrupting me with—"And did they say this, sir? Did they really dare to speak so of a man who for years past—. But I say nothing, sir; mark me, I say nothing; but this I will say, that the public service is the most thankless—the most—. And they really said this, did they?"

"They did, indeed; but you have it in your power nobly to refute the calumny. Join the Whigs, who, by the bye, have always dreaded your influence, and those dangerous powers of oratory which—"

"What, then, you heard of the speech I made during my mayoralty? It certainly did create a stir at the time," added the alderman, recovering in some degree his self-complacency.

"And no wonder. You are aware, of course, sir, that the living of St. Andrew is just about to be vacated by the promotion of the present incumbent to a deanery?"

"I never heard a syllable of it," said the alderman, musing.

"It is the richest in all Humbug, I'm told."

"So they say; what then?"

"Oh, nothing. I was merely thinking that, as you intended your son for the church, it would be the very thing to suit him. The patron, you are aware, is a staunch Whig, and, as I have good reason to believe, exceedingly anxious that a person of your rank and ability should be returned for the borough."

"My dear sir," said the alderman with animation, "your arguments are so convincing, and the justice and necessity of the case so apparent, that—that—in short, Mr. O'Blarney, I accept the flattering offer of the committee. I will show ministers what it is to overlook—I mean, sir, that by deeds as well as words I will prove that I have the public good at heart. But you are quite sure the living is about to fall vacant?"

" I heard so from the incumbent's own lips."

" What a capital thing for Tom ! Not that this has the slightest weight with me. I am not a man to be biassed by interested motives, as I think I have sufficiently shown in the sacrifices I have already made for my king and country ;" and the alderman looked the very image of patriotic benevolence.

At this moment we were interrupted by a light tap at the door, and his bailiff entered the room. " Beg pardon, sir, but it was missis' wish that—"

" Your mistress should have known better," replied Mr. Snodgrass sharply, " than to send you here, when she knew I was busy. What do you want ? "

After sundry preliminary hems and haws, the bailiff commenced a somewhat copious narrative of the distresses of one of Mr. Snodgrass' tenants, who, with his wife and three children, had been burnt out of house and home a few nights previous ; and, as a last resource, had requested the bailiff to lay his case before the alderman.

" Burnt out ! Starving wife and family ! Aye, aye, the old story. What business has a poor man with such a litter ! Pretty thing, if all my tenants who have families were to apply to me for support !"

" Missis says, sir, says she, if you can only assist them just till they can—"

" What ! assist a fellow from whom I have not received a farthing's rent for the last year ?"

" But the man and his family are actually starving, sir," replied the honest fellow, waxing bold in a good cause.

" Starving, John ! How can that be ? There's lots o excellent soup and meat twice a week at the workhouse. I tasted the soup once myself, and really"—making a wry face, as if he had swallowed physic—" it was not so much amiss."

" It is but a small matter, sir, that is—"

" Small or large, I can do nothing ; so leave us. Mr. O'Blarney and myself are busy."

Aware that all further expostulation was useless, the bailiff quitted the room, and Mr. Snodgrass continued— "As you were saying, Mr. O'Blarney, when this blockhead interrupted us, I feel conscious that I have it in my power to be of some little service to my country. What is fortune to a man who has the good of his fellow-men at heart! But how are we to win over the corporation?"

"Leave that to the committee, sir."

"And the Dissenters?"

"You can subscribe a hundred pounds to their Institution."

"Humph! won't fifty— But no matter; it shall be as you say."

"I am to presume, then, all is settled?"

"Unquestionably; for if I expend my last shilling, I am resolved the citizens of Humbug shall see that Miles Snodgrass is not quite the fool they take him for. But the Whigs are sanguine of success, you say?"

"So the committee assures me;" and with these words, lest I should be closer pressed on the subject, I abruptly took my leave.

CHAPTER III.

PREPARATIONS FOR AN ELECTION.

WHILE I was acquainting the committee next day with the success of my first electioneering manœuvre, and arranging with them all the necessary preliminaries for putting Miles Snodgrass, Esq., of Calico Lodge—so he loved to entitle himself—into nomination, a footman, bending beneath a weight of gold lace, thrust into my hands a letter from the worthy alderman, requesting the favour of my company to dinner—"quite in the family way," as the P.S. considerately assured me.

Of course I was all compliance, and, having duly despatched my reply, sat down, and in concert with the more active members of the committee drew up the following leading article (by way of feeler) for the next day's *Flying Reporter :*—

" It is with no slight satisfaction we announce the important intelligence that Miles Snodgrass, Esq., of Calico Lodge, has allowed himself to be put in nomination for the borough of Humbug. We need scarcely inform our readers that for many years Mr. Snodgrass has been what is called a friend to ministers. Had these misguided men remained consistent, and adapted their measures to the wants and wishes of the people, he would have been so still ; finding, however, that it is no longer practicable to act with them, he comes forward with the avowed determination of henceforth owning no party but that of the country. 'Measures, not men,' is his motto. Electors of the borough of Humbug, remember your duties. The eyes of Europe are upon you ! Rally round the banners of Snodgrass, who has already sacrificed so much, and is prepared to sacrifice his all in your behalf. He will well and truly represent your interests ; whereas that pensioned hireling Lord Gilchrist, whom the faction have put forward, will but make you subservient to his own base purposes."

This feeler roused the bile of all the Humbug Tories. The corporation in particular were astounded, though, like experienced tacticians, they kept their feelings to themselves. Among them was one Alderman Slyboots, a man who, on the partial secession of Mr. Snodgrass from public life, had succeeded to much of his influence with the fraternity. This person it was a great object with me to gain over. But in vain I pumped, sounded, and tried to get a clue to his weak points. He was too well aware of his position, to compromise his importance by siding prematurely either with a Snodgrass or a Gilchrist.

But though the corporation with their Corypheus Slyboots were thus reserved, not so with the Tory organ, the *Miraculous Express,* which, the very day after the publication of my leader, replied in the following classic terms :—

"Our contemporary, the *Flying Reporter*, announces the astonishing fact that Iscariot Snodgrass intends to offer himself for this insulted borough on what he calls the Independent interest—that is to say, on the interest of the Great Unwashed! 'Mr. Snodgrass,' quoth our contemporary in his usual pompous style, 'comes forward with the intention of henceforth owning no party but that of the country.' Now the plain English of this is—Snodgrass has ratted! He has surrendered himself up, bound hand and foot, to the Radicals and the Atheists! But we have our eyes on this worse than Judas. Meantime, Tories of Humbug, look well to yourselves! Up, and be stirring in all quarters. You have a glorious example before you in the patriotic, the high-souled Slyboots, who is night and day at his post."

From the period at which this wordy warfare commenced, down to the close of the election, all was uproar in the borough, each party striving which should outbribe the other. Among other "signs of the times," the price of various household utensils rose in a most extraordinary manner. Tongs and pokers looked up. Coal-scuttles were above par. I myself gave one elector five pounds for a saucepan without the lid ; a second, ten for a bedcandlestick ; and a third, no less than fifteen for a cracked tea-cup ! Oh, virtuous times ! Oh, virgin purity of election ! Perish the wretch who could have the heart to corrupt ye by the ballot !

CHAPTER IV.

A FAMILY PARTY.

THE hall-clock was just on the stroke of six as I entered Mr. Snodgrass' drawing-room, where I found all the family present, except the eldest and youngest sons, the former of whom was putting the finishing stroke to his education at Cambridge. His mother spoke in

raptures of this young man's precocity, in which she was
joined by Miss Anna Maria Snodgrass, a spinster addicted
to Sunday-schools and the patronage of all the rising
geniuses of the district; and whose face, broad at the
forehead and peaked at the chin, like a kite—and which,
by the bye, she rarely showed but in profile—gave unde-
niable token that she was of an intellectual turn of mind.

The youngest daughter, Isabel, was in every respect the
reverse of her sister. The one was grave and predisposed
to sanctity; the other, all smiles and ecstacy. The one
was a blue, the other a tom-boy. The one seemed
astonished at nothing; the other at everything. The one
was tall, lean, and straight from head to foot like a bed-
post; the other, short, fat, and remarkable for a fine
expanse of foot, which, spreading out semi-circularly, like
a lady's fan, at the toes, lent peculiar weight and safety
to her tread.

As for Mrs. Snodgrass, she was a plump, buxom relic
of the old school—a cross between the mistress and the
housekeeper. She dressed invariably in the brightest
colours, wore pockets, and persisted in carrying about with
her a huge bunch of keys. In temper, she was the perfection of homely, hearty good-humour, and was fond of sea-
soning her talk with parentheses, and indulging in allusions to her brother, a barrister in some practice at the
Chancery-bar.

During dinner, a more than ordinary taciturnity prevailed. The alderman in particular, who held all conversation during meals as an act of folly, if not profaneness,
said little or nothing. The very utmost licence of speech
he allowed himself, even on that subject which lay next
his heart, the election, was a stray remark or two, thrown
off between the courses. "Why, yes," he would say on
such occasions, in reply to observations previously made
by one or other of the party, "your opinion of Gilchrist
is very just, Maria.—Izzy, are those artichokes near you?
And as for the corporation, O'Blarney, I agree with you
that with a little dexterous management we may contrive

to win them over.—Mrs. S., that haunch looks so tempting that I really think I must venture again.—Besides, Slyboots is almost the only man among them all whose principles may be said to be fixed.—Maria, I'll thank you for a wing of one of those partridges ; don't trouble yourself, O'Blarney, Maria is a capital carver."

I *did* trouble myself, however, and with my usual luck ; for in attempting to anatomise the bird, I happened —bashful men are always awkward—to baptise Miss Snodgrass with the gravy, and despatched a leg over the way to her sister. This catastrophe elicited a loud laugh from the frolicsome girl, for which her mother thought fit to apologise : "She is so full of life, Mr. O'Blarney— (Izzy, my dear, you've got no vegetables ; you know I dislike your eating meat without them)—quite the child of nature ; indeed, her spirits are too much for her strength."

"I was not laughing at Mr. O'Blarney, mamma," replied Isabel, and was proceeding still further to vindicate her innocence, when her father bluntly checked her by saying, "Hold your tongue, child, and attend to your business ;" shortly after which, the cloth being withdrawn, he took off his spectacles, placed a dry crust beside him which remained over from the cheese, and looked about him with the benignant air of one who has just fulfilled a sacred duty. There is nothing like a good dinner to bring out the humanities.

"John," said Mrs. Snodgrass, as the footman was arranging the dessert, "you have forgotten to place a chair for Master Samuel."

The man hastened to repair his omission, after which the bell was rung twice, and almost instantly followed by the entrance of a mischievous-looking urchin, about six years old, with his hair combed straight over his forehead, and his face shining with soap and water.

This imp had no sooner taken his seat than he began helping himself to everything within reach of his talons. I was convinced by this that he was a spoiled child ; so, coaxing him towards me with the offer of an orange, I planted him on my knee, and, patting him on the head, said, "Well, my fine little fellow, and what's your name?"

"Samuel Charlton," replied the boy, as demurely as if he were answering the first question in the catechism.

"I have named him Charlton," observed his father, with emphasis, "after a gentleman of that name, to whom I dedicated the printed copy of a speech I made during my mayoralty."

"I see you're fond of children," said the gratified mother; "Sam takes to you quite naturally. Would you believe it, Mr. O'Blarney?"

"O'Blarney!" said the urchin, with a grin, "what a funny name!"

"Sweet simplicity!" resumed the good lady; "would you believe it, sir—Maria, do pray take that knife out of Izzy's hands—young as he is, he has already got the multiplication table by heart! Sammy, dear, hold up your head, and tell the gentleman how much twice nine makes."

"Ten!" screamed the lad.

"Oh, fy! guess again."

"Eleven!"

"No."

"Twelve!"

"No."

"Eighteen!"

"Right, Sam," said his father; "that lad, I'm thinking, Mr. O'Blarney, will make a figure in the world."

I was just about to reply, when a sudden acute twinge caused me involuntarily to cry out, "Oh, murder!" and, on directing my attention to the part affected, I caught the promising Samuel busily engaged in driving his father's toothpick into my knee.

"Dear me! what's the matter?" inquired Mrs. Snodgrass, with an air of much concern.

"A mere trifle," I replied, striving hard to look good-natured; "the sprightly little fellow has been boring a

hole in my knee-pan, that's all ; but children, boys especially, are so engaging at his age ! It s quite impossible
to be angry with them."

I thought Isabel would have gone into fits at this explanation, which so tickled her brother, who even at that
early age was impressed with a notion that he was a wag,
that he played off a variety of other tricks, until at length
his pranks became so intolerable that his mother, in self-
defence, was compelled to order him up stairs to bed.

But here ensued a scene which baffles all description.
Notwithstanding his mother's coaxings, the brat refused
to stir; and, while the nurse was preparing to carry him
up stairs, freed himself by a desperate effort from her
grasp, clung to the green baize for protection, pulled it
half off the table, and brought plates, glasses, and de-
canters to the ground.

In an instant all was confusion. The alderman started
up to save as much as he could from the wreck, but happening to make a false step was thrown forward on Mrs.
Snodgrass, who, upset by the shock of this novel impetus,
plunged backward with a scream ; while, to make matters
worse, a tom-cat, on which her husband had trodden,
roused from a nap on the hearth-rug, dug his claws into
his calf; so that, what with the yellings of the cat, the
screaming of Mrs. Snodgrass, and the astonishment, mixed
with laughter, of the rest of the group, the scene was one
of the richest farce I ever remember.

In about half an hour tranquillity was restored, and the
alderman, having appeased his wrath by a bumper of
claret, said, " You'll excuse what I am going to say, Mr.
O'Blarney—curse the cat, how she has scratched my leg !
—but the fact is, sir, I always make a point of taking a
nap after dinner ; no matter who may be here, I never
give up my nap ; but help yourself, don't mind me. Mrs.
S., you'll take care of Mr. O'Blarney ;" and so saying,
without further ceremony, the alderman threw himself back
in his arm-chair, and in a few minutes was fast asleep.

" Have you read ' Kenilworth ?'" asked Miss Snodgrass,

6

as she beheld her father's chin give its first decided bob against his chest.

"I cannot say I have; my time of late has been too much occupied for such reading."

"That's just my case, Mr. O'Blarney," observed Mrs. Snodgrass.

"La! mamma, how can you say so! you know it is not a month since you finished the tale."

"Oh! true, love, I remember I read it at the recommendation of my brother the barrister; and, if I recollect rightly—Izzy, don't sit with your legs crossed—there was something in it about a grand dinner given at Kenilworth Castle, which reminded me, as I mentioned to you at the time, of your father's mayor's feast."

"So Lord George Gilchrist has really arrived in the neighbourhood?" interrupted Miss Snodgrass testily.

"Yes," I replied; "are you acquainted with him?"

"Not at all. I have seen him once or twice; he is quite a young man, apparently not more than thirty."

"Do you call that young, Maria?" inquired Isabel; "I call it being quite old."

"Old!" said Miss Snodgrass; "you don't know what you are talking about, child."

"His lordship must have felt it a great sacrifice to quit town at this gay season," I observed; "and for such a troublesome business as an election, too. Of course, you know what a London spring is, Miss Snodgrass?"

"I am ashamed to say I never was in London but on one occasion, and then for a very short time. For the last five years papa has regularly talked of indulging us with a trip there, but one thing or other always interferes to prevent it. In the first place he hates being put out of his way; then mamma has her objections—"

"I have objections certainly, Maria. To say nothing of the trouble of packing up, and the chance of damp sheets in one's lodgings, the expense of a season in London is, I am told, beyond what could be conceived."

"Expense, my dear madam!" I replied, in no little

alarm; "surely you must be under a misapprehension!"
I then proceeded to expatiate on the advantages of an
occasional residence in the metropolis; to Miss Snodgrass
I talked of the agreeable tone of its literary society; while
I whetted her sister's curiosity by dwelling on its various
public exhibitions, balls, theatres, dances, and so forth.

The bait took as I desired. "O mamma!" said Isabel,
jumping up, and clapping her hands in ecstacy, "how
delightful! Do, pray, let us leave this horrid dull place.
I shall never be happy till I go to London. There's Mary
Andrews goes once every spring, and she's a year younger
than I am. Oh! I do so want to see all the sights. And
the dancing, too! I'm so fond of dancing, you can't think!
When shall we set off, ma?"

Before her mother could reply, the alderman woke up
from his nap, which was the signal for the ladies' retiring
into the drawing-room. When the door had closed on
them, he said, putting on a look of official dignity, "I
never talk of business before women; but, now they're
gone, we can discuss matters at our ease." He then inquired minutely into all the particulars of my reception
by the committee, complimented me on my address to the
electors, and vowed that, if he expended his last shilling,
he would let people see he was not quite the fool they
took him for.

Of course I was all admiration of such conduct. "But,"
I added, in my most persuasive manner, "Mr. Snodgrass
must be aware that in contests of this nature ready money
was the main desideratum; if, therefore, he would place
at my disposal certain sums which were requisite for the
service of the committee, who had done me the honour to
place themselves under my guidance, I would stake all
my Irish estates on the chances of his success."

This direct allusion to money-matters put the old fellow
on his mettle. In an instant he was all caution.

"Ahem! we'll talk of this to-morrow. Help yourself."

"But, my dear sir, consider that in these cases prompti-
tude is the life and soul of business."

" True, very true, but still—"

" I know what you would say; but remember, sir, the old adage, 'Nothing venture, nothing gain.' An election—J. will not deny the fact—is like everything else, a lottery; but, in this particular instance, it is a lottery in which a prize is all but certain. And what a prize! To you, sir, whose eloquence is so well known, it must be beyond all price. I almost fancy I see you rising for the first time in the House. Ministers are in despair—the Opposition in ecstacies ; while the *Times,* next morning, in noticing your triumphant début, says, 'Loud cheers from all parts of the House followed the conclusion of the honourable member's speech.'"

" Enough, enough," said the alderman, in that peculiar manner which betrays marked satisfaction, while it would fain affect indifference ; "nothing, as you say, is to be done without ready money," and he acceded without further hesitation to my demand ; but then, as if glad to get rid of an ungracious topic, he rose from his seat, and led the way to the drawing-room.

During tea-time I took my station beside Miss Snodgrass, who had a thousand gossiping nothings to say about Lord George and the election, while her father occupied himself by poring over the contents of the London newspaper.

When the equipage was cleared away, my fair neighbour went into the back drawing-room, and returned almost immediately after with—*horesco referens !*—a splendidly bound album, which she placed in my hands, adding, " I am sure you are fond of elegant literature by your conversation, though perhaps you are too modest to say so" —it is astonishing what keen insight women have into character—"remember, therefore, that I shall depend on you for a contribution ; nay, no excuse, you are compromised."

" Compromised !" said her father, throwing aside his paper, "who says I am compromised?" then instantly recovering himself, he added, in a gayer tone, " Pooh ! pooh ! my brain is always running upon politics."

"The choice of subject," continued Miss Snodgrass, taking no notice of this interruption, "I leave to yourself, though I had rather it should be something in verse, for of all things poetry is—"

"A pack of rubbish," said the alderman ; "if I had my will, I'd clap every poet in the stocks ; I never had dealings with any but one, and he—"

"I know whom you're thinking of, papa—poor young Atkinson, your clerk, whom you dismissed last year for setting fire to his bed-curtains. But you should make allowances for the eccentricities of genius."

"Genius, forsooth ! why, the fellow could not cast up a sum in addition. But enough of him. O'Blarney, do you play whist ?"

"No."

"Sorry for that ; for Mrs. S. and myself love a quiet rubber, now and then. Backgammon ?"

"No."

"Well, then, suppose you sing us a song or two, Maria. Mr. O'Blarney, I dare say, is fond of music.'

To be sure I was : indeed, it was quite a passion with me—a confession which raised me still higher in the good graces of the young lady.

But let no man vaunt his love of music. It is a dangerous boast, and never fails to carry its own punishment along with it. Miss Snodgrass chirped one, two, three Italian airs ; then came a duet with Isabel ; then a French canzonet ; and lastly, the well-known "Oh ! 'tis love, 'tis love !" sung with a twist of the mouth peculiarly provocative of that passion.

But as all sublunary matters must have an end, so a termination was at length put even to Miss Snodgrass' musical displays ; and at a late hour I quitted the Lodge, but not before the alderman had insisted on my making his house my home, whenever I found it convenient.

CHAPTER V

A CONTESTED ELECTION.

THE day of the election had now arrived, and all Humbug was alive with the hum of thousands passing through from the neighbouring villages towards a large field that skirted the town, in the centre of which (the Guildhall being under repairs) the hustings were erected.

At the appointed hour the official gentry made their appearance, followed by the Tory candidate, Lord George Gilchrist, who had no sooner taken his station than a loud uproar announced the advent of the great hero of the day —Miles Snodgrass, Esq. ! He arrived in imposing state, in a carriage drawn by four horses, profusely decorated with ribbons. Beside him sat the whole existing dynasty of the Snodgrasses, radiant with the colours of the rainbow, and simpering benignly at the crowd which deafened them with huzzas.

And now the great man alights ! The cheers are tremendous. He ascends the hustings ! The cheers are redoubled. Already he is within a yard of his opponent, when—oh, death to the dignified and the picturesque !—his foot slips, an irreverent exclamation escapes him, and he is precipitated, by the force of gravitation, head-foremost into the arms of an elderly Whig who is eyeing him with evident pride through a pair of green spectacles. Luckily, no damage was sustained, and, in a few minutes, the alderman re-appeared, emerging from the sea of heads that blackened beneath him, like Achilles from the waters of the Styx.

When the confusion which this little incident occasioned had subsided, the rival candidates were proposed, seconded, and so forth ; after which, polling commenced, and terminated in a majority of *ten* in favour of Lord George.

His lordship first came forward to return thanks. He

was all smiles and sunshine ; eulogised Church and State ;
deprecated the slightest innovation on a Constitution
which was the envy and wonder of surrounding nations,
and which the wisdom of our ancestors had rendered perfect ; and he would have wound up by a peroration of (no
doubt) surpassing splendour, had not his eloquence been
cavalierly abridged by a loud, universal groan, as if ten
thousand individuals were at one and the same moment
seized with the colic.

Mr. Snodgrass followed. " Gentlemen," said he, " gentlemen, this is the proudest moment of my life (*loud
cheers*), for which reason, my heart (*cheers*)—wherefore, I
say, gentlemen, I feel it an unparalleled honour to be
called on by so numerous and respectable a constituency
to represent the free and independent borough of Humbug.
Rely on it, if you return me (*cheers*), I will act only in
accordance with your interests ; for I am attached to the
excellences, not the defects, of the Constitution ; for, born
and *eddicated* a Briton, I glory in the name (*enthusiastic
applause*); but, though a— ahem !—Briton—ahem !—I am
attached to the excellences, not the defects, of—I mean, I
glory in the name of—that is to say, born and *eddicated*
a—" Here the worthy alderman paused a few moments,
evidently overcome by his emotion ; after which, he proceeded to state that he was strictly independent in his
principles, being attached neither to Whigs nor Tories ;
that he was favourable to a moderate reform, a reduction
of taxation, a modified system of free trade ; and concluded, amid loud applause, by saying that, though last
on the poll, he hailed the omen as being auspicious of
future victory.

At the close of this matchless specimen of eloquence,
the candidates quitted the hustings, and, accompanied by
the dense crowd, with the exception of a few who lingered
behind to witness a fight between two bricklayers of opposite politics, made the best of their way back to their
respective hotels and taverns.

In England nothing can be done without a dinner.

The rival candidates, well aware of this, had each provided one worthy of the occasion ; and as evening drew on, the effects of such unrivalled cheer began rapidly to develop themselves in the speeches of the influential electors at the leading hotels ; and more especially in the gait and gestures of the bludgeon-men, who kept sallying forth, in small parties of two and three, from the lower public-houses towards the market-place.

It so happened, that just as a group of these, composed equally of Snodgrasses and Gilchrists, had turned out from their respective quarters for fresh air, but in reality for an adjustment of differences after the usual electioneering fashion, a showman, in the interest, as was suspected, of the Gilchrist faction, announced a series of necromantic entertainments in the market-place.

This announcement, from a supposed Tory, was resented as arrant presumption by the Whigs, who insisted on the man's instant evanishment. In vain the poor conjurer assured them that he was of the *juste-milieu* in politics, and cared nothing for either party ; the Snodgrasses were bent upon a row ; upon which the showman, like many a temporising politician before him, finding that he could make nothing by duplicity, at once threw off the mask, and called on the Gilchrists for support.

When did Briton ever turn a deaf ear to the cry of misfortune? The appeal was answered on the spot by a battle between the two factions, both of whom, being reinforced by detachments red-hot from the public-houses, set to work with the fixed determination, as one of the ringleaders observed, of "having it out."

And now commenced a conflict to which it would require the genius of a Fielding to do justice. There was not a moment's delay on either side. Legs, arms, lungs—each was put into instant, active requisition ; heads violated the "fitness of things," by taking up a position where heels should be ; bludgeon jarred against bludgeon ; sculls gave out hollow sounds like drums ; old women and apple-stalls were strewed here committeemen and constables there; while, by way of adding to the uproar, every bell in the town was set a-ringing, every dog in the town a-barking; maid-servants squalled from the house-tops; ladies went into hysterics in the drawing-room; cooks resolved themselves into dew in the kitchen; crash went windows, doors, and lamp-posts; down from all quarters came shutters, pails, and bow-pots; up flew flags, staves, brick-bats, cabbage-stumps, dead dogs, cats, and turnip-tops; until, at length, the entire market-place, from the parish-pump in the north to the piggeries in the south, was strewed with pyramids of bodies like a new-mown field with haycocks.

Mr. Snodgrass and myself, together with our committee, were seated over our wine at the Cock and Toothpick, when the tidings of this terrific *mêlée* reached our ears. At first, we concluded it was merely a slight squabble got up to diversify the evening's entertainments; but soon the sounds of war deepened, and presently in rushed a waiter with his head bound up, who conjured us to save ourselves by flight, as the Tories, having defeated the Whigs, were already in full march for the hotel.

While debating what was to be done in this emergency, the landlord staggered into the room, ghastly as a newly-shrouded corpse. "Fly! fly! save yourselves; five hundred of the Gilchrists will be down on us in an instant— and the house not insured too!"

Hardly had these words escaped the poor fellow, when, bang! came a brick-bat through the window, caught him in the midriff, doubled him up, and shot him right under the chairman. This hint was followed up by a huge volley of stones, which had the immediate effect of scattering us in all directions. Some flew up, and some down stairs; while others, among whom was Mr. Snodgrass, dived with incredible agility into the subterranean abysses of the coal-cellar.

As for myself, I sallied out at the back entrance of the hotel, and, snatching a Gilchrist shillelagh from a drunken Tory who was stretched full-length in the gutter, fought my way to the market-place, where the very first object that caught my eye was a smooth, round, bald-pate popping cautiously in and out of a cobbler's stall. The sight of this polished sconce, shining in the moonlight, was too tempting to be resisted by one in my frolicsome and pugnacious mood; so, stealing up on tip-toe towards the stall, I waited till the skull was next popped out, when I let fall my shillelagh upon it— quite a gentle pat—but instantly such a shout was set up of "Murder!" and "Thieves!" that I had nothing left for it but to make a precipitate retreat.

Meantime, the battle in front of the Cock and Tooth-pick continued to rage like a hurricane, and it is hard to say what might have been the ultimate consequence had not a squadron of Dragoons, who were quartered within a few miles of the town, been seasonably apprised of the uproar. By the exertions of these warriors, the siege of the Cock and Toothpick was raised, and order, with some difficulty, restored ; but it is melancholy to be compelled to add, that at least a dozen sterling patriots spent the remainder of the night in the watch-house.

CHAPTER VI.

SYMPTOMS OF SOCIALITY.

LATE in the evening, I returned with Mr. Snodgrass to Calico Lodge, where he insisted on my taking up my quarters for the night. He was in the highest possible spirits, full of good cheer, eloquence, and patriotism.

"Well, O'Blarney," he asked, "what do you think of our chance now?"

"Nothing can be more promising; Lord George, I have every reason to believe, has nearly exhausted his strength."

"So they say. Nevertheless, I am not without my fears about the corporation. Our canvass in that quarter has not been such as I had a right to expect. However, the majority, you say, will remain neutral?"

"Such is the general impression of our committee; and the circumstance of Alderman Slyboots not taking the decisive part it was supposed he would, strengthens the notion."

"Ah! you know not that fellow. He is a sly, smooth dog; says little, but is always plotting some mischief. I disliked the look he gave me when we met on the hustings, especially when I saw him, shortly after, busy in close whispering with Lord George."

"But are there no means of winning him over? Suppose the ladies pay a visit of inquiry to Mrs. Slyboots on Monday. I am sure her husband must have caught cold from his long exposure to the air on the hustings. By the way, if I mistake not, he has a daughter of whom he is justly proud; how lucky that you are on the eve of visiting London, and that there is just room in the carriage for one! You understand me, Mr. Snodgrass?"

"Perfectly; the idea is excellent. And now tell me, what did you think of my speech? Egad, I thought Lord George looked a little jealous."

"Particularly when you alluded in such energetic terms to your having been born a Briton. He appeared quite vexed to think you had anticipated him in that noble burst of patriotism."

"Aye, that idea struck me while I was on my way to the hustings. I had always a knack at public speaking. I remember old Lord Leatherhead used to say, 'Take my advice, Mr. Snodgrass, and enter the House. A person of your eloquence and sound principles cannot fail to make a figure. I wish we had many such in Parliament.'"

"The very remark poor Sims was making, when he was knocked down by the butt-end of a bludgeon."

"What, during that dreadful hubbub at the hotel?"

"Yes, we were just stepping out together to see what could be done to restore order, when an Irishman, mistaking him for one of Lord George's voters, levelled him by one handsome flourish of his shillelagh."

The alderman laughed heartily at this account; perceiving which, and conscious of the importance of keeping him in good humour, I added, "But this was not the only ridiculous incident I met with during the bustle. On escaping from the hotel, I turned into one of the more quiet streets, when suddenly a dumpy parish beadle, close pressed by one of the Gilchrist party, bounded into an inn-yard, near which I was standing. Just as he entered, a fierce little terrier made a bite at his leg, which so alarmed the poor fellow that he turned round and bounded back again into the street, coming with his head like a battering-ram full tilt against his pursuer, whom he shot off the pavement just as you may have seen a sack of coals shot out of—"

Whether there was a particular something in this invention, or in my mode of relating it, supremely absurd, I know not; but, before I could bring it to an end, I turned, and behold!—the alderman in convulsions! Such a hurricane of hah, hahs! His whole frame shook and heaved beneath the jolly tempest, until, at length, I myself caught the infection, and laughed till I was nearly suffocated.

When the storm had spent its strength, Mr. Snodgrass, wiping the tears from his eyes, said, "O'Blarney, my excellent young friend—oh, how my sides ache!—you and I have not yet taken a glass of wine together. I tried to catch your eye once or twice at dinner; but some committee-man or other perpetually interfered. We must repair this omission;" and rising, though not without difficulty, from his seat, he rang the bell for the butler.

In a few minutes, having received due directions as to the particular bin in which it would be found, the butler re-appeared with a bottle of champagne, at the same time placing a small packet of books on the table which had just arrived by the coach from London.

The alderman eagerly opened the parcel, which contained Hansard's Parliamentary Debates for the two preceding sessions. "I have ordered these," he said, "to enable me to get some insight into the mode of doing business in the House. When a man becomes an M.P.," he added, with dignity, "he must study, not to please himself, but his country."

"Your ideas do credit to your patriotism, sir. Capital wine this—quite a nosegay."

"You may well say that. Slyboots, who is the best judge of wine I know of, would have given me my own price for it;" and the alderman was proceeding to enlarge on this favourite theme, when suddenly—owing, I suppose, to the excitement of his nerves, and the zeal with which he had pledged and been pledged by his committee—his eyes began to twinkle and his articulation to thicken.

At this auspicious crisis I resumed the subject of the election. "Mr. Snodgrass," said I, "there are a dozen refractory voters of whom, to their shame be it said, I can make nothing. Would you believe it, sir, the fellows have the face to ask ten pounds each for their vote! What is to be done? I am really afraid we must bribe the rascals, for it would be a thousand pities to risk all for such a trifle. However, you are the best judge."

"Don't mention it ; you shall have the sum instantly; I have set my heart on gaining the election ;" and, hurrying into the back room, he returned in a few minutes with a cheque for the amount, which he requested me to see duly apportioned.

"And now," said I, "that this troublesome business is settled, permit me to propose a toast. 'Success to the Hon. Member for Humbug!'"

"Hear, hear!" replied the alderman, as if he were already seated on the Opposition bench.

"I really never saw papa so animated before," said Miss Snodgrass, who, with her mother and sister, just then entered the room.

Mrs. Snodgrass was about to make some reply, when the alderman interrupted her by ringing for a second bottle of champagne, which was no sooner produced than it was emptied with as much zeal as its predecessor.

The alderman—accidents will happen to the best of us —was by this time in that peculiar state which the experienced in such matters have agreed to call "half seas over." "My excellent young friend," he began, in a sort of muttered, disjointed soliloquy, "you are, without exception, the cleverest fellow I ever met with. Ah, Izzy, you there? Why, how the child grows! No wonder my speech made such a hit! How jealous that Gilchrist was! And to laugh at me too! Well, let them laugh that win. That's my maxim, and a fine old Tory maxim it is."

"Whig, you mean, sir," I replied.

"Right, right—I love a Tory maxim. Depend on it, sir, the Tories are the only men fit to govern this country." Then, in a more solemn tone, while he shook his head with an air of uncommon gravity, he added, "Excuse what I am going to say, but really, my young friend, I cannot help thinking that you are not quite so—you understand me. Temperance, O'Blarney, temperance is the life and soul of business. Look at me now, I'll do—"

What the alderman *would* have done is now a rather difficult problem, but what he *did* admits of more easy solution. Overpowered by champagne, and a long-continued flow of eloquence, he muttered a few more inarticulate sentences, and then sunk fast asleep in his arm-chair.

"Papa's exertions," said Miss Snodgrass, who could not but perceive the state of the paternal intellect, and wished indirectly to apologise for it, "have been too much for his strength—I never saw him so overcome before;" and then, by way of diverting my attention, proposed that as the night was so calm and the moon so brilliant, we should take a stroll upon the lawn.

To this the more prudent mother objected, alleging the extreme lateness of the hour; her opposition, however, was overruled, and we all set out together, leaving the unsentimental alderman in quiet possession of his arm-chair.

We walked, as Pope wrote, in couplets. Isabel and her mother went first; Miss Snodgrass and myself followed;

and, as we rambled together about the lawn, on which the moonshine lay as on a carpet of rich green velvet, our conversation took a more confidential tone than usual; for single ladies hovering on the dismal verge of thirty are not apt to be over-reserved or fastidious when wandering alone at midnight with an agreeable and (if I may use the expression) a good-looking single man, whom their parents have honoured with their esteem.

After a quarter of an hour's stroll, during which we exchanged a thousand sentimental nothings, Mrs. Snodgrass and Isabel rejoined us, with a summons to the drawing-room, lest, peradventure, as the careful dame alleged, we might catch cold from the heavily-fallen dews. Accordingly, we all returned to the house; and on ascending the steps that led to the hall-door, I turned round to point out to Miss Snodgrass the effect of moonlight on the gravel-walk, when I observed with astonishment that her spare, tall figure threw forward a shadow that reached full twenty yards down the avenue.

CHAPTER VII.

SYMPTOMS OF SENTIMENT.

THE next day being Sunday, the whole family attended church as usual, with the exception of the alderman, who was closeted with me, talking over electioneering matters, and referring every now and then to the Parliamentary Register, in which he seemed to take prodigious interest, as recognising in it the future record of his eloquence.

When the family returned home, he despatched his wife and Isabel, as had been previously arranged, on a formal visit of inquiry to Mrs. Alderman Slyboots, while he himself, knowing there was not a moment to be lost, set out on another visit to a couple of Humbug tradesmen, on whom, with all my eloquence, I had hitherto made no impression.

The house being thus comparatively deserted, Miss Snodgrass considerately proposed that I should accompany her to afternoon service at the parish church—a proposition with which I was by no means unwilling to comply.

On our road thither, we were joined by two young ladies who visited at the Lodge, and to whom Miss Snodgrass introduced me. They were lively, chatty, agreeable women, but rather too much so for Maria, who, as I have before observed, was predisposed to sanctity and sentiment, and to whose delicate nerves anything like vivacity, especially from the youthful and good-looking, gave a shock like a galvanic battery.

The service concluded, our party took leave of each other at the church-door, and Miss Snodgrass and myself returned to the Lodge, by what she called "a short cut" across the fields.

Our conversation turned of course on the sermon we had just heard. "Well, what do you think of our minister?" inquired the lady. "He is a great favourite with papa; but, for my own part, I cannot say I like him."

The secret of this dislike was, that the Rev. Mr. Jenkins was old, ugly, and had lost half his teeth.

"If you wish to hear an eloquent preacher," resumed Miss Snodgrass, "you should accompany me on Wednesday evening to the meeting-house in Pump-street. The Rev. Mr. Cant, who officiates there, has the gift of tongues to a greater degree than any minister I ever heard."

"Is he married?"

"Married!" replied Miss Snodgrass hastily. "Oh, dear, no; his only bride is his church, and it is delightful to hear him lecture on this subject. His feelings rise so naturally from his heart, his language is so appropriate, and his voice and manner so persuasive, that I always feel myself a better Christian after—"

"That is impossible, madam," said I, gallantly interrupting her; "perfection cannot be improved!"

"Ah! you gentlemen are such flatterers. However, whatever may be my defects, want of charity, I trust, is not among the number. By the bye, Mr. O'Blarney, what do you think of the two Misses Thompson, who left us just now? They are great admirers of Mr. Cant; but their mode of showing it is so bold and undisguised that I am sure it must give pain to a delicate mind like his."

"Unquestionably it must; but, indeed, the Misses Thompson, from the little I have seen of them, are just what—"

"Hush! I will not hear you say a word against them. As for Harriette, though she is decidedly not handsome, yet I can assure you she is uncommonly amiable. Emily, too, is full of vivacity, and, except that she dresses rather too much like a girl of sixteen, has a thousand good qualities."

"Heaven knows she has need of them! for both in face and figure, the poor young lady—"

"Young, did you say? You would be surprised if I were to tell you dear Emily's age. But no, I will not be uncharitable enough to betray her secret."

"Noble sentiments! Ah! Miss Snodgrass, an enlarged mind like yours can afford to be indulgent to—"

"Oh, fy! Mr. O'Blarney; not a word against my Emily. I shall really be quite offended if you go on. If she does affect that dangerous character, a wit, it is not for us to condemn. But, to turn to a more pleasing theme, I have seldom read prettier lines than those which you were kind enough to contribute to my album." (I had returned the book the preceding day, with some stanzas which I had copied from an old pocket-book, entitled "Perfection, a Sketch from Life.") "I assure you, mamma considers them quite the gem of the volume. Are they really a sketch from life, Mr. O'Blarney?"

"Wholly so. The original is—"

"Who?"

"Yourself!"

7

"Oh, flatterer!" simpered the lady, patting my arm coquettishly with her hand.

"Yes, Miss Snodgrass, you indeed are the original; and would that I had the descriptive powers of a Thomson to portray that indefinable grace of manner—that richly cultivated mind—that classic outline of face—"

"Is Thomson one of your favourite poets?" interrupted Miss Snodgrass, averting her head, so that I might see it in full profile.

"He is, indeed."

"I am delighted to hear you say so; for his 'Seasons' have long been the companion of my solitary walks."

"Of course, then, you remember his divine sketch of Musidora?"

"Perfectly."

"Ah, Miss Snodgrass, despite what has been so often said and sung to the disparagement of our sex, how much easier is it to meet with a Damon than a Musidora! Real life will often supply us with the former; indeed, at times, in moments of weakness, I have been half tempted to persuade myself that in the impassioned, and still more in the disinterested nature of Damon, my own character was— But how am I betraying myself! Ten thousand pardons, Miss Snodgrass, but really feeling is such an egotist! As for Musidora," I added, striking into a more playful mood, "I am far too much a man of the world to venture on the hazardous task of praising one accomplished woman in presence of another;" and I bowed with inexpressible grace.

We had by this time reached the gates of the Lodge, when the fair Maria proposed, as there was just time before dinner, that we should take a stroll across the lawn towards the summer-house. To this I readily assented, and we crossed over to the arbour; which was built in the simplest form possible, contained one small bench and table, and was thickly overgrown with parasitic shrubs.

"Here," said Miss Snodgrass pensively, "while the

weather permits, I pass hours in company with Cowper, Grahame, or Thomson. The spot, though retired, is far from gloomy, for the copse behind us is full of music ; and in the long summer twilights, Philomel—"

"Oh, don't say a word in praise of the nightingale, Miss Snodgrass ; it is a distrustful, querulous bird, and always lives and sings alone. Trust me, there is no true enjoyment but in union. You remember, I dare say—to return once again to our favourite poet—Thomson's exquisite picture of domestic bliss, especially that passage which relates to what the divine bard calls 'an elegant sufficiency.' How often have I thought that where impassioned love— But I am sure I must be wearying you—"

" Not at all ; I am never tired of listening to the praises of my favourite minstrel."

" Well, then, often and often have I thought that where love, such as Thomson portrays, goes hand in hand with 'an elegant sufficiency,' the union must realise all that man or woman ever yet conceived of happiness. Oh, the perfect bliss where two fond hearts blend together as one —where the husband's smile reflects its happy sunshine on the countenance of the wife—where, if the one is sad, the other cannot choose but droop also—where the only struggle between them is as to which shall evince the fullest and most entire affection—while Time, as he rolls over the heads of both, must content himself with mellowing what he feels he cannot destroy ! Would to God that such a lot were mine ! It is not to the cold, heartless world that feelings like these are to be breathed ; but, if I may be permitted to use such a term, in the presence of a congenial spirit, when the scene, the hour, prompt alike to candour and feeling ; then, indeed, they may with some propriety be breathed, and possibly even forgiven ;" and I concluded in a low, suppressed whisper.

" Oh, Mr. O'Blarney !"

" Ah, Miss Snodgrass !"

" Pray forgive my weakness," interrupted the susceptible lady, averting her head ; " but, indeed, indeed, your touching picture of domestic— But I am so silly ! What must you think of me !" she added, with a faint smile.

"Forgive, madam ! Nay, it is I who should ask forgiveness ! I who have drawn tears from those lovely eyes ! I who, agitated and wholly overpowered by a passion, pure, fervent, disinterested as ever—"

"For God's sake, Mr. O'Blarney, be composed ! I must not—dare not hear this."

"Say, then, that I am forgiven."

"Hush, I implore you, hush ! I hear a footstep. Oh, that horrid John !"

This was said in allusion to the footman, whom we now saw advancing towards us. "One word—but one little word," I continued, "and I release you from my frantic persecution. Say, dearest Maria, idol of this devoted heart, say but that you—"

"Oh, I know not ; ask papa."

What acuteness women have in all matters relating to matrimony ! They absolutely snuff an offer, as Job's war-horse snuffed the battle, "afar off." However, I had no time to moralise ; for just as I had imprinted a sonorous Milesian kiss on the lady's half-averted lips, the footman approached with a message from Mrs. Snodgrass, that the first bell was just about to ring for dinner.

CHAPTER VIII.

A DISAPPOINTED CANDIDATE.

LATE on the fourth day, to the consternation of the Independent party, the election terminated in favour of Lord George by a meagre majority of—twelve ! This result was chiefly owing to the manœuvres of the corporation, most of whom were Tories, and, though with admirable tact they kept their opinions to themselves till the proper season came for putting them forth, looked on the apostacy of one of their fraternity as a sort of re-

flection on the whole body. Even Alderman Slyboots—
"unkindest cut of all!"—was found among the number
of Mr. Snodgrass' opponents, and gave a plumper, like
himself, to Lord George.

This defeat was a grievous blow to my interests. It
at once demolished all the fine castles which, for weeks
past, I had been erecting in the air; for, by the aid of
the alderman's influence, I had hoped, not only to establish myself among the *élite* of Humbug, but peradventure
even to become nearly connected with his family.

But if my disappointment was great, far greater was
the alderman's. On him the disastrous tidings burst like
a thunder-clap. Never once had the possibility of a defeat
entered into his calculations, so effectually had his pride,
his ambition, and, above all, his vanity, conspired to mis-
lead his judgment, and with such persevering flattery
had I kept alive his wildest fantasies. He had entered
upon the election, not coolly and deliberately like a man
of the world, but with all the red-hot enthusiasm of a
school-boy; for the time being it was his one engrossing
hobby; and for me, as the author of all his agreeable self-
delusion, he felt, of course, while it lasted, the utmost
respect and friendship.

But the spell of my influence was now broken; and just
in proportion as I had risen, so did I fall in the alderman's estimation. For one whole week he confined himself to the retirement of Calico Lodge, admitting no one
to his presence but an attorney, whom he engaged to
prosecute minute inquiries into the way in which I had
disposed of certain electioneering sums intrusted to my
superintendence; his suspicions being roused by the singular circumstance of the election having been lost by
the very same number of votes which he had supplied me
with funds to purchase!

The result of these inquiries was, I soon found out,
unsatisfactory; for when I ventured, a few days after
the election, to send in my card, I was informed that my
presence at the Lodge was no longer desirable.

A man of more brass than I can possibly pretend to would have insisted at once on being confronted with the alderman and his attorney; but my disastrous diffidence in this, as in every other instance, got the better of me. I imagined, too, that by remaining quiet for a time, the storm would blow over, and Mr. Snodgrass be brought to regard my conduct with a more unprejudiced eye, especially as I had every reason to believe I should find a warm advocate in his eldest daughter; so I allowed the golden moment to escape, and the sand in the hour-glass to run out, till it became almost too late to retrieve myself

At length, stung into resolution by the slanderous whispers that began to gain ground in the borough, I determined, *coute qui coute*, on obtaining an interview with the alderman, which, with some difficulty, and after repeated applications, I was lucky enough to accomplish.

Just as I was turning an angle of the road that led sharp round to the gates of the Lodge, I suddenly encountered Mrs. Snodgrass on her way on foot to Humbug. The good lady recognised me in an instant, but looked shy, embarrassed, and more inclined to retrograde than advance; on which, with as much easy assurance as a man of my peculiar temperament could muster, I hastened forward to accost her; and, after alluding delicately and feelingly to the unfortunate prejudice which I understood her husband had of late been persuaded to entertain against me, I observed that I was now, by his express desire, on my way to pay him a visit, when I had no doubt I should be able to explain everything to his perfect satisfaction.

The mention of the word "visit" convinced the good-natured dame that the quarrel was about to be made up between her husband and myself, and in an instant she became as friendly and communicative as ever.

"Well," she exclaimed, "I always said everything would be cleared up; though, to tell you the truth, Mr. O'Blarney, the alderman has been in a sad way about you. Some one has put it into his head that you've been making a cat's-paw of him, though, as I told him at the time, 'My dear Mr. S.,' said I, 'what matters it what people say? they will talk, you know; so let 'em, and when they're tired they'll hold their tongues.' Those were the very words I used, Mr. O'Blarney; for I knew you must have a good heart by your taking so much notice of Sam."

"Ah, my little playfellow Sammy!" said I, with affectionate vivacity, "how is the dear little fellow? It may be a weakness, Mrs. Snodgrass, but I never see children without feeling my heart warm towards them, as if they were my own. And your fair daughters—are they, too, in good health?"

The old lady shook her head. "Very odd, Mr. O'Blarney, but Maria takes the loss of the election more to heart than even Mr. S.! I can't conceive what's come to the girl. She says nothing except that she is resigned to the visitation, and that if it be the will of God she must submit. But she was always of a serious turn, you know. I'm sure, what with one thing and what with another, I have not a moment's peace. There's Mr. S., he does nothing but sit and sulk from morning till night; I'm afraid he's in a delicate way, for he eats a mere nothing to *sinnify*. In short, Mr. O'Blarney, we're all in a peck of troubles. However, I'm glad you're going to clear up matters with the alderman. I always said you could if you would; and perhaps, if you find him out of humour, you'll just give in to him a bit; he means well, though he's a little hasty. I'm sure, if my good word is of any service, you're welcome to it; for I never will believe any harm of a man who is fond of children; and so I told the alderman last night, when he was snubbing you before Maria."

"And did Miss Snodgrass not condescend to say one little word in my behalf?"

"She! Lord bless you, she's grown as mute as a fish! Between you and me, Mr. O'Blarney"—and here the good lady put on an air of uncommon slyness—"I'm afraid the girl's had a call. Sad business! Mr. S. hates the Methodists. He says they're enemies to the Constitution ; and so they are, for this cant has done a deal of harm to Maria. She's not half the girl she was."

"I'm glad to see that you at least bear up against these afflictions, Mrs. Snodgrass."

"Who, I? Oh, I've lots of trouble too, only I haven't time to be down-hearted. Who would look after the servants, if I were to lay up? But I must not stay gossiping ; so good-bye, Mr. O'Blarney. I wish you success with Mr. S. ; but, pray, don't take him up too short, if he should be a little hot at first. It's merely a way he's got ; my brother, the barrister, has just the same ;" and, without allowing herself time to complete the sentence, the old lady vanished at a brisk pace round the corner.

Far different was my interview with the alderman. Six publicans, on whose faces tribulation was written at full-length, and in the clearest type, were just quitting the house as I reached the hall-door—a circumstance which, taken in connexion with the sinister glances of the footman, and the suggestions of Mrs. Snodgrass, convinced me that I should have need of all my temper and address.

No sooner had I announced my name than the servant showed me into a small parlour, while he went and informed his master of my arrival ; and returned almost immediately with a bluff answer, which lost nothing of its rudeness by his mode of delivery, to the effect that I must wait a while, for the alderman was engaged.

For fully an hour I remained in this state of suspense, till at length, when tired of waiting, and I was making up my mind to depart, the study-bell rang, and I heard the alderman's surly voice in the passage, desiring the footman to "send in that fellow."

On entering the study, Mr. Snodgrass, who was seated at the table, neither looked up nor rose to meet me, but kept his eyes riveted on the table. His personal appearance was by no means improved by his late disappointment. His face was yellow as a crocus ; a beard of at least two days' growth threw his chin into what artists would call a fine shadow; and he perpetually shifted his position, like a man in a high state of nervous excitement. I could not but feel for his situation, and was just beginning to express my regret at finding him so much of an invalid, when he interrupted me fiercely with, " Aye, you may well condole with me ; none but an egregious block-head would have listened for an instant to such an Irish adventurer !"

I made allowance for this outburst, and calmly replied, " Mr. Snodgrass, you do me injustice. I am no adven-turer, sir, but a man who, wishing well to the cause of good government, has endeavoured to procure for that cause the ablest advocate. It was on this principle, and this only, that I sought to interest you in behalf of the Independent party. I was prepared for a more difficult task than I encountered ; for you were already half a Liberal when I stepped in to confirm your faith."

The alderman here started from his seat, and his eye happening to fall on a volume of Hansard's Parliamentary Debates, which lay with a paper-cutter in the leaves on the table, he flung it with violence on the floor, exclaim-ing, as he resumed his chair, " Who placed this book here ? You're all leagued to drive me mad ;" then, as if recol-lecting himself, he added, " What is this matter that you say you have to explain ? Tell it at once, and be off."

" Language like this, Mr. Snodgrass, scarcely deserves a reply. However, to show you that I am not vindictive, and can make every allowance for your situation—"

" My situation ? what do you mean by that, sir ? Think of your own. Yet what, after all, is yours compared with mine ! I have lost everything. For the money I care nothing—it is gone, and there's an end of it ; but where is my standing with the corporation ? where my borough influence ? where my character for consistency ?"

" Have courage, sir, and all will yet be well."

The alderman took no heed of my interruption, but, as if unconscious he was overheard, continued, " To be bam-

boozled, lampooned, paragraphed, and held up to ridicule by both parties ; a man of my years and station to
be treated in this manner, and all through the trickery
of an obscure Irish adventurer—'tis not to be—Ah, what,
you're there still, sir ? laughing, no doubt, in your sleeve,
at my egregious folly."

"Folly, Mr. Snodgrass !"

" Well, wisdom then, if you like it better, for wise
indeed I have shown myself to be your dupe ! You knew
from the first I had no chance. But what did that matter
so long as you could feather your own nest ? But proceed
with your story, sir."

" It is very plain and simple. In one word, Mr. Snodgrass, for I perceive you are not in a fit state calmly to
consider the details of my proposition, I have every reason
to believe that Lord George's election has been carried
solely by means of the most notorious bribery and corruption ; and that, if you think fit to petition against his
return, there can be no doubt that the House will decide
in your favour. To be sure, we are far from immaculate
ourselves ; but fortunately our manœuvres have been
managed with skill and secrecy, whereas Lord George's
party have been openly boasting of theirs."

" Well, sir, and what then ? "

" Merely this—that it remains with yourself to decide
whether you will choose to affix M.P. to your name or
not. Your chance is, I am persuaded, better than ever ;
for the House entertains such a well-bred horror of bribery, that the mere charge is almost enough to insure the
condemnation of the luckless wight against whom it is
brought."

" Indeed !" said the alderman, drawling out the word,
as if he were half-asleep ; " and pray, sir, for your valuable assistance in this matter, what further sums may be
necessary ? Will another hundred pounds satisfy you ?"

" I understand your sneer, and, as an honest man, meet
it with the contempt it deserves."

" What ! and have you the impudence to call yourself

an honest man? Honest, forsooth! Ha! ha!" and the old savage grinned in my face like a hyena.

This stung me to the quick; "Oh, Mr. Snodgrass, Mr. Snodgrass," said I—for I could not but perceive that all hope of reconciliation was at an end—"it grieves me to the soul to see such powers of sarcasm and eloquence as you possess thrown away on an obscure individual like myself. Reserve it, I beseech you, for those apostate ministers whose reduction of the five per cents.—"

These words wrought quite a talismanic effect on the alderman. "Quit the room, sir!" said he; and then jerking the bell-rope with such fury that the handle came off in his hand, "John," he added, as the servant entered the room, "turn this fellow out of the house, and, d'ye hear, take care that he never shows his face here again."

Such language was beyond all bearing. Nevertheless, though I resolved the alderman should smart for it, I would not lose my temper, but in the mildest possible terms continued, "With respect to this election, Mr. Snodgrass, which seems to have disturbed that enviable and serene sagacity which all who know you appreciate, and none more highly than myself, there is yet one way left by which I think you may manage to disincumber yourself of the pecuniary obligations attending it."

In an instant the old man was all attention, and making a sign to the servant, who had hitherto been lingering near the door, to quit the room, said, "Free myself from these election debts, did you say? Where—when—how? Explain yourself, my excellent young friend. I am hasty, it is true, but always open to conviction."

"Oh, my plan is scarcely worth mentioning; it merely regards pecuniary matters, which, as you observed just now, weigh nothing in your estimation compared with the loss of your character for consistency."

"True, I did say so, nevertheless—"

"You are anxious to hear it. Be it so, though I am by no means sanguine that a person of your distinction will adopt it. However, such as it is, it is at your

service.   You may have heard, sir, in the course of your
long—commercial—experience—" said I, pausing between
each word, "of—"

"Yes, yes, very good, go on."

"Of an—act—entitled—the—Insolvent Debtor's Act
It is one of singular—"

"Knave! swindler! rascal!   Is it thus you   add
insult to injury!"

"You complain of your debts. I propose to you a
remedy. Am I to be blamed for this?"

"How dare you, fellow, throw out such hints to a man
of my character?"

"Character, Mr. Snodgrass! Why, yourself assured
me just now that you had none left, and, as a gentleman,
I felt bound to believe you!"

"Quit the room instantly, sir! I disgrace myself by
holding conversation with you."

"There is no need of bluster, Mr. Snodgrass," said I,
moving with unruffled dignity to the door; "I quit your
house far more readily than I entered it, fully convinced
that when you have regained your senses, you will do me
that justice which your blind passion just now withholds.
Infatuated old man! where now is that keen political
foresight which, detecting at one glance, as it were, the
great public embarrassments that must ensue from the
reduction of the five per cents., nobly—"

"The five per cents. again! By Jove! I'll—"

Just at this instant a gaunt, sulky publican forced his
way into the room, and, after stammering out one or two
awkward words of condolence, approached Mr. Snodgrass,
and thrusting forward something that bore the semblance
of a bill, was just commencing with, "Touching this little
account," when the alderman snatched the paper from the
dun's talons, and, throwing it to me, exclaimed, "This,
fellow, is your affair, not mine. You have had the money,
and must and shall be responsible."

"Responsible! And for your debts too! No, no, Mr.
Snodgrass, I have no objection to be just, but I really
cannot afford to be generous."

"Wretch! this impudence surpasses belief! What, have you not had my cheques for the tavern bills, as well as for those twelve voters, to not one of whom you ever paid a sixpence? Nay, more, sir, have you not, throughout the whole business, been bent on my own ruin? Yes, sir, my ruin, I say."

"Not I, Mr. Snodgrass, but the five per cents. have been your ruin."

"Hang the five per cents.!" thundered the alderman. "What's that to the purpose, you—"

"Aye, what indeed?" interrupted the publican, who began to tremble for his account. "I shall look to you for payment, Mr. Snodgrass. I know nothink of this here gemman. These are hard times, Mr. S., and I mean no offence, but justice is justice, and law's law, sir; and so, sir," putting on his hat with a vehement thump on the crown, "I wish you good-morning, sir."

"And I shall follow this worthy man's example. Possibly, Mr. Snodgrass, you and I may never meet again; I avail myself, therefore, of this opportunity to declare that, despite your conduct towards me, which I must say has been marked by flagrant ingratitude, from my soul I pity and forgive you;" and I stalked in sullen majesty from the apartment.

CHAPTER IX.

A DISAPPOINTED CANDIDATE'S REVENGE.

HAVING rarely known a contested election terminate without a quarrel among the losing parties, I was not in the slightest degree surprised at the alderman's indignation; though I had no idea he would carry it to the extreme length of holding me publicly forth as an adventurer and a swindler. True, certain sums intrusted by him to me for distribution did not exactly reach their destination; but surely this did not justify the atrocious placards and paragraphs that now daily appeared against me! The truth is, that in the hurry and bustle necessarily attendant on a contested election, the money had been overlooked ; but I put it to any man of feeling and delicacy, whether, under the peculiar circumstances of the case, such an act of forgetfulness was not perfectly natural; or, if an error, whether it were not one of omission rather than of commission.

But I have a better plea to urge than that of mere omission. As principal agent for Mr. Snodgrass, it was of course necessary that I should make a parade of superior respectability—in fact, keep all but open house. Now, this could not be done on the weekly pittance I received from the *Flying Reporter*, and I was compelled in consequence to appropriate a portion of the sums received from the alderman; and pray, to what more fitting or laudable purpose could I devote his money than to secure the interests of his election ? For myself, individually, I neither asked nor received one farthing for my labours; they were undertaken solely with reference to the public good; and the reward I met with for such heroic disinterestedness was, first, to be denounced as a swindler ; secondly, to be dismissed from my editorial functions!

In this predicament, with a name tainted throughout Humbug, and but one paltry hundred pounds left in my exchequer, I felt I had no alternative but to appeal once more to the sense and justice of Mr. Snodgrass. Accordingly, after much deliberation and blotting of paper, I despatched an argumentative and pathetic letter to the Lodge, to which no reply being vouchsafed, I allowed a week to elapse, and then sat down and penned a second to the following effect :—

" *Wellington-place, Humbug*, 1821.

"SIR,—The pertinacity with which you persist in blasting the character and fortunes of one who never injured you is, I hope and believe, without parallel in the annals of human depravity.

"In justification of such conduct, you allege that I have appropriated to my own use a considerable portion of certain sums which you had intrusted to me for electioneering expenses. To this vague charge I have but one reply to make. Produce your vouchers" (I knew he could not), "or else confess that you have wantonly slandered a name which the breath of calumny has never yet dared to taint.

"One or other of these alternatives I feel that I have a right to insist on. Should neither be acceded to, then, as a matter of course, I shall demand that satisfaction which one gentleman never withholds from another whom he has aggrieved.

"You have been pleased, I perceive, in one of your numerous placards, to allude in terms far from flattering to what you call my 'immeasurable impudence.' Ah, sir! did you but know me as I feel that I deserve to be known, you would be convinced that, if there be one infirmity beyond another which I inherit from a long line of ancestors, it is an extreme coyness of disposition —a shrinking sensitiveness which has ever stood between me and good fortune. Had it not been for this distressing affliction, I should, long ere now, have done myself the honour of proposing for the hand of your eldest daughter, who has already condescended to evince an interest in my behalf, which needed but time and the sanction of her respected parents to ripen into a tenderer sentiment.   "I am, sir,
                              "Yours, &c.,
                         "TERENCE FELIX O'BLARNEY.
"To Miles Snodgrass, Esq.

"P.S.—If you could, with perfect convenience to yourself, accommodate me with the loan of three hundred pounds, till my father's agent remits me my usual half-yearly allowance, I shall esteem it an act of courtesy more than sufficient to atone for that inexplicable conduct which has so deeply wounded my sensibilities."

This modest missive, strange to say, shared the fate of the former; on which I despatched a third, wherein I specially requested that Mr. Snodgrass would "do me the favour to consider himself horsewhipped;" and, not satisfied with this revenge, wrote and printed for general distribution a most combustible pamphlet, in which, after defending my own conduct during the election, I attacked the public and private character of the alderman; branded him as an apostate, a liar, a coward; and, in short, laid about me with such zeal, that Mr. Snodgrass, stung to the quick, commissioned his attorney to enter an action against me for libel.

This was the very thing I most desired, for it not only afforded me an opportunity of publicly vindicating my character, but also of mixing up my case with the great question of the liberty of the press.

But let no man trust to his innocence for acquittal by a British jury. Law is a game of hazard, where luck decides everything. Within a fortnight from the publication of my pamphlet, the assizes took place; and among the trials which engrossed public attention was that of "Snodgrass v. O'Blarney," in which, after the plaintiff's counsel had inveighed elaborately against the licentiousness of the press, and the defendant's had insisted, with equal pertinacity, on its perfect freedom as the "Palladium of the British Constitution"—both, in the fervour of their eloquence, losing sight of the main features of the case—the jury brought in a verdict of guilty; and I was sentenced to six months' imprisonment, and a fine, which I had no earthly chance of ever being able to liquidate.

CHAPTER X.

PRISON ASSOCIATES.

WHAT a change had the last few days wrought in my condition! But one short month before I was in no inconsiderable repute in Humbug; I was now the proscribed inmate of a county jail. My position was indeed a hopeless one, and the mean, dark, cheerless apartment I inhabited was by no means calculated to raise my spirits. The walls were constantly dripping with wet ; the floor was begrimed with dirt ; and the only furniture consisted of a rickety wooden chair, and a small deal-table, on which lay two or three dogs'-eared tracts.

" How many last moments," thought I, as, for lack of better employment, I turned over the well-thumbed pages, " have been spent in communion with these books ! How many hot, scalding tears have been dropped on them ! What a tale their very look tells, of every emotion that can raise or depress humanity ! Repentance has leaned on them as her last resting-place on this side of eternity ; Despair has dashed them from her presence as a curse. They have softened the grim features of Death till the spectre wore almost a smile ; they have darkened them till it were madness to look on his frown. Silent but expressive moralists ! would that ye could impart your lessons in some more social fashion ! But, alas ! ye do so in darkness and in solitude to the wandering brain and the broken heart that quit ye only for the scaffold."

My soliloquy was here broken off by the entrance of Mr. Graves, the turnkey, who, affected by my prompt munificence—for I had slipped a guinea into his hand only the day preceding—came to propose to me "a turn" in the courtyard, to which I readily assented.

I found it filled with prisoners, chiefly of the male sex, some of whom were pacing up and down in groups of twos and threes ; others playing at hustle-cap and chuck-farthing ; and others seated on a bench enjoying the philosophical luxury of pipes and tobacco.

While the turnkey was pointing out to my notice some of the more notorious among them, which he did with an emphasis amounting almost to reverence, we were joined by a grave, stout, formal personage, with an enormous bullet-head, firmly fixed (with little or no intervention of neck) between two massive shoulders.

8

This stranger, whom I soon discovered to be a piquant mixture of the scamp and the pedant, making me a profound obeisance, while at the same time he eyed me from head to foot with an air of scientific discrimination, expressed his regret at my presence in a place so ill-calculated to improve my moral or physical condition. "But, sir," he added with amazing pomp of manner, "you have the consolation of knowing—no matter what be the cause that brought you here—that you are, like myself, the victim of destiny. Vice and virtue, sir, are mere matters of impulse, as I endeavoured to show in a little treatise I lately wrote, entitled 'Death the Fulfilment of Destiny,' for which a man is no more to be blamed or praised than he is for being short or tall, thin or stout. For my own part, I have come to the conclusion that, do what we will, neither the best nor worst of us can control our actions, being alike mere spokes in the wheel of fate ; and that the sum and substance of all human wisdom may be comprised in this one sentence—what will be, will be."

"A very sagacious conclusion, Mr.— I beg your pardon, but may I ask whom I have the honour of addressing ?" I inquired, not a little amused by my new companion's loquacity.

"Stubbs, sir—Justinian Stubbs, late professor of languages at the Humbug Charity School—a gentleman and, I trust I may add, a scholar, who, by one of those sudden vicissitudes to which the best of us are liable, has been but just subjected to the unchristian persecution of the pillory."

"Indeed !"

"Yes, sir, the humble individual before you has 'fretted' —I would add 'strutted,' but the quotation would be inapplicable—his 'little hour' in that elevated position."

"May I inquire the cause of such an accident ?"

"Oh, certainly, sir ; I need have no reserves with one of your respectability. It was my fate some months since to be detected in certain verbal inaccuracies touching the amount of a few corporation subscriptions for the Humbug

Charity School, and to be publicly exhibited, in consequence, to the gaze of the most unpolished rabble I think
I ever saw."

"They certainly did let fly uncommon sharp," interposed
the turnkey ; "the cabbage-stumps flew like anything."

"Vulgar beast !" whispered the fatalist.

"You could scarcely have expected otherwise, Mr.
Stubbs," I replied ; "the pillory is no place for the cultivation of the gentilities."

"Sir, your position is unanswerable. After the most
impartial consideration I can give to the subject, I find it
impossible to reconcile myself to the idea that it is either
an elegant or creditable exhibition. Still, like everything
else, it has its redeeming points."

"How so ?"

"Why, sir, if it pander to the malignant tastes of the
oppressors, you must at leaast allow that it teaches the
oppressed a lesson of forbearance ; enables him to put in
practice the precepts of philosophy ; to endure adversity
with becoming resignation."

"Sweet are the uses of adversity," I observed.

"You are right, sir ; and the poet who broached that
wholesome truth must himself have tasted them in the
pillory. It is the very Paradise of such sweets."

"You seem to entertain a very soothing recollection of
them."

"And why not ? On me, sir, the pillory had no effect
but what was strictly salubrious. Conscious that I was
the victim of destiny, I bade a philosophic defiance to the
storm that hurtled round me. Besides, I reflected that
the pillory was classic ground, and derived inexpressible
comfort from the consideration that, though I was nearly
pelted out of all shape there, I yet had not my ears
cropped, like that illustrious sage Defoe."

"Why, no," said I, with an arch smile, "it is plain they
are as long as ever."

"You're a wag, sir, I conjecture ; and inasmuch as a
little seasonable facetiousness in nowise detracts from,

but rather gives an agreeable relish to, the grave discourse of wisdom, I partake your mirth. By the way, talking of such trifles—the by-play of the mind, as the learned Helvetius calls them—could you oblige me with a shilling?"

The abruptness of this request, following, as it did, on the heels of such high-flown sentiments, not a little astounded me. However, I acceded to the fatalist's petition, who instantly left me, with a low bow and a profusion of apologies.

When we met again next day in the courtyard, our conversation turned on my late electioneering experiment on Alderman Snodgrass, in which Mr. Stubbs found much food for condemnation. My resolution to abide the result of the trial especially astonished him. "Doubtless," said he, "it was a honourable, even a heroic determination, but utterly lost, as you now find to your cost, on an unreflecting age like the present. You should have quitted Humbug, sir, the instant your degenerate patron had lost his election. Of what consequence were the opinions of the rabble? It is the unerring test of a great mind to treat them with a lofty indifference. Speaking on this point, the learned Helvetius—"

"I confess my weakness, Mr. Stubbs; but society, you know—"

"Society!" interrupted that eminent philosopher; "talk not to me of society, sir. It is diseased to the heart's core. There is no moral harmony—no nice adjustment of parts—no consentaneousness as a whole, in the present state of things. What is our social code but a huge conglomeration of blunders? Look at me, sir; I am an instance in point. Why am I here?"

"Because you can't get out, I suppose."

"I am here," resumed the fatalist, "because the mental abstraction necessarily attendant on philosophic pursuits like mine rendered me on a certain occasion oblivious of worldly discretion. Accident was in my case misconstrued into design. Hence the pillory and a year's imprisonment! But I have one consolation—it could not have been otherwise."

We were here interrupted by the approach of a flippant, light-haired, red-faced young fellow, who, taking a cigar from his mouth, and addressing me with an air of affected courtesy, exclaimed, "Proud to have the honour of your acquaintance, sir; I presume, like the rest of us, you are the sport of Fortune. Singular, how the blind goddess always persecutes the diligent and the deserving! However, what will be, will be; a vulgar truism, but not the less valuable on *that* account—eh, Stubbs?"

"Vulgarity," observed the schoolmaster, taking out an iron snuff-box, and offering me a pinch, "is of two kinds, physical and intellectual. The physical may be said to consist in a perverse indulgence in such habits as have a tendency to stultify or brutalise the mind. Now smoking is one of these habits; wherefore—"

"You are out there, Stubbs, quite out," replied Wilde (such was the name of my new acquaintance); "I am a smoker myself, and have been so for years. Snuff-taking, I grant you, is a vulgar habit. I never snuff."

"Snuff-taking!" rejoined the philosopher; "nothing can be pronounced vulgar that tends, in however humble a degree, to stimulate the faculties of thought, and— But I see an old acquaintance yonder; I must go and join her;" and away he posted to recreate his epigastrum with a glass of the best British, or Falernian, as he called it, which an old woman, in a scarlet hood, had just smuggled into the prison.

No sooner had he quitted us than Wilde, pointing after him, said, "There goes one of the biggest rogues in all England, who, while he grasps you cordially with one hand, will pick your pocket with the other. He sounded the depths of mine within ten minutes of our first acquaintance, while I was listening to a long story about Helvetius."

"Bless me!" said I, "I have heard twice of that author already. I had no idea he was such a suspicious character."

"Then, sir, rely on it, you have paid dearly for your

knowledge.   Stubbs is no advocate for gratuitous instruc-
tion."

" No," I replied, after a diligent examination of my
pockets, "fortunately all's right.   Nevertheless, I thank
you for your caution ; when I next hear of Helvetius, I
will take care it shall be at a respectful distance."

" I am not unreasonable enough," continued Wilde, " to
condemn our friend for wishing to keep his hand in practice—such a wish is creditable to his ambition as an
artist ; but that he should affect the moralist all the
while —this, sir, is what enrages me.   Confound such
canting scoundrels !   Give me the knave who has manli-
ness enough to avow his vocation.   I have no notion of a
man being above his business.   For, after all, sir, what
difference is there between the thief and the conqueror ?—
between the plunder of individuals and that of nations ?
I protest I can see none.   But perhaps I am partial."

" The main difference lies in this, that society binds a
laurel wreath round the brow of the conqueror, while it
adjusts a rope to the neck of the thief.   I trust, Mr.
Wilde, you are in no danger of the latter distinction ?"

" God forbid ! I am, indeed, condemned to undergo—
excuse my speaking professionally—the last penalties of
the law for an awkward sort of night blunder, made on
the premises of Alderman Squarestern last spring (one is
apt to make mistakes in the dark, you know) ; but, luckily,
on my trial a doubtful point arose, which induced the
judge to grant me a respite till he had consulted the
whole twelve."

" And can you feel at ease while in such a state of suspense ?"

" Suspense !   Nonsense !   My attorney says—"

" Mr. Wilde, Mr. Wilde," said I, in a solemn but affectionate tone, " the less you have to do with attorneys the
better.   Rely on it, sir, they are not safe or creditable
associates for gentlemen of your character.   But I beg
pardon for interrupting you.   What about your attorney ?"

" Why, he assures me that the point in question is all
but decided in my favour already."

"My dear sir, I am transported to hear it."

"No personalities, I beg. I hate that word 'transported;' 'tis a villanous phrase, and should never be used among decent folks. Another man, now, would be offended by such an expression; but I am a citizen of the world, and take things coolly."

"And the adventures of such a cosmopolite must be well worth hearing. If it be not exacting too much from your politeness, may I beg a sketch of—"

"Oh, certainly, sir; your request is most flattering. At present, however, I can say nothing on the subject, for I see Graves yonder preparing to lock up; to-morrow, my history, such as it is, shall be at your service."

Accordingly, on the following day, when we came out for our usual hour's airing, Wilde, true to his promise, seated himself on the stump of an old tree, close under the wall, and gave me the following rambling outline, which I here repeat pretty nearly as I heard it, of his past life.

CHAPTER XI.

THE SAYINGS AND DOINGS OF MR. JONATHAN WILDE THE YOUNGER.

"I AM a zealous advocate for family pride, which, I think, you will scarcely wonder at, when you hear the name of the individual whom I have the honour to call great-grandfather. By my father's side I can boast no illustrious pedigree; but my mother was lineally descended from the renowned Jonathan Wilde, and was the only sister of four brothers, all men of capacity in their line, but all equally unfortunate. The eldest of these worthies—pardon my prolixity, but I love to talk of my ancestors—was transferred from his happy home at Whitechapel to Botany Bay; the second died of a broken heart in Horsemonger-lane; the third fell a victim to a severe cold, caught while gazing at one of the prettiest prospects in all Berks from a damp pillory; while the fourth got his head accurately bisected at an Irish wedding.

"By these successive calamities, added to the premature death of both my parents, I was left with nothing but ten remarkably docile fingers to rely upon for support. Luckily, however, there dwelt in my neighbourhood a certain butcher, who, observing what he called my 'predicament,' took me into his employment as an errand-boy; and shortly afterward, fancying that he discovered in me evidences of superior genius, despatched me to a neighbouring grammar-school, where I soon became distinguished by my thirst for letters, inasmuch as I had got the 'Forty Thieves' and the 'Newgate Calendar' by heart—two works which made a deep impression on my youthful mind.

"I had remained but two years at school, when I was expelled, together with a lad named Fusby, for tying crackers to my master's coat-tail. The joke scarcely merited such retribution; so, by way of revenge, and also as a pleasing memento of my school-boy days, I abstracted the pedagogue's watch and seals; after which I wrote him a courteous but spirited note, wherein I assured him that my mind soared far above the idea of dependence, and that in future I should look on myself as my own master.

"You will scarcely believe that for this harmless frolic I was taken up, tried, tied to a cart's tail, flogged, rubbed down with vinegar, put into the black hole to dry, and then imprisoned for three tedious months; at the expiration of which time, finding myself independent alike of money, prospects, and connexions, I was compelled, in self-defence, to commence business as a conveyancer.

"It was at the Surrey Theatre—I linger on the recollection with a pleasing melancholy—that I made my first appearance as an artist in this line. The house was crowded, and, as good luck would have it, I chanced to stand next an asthmatic old man, to whom I imparted my suspicions of there being thieves in the house, and hastened to prove the fact by decamping with his snuff-box.

"This exploit at once got me into repute among my contemporary artists, and inspired me with such self-confidence that, for upwards of a twelvemonth afterward, I wrought successfully, night and day, at my new vocation ; and one evening, on the steps of the Opera House, had the honour of a personal interview with the Prince Regent."

"Indeed !" said I, "how came that about ?"

"Why, sir, in attempting to ease his Royal Highness of a remarkably handsome gold snuff-box, I happened to make a false step and stumble up against him ; whereupon he turned round with a smile, and made me such a gracious bow that I have been the most loyal of men ever since. But in politics I was always a Tory, though I cannot say I have fingered so much public money as Lords E—— or B——. However, a man can but do his best.

"It was at this period of my life that I became acquainted with the immortal Ikey Singleton. We shook hands (strange enough !) in the coat-pockets of a clergyman, who had stuck himself at the back of one of the dress-boxes in Covent Garden, and against whom our professional dexterity was at one and the same moment employed. Ikey was a great man, sir ; still I cannot but think he was overrated. Certes, his mode of effecting transfers was prompt and intelligent ; but it wanted originality. You might know him anywhere by his style. With his contemporary Slender Billy it was otherwise. He was all versatility, and had the finest conception of a burglary of any man I ever met with.

"But to return from this digression, into which I have been led by my respect for departed genius. Scarcely had I achieved notoriety by the felonious capabilities of my fingers, when my mind, fitted for nobler pursuits, began to languish for pre-eminence in the higher branches of *the* profession. Ah, sir! ambition has been my ruin, as it has been that of many a great man before me. On sounding my old schoolfellow Fusby on the subject, he readily entered into my feelings, and agreed to join me in an attempt on a house in Brunswick-square, where I had previously ascertained that a rich old bachelor resided.

"Punctual to the moment, we proceeded to effect a lodgment in his kitchen ; but, unluckily, while we were ascending towards the drawing-room, a stout scullery-girl, unperceived, had watched our motions, assaulted us both with her fists in so cowardly and unprovoked a manner that we were compelled to make a precipitate retreat. Detection was the inevitable consequence. Fusby, however, escaped by turning King's evidence ; while I was tried, convicted, and transferred to his Majesty's colony at Botany Bay, where I was immediately placed in the service of a Scotch emigrant, who held vast pasturages in the neighbourhood of Sydney.

"I cannot say much for the society in this quarter of the globe. Your Australian colonist is, at best, but semi-barbarous ; so much so, that whenever I chanced to fall in with a kangaroo, I invariably made a point of taking off my hat to him, to mark my sense of his superior intelligence and respectability. Conceive the innate vulgarity of a wretch who could think of nothing better for me to do than associate with his own sheep! Yet this was my sole occupation. From morning till night did my master compel me to keep company with his merinoes, till at length—such is the force of habit—I actually began to 'ba-a' in my sleep, as naturally as if I had been a ram.

"For many wearisome months I submitted to this monster's tyranny with the meek resignation of a Christian ; but when, not content with making me do duty as a sheep-dog, he set me also to superintend the education of his pigs—by Jove! I could stand it no longer : so, seizing the first favourable opportunity of flight, I set off for Cape How, whence I secretly embarked in a free-trader bound for England.

"The voyage home was long and stormy, and our little vessel went staggering over the Pacific just as if she were dead drunk. For weeks together I was constantly dripping like a parish pump, and knew not what it was to eat a meal in safety. You see this scar on my left cheek? It was made by a fork, which, taking a slanting direction, one squally day at dinner, when I was attempting to convey a small bit of stale pork to my mouth, ran clean through, and, I fear, has spoiled my beauty for life. But this is a trifle. The worst is to come.

" Late one night I was roused from an uneasy slumber, by the cry of ' Breakers ahead!' and, on rushing on deck, found the ship in strong hysterics, kicking, and plunging, and groaning among a cluster of sharp white jagged rocks. Ah! sir, that was an awful spectacle, worse even than the black cap on a judge's head! The waves ran mountains high; and as each fresh one broke over us, our poor little vessel trembled from stem to stern, and finally went to pieces; while I, after floating about some time on the fragment of a mast, was lifted up by an enormous billow, and hurled far on land in a state of utter insensibility.

" On recovering consciousness, I found myself stretched on a sandy coast, surrounded by a host of peculiarly loquacious savages, who, as I afterward learned, were discussing the interesting point as to whether or not they should eat me! Fortunately, the humane interference of one of the chief's wives—I was always a favourite with the ladies—saved my life; and, instead of being cooked myself, I was taken up into the country, and set to cook for others.

" Folks in England are in the habit of talking of savages as wholly uncivilised. Never was such arrant presumption! They defraud, bully, lie, and make war upon each other, quite as readily as we do here; and, in point of manual dexterity, might put to shame the best-instructed artist in the metropolis. I assure you, sir, I felt quite humiliated to think, after all my practice, how much I had still to learn in this respect.

"You wonder, no doubt, why I quitted such a civilised people. My reason was this. When I had remained with them the best part of a year, I began to acquire such a plump and tempting rotundity as to excite the epicurean propensities of the high-priest—a noted cannibal; and not relishing the idea of being served up, hot and smoking, at one of his dinner-parties (for he was remarkably hospitable, and gave capital entertainments), I made no more ado, but hurried off to the sea-coast; where, a few days afterwards, I was discovered by the crew of a homeward-bound English merchantman, which had put in there for fresh water, and safely conveyed to Liverpool; from which place I instantly made the best of my way to the metropolis.

"Here, for four subsequent years, my professional tact, sharpened by experience, enabled me to live in comfort, if not in affluence. Like my illustrious ancestor, too, I became the captain of as choice a gang of spirits as ever rode a mare foaled of an acorn; assisted by whom I levied contributions on all classes, with an impartiality which I shall ever reflect on with satisfaction. But where, you will ask, are all these great men now? Alas! one languishes in the hulks at Woolwich; another treads the horrid flats of Australia; a third takes compulsory exercise at Brixton; a fourth—but I have no heart to proceed. I must weep a while.

"The rest of my tale is brief. My gang dispersed—my person proscribed—my fame blown far and wide—I was compelled to quit London and seek some more fitting scene of action. This I fondly hoped I had found in Humbug. But the eye of the law—or, as our friend Justinian would say, of destiny—was on me; and scarcely had I resumed business, when I was taken up, convicted, and—here I am. And thus, sir, conclude the adventures of the last and least worthy of the Wildes."

CHAPTER XII.

THE DEATH-WARRANT.

WILDE was in the habit of conversing with me in this flippant style whenever we happened to encounter each other in the courtyard. As I became better acquainted with him, however, I found that he was at best but a lively bore, full of levity, which he mistook for wit, and without one atom of real moral or physical fortitude. I was disgusted, besides, with the rhodomontade spirit in which he boasted of his past achievements, just as if, under any circumstances, they were not to be deeply regretted. Hundreds are scamps from necessity; but he who is a scamp from choice is a wretch whom all men are equally interested in persecuting to the death. This is one of those sapient moral saws which I owe to my intercourse with the casuist Justinian, who, whenever we conversed together on the subject of our mutual acquaintance, always shook his head, gravely and distrustfully, as Socrates may be supposed to have done when pondering on the irregularities of the young Alcibiades.

Meanwhile the time drew on when Wilde's destiny was to be decided, and, unknown to himself, I could detect a very visible alteration in his feelings. He began to shrink from the society of his former crony Justinian, who, like a true Job's comforter, exhorted him to prepare himself for the worst; and he clung more tenaciously to me, with whom he held repeated discussions on the subject of his chances of acquittal; and though both of us came to the same conclusion—I from good-nature, and he from sheer incapacity to brave the worst—still it was impossible not to see, from his strange, fitful alternations of mirth and melancholy, that an uneasy something was perpetually hanging about him.

One night, by permission of the turnkey, and at Wilde's earnest intercession, I accompanied him to his cell. He was in rather more equable spirits than usual, abounding in anecdotes of his past life, and speculations as to his future course of conduct. He was tired, he said, of his old habits, and had serious thoughts, if only for the novelty of the thing, of turning over a new leaf. I approved highly of his project, and was dwelling on its advantages, when suddenly, " Hark !" exclaimed the poor fellow, turning on the instant as white as a corpse, " I hear a footstep."

" Nonsense," I replied, " 'tis mere fancy ; or, perhaps, they're locking up for the night."

But the quick instinct of fear was correct ; for, while I was yet speaking, we heard a heavy, measured tread, accompanied by the clanking of keys, proceeding along the passage. An instant, and the step was at the door.

" It is the turnkey," said Wilde, fetching a breath from the very bottom of his heart ; and as he spoke the door opened, and in walked that important official with a written paper in his hand.

I looked anxiously into his face, and saw at once that there was no hope. Wilde, too, caught the glance, but instantly closed his eyes, and waved off the man with an impetuous movement of his hand.

" Jonathan Wilde," commenced the turnkey, clearing his throat with a few solemn hems, " it is my painful duty—"

" Not a word—I will not hear a word. It is false as hell, and you know it. Come, come, Mr. Graves, confess now you are joking ;" and the poor wretch clutched the turnkey by his arm like a madman.

But the man only shook his head.

" Liar ! It is—it must be false. O Mr. Graves ! my best, my only friend, as you hope for mercy hereafter— as you would not have the curse of a dying man on your—" Then abruptly breaking off as the word " dying" struck. on his half-bewildered brain—" Dying, indeed ! Faith, this is excellent. Hah ! hah ! hah ! Who's afraid !" and he broke out into a fierce laugh, while the blood, surging upward to his forehead, gorged the veins there till I thought they would burst.

"Mr. Wilde," resumed the turnkey, "my duty, however painful, must be performed. Prepare yourself for the worst—you have but two days to live."

A moment's pause succeeded this awful intimation. At length, "O'Blarney," said Wilde, in a whisper, such as a curse is breathed in, "take my hat off—quick—quick—it binds my temples."

"Hat, man! sure, you're dreaming. You've got no hat on." But he heard me not. Sense and feeling were alike crushed out, and, dashing his doubled fists against his forehead, he dropped, as if shot through the heart.

CHAPTER XIII.

A CONFLAGRATION, AND AN ESCAPE.

A FEW days after this sad occurrence, as, full of serious and painful thoughts, I was gazing on the stump of the old lime-tree where I had last seen Wilde seated, I was joined by Mr. Justinian Stubbs, who, observing my melancholy, said, "Doubtless, sir, you are thinking of the poor young man who made such a disastrous exit the other morning. It was a sad business, certainly; but is so far satisfactory, inasmuch as it confirms the great philosophic axiom, that what will be, will be. Our defunct friend, sir, was born to be hanged. Often and often did the humble individual who has the honour to address you delicately hint to him this ungracious truth; but the young man, with a thousand estimable, and some few brilliant qualities, was strangely regardless of all that militated against his own view of a question. However, I do not blame, I only pity him. It was a shocking case. Do you take snuff?"

"You would indeed have pitied him, had you witnessed his death."

"I believe you, sir; death is at all times an awkward matter, as I showed, and, I flatter myself, with some success, in my treatise on the subject. 'Death,' I observed, 'being the inevitable fulfilment of destiny, it is sheer folly to attempt to retard or deprecate its approach.'"

"Poor Wilde!" said I, interrupting the flow of the fatalist's eloquence.

"You're affected, sir, and your feelings do honour to your heart. Nevertheless, it is as well to bear in mind that undue feeling is injurious to philosophy, which, after all, is but the perfection of phlegm. Besides," added Justinian, with wonderful composure, "we must all die, you know."

"True; and in the majority of cases, death is rather a blessing than a curse; for what is life but a synonyme for sorrow, and the world itself but a melancholy mausoleum raised to the memory of blighted hopes and buried loves?"

"Mr. O'Blarney," replied the sage condescendingly, "permit me to congratulate you on the exceeding eloquence of your last remark. I confess I am partial to a striking, conversational style; it shows character. But enough of this for the present; Graves is beckoning us;" and, putting his arm through mine, the fatalist and myself strolled back to our respective cells.

In the course of the evening, while I was still sadly pondering on Wilde's melancholy end, my meditations were put an end to by a tremendous uproar, and the shouts of many hundred voices outside the prison-gates. A few minutes after, the turnkey rushed into my apartment, breathless with astonishment and consternation.

"Hey-day, Mr. Graves!" said I, "what's the matter now? You seem completely at your wit's end."

"Matter! Why, that Corn Law business has turned all the people's heads, I think. The Radicals have been holding a public meeting this morning about it; and, having broken every window in town, and set fire to the mayor's house, they have now come up here in a body of eight hundred or a thousand strong; and swear, if we don't set all the prisoners free, they'll burn the jail down. I'm blessed if I know which way to turn."

"Have you not sufficient force within to beat them off?" I inquired, and my heart leaped with delight at the probability of my liberation.

"Force! bless your heart, what can force do against a —hark! there they go again. They're at it now in right earnest."

Knowing well the innate ferocity of all mobs, I proffered Mr. Graves the most disinterested advice in my power, by exhorting him at once to throw open the prison-gates; "Otherwise," said I, "you may rely on it your life will be in jeopardy, and it will be but a poor consolation to you when dangling from the prison-wall to know that you have done your duty. Our first duty is to our own necks; our second, to our country."

But the man was deaf to my exhortations. "Bless your soul," he argued, "if I were to do as you—O Lord! O Lord! what shall I do? Hark, how they're banging away at the gates!"

"Break open the doors—set fire to the jail—down with the parson-justices—no taxes—no Corn Laws—Hunt for ever!" thundered a thousand hoarse voices outside the prison-walls.

These shouts were followed up by a terrific attack on the gates. Hammers, brickbats, bludgeons, and huge beams of wood were all at once pressed into the service of the mob, who cheered each other's progress in the work of destruction by repeated huzzas, which were as loudly replied to by the prisoners.

In little more than half-an-hour from the commencement of the assault, the efforts of the rioters were crowned with success. The huge brazen gates groaned, yawned, and finally gave way beneath the rush of an infuriated rabble, who poured like a cataract into the jail, bearing down all before them.

My apartment, being nearest to the gates, was the first

9

they entered. The turnkey made no opposition—indeed, from the first he had stood stupified, like one bereft of all his faculties ; but holding forth the keys, mechanically as it were, thrust them into the hands of the foremost rioter, who acknowledged the receipt by a blow which compelled poor Graves to salute his mother earth.

To rush out with the keys, unlock all the cells, and then set fire to the jail, were the acts of almost one and the same moment. I profited by the confusion, and, forcing my way over heaps of drunken rioters who lay sprawling in all directions, gained at length the exterior of the prison.

Here the very first person that met my eyes was the sage Justinian, who was engaged in an animated altercation with the ordinary, whom he had unscrupulously seized hold of by the collar.

"D—n your eyes, you old cove !" said the philosopher, surprised for the moment out of his usual dignified equanimity, "tip us your castor, and be quick about it ;" with which words he snatched the hat (a shovel of the first water) from the sconce of the astounded ecclesiastic, who had barely time to pronounce his opinion of this act of sacrilege when he found himself stripped also of his coat.

"Please your reverence," snuffled Justinian, while he hastened to invest himself with the ordinary's coat, and offered his own in lieu of it, "exchange is no robbery. We have warrant for it in Scripture. But come, O'Blarney —Scroggins, I should say—we have no time to lose ;" and making a formal obeisance to the parson, who, having hastily shoved his hand through the ragged elbows of the fatalist's coat, kept thrusting and driving away with both arms in a state of the most ludicrous irritability, we made the best of our way to Humbug, just as the fire began to mount aloft above the prison-walls.

Scarcely had we lost sight of the jail, when the loud, sullen clangour of the alarm-bell convinced us that the authorities of Humbug were on the alert. This induced us to pause a while and arrange our future plans, which we were busily discussing, when we heard a heavy tramp of horses, and presently a squadron of cavalry, with their drawn swords flashing like meteors in the night, came galloping towards us.

There was no time for flight or concealment. The soldiers were on us in an instant ; on which my companion, with admirable readiness addressing the commander of the troops, who had just halted for the purpose of taking a close survey of our persons, said, " For God's sake, sirs, be quick, or you will be too late ; the jail is already on fire in every part ;" and he pointed to where the blazing conflagration towered high up into the sky—a vast fiery beacon, seen for miles and miles round the country.

"Who are you, sir ?" replied the officer. " I have orders to stop all suspicious persons."

"Who am I !" said Justinian, with well-feigned surprise ; " why, sir, I am the prison ordinary, and this is Mr. Graves the turnkey. We have but just effected our escape from the rioters, and are now on our way to Humbug."

" Enough, sirs, I have no time to hear more. Pass on ;" and, giving the word to the soldiers to move forward, the officer put spurs to his horse, and the whole squadron vanished in the direction of the jail.

As we entered the town, we found fright, astonishment, despair depicted on every countenance. All the shops were shut ; the lamp-lights in many of the principal streets were smashed ; and in the one large square (the West-end of Humbug) groups of urchins were indulging in minor matters of mischief, proportioned to their tender years—such as pelting stones at the drawing-room windows, or at the heads which were every now and then thrust out of the upper storeys ; while more than one special constable, kept in countenance by the solemn parish beadle, who blushed deeper than his scarlet coat at this affront to all legitimate authority, looked tamely on.

When we reached the open space before the mayor's house, a far more fearful sight was revealed to us. The whole building was one enormous mass of living fire; and beneath its lurid light danced and shouted a band of ghastly, half-naked wretches, in the most frantic state of drunkenness. Others of the rioters, scarce able from their excesses to stir hand or foot, lay wallowing like swine in the middle of the road; and one, in particular, was stretched in a pool of red-hot lead, close to the building, writhing, shrieking, and blaspheming, like a tortured fiend—his teeth clenched, his white shivering lips apart, and his eyes in a stony stare, such as is seen in tombs!

A groan of horror burst from the mob, as they witnessed this appalling object. "Save him, for God's sake save him!" was the general cry. But not a soul stirred. Fear had frozen up the faculties of the whole multitude. They stood, fixed and spell-bound, like the statues in the Oriental City of the Dead.

At length, one more intrepid than the rest sprang forward to where the wretch lay convulsed in his last agonies; but scarcely had he made this movement, when a stentorian voice behind him shouted out, "Stand back, the roof is falling." The crowd caught up the cry. "The roof is falling," roared out one and all. "See, the walls are giving way. Stand back, sir, for your life."

This warning induced the stranger to pause, and casting one brief glance upward at the blazing building, which enabled him to take in the whole extent of his danger, he darted back among the mob just at the moment when the walls, after tottering and rocking as if under the action of an earthquake, came down with a crash, involving the whole fabric in their fall.

Awe-struck at this catastrophe, I hurried forward with Justinian towards the market-place. On our way thither, at the bend of a dingy, narrow lane, we saw beneath the dim glimmer of a lamp at the door of a small house, a forlorn, solitary female figure, sitting with her head buried in her hands. Whatever may be my *sang-froid* as far as man is concerned, I cannot, unmoved, pass a woman in affliction. I halted accordingly, and, addressing a few kind words to the poor creature, inquired whether I could render her any service ; but she made me no other reply than a low moan ; and I was again moving on, when one of the neighbours came up, and in answer to my questions informed me that the mourner was a widow, whose husband had been killed in the forenoon at the riots before the Guildhall ; and that from the moment his corpse had been brought into her house, she had persisted, despite the intreaties of her neighbours, in sitting where we now saw her, like one bereft of reason.

This explanation shot a sudden pang to my heart, for it brought to my mind my own wife ; while to give a still more subdued tone to my feelings, I could hear, as I stood listening to it, the merry in-door laughter of the poor widow's unconscious children. " What a contrast is here !" thought I. " Joy riots within, while a fond, warm heart is breaking without ;" and with a sigh, which I could not, for the life of me repress, I left the disconsolate mourner still sitting, apparently indifferent to all things, at the door of the house which contained her husband's remains, like Memory keeping watch beside the grave of Love.

A few minutes' brisk walking brought us to the market-place, where some hundreds of men and boys were assembled, listening to and laughing at the ravings of a half-witted religious enthusiast, whom I recollected to have seen occasionally among the debtors in the courtyard of the jail ; and whose imagination, kindled by the scenes he had witnessed during the day, was now venting itself in all sorts of prophetic anathemas. " Woe, woe unto ye !" he exclaimed, " ye scribes and pharisees ! Ye have been weighed in the balance, and found wanting. The handwriting on the wall has gone forth against you. Lo, yonder it is graven in dark characters on God's own palace !" and he pointed with his long lean right arm to the black body of cloud which hung in the still air, like a funeral pall, above the city.

He was proceeding in this frantic style, when a small knot of special constables made their appearance, on which the rabble, true to their own instincts, from the days of Jack Cade downward, scampered off in all directions. Justinian, too, took the hint, and whispering in my ear, "Now that the civil power is beginning to recover its senses, we may as well be cautious," drew me away from the market-place into one of the long dark streets in which Humbug abounds.

CHAPTER XIV.

THE FAREWELL.

JUST as I had passed the memorable Cock and Tooth-pick, which stands at one corner of the market-place, I saw a carriage, the dashing panels of which I at once recognised as it entered the Inn-yard, and farther on, at the distance of about a hundred yards, the plump figure of Alderman Snodgrass, who, it was clear, had but just reached Humbug, and was busy receiving information from, and giving directions to, some three or four tradesmen. The unsuccessful M.P. was as full of bustle as ever, talking at the very top of his voice, and turning every now and then a wrathful glance in the direction of the prison.

Though aware of the hazard of accosting my implacable persecutor, I could not resist the temptation, so stood unperceived beneath the shade of an old wall till the gossips had retired, when just as the alderman was following, I stepped forward, and, making him the profoundest of bows, addressed him as follows :—"I am most happy, Mr. Snodgrass, in this opportunity of again meeting with a gentleman whose discernment and generosity of spirit have, no doubt, taught him by this time to do me justice. I hope, sir, all the members of your excellent family are well ; and that the fair Miss Maria— But excuse my enlarging at present on this delicate topic ; it is my intention to pay my respects to the young lady to-morrow, when I trust that my modesty may not again prove a bar to my good fortune. You look well, Mr. Snodgrass, whence I conclude that the little unpleasantnesses of the election are already forgotten, and, above all, that affair of the five per—"

During all this time the alderman had stood like one bewildered; but no sooner had I mentioned the words "five per cents.," than the blood rushed to his face, and he gave vent to his astonishment and wrath in such broken sentences as, " Well, I never!   Gracious heavens, is it possible!   Prodigious impudence!   But you shall not escape me this time;" and, seizing me by the collar, he endeavoured to drag me back to the Inn-yard, when I freed myself from his grasp, while Justinian, who was but a few dozen yards in advance, attracted by the scuffle, turned back to offer me his aid.

His presence did not in the slightest degree daunt Mr. Snodgrass, who swore he would not rest satisfied till he had again seen me consigned over to justice, hurling, in his passion, a thousand coarse epithets, such as " rogue, swindler, vagabond," in my teeth; whereupon, seeing a raw-looking constable a few yards ahead, I requested Justinian to prevent the alderman's escape, and, running up to the man, said, " Are you a stranger to Humbug?"

" Eez, I be; I war only swore in this morning."

" Well, then, follow me; I want you to take charge of a suspicious character."

The man obeyed my commands, which were given with an air of authority; and when we reached the spot where the alderman was still struggling in Justinian's grasp, I said, pointing to him, " Arrest that man.   This gentleman and myself have proof that he is one of the incendiaries who set fire to the jail."

The constable instantly laid fast hold of Mr. Snodgrass, who roared out, " Hold off, villain! or you shall pay dearly for this assault.   Do you know who I am?"

" Ecz; you be one of the incendiaries like."

" Rascal, I am Alderman Snodgrass, a county magistrate!"

" A loikely story, faith!" said the constable, leering at me with a knowing wink.

" Alderman Snodgrass !" said I, " how dare you use the
name of that much respected individual ? Take him
away, constable."

"Aye, away with him," said Justinian, who saw at
once the real state of the case ; "away with him to the
watch-house, and we will follow and give evidence against
him. Alderman Snodgrass, indeed! What should a
person of his rank want wandering alone at midnight in
this suspicious manner ?"

During this brief discussion, Mr. Snodgrass kept struggling and vowing vengeance against all three of us ; but
the more he roared, the tighter hold the clodhopper kept
of him ; until at length, despite his magisterial dignity,
I had the satisfaction of seeing him safely walked off to
the watch-house.

For appearance' sake we followed the constable and his
prisoner for a few minutes, but when we came within sight
of the Inn we gave them both the slip, and, turning down
a narrow arched passage, were instantly lost to sight in
the gloom.

After threading a variety of lanes and alleys, we reached
a low, dingy brick building, with a square courtyard
before it, at the end of which a solitary lamp was burning. Here, making a sudden halt, " My friend," said the
philosopher solemnly, "do you see yon edifice ?"

" Yes, what of it ? It looks like a lock-up house."

"A what !" replied Justinian, drawing himself up with
an air of hauteur, "a lock-up house ! Sir, that building,
meanly as you may be pleased to think of it, is neither
more nor less than the celebrated Humbug Charity
School ! Within the walls of that edifice the obscure
individual before you first projected his ' Treatise on
Destiny.' I am a total stranger to literary vanity, as
doubtless you have long since perceived ; but I certainly
do pique myself on the composition of an essay which has
for its sublime object the overthrow of all existing social
abuses, and the introduction of a more enlightened code
of ethics. Hail, consecrated fabric ! within whose—'

His meditations were here abruptly put an end to by a cry of "Stop thief!" which proceeded from the upper end of the street, and was followed by a crowd of boys and men, who came rushing forward in the direction where we stood. This ominous interruption wrought the same talismanic effect on Justinian's nerves that the invectives of Cicero wrought on Catiline. His enthusiasm was below zero in an instant. Abiit—excessit—evasit—erupit!—in plain English, he bolted.

In vain I conjured him to stop, assuring him that there was no cause for apprehension. The more nimbly I cried "Stop," the more nimbly he shot forward; while I, though a far better hand at running, could with difficulty keep up with him, such an impetus had fear given to his muscles, and so completely was I convulsed with laughter.

Away he flew, up this street, down that, and whenever he showed symptoms of flagging I kept him at full speed by maliciously crying out, "On, on! they're just behind us." Having at length cleared the town, he stopped an instant to draw breath; when, suddenly looking behind me, I again exclaimed, with affected dismay, that the constables were close at our heels.

"Oh, mercy!" cried the philosopher, perspiring like an alderman in the dog-days; "it's all over with me, so I may as well die here."

"Nonsense, man! I tell you we must run for it."

"Run for it! Ah! it's all very well for you to talk of running; but for me, with this weight of— However, I suppose there's no help for it;" and he made one more desperate effort, when, having reached the high-road, he shot across it, and thence head-foremost, through a quickset hedge, into some secluded meadows, leaving Humbug a few hundred yards behind.

Here, halting to wipe the perspiration from his forehead, he was beginning to pour forth his plaintive lamentations, when a spectacle presented itself which, for the moment, banished every other consideration from his mind. This was no other than the full, unimpeded view

—the first time we had yet witnessed it in all its subli-
mity—of the blazing prison, which, notwithstanding that
the night was black as the raven's wing, yet brought out
every house, tree, hedge, and barn throughout the neighbourhood as distinctly as if it had been mid-day.   For an
instant, all would be gloom, as volume after volume of
smoke swept across the sky ; and then a broad, red, un-
interrupted column of light would shoot up into the
lurid atmosphere, till the very clouds themselves seemed
on fire.   Even from the spot where we stood we could
hear the hiss and roar of the mighty conflagration, blended
at intervals with the heavy rumbling of the engines, the
clang of at least a dozen alarm-bells, and the shouts of
the rioters, who, as the blazing billows surged upwards,
and spread over an airy reach of miles, made the welkin
ring again with their huzzas.

After gazing our fill on this terrible spectacle, Justinian,
who had by this time partially recovered his wind, seated
himself on a hillock, and began to moralise on the subject.
" A fire," said he, taking a long, solemn pinch of snuff,
"is a fine theme for philosophic contemplation.   I recognise in it the principle of good struggling with that of
evil.   See, the firemen are endeavouring to put it out.
They are the representatives of bigotry, who are interested
in stifling the blaze of truth.   But it will triumph in
spite of them ; for what will be, will be."

" But you don't take into consideration the poor wretches
who have lost their lives in the flames."

" Young man, my philanthropy, I say it with honest
pride, is altogether on a comprehensive scale.   I sympathise with humanity in the aggregate, not in the
particular ; for so long as society continues in its present
sophisticated state, grounding the laws that regulate
meum and *tuum* on the shifting sands of conventional
opinion, instead of on the immutable rock of instinct,
so long will it be the duty of those who, like myself,
cherish virtue for its own sake, to suspend their sympathies for individuals, in order to devote them exclusively to the interests of the mass."

I could with difficulty repress a smile while the philosopher made these remarks; he made them with such sublime fervour of manner and intonation. One is prepared to meet with animation in the young; but to see a fat middle-aged man enthusiastic is as novel and grotesque a sight as would be that of a prize-ox starting at Epsom for the Derby.

Justinian was proceeding still further with his sage speculations, when, finding that I was beginning to get a little ennuied, he adroitly changed the theme, and, lowering his lofty tone, said, "My friend, pardon the suddenness of my resolution, but I must here bid you farewell. Fain would I proceed, but a certain twitching in the calves of my legs—to say nothing of my ribs, which ache just as if I had been pommelled with a dozen bludgeons—warns me that I must either sink with fatigue, or make the best of my way to Humbug. Will you accompany me?"

"Never!—the alternative is too hazardous."

"Oh, as to that, so far as I am concerned, I feel convinced, notwithstanding my late unaccountable panic, which I attribute rather to a deranged state of the nervous system than to any inherent lack of moral fortitude, that this disguise will afford me quite sufficient protection, while you—"

"'Tis of no use talking, Mr. Stubbs; my resolve is taken."

"And whither does your destiny lead you?"

"I know not. Possibly to South Wales, which is easiest of access from this neighbourhood, where I shall remain secluded till my late adventures are forgotten. Bad as it is, I have no other resource left. A licentious press has ruined me for ever in this neighbourhood."

"Arcadian simplicity! The idea is not amiss in theory, but defective, I fear, in—"

"Practice. Possibly so; but, to say the truth, I am sick to death of all literary and political turmoil; so, for a season or two, I shall content myself with peeping at the world through 'the loop-holes of retreat.' I have been an active agent long enough. I now intend to become a mere passive spectator of other men's doings."

"Farewell, then," said Justinian, grasping me fervently by the hand; "not a moment is to be lost: so farewell, my friend, for ever! A few days since, and I could have borne our parting with indifference; but now—forgive the starting tear—I feel the man triumph over the philosopher;" and he applied the ordinary's handkerchief to his eyes.

I was not a little astonished at this pathetic ebullition; but before I had time to recover myself, Justinian, who had marked my emotion, continued—

"I see my sensibility surprises you, and no wonder, for I am not apt to be thus overcome; but the truth is, my young friend, from the very first moment we met, there was a certain something about you that irresistibly won my affection!"

"You are pleased to be complimentary, Mr. Stubbs."

"No; I am too sad to be insincere. I thought I could sympathise only with the *many*. Alas! I feel I have a tear for the *one*. But I hear footsteps: let us hide ourselves;" and, accordingly, we both squatted down under the hedge, till a ploughman, who was mounted on a huge dray-horse, had galloped past us. When we ventured forth from our hiding-place, the philosopher, after again bidding me farewell, and straining me to his breast, in what he called "a long and last embrace," hurried back as fast as his legs would carry him to Humbug.

No sooner was he out of sight than, a strange presentiment flashing across my mind, I plunged my hand into my coat-pocket, and found that this accomplished rascal, while busy hugging me in his arms, had actually found means to elope with my pocket-book! I have detested the word "philosophy" ever since.

But other ideas soon diverted my attention. Just as I turned to pursue my solitary route, the church clock of St. Laurence struck twelve; and while I yet stood listening with involuntary awe to the echo of the last stroke as it rolled away in the distance, a wild yell of exultation caught my ear, and instantly the prison-walls fell in with a tremendous crash, while millions of sparkles, followed by a dense body of smoke that blackened the entire firmament, announced that the work of destruction was consummated. Such was the joyous illumination that ushered in the passing of the Corn Laws.

BOOK THE THIRD.

THE VILLAGE DOCTOR.

CHAPTER I.

THE VALE OF TOWY.

IT was on a warm, mellow summer evening, when the sheep were browsing on the Black Mountains, and the vale of Towy, which lay beneath him, caught a thousand glowing tints from the west, that a stranger, manifestly young, intelligent, and perhaps handsome, but with his expressive features sicklied over with melancholy, stood alone, with folded arms and downcast eyes, on the highest summit of Llynn-y-van. That interesting stranger was—*myself!* Disgusted with England, I had no sooner quitted Humbug than chance, or perhaps that ruling destiny which, do what we will, still sways all our motions, led my steps in the direction of South Wales.

As I stood among the lofty peaks of the Caermarthen Alps, and glanced my eye abroad over the far-spreading landscape of hill and dale, wood and water, sylvan meadow and sunlit rock, that lay in unequalled loveliness beneath me, all my gentler sympathies were called forth by the sight ; and I exclaimed aloud, " Yes, here indeed is a Paradise in which even I may find repose ! Here, like the patriarch of Eld, will I set up my tent, and enjoy the sweet solace of pastoral life. Hope, thy visions have faded ! Ambition, thy dream is at an end ! On the summit of this wind-swept crag, in this saddening twilight,

I bid ye both farewell! Lo! I shake the dust of England from off my feet, and descend to pass the threshold of a more auspicious clime. Within this secluded valley I shall find gentle hearts and unsophisticated heads; the busy slanders of the great world cannot pierce these mountain ramparts. Here, then, I may be free from persecution and detection. Hark! the bells from yonder village warn me onward. See, even while I speak, day drops behind the groves of Grongar Hill!"

From this high-flown soliloquy, the reader will at once perceive that I am a man who can accommodate himself to circumstances. I can indeed—and I thank God for the fortunate temperament—conform to the peculiarities of every position into which circumstances may throw me. No mode of life, no turn of thought, comes amiss. With the satirist I can sneer, with the good-natured I can laugh, with the hypochondriac I can sigh. In fact, it was ever my opinion that the golden rule of wisdom consisted in being all things to all men. I was now to adapt myself to a new fashion of society, and lo! I felt already prepared for the change. Strange, that a man so invincibly shy and bashful should possess such antipodean qualifications.

On I went, right down the mountain-side, till I found myself trespassing on the boundary-line of a bog, and ankle-deep in mud. This would have damped the enthusiasm of many a less resolute pedestrian, especially as night was fast blackening around me; but I was stout of heart, and struggled bravely through the morass, advancing at the satisfactory rate of two steps back for every one I made forward.

Just as I had reached a bit of elevated ground, which afforded me a secure footing, I caught sight of a copse, beyond which lay something like a high-road. Scrambling, with sore detriment to my hands and feet, through this jungle, I at length gained the desired point, where I met with a countryman squatted on a hillock, and tying together a broken leash, in which he held a goat.

Had this rencounter, at such an hour, occurred in a

more civilised country, I should, as a matter of course, have been robbed, murdered, and buried in a ditch, to be dug up again a fortnight after in a state of perplexing decomposition ; but civilisation has made less progress in Wales than in England, for the schoolmaster is more domestic, and less abroad at night.

The man replied to my inquiries by informing me that Llandwarrys (such was the name of the nearest village) was at least three miles off; but this news, though it surprised, did not disconcert me ; so I pushed forward again, amusing myself, as I proceeded, with framing shapes out of the odd shadows that twilight flung down upon the earth. One in particular, thrown by a short, squat blackthorn across my path, struck me as bearing a flattering likeness to old Snodgrass.

The last gleam of day had now faded off the horizon. There was clearly not an instant to be lost ; so, holding on, as well as I could, a mean course between the broad ruts—and such ruts !—of the cross-road, I kept up my confidence by anticipating the various comforts that awaited me at my journey's end.

But fancy ill accords with an empty stomach. You may blunt grief by reflection, and passion by philosophy, but I have yet to discover what mental specific can take the edge off a craving appetite. Hunger is not to be argued into submission. It is a stubborn Catholic, that knows its rights and will maintain them.

By this time, darkness, with a giant's step, had traversed the whole landscape. My very pathway not a yard before me looked dim and doubtful, and, so far from leading out of, seemed only to lead me farther into a labyrinth.

At length, after incredible toil, and a thousand turnings, now to the right and now to the left, I was lucky enough to stumble up against the low paling of a cottage-garden which jutted out beside the cross-road. Availing myself of my good fortune, I knocked at the half-open door, and was received by the tenants with the usual Welsh hospitality. The night's meal was just at an end, but the friendly cottagers relaid the cloth, and placing a home-baked loaf, a lump of cream-cheese, and a jug of delicious Welsh ale on the table, told me to commence the onslaught.

A hungry traveller needs no persuasives; so I set to in a steady spirit of determination, when, having satisfied the claims of the gastric juice, I commenced putting divers questions touching the distance to Llandwarrys, and the possibility of reaching it in time to obtain accommodation for the night.

Not a little to my mortification, I found that I was still three miles off, even taking the nearest road, which was difficult to find in the dark; I had better, therefore, added my informant, wait till the moon-rise, when I should be able to find my way to the common, at the farther end of which the town was situated.

This advice was too reasonable to be rejected; I therefore acceded to it at once, and, after an hour's halt, had the satisfaction of seeing the first beams of the rising moon glimmer in at the lattice.

"Now," said mine host, "you may proceed with safety; but as the first part of your road may perhaps give you some little trouble, I will accompany you as far as Llyn-ym-dwarrys, when you will be within a mile of the town, and can no longer make a miss of your way." He then proceeded to put on a pair of thick wooden clogs, and whistling to his dog, which came bounding over the garden-fence at the well-known summons, led the way down the cross-road.

It was a fine starlight night, with a brisk wind that kept hurrying the clouds in rapid succession across the moon's disk, and chequering the landscape with spectral varieties of light and shade. Now and then the breeze came in sharp, shrill gusts, that whirled the dead leaves by hundreds across our path, and brought to our ears the hooting of the owl or the trickling of many a shy streamlet.

We had held on our course for some two miles or more, and I was beginning anxiously to speculate on the chances of a speedy termination to it, when, on rounding the brow of a low hill, we at length came in sight of Llyn-ym-dwarrys. I have seldom seen a more picturesque landscape than the one now presented to my eyes. Before me the country lay open for miles, with every rugged feature softened into beauty by the mellow moonlight. Right through the centre of the common lapsed the Towy, forming, at the most distant extremity, a broad sheet of water, like a lake, whose surface, as the quick wind swept over it, glistened with a thousand silvery spangles. At a few yards from this estuary stood Llandwarrys, conspicuous by its one dim, grey church-spire.

My companion here made a halt. "Yonder is the town," said he; "you have now only to keep straight ahead till you reach the churchyard, when you must turn sharp round by the yews, which will bring you right opposite the Red Lion. Good night, sir. Come, Rhys," continued he, whistling to his dog, "We must be quick back, or the old woman will think we're going to make a night of it at Cevengorneth."

The lights were still twinkling in the houses of Llandwarrys as I passed the churchyard. In a few minutes more I had entered the town, and was safely housed in the snug sanded front parlour of the Red Lion. What luxury was mine at this moment! Epicures may talk of the pleasures of the palate, and poets of those of romance, but I contend there is no enjoyment equal to that which a jaded traveller experiences when, his day's toil fairly at an end, he exchanges two tight boots for a spacious pair of list slippers.

CHAPTER II.

A WELSH VILLAGE AND ITS CONTENTS.

THE town, or, more strictly speaking, the village of Llandwarrys is situated in the centre of the luxuriant vale of Towy. On every side it is barricaded by double ranges of hills, the most elevated of which are the Black

Mountains, whose monarch Llynn-y-van may vie in colossal magnitude with the proudest eminences of North Wales. The town consists of one long straggling street; and its church, remarkable for a grove of yews that tower like majestic mourners above the tombs, stands alone, just outside the town, on the verge of Llyn-ym-dwarrys, through whose common slowly winds the Towy, spanned by a wooden bridge, which nis free mountain spirit makes a point of indignantly sweeping away once a year, when the winter floods pour down from the adjacent highlands.

The great charm of Llyn-ym-dwarrys is its perfect rusticity. No Welsh Nash has yet defaced it by Regent's Park conceits. It is just what Nature intended it should be; a vast circular carpet of the freshest, greenest turf, placed at the base of hills studded with flocks of sheep, and sheltering whole villages in their recesses. In one part it rises into gentle undulations, on which are perched cottages with their pretty strips of flower-garden in front, and of kitchen-ground behind; and, in another, it forms shelving declivities, the sides of which, at the fitting season, are enamelled with heath-bell; moss, fragrant as cinnamon; primrose-tufts, whereon the homeward-bound bee loves to rest her weary wing; celandine, and the creeping wild strawberry-plant.

Two ranges of hills, as I have already observed, sentinel this miniature paradise. The nearest are robed to the very summit in Nature's richest drapery, while the more distant are abrupt, barren, precipitous, and rear up their bluff fronts to the sky, as if disdaining all connexion with earth. More aristocratic-looking mountains I never yet beheld.

It was in one of the cottages that adorned this lovely common that I took up my abode. Apparently no situation could be more attractive or commodious. It stood within a stone's throw of Llandwarrys, yet enjoyed perfect seclusion. A small but productive garden was attached to it, which, stretching up a little green, sunny knoll, afforded a delicious glimpse of the surrounding scenery.

My establishment consisted of a stout lad and lass, whom I selected from among a host of applicants for their rustic manners and appearance. Both seemed models of simplicity—both in perfect keeping with the patriarchal character of the valley they inhabited.

For the first ten days or fortnight my time passed wholly to my satisfaction. A stroll about the common— to the ivied bridge of Pont-y-kle-kys, to the nearest uplands, or the more distant Grongar Hill, occupied the best portion of my mornings; while my evenings were passed in chit-chat with any one whom I might chance to fall in with; and at night my landlord, Mr. Davis, would drop in at the cottage, and, over the old national relish of a Welsh rabbit, initiate me into the politics, &c., of the neighbourhood.

It was through the medium of this gossip, assisted not a little by the ennui which, despite my vaunted ability to conform to circumstances, began to creep over me, that I got introduced to the club of village dignitaries who assembled almost every evening, for the purpose of social compotation and chit-chat, at the Red Lion.

I should previously have mentioned that, owing to its secluded site, being full thirty miles distant from the nearest English town, wholly removed from the usual route of tourists, and holding out no inducements to manufacturing or agricultural schemers, Llandwarrys possessed all the agreeable strangeness of novelty. The majority of its inhabitants—of course I speak not of the more wealthy or patrician classes, but of those whose occupation or any other cause wedded them to the district —were "full of mark and likelihood," and kept the even tenor of their way, from the cradle to the grave, precisely as their fathers had done before them.

Shy, sequestered nooks like Llandwarrys are still to be met with, or were at least fourteen years ago, in the interior of Wales; for it is not, like the Highlands, or the northern lakes, a country which every one makes a point of visiting ; but, to a certain extent, an untrodden soil, where a strange face is seldom seen, and where the tradesmen and small farmers, wholly occupied with their own concerns, busy their heads but little with those of the great world.

The Red Lion, where the club to which I have just alluded were in the habit of assembling, was one of those snug, old-fashioned inns now so rarely to be met with except in the east of England. It had a deep, wide brick porch, from whose roof swung a magpie in a wicker-cage. This porch opened into a tolerably-sized hall, wherein stood an oblong oaken table, grievously notched, albeit hooped with iron ; and a few high-backed arm-chairs of the same material. Opposite the window was the fireplace, within whose ample range four men might sit with ease : and on the walls hung, on one side, a book-shelf, containing a few odd volumes of Swedenborg's works, and, on the other, a glass case, in which was a stuffed salmon reclining at full-length on some bits of artificial grass.

Among those who were oftenest to be met with in this cosy outlandish hall was, first and foremost, the auctioneer—a person who, in an isolated Welsh district, usually enjoys great consideration. He was a duck-legged, pompous little being, fond of making allusions to a professional visit which he paid to London in the year 1814, when he had the rare luck to see the allied sovereigns, and squeeze the horny fist of Blucher. This was the one leading incident in his life from which he always dated.

Next came a half-pay officer ; a grim-looking dog, snappish, disputatious, egotistical ; with a dried liver, and cheeks sallow and wasted, which went in like the two sides of a fiddle, and spread out again at the chin and forehead. This warrior, or the "captain," as he was commonly styled, held it as the chief article of his creed that whatever is, is wrong, and was never so happy as when setting people by the ears together. His favourite hobby was India, about which, like General Harbottle, he was fond of telling marvellous stories. In person he was remarkably prim; wore a blue frock-coat, a little white at the edges in front, and buttoned close up to the throat; stiff black stock, and boots pieced, but polished —for he prided himself on a small foot—with singular attention to effect. On warm sunny days he might be seen sitting on the parapet of the Towy bridge, rocking his legs listlessly to and fro, humming a fragment of some old mess tune, or taking brisk turns up and down the bridge, and jerking out an impudent " Hem !" whenever a petticoat approached him. When heated with argument, he had a trick of giving sharp, irritable tugs at his shirt-collar.

Third in station was the attorney; who exacted respect by virtue of his profession, and who was withal so cautious of what he called committing himself before court, that, in alluding to any particular individual, he never mentioned more than his or her initials. This fellow, like his prototype Rondibilis, had the keen scent of a staghound for a lawsuit, whence it came to pass that he was more reverenced than loved by his neighbours, many of whom he had contrived to render singularly poetical about the pockets.

The fourth was my landlord the apothecary; a good-natured, silly creature, blessed with a widowed sister, who superintended his establishment, and of whom I shall presently have occasion to speak. His chief occupation consisted in sauntering about the neighbourhood, with his hands in his breeches-pockets, and talking to any one who would talk with him. He had projecting eyes, like a lobster, with a vague, unmeaning stare, and usually kept his mouth ajar—I suppose from a habit he had acquired of swallowing every extraordinary story he heard or read.

Lastly, came the curate of Llandwarrys; an amphibious phenomenon, compounded, in nearly equal portions, of parson, poacher, and pugilist. He was social and bibulous, with a prodigious face, the thickest part of which was downward, like a bee-hive, a fist like a quartern loaf, and an inordinate love of song. His favourite *arietta* was " Cease, rude Boreas," which, when in fine voice, he generally sung right through, with a lavish expenditure of wind that might have put a hurricane to the blush. I never heard this tempestuous bravura (the parson called it an air !) but once, and was deaf for two days afterward.

A few farmers from the adjacent villages, on their way home on market-days, occasionally joined this coterie : now and then, too, a traveller from Humbug, or the other large towns on the borders, would drop in ; but these were merely chance customers, whereas the above were regular fixtures at the Red Lion.

Till within a few months of my arrival, these dignitaries had been in the habit of mustering at the Castle ; but a slight of some sort or other having one evening been put on them by the landlady, a pert, pretty widow, who had but recently resigned the office of chambermaid at the Pulteney Hotel, Bath, the whole coterie instantly transferred their patronage to the Red Lion. The consequence of this elopement was a schism between the rival landladies, which, extending more or less to all their dependants, produced a violent party-spirit in the town, sorely to the endamaging of its peace and respectability.

Such was the state of public feeling in Llandwarrys at the time I came to reside there. On my first introduction to the Red Lion, I was looked on as a sort of intruder by the club ; for, strange to tell, many of the old prejudices against the Irish still exist in the more sequestered nooks of Wales ; but gradually, by listening to the anecdotage of one, submitting to the law laid down by a second, laughing at the dull jokes of a third, and adopting the opinions of a fourth, I conciliated the good-will of all parties.

CHAPTER III.

HOW TO MAKE THE MOST OF ONE'S SITUATION.

I HAD now been nearly a month resident at Lland-warrys, and the pittance I had been able to preserve from the wreck of my fortune at Humbug—independently of that portion with which the philosophic Stubbs had eloped—was fast dwindling away. My domestics, whom, in the innocence of my heart, I had imagined void of guile, materially assisted the diminution of my funds. Two more assiduous conveyancers never yet carried on business in the metropolis. Nothing escaped their clutches.

But this was far from constituting my sole grievance. As autumn drew on, the cottage, which, under the in-fluence of sunshine and dry weather, I had fancied so attractive, became not only damp, but positively un-tenable. The walls and ceilings began to thaw, like Falstaff in the dog-days; while that domestic insect which Sir J. Banks once endeavoured to boil into a lobster took possession of every nook and cranny in my bedchamber. To wind up the sum of my household an-noyances, a flood one night came down from the moun-tains, burst open my pantry-door, and committed a bur-glary on all that my servants had left untouched.

When I rose the next morning, the valley was one broad sheet of water. The Towy roared and chafed like an angry sea; and I just reached my ground-floor in time to see two boiled fowls swim off in hasty pursuit of a cold turkey; and a fillet of veal "clear out" from the lower pantry-shelf, for a voyage down the Towy to Llandilo.

I should observe, in addition to these vexations, that my pursuits answered the purpose neither of amusement nor utility. My horticultural experiments just sufficed to convince me that a man must have an innate genius for superintending the education of fruits and vegetables; my reading, which was chiefly restricted to the bulky

tomes of Emmanuel Swedenborg, served only to bewilder
or set me asleep; and when, with rod in hand, I took a
saunter along the banks of the Towy, I was constantly
hooking the calf of my leg, jerking my hat into the water,
or pulling up a huge weed in mistake for a salmon. The
fish, I have often thought since, must have entertained a
very mean opinion of my abilities.

On specifying these grievances to the apothecary, he
consoled me by the assurance that they were mere matters of course, to which a few months' endurance would
not fail to reconcile me. But this consideration, though
well enough so far as it went, had not quite the effect
that he anticipated. Like the widow in Voltaire, for
whose benefit the sage Memnon drew up a consolatory
catalogue of all the wives who had lost husbands before
her, I refused to be comforted; and by way of effectual
safeguard, as well from peculating domestics, damp walls,
solitude, and, worse than all, consumptive finances, I proposed to the apothecary for the future to take up my
abode with him.

For the better enforcement of this abrupt proposition,
I pointed out tho various services I might be the means
of rendering him in his vocation. I stated that medicine
had been my favourite study ever since the period when I
first commenced it, under the auspices of a celebrated
physician in the county Galway; that I was conversant,
in all their forms and varieties, with the infirmities of
poor, weak, shivering humanity—though I did not for a
moment presume to compete with him in medical ability;
and that, such being the case, I considered it almost a
matter of course that a mutual connexion would turn out
profitable to both of us. I concluded with the payment
of my quarter's rent.

How eloquent is egotism! Where is the man who does
not kindle into enthusiasm when Self is the hero of his
story? The apothecary partook in some degree of my
emotion. In common with the rest of the world—that is
to say, of that illustrious and influential portion of it

which constituted the club at the Red Lion—he held my talents in exceeding respect ; and was prepared to augur well of my success in business, from having so recently witnessed the skill with which I had converted into friends and admirers those who had at first received me as an alien and an intruder.

Still he had his doubts of the propriety of my partnership project. I was young—I was a stranger—I was inexperienced. Granted ; but I was industrious, persevering ; at home in the theory, if not quite so much so in the practice, of medicine ; and was, besides, in possession of a recipe (imparted to me by the famous Dr. Killquick, of Galway) which had effected the most miraculous cures.

I saw that the apothecary was staggered by my reasoning, so followed up blow after blow with all the zeal I could muster, for I felt that everything depended on perseverance ; and, after a week of doubts and demurrings on his part, I had the satisfaction of finding my efforts crowned with success. Drop by drop, water will in time wear out the toughest rock.

CHAPTER IV.

A SECOND MATRIMONIAL CATASTROPHE—THE PROGRESS OF QUACKERY—A FIT OF THE HORRORS.

About this time another and more momentous change took place in my domestic condition. I allude to my marriage with the apothecary's widowed sister—a catastrophe which took place after a month's acquaintance with the lady, on an erroneous supposition that she was worth money.

And here it may be possibly urged that I was guilty of a grievous backsliding, inasmuch as my first wife was most probably still alive. I plead guilty to the charge ; but may state, in extenuation, that such was the havoc which repeated disappointments had wrought on my me-

mory, that not till the nuptial ceremony was concluded
did it occur to me that I had committed bigamy. When,
however, the dreadful conviction flashed on my mind, the
shock it occasioned was inconceivable !

I should be trifling with the credulity of my readers,
and militating against the sacred interests of truth—
which, with me, are paramount to every other consideration—were I to assert that my second wife realised all
that a romantic fancy could conjure up of loveliness and
sensibility. She was neither a Helen nor a Juliet; and
for these reasons, which I take to be conclusive on the
point :—In the first place, she was ancient, irascible, and
jealous ; secondly, she was as unimaginative as a steam-
engine ; thirdly, she had a long lean neck, like a vinegar-
cruet ; and lastly, she was remarkable for her thriftiness ;
and, when displeased with what she called my extravagance, was fond of instituting comparisons between me
and her first husband, which made me, notwithstanding
my general forbearance, more than once express a wish
that he and I could change places.

It was some weeks, however, before my wife's peculiarities fully developed themselves. For the first fortnight or so, she was all smiles and civility ; for her brother's business, from the time I took a share in it, and
began to bestir myself, exhibited such a satisfactory increase as to enable us to indulge in the luxury of an
assistant, and even give occasional dinners to our friends
at the Red Lion.

It was just about the close of the honeymoon that, after
trying a variety of Dr. Killquick's recipes with but indifferent success, I hit upon one of which, from having once
tasted it, I retained a very vivid recollection. I had observed that the lower classes of the Welsh, like the Irish,
were inordinately fond of stimulants, so persuaded myself
that I had but to hit this prevalent fancy to bring myself
into repute among them.

The recipe in question possessed all the requisite ingre-
dients for notoriety ; so much so, that when I explained

its character to Mr. Davis, that unsophisticated apothecary opened his mouth wider than ever at the idea of such an experiment being tried on Christian bowels.

"Why, you must be joking, surely!" said he; "the dose you speak of would kill a crocodile!"

"Nonsense; Dr. Killquick tried it with wonderful success in Ireland."

"Likely enough; but Wales is not Ireland; so, for Heaven's sake, think better of it."

But I was deaf to all his expostulations. I was convinced, I replied, that the experiment would succeed; and justified myself for making trial of it, by the parallel case of the celebrated town-quack Dr. Fingerfee.

O Quackery! to him who is inspired by thy spirit the road to notoriety lies equally open, whether in a crowded city or a secluded Welsh district. While Genius trudges afoot, and by many a thorny, circuitous route ascends the hill of fame, thou bowlest along in thy chariot, and attainest the same sunny eminence with scarce an effort. Genius is the simpleton who made his pilgrimage with raw peas in his shoes; Quackery, the knave who had the sagacity first to boil them.

The "Infallible Resuscitating Elixir," as I styled my new specific, was a medicine composed, in nearly equal quantities, of bark, brickdust, gin, and gunpowder, boiled over a slow fire, and flavoured with Scotch snuff! Its success at first was equivocal; but, when its virtues had been duly insisted on in all the public journals, it brought a world of patients of the lower orders to my shop; and I had the tact to confine it exclusively to them (well knowing that your civilised stomach is apt to be fastidious), just as if it were the balsam of Fairy Blas, whose singular property it was to kill one-half of the community while it cured the other.

The neighbouring small farmers and their serving-men were among the first to honour my elixir with their patronage. The bark was so bracing, the brickdust so cleansing, the gunpowder so stimulating, the gin so pa-

latablo, that, no matter what the disorder might be, one
ingredient or the other was sure to suit. If the bark
failed, there was still a chance for the brickdust; while
the gin, acting in spirited accordance with the gunpowder, produced an internal commotion, which, in cases
where the gastric juice was languid, wonderfully facili-
tated digestion.

To be sure, it was my lot now and then to lose a
patient; and once, I recollect, a low, obnoxious, pettifogging attorney died under the potent stimulus; but,
singularly enough, his death, so far from proving injurious, actually did me service. I was looked on as a vil·
lage Brutus who had destroyed a village Cæsar; and
though I declined the flattering distinction, yet my neighbours still persisted in giving me the credit of the deed.
Nay, so grateful were they to me for having rid them of
an arrant rogue, that a few of those who had most suffered by him actually talked of purchasing me a piece of
plate, in commemoration of the patriotic action! But my
modesty would not hear of such a proposition.

One of my most tractable patients was a tippling little
exciseman, with a polypetalous proboscis, whose countenance, whenever he stooped to tie his shoe-strings, blushed
deeper than a mulberry. This annoyed him exceedingly,
for he fancied himself an Adonis; so applied to me for
relief, and I at once prescribed the elixir, together with
periodical blood-lettings. But, unfortunately, his disease
was beyond the power of medicine; for, notwithstanding
he took a hearty draught every day, and always, as he
said, felt the better for it, though "a little sickish at
first," he grew gradually worse. The gunpowder, I rather
suspect, disagreed with him; for he went off one night
like a shot, after having taken it twice during the night
in currant-jelly.

I did not quit this worthy man's bedside until the last
thread of life was fairly spun out, when, with a doleful
heart and moralising frame of mind, I made the best of
my way home.

It was a dark, moonless night, and my road lay across the common, and close beside the yews in the churchyard. I know not why it was, but when I neared the old wall that bound in the last resting-places of the dead—when I heard the wind moan and sigh through the trees, that, slowly waving their gaunt arms to and fro, looked like fiends holding watch and ward above the charnel-house—my pace instinctively quickened, my heart beat quick and loud, and a nervous, undefined apprehension of something horrible flitted darkly across my mind. Involuntarily I thought of my patients, one or two of whose graves lay close underneath the wall which I had yet to pass. "If they could rise," said I, endeavouring, but in vain, to banish the awful supposition, "from the earth wherein they lie full six feet deep—if they could rear up their shadowy forms across my path, what, in the name of Heaven, should I do or say? How convince such sceptics that their exit from life was the work of fate, not of mortal agency? Disembodied spirits, I have heard, are— Hah! whose are those eyes glaring full on me from between the chinks of yon tombstone? Methinks I should know that threatening countenance! Hark! is that a voice? Fool, 'tis but the wind!" and I rushed homewards with the speed of an antelope. Singular what a repugnance medical men have to pass a churchyard after dark!

I found my wife up and waiting to let me in, with her brow clouded, her eye full of tempest, and her temper in a high state of acetous fermentation.

"So, sir, this is a pretty time for a married man to be abroad! I dare say you will tell me you've been attending one of your patients. But I know better; there's my brother has been in bed these two hours."

Without vouchsafing any answer, I strode past my wife into the parlour, where I found the fire just out—one or two of the large cinders having been carefully put aside on the hob—and the rushlight glimmering in its socket. At a small deal-table, on which was placed an old towel by way of cloth, stood my scanty supper of bread and cheese, with a few leeks in a cracked plate, and a small jug of still smaller beer, which on emergency might safely do duty as vinegar.

I glanced at the sorry repast with an expression of countenance, I fear, in which resignation was less apparent than disgust. My wife understood the hint, and exclaimed peevishly, "You need not turn up your nose so, Mr. Fitzmaurice"—such was the *alias* I had assumed on entering South Wales; "the supper is quite as good as you have a right to expect at this hour. But it's no use talking—"

"None in the least."

"For the more one does the less thanks one gets. Good nature is always sure to be imposed upon. Ah! times are sadly altered since poor dear Mr. Evans—"

"Hang Mr. Evans!"

My wife took no notice of this smart repartee, but continued, "I'll tell you what it is, Mr. Fitzmaurice, I've just been looking over our last month's bills, and have come to the resolution of keeping no more dinner— What do you sit there for, kicking the legs of the table, just as if they cost nothing?"

"Pray, go to bed, my dear; this is no time for discussing such matters."

"Aye, that's always the way you put me off; nothing I say or do is done at the proper time."

"Well, well, we'll talk of these things to-morrow. At present, I have some medicine to make up; so light two fresh candles and leave me."

"Two fresh candles, Mr. Fitzmaurice! where am I to get them at this late hour?"

"What, are there none in the house?"

"None, but a rushlight."

"That must do instead, then; so fetch it quickly, and go to bed. I'm sure your delicate constitution must suffer by sitting up so late."

Sullenly, and with many an ominous shake of the head

my wife drew forth a rushlight from the cupboard, and, having lit and placed it on the table, admonished me to be sure to put it out when I had done with it, and quitted the room.

Left to my own reflections, I sat wistfully down—for, to eat, and, above all, to digest my supper was wholly out of the question—and busied myself in contrasting my present with my past situation. I called to mind the ambitious dreams that beset me on my first commencing my theatrical career : on the hopes which buoyed me up on my road to London ; and more especially on my connexion with the Snodgrasses, which I had once thought would fairly set me on the high-road to fortune. All these had now passed away, and here I was, the child of mystery and misfortune—an *alias* and *alien*, rooted in an obscure, semi-barbarous Welsh village; unable, from the peculiar delicacy of my position, to venture openly forth again into the world ; and raised from utter penury only by my marriage with a skinflint, and my chance profits as an apothecary in the healthiest situation in all Wales.

The solemn silence of the hour—the spectral gloom of the apartment, lit only by a miserable rushlight, which threw its flickering "darkness visible" on walls naked as unfigleafed Adam, and old-fashioned mahogany chairs with elbows as high as the cheek-bones of a Scotchman—the excitement produced by the sudden death of the excise-man—the thrilling recollection of the churchyard which I had so lately passed ; all these various associations deepened my despondency, till, fairly worn out with exhaustion, my head dropped on my chest, my arms fell lifeless and flaccid by my sight, and I sunk fast asleep in my arm-chair.

But, alas! even slumber itself failed to bring relief. The grimmest, most fantastic, and most ridiculous visions passed and repassed before my mind's eye. I dreamed that I was seated in my shop, gazing upwards at the shelf where stood, ranged in due order, a row of elixir-bottles, when—whizz! out flew the corks, and out too from each bottle popped the head of a defunct patient! I was astonished at their numbers; but surprise was soon lost in horror, for, just as I was attempting an escape, the goblins leaped with a bound on the floor, pulled me back by the coat-skirts, caught hold of me, this one by the legs, and that by the arms, and chucked me head-foremost into the mortar. I implored pity, but in vain — the phantoms were inexorable; on which, making a desperate effort, I just contrived to lift my head above the vessel, when suddenly the ghost of the exciseman—I knew him by his nose!—starting up from the inside of a pill-box, forced open my reluctant jaws; drenched me with my own elixir; and then, with a refinement of cruelty worthy of Procrustes, caught up a pestle, and kept pounding and pounding away at my ribs, till in the agony of my struggles I awoke—to find the rushlight just expiring, and my wife stooping down beside me to pick up the nightcap which I had dislodged from her head.

"Gracious heavens! Mr. Fitzmaurice, are you mad? or are you going to murder me by way of gratitude for my affection? Why, it is now near daybreak, and the rushlight burnt out too! Fitz! Fitz! your extravagance is past all bearing!"

Too much depressed to reply, I rose from my seat, my limbs stiff with cold, my nerves shaken with agitation, and hurried upstairs to bed.

CHAPTER V.

A SKETCH OF AN ANGLO-INDIAN.

As I was seated one morning with my wife and her brother at a late breakfast, a lad on horseback came with a message from a gentleman named Rupee, requesting that either Mr. Davis or Mr. Fitzmaurice would instantly hasten over to him, for that he had just had a relapse of an old complaint, and scarcely expected to survive the day.

"Rupee—Rupee ?" said I musingly ; "don't know the name. Do you ?" turning to Mr. Davis.

"Oh, yes," replied my brother-in-law ; "it's the old bachelor who lives up at the Lodge, about three miles hence. He is a shy, whimsical sort of fellow, and with the exception of Captain Caustic, whom he picked up somewhere in India, is scarce known to a soul in the village. I called on him once or twice, at his express desire, but could make nothing of him. Possibly you may be more successful ;" and so saying, Mr. Davis quitted the breakfast-table, and desired the messenger to say that Mr. Fitzmaurice would follow him within the hour.

On reaching Tippoo Lodge, I found the "nabob," as he was called, though the day was far from inclement, seated in an arm-chair by a blazing fire, with a red worsted night-cap on his head, and a flannel dressing-gown wrapped tight round him. Close beside him stood a Pembroke-table, on which lay a dog's-eared copy of Hervey's " Medi-tations among the Tombs," and the last number of the *Asiatic Journal*, with a paper-cutter fixed in the obituary ; and on the hearth-rug, at his feet, an ugly, spiteful, wiry little terrier, called " Venus," into whose good graces, at the hazard of my fingers, I tried in vain to ingratiate myself.

Mr. Rupee was a thin, adust, spindle-shanked duodecimo of a man, under-jawed like a shark, with a low, querulous voice, a fishy eye, and a hatchet-face, on which lingered one or two dry streaks of red, like the bloom on a stale apple. Yet, notwithstanding this apparent fragility of constitution, the old fellow was as tough as whipcord. People who dry up as they grow old often set death at defiance for years.

On my inquiring how he felt himself, the nabob heaved a deep sigh, and said, " Very ill, sir, very ill. I can just say I'm alive, and that's all. When I sent for Dr. Thick-scull last week from Caermarthen, he told me he feared my lungs were affected."

11

" Why—I—must—confess—I *do* see—symptoms of—"

" Bless me, you don't say so!   I hope there's nothing *very* alarming."

" Ahem !"

" Ah, just what I feared ; but is there no hope ?"

" Permit me to feel your pulse, sir."

Tremblingly Mr. Rupee held forth his wrist, while I counted the pulsations with Mr. Davis' stop watch ; and then shaking my head gravely, said, " A little feverish, sir. The—the system—"

" Is breaking up—so Thickskull feared."

" Not *quite* so bad as that ; but these east winds are evidently too searching for a delicate constitution like yours."

" My dear sir, you've just hit it.   Ah, what a blessing is health !   Within the last twelvemonth I'm sure I must have drunk out an apothecary's shop ; yet—would you believe it ?—I feel no better than when I began.   It's astonishing how I bear up against such a complication of maladies ?   Have you taken tiffin yet, Mr. Fitzmaurice ?"

" Tiffin, sir ?"

" Oh, I forgot you were never in India ; lunch, I should say.   I always try to pick a bit about this time of day."

So saying, he rung the bell, and immediately his butler, who seemed thoroughly to understand his master's humours, answered the summons by placing on the table a tray containing some anchovy sandwiches, and a bottle of East India madeira.

When the man was gone, Mr. Rupee set to work with his tiffin, at which he displayed far from contemptible prowess ; observing between whiles what a treasure he had secured in Roger, who, having accompanied him home from India, and being, like himself, a martyr to ill-health, was a sort of privileged domestic.   " He is a kind, considerate creature," added the nabob ; " always so careful to prevent my sitting in a thorough draught.   And so full of feeling, too !   I never heard him bang the door to yet.   I'm sure I don't know what I should do without him."

"That madeira is a fine restorative, sir; it has given you quite a colour already."

"Ah, my dear Mr. Fitzmaurice, that colour you speak of is no symptom of health. It's hectic, mere hectic. But that's always the case with me. People are perpetually complimenting me on my good looks—I remember it was the same thing at Cheltenham—at the very moment, perhaps, when I'm within an ace of death. But I must confess I *do* feel a little better, though I'm too apt to be sanguine."

I forget what reply I made, but it was something that mightily pleased the nabob. Indeed, I very soon found out the way to ingratiate myself with him, which was by listening attentively to the prolix catalogue of his maladies. Men who live in solitude are necessarily arrant egotists. Mr. Rupee was the greatest I ever met with; but then in proportion to his egotism was his esteem for those who could put up with it.

I stayed with the old proser about half-an-hour, chiefly busied in giving him directions (as agreed on with Mr. Davis) for the future management of his constitution; which done, I took my leave, when, just as I was closing the door, he called me back, and said, "I may depend, then, on seeing you to-morrow, Mr. Fitzmaurice—that is, if I happen to survive the night? Perhaps, also, you will stop and dine with me. Caustic will be here. He's an old Indian chum of mine—a little bit of a croaker; but we have all of us our weak side."

I replied in the affirmative; on which he half-rose to wish me good morning, at the same time requesting me to shut all the doors after me.

Next day, at the appointed hour, I made my appearance at the Lodge, where I found the captain already arrived, lounging up and down the gravel-walk with the nabob. It was curious to mark the contrast of character that these two originals presented. Though both were hypochondriacal, yet both showed it in a different way. The nabob's grievances were of a plaintive, subdued cast; the captain's took an irascible, domineering turn. The

one was discontented from fancied ill-health ; the other
from straitened finances — which confined him, sorely
against his inclination, to the inglorious solitude of a Welsh
village.

"A fine day, gentlemen," said I, advancing towards
them.

"Humph!" replied Caustic ; "well enough for Wales."

"You must find this snatch of sunshine very agreeable,
Mr. Rupee."

"Sunshine!" retorted the captain, pointing towards the
western mountains, above which the orb was stooping ;
"do you call that thing a sun? Why, sir, it has not
strength enough to blister a gooseberry-bush. God, how
cold it is!" and he made off with all speed into the dining-
room, just as Roger came up to summon us to table.

I forbear to describe the particulars of the dinner.
Suffice it to say, that, notwithstanding my remonstrances,
Mr. Rupee insisted on fixing me with my back to the
fire ; and, what was still worse, directed my particular
attention to a dish of curry ; and when, rather too cavalierly perhaps, I declared my indifference to it, "What,
no curry!" said he, in a tone of astonishment. "No
curry!" chorused the captain ; and instantly I fancied I
saw a look of contemptuous commiseration exchanged
between them.

When the dinner was at an end, the nabob began to
catechise me on the subject of the vale of Towy, whose
salubrity, he said, had been warmly insisted on by both
his medical men ; on which Caustic observed—

"Employ two medical men! I wonder you're alive to
tell the tale! But you will not persuade me that you
settled here solely for your health's sake."

"Not altogether. My chief inducement was the circumstance of my having been born in the valley. Ah,
Mr. Fitzmaurice! when, five-and-forty years ago, I scaled
the summit of those hills behind us, I little thought the
time would ever arrive when I should be compelled to
creep like a snail about their base. I never feared an

east wind then. But the climate's nothing like what it used to be. The very people are changed—and for the worse, too ; so that, notwithstanding my inclinations, I'm afraid I must hurry back to Cheltenham."

"Cheltenham !" said I, not a little alarmed at the idea of losing such a promising patient, otherwise than in a professional fashion ; "my dear, dear sir, you must be mad to dream of such a thing."

"Why so ?"

"Why, sir," I replied, a bright idea suggesting itself on the spur of the moment, "a medical friend of mine writes me word that the influenza is raging there to a most alarming extent, and proves particularly fatal to those whose constitutions have been debilitated by a residence in the East. Out of ten Indian patients, he assures me, he has had the misfortune to lose not less than seven."

"Bless me, how fortunate that I have been told of this in time ! The influenza ! Of all disorders, the one of which I have the greatest horror. I remember—"

"Pass the bottle, Rupee," said the captain impatiently ; "this wine is of the right sort. Do you recollect Major Tipple ? The last time I tasted madeira like this was at his quarters at Calcutta, the night he played Romeo so admirably at our private theatricals."

"Ah, poor Tipple ! I recollect him well. He was a good-natured fellow ; no one's enemy but his own."

"Yes ; and what a devil among the women ! But I say, Rupee, if I mistake not, you've indulged a little in that line yourself. But you were always a sly dog, close as wax, no getting anything out of you."

"He ! he !" faintly simpered the nabob ; "you are so facetious, captain ; such a wag. He ! he ! he ! But I have done with all those follies now."

I have generally remarked that men who have spent the best part of their lives in the East have but three leading topics of conversation—wine, women, and the jungle-fever. Now these, together with a few supplemental ones, such as tiger-hunts, private theatricals, &c.,

having been fully discussed, I imagined that I might possibly slide in a word—for hitherto I had been little better
than a listener ; so I inquired of Mr. Rupee whether he
had read the *Observer* of the preceding week, containing
full particulars of his Majesty's landing and reception in
Ireland, and the presentation of Mr. O'Cromwell at
court.

" The devil's in it," thought I, " if the illustrious Agi-
tator can remind either the one or the other of any old
Indian crony, for he is a phenomenon restricted to the
Emerald Isle." But I reckoned without my host. The
name O'Cromwell reminded Captain Caustic of an Ensign
O'Cromwell, who was shot in a duel on the ramparts at
Sincapore ; and this again brought on an inquiry from
Mr. Rupee, as to whether that was the same O'Cromwell
who had distinguished himself so highly at Seringapatam.

From the moment that the ominous word "Seringapatam" escaped the nabob, I foresaw that Caustic, like my
Uncle Toby at Dendermond, would indulge me with the
full particulars of the siege ; so, in order to extricate myself from the infliction, I said—such assurance will desperation lend even the most modest of men !—" I am going
to make a very bold request, Mr. Rupee, but will you
favour us with that charming Welsh air, ' Ayr-hyd-yr-
nos ?' If I mistake not, it is admirably adapted to your
style of voice."

The captain laughed outright at this proposition.
" What, Rupee sing !" said he ; " why, you might as well
ask an old crow to chant ! Only look at him. Has he
got a singing face ?"

" Caustic is so odd," observed the nabob, gently deprecating his sarcasm ; " but he speaks the truth. I never
did sing in all my life. How should I ? Where am I to
find the wind, when, as Thickscull says, my lungs are
affected ?"

Mr. Rupee was proceeding to enlarge on this favourite
theme, and I was giving him purposely my undivided
attention, when Caustic, who by this time perceived my

drift, and seemed to take a malicious pleasure in thwarting me, turned back the conversation into the old channel, by saying, "You mentioned Seringapatam just now, Fitzmaurice. It was there that I smelt gunpowder for the first time."

"And a villanous smell it is; I am surprised you can like to talk of it."

"I remember the year of the siege," said the nabob, "as well as if it were yesterday. I was at Hyderabad at the time, laid up with my first attack of—"

"Pooh, pooh!" interrupted the captain, "what was your attack compared to mine?" then smiling grimly at this bright pun, he commenced his details of the siege as follows:—

"Do you see this plate of **biscuits**, Fitzmaurice?"

"I see the plate, but we've despatched the biscuits."

"No matter; imagine that this plate forms the main body of the fortress of Seringapatam, and that these nut-crackers" (placing a pair on each side the plate) "are the two wings, or bastions to the north and south. You comprehend so much, I presume?"

"Nothing can be clearer," was my reply; on which the captain, dipping the edges of a doyley in a finger-glass, and describing a circle which took in both plate and nut-crackers, proceeded to say, "You must next suppose, sir, that this is the outermost line of ramparts, in which the British columns, headed by Colonels Sherbroke and St. John, have just effected a breach. Now then—"

At this instant the door opened, and, to my inexpressible relief, old Roger thrust his head into the room with the tidings that a special messenger had just arrived from Talleen from Mr. Evans, who was anxious to see Mr. Fitzmaurice as early as he could make it convenient.

"Why, you're not going to leave us?" inquired Caustic.

"I'm sorry to be compelled to quit you just at the moment when I was beginning to get so interested in your story; but business must be minded, you know."

"Pooh, pooh! where's the hurry? Evans won't die

just yet ; and if he does, no great odds   It's only one
attorney the less."

But I persisted in my intentions, on which Mr. Rupee,
making a faint effort to rise from his seat, said, " Excuse
my accompanying you to the door, Mr. Fitzmaurice, but
it's not safe to venture into the air on a night like this.
But won't you take some nice warm barley-water before
you go ? My cook makes excellent barley-water. Just
allow me now to order a basin for you, with a small tea-
spoonful of brandy in it."

With many thanks I declined the horrid proposition,
and made a precipitate retreat home, where I found Mr.
Davis cozily seated in the parlour, over a jug of cwr.

"Well, Fitz, what news ?" said he ; " how have you
managed matters with the old croaker ?   Failed, of
course."

When I told him that, so far from failing, I had succeeded in inspiring Mr. Rupee with a full and lively faith
in my medical abilities, he uplifted his hands and eyes in
astonishment. " Well, this is really miraculous ! To convince a man so hard of belief as the nabob, that you
actually understand his case ! Astonishing ! I could not
do so.   How did you go about it ?   What did you say ?"
Then, with a low, chuckling laugh, like the quack of a
young duck, " Upon my word, Fitz, you are, without exception, the most impudent dog I ever set eyes on ! I
thought I was not deficient myself ; but I see I am a
child compared to you."

I did not contest the point ; for I felt that to attempt
to imbue a man like Mr. Davis with right notions of
character was as absurd as to carry coals to Newcastle ;
so I left him to his ale, and retired to bed.

CHAPTER VI.

A ROYAL PROGRESS ; OR MUCH ADO ABOUT NOTHING.

IT was now August, a month destined to be ever memorable in the annals of Llandwarrys, when the broad light of royalty shone full on the bewildered vale of Towy. His Majesty George the Fourth having, on his return from Ireland, encountered some refractory weather in the Channel, was compelled, contrary to his original intention, to land at Milford Haven, and so return home by way of South Wales.

This intelligence created an extraordinary—I might even say an unparalleled—sensation throughout the valley, scarcely an inhabitant of which had ever seen a king except on a sign-post ; and more especially did it keep our gossiping little town on the *qui vive*, as Dwarrys Castle, where his Majesty made his first halt, was but a few miles distant.

It being, therefore, taken for granted by our club that the king would not omit the opportunity, on his progress through the town, of halting to receive the congratulations of his faithful subjects, and peradventure—such was the absurd extravagance of the hour !—of taking a hasty collation with them at the Red Lion, a special meeting was summoned, at which it was resolved that arrangements should be made for escorting his Majesty through the town ; that a repast, under the surveillance of the parson, who was "Sir Oracle" on all culinary matters, should be prepared in the very best room of the Red Lion ; and that a loyal address should be drawn up, to be read by the auctioneer, who knew better than any one else in the district how such forms were managed in London.

These resolutions, however, were not carried without a strenuous opposition from Captain Caustic, who, being more a man of the world than all the rest put together, kept "pooh, poohing" away at every fresh suggestion ; till,

finding himself left in a minority, he damned the committee for "a pack of fools," and washed his hands of the
concern.

The landlord, landlady, and indeed all the household of
the Red Lion were in ecstasies at the anticipation of the
honour assigned to them. To receive a king—a real king
—beneath their humble roof! Was ever roof so honoured!
In the frenzy of their loyalty, these simple-minded publicans sent for an artist, who usually officiated as house-
painter in the neighbourhood, and commissioned him to
prepare forthwith a "Royal George," in lieu of the old-
established sign — a task which, considering the time
allowed, was executed with surprising ability.

When this *chef-d'œuvre* was hoisted, all Llandwarrys
rang with acclamations, sorely to the annoyance of the
landlady of the Castle, who kept watching the progress of
the workmen behind the blinds of her parlour-windows,
observing between whiles, " It was a shame and a scandal
on folks of station and respectability that a paltry Welsh
innkeeper should have the honour of receiving his Majesty;
when she, who had lived for upwards of six years at the
first hotel in Bath, was thrust aside like an old gown,
just as if she were nobody. But, thank God! she had no
silly pride or envy about her—not she! She could make
both ends meet at the end of the year, which was more
than some folks could, much as they might think of
themselves."

In the course of the evening, motives of curiosity led
me into the Red Lion, where I found its mistress, who
up to this time had been all sunshine, in pretty nearly as
irritable a mood as her rival. Her husband, who had
been despatched in the forepart of the day on some important mission to Llandilo market, had stopped to drink
his Majesty's health at so many public-houses that he had
wholly lost sight of the object of his journey, and had but
just returned home, as drunk as any loyal Briton could
reasonably desire to be.

On entering the parlour, I found this poor sinner of a

publican pinned up in a corner, the very picture of helpless resignation, while his enraged wife stood before him
with her doubled fists thrust close into his face, by way
of giving point to her philippic. "Oh, you good-for-
nothing brute! is this the return you make for all my
kindness to you? What do you think his Majesty would
say, if he were to see you in such a pickle? A precious
example you're setting to all the servants! There's David,
who's been gone ever since two o'clock to Llandovery;
I'll lay my life, he'll come back just as drunk as yourself.
And who's to blame if he does? Now, don't attempt to
answer me"—for the good man was beginning to expostulate—"or I'll knock that fool's head off your shoulders."

In this energetic style, despite all my efforts to restore
harmony, the angry dame ran on for the best part of half-
an-hour, till the opportune return of David, unexpectedly
sober, and bending under the weight of a well-laden fish-
basket—the dropping-in of a more than ordinary number
of guests—and, above all, the promise of her contrite
spouse to go to bed and "sin no more," restored her to
good-humour.

Early on the following day, crowds of farmers, &c., all
bedizened in their holiday-suits, came pouring into the
town, on their road to the spot where the procession was
appointed to meet his Majesty. Smiles beamed on every
face—expectation lit up every eye; and the day being
clear, dry, and sunny—that is to say, the showers collected
by the neighbouring mountains not pouring down *oftener*
than twice or thrice an hour—the whole scene was one of
the most animated it is possible to conceive.

Even my wife partook of the general cheerfulness.
"Well, Fitz," said she, in the blandest of tones, as she
entered the parlour after breakfast, fully equipped for
walking, "are you ready?"

"Yes; but where's Mr. Davis?"

"Oh, he's gone to the Red Lion to assist the parson in
preparing the collation."

"Collation, indeed!" said I, bursting into a laugh, for

the whole business struck me in the same ridiculous light as Captain Caustic. "However, come along, Mrs. Fitzmaurice ; there's no time to be lost, since you're bent on seeing the sight ;" and, drawing her arm through mine, we set out for the place of rendezvous, which was a broad open patch of common jutting on the Llandilo road, and about two miles distant from Llandwarrys.

During the first part of the walk our chit-chat was remarkable for its social tone ; but unluckily, when about half-way, we were met by a ragged Irish beggar-woman, young and somewhat pretty, with an infant in her arms, who stopped to implore charity for herself and child.

The sight of this poor forlorn creature presented such a contrast to the cheerful scene about me that instinctively I thrust my hand into my pockets, which my wife perceiving, looked at the petitioner with supreme contempt, and was hurrying me on, when I threw her a half-crown, accompanying the donation with a smile. This so incensed the astringent virtue of my wife that in an instant she became herself again, and, tossing her head back, said, "Well, I'm sure, Mr. Fitzmaurice, this is pretty conduct to observe in my presence !"

"Conduct, my dear ! I don't understand you."

"Don't dear me, Mr. Fitzmaurice ; I want none of your dears, sir. What business have you to be giggling at every trolloping hussy you meet on the road ? I would not have believed such a thing possible, if I had not seen it with my own eyes."

"I was merely giving the poor woman a trifle from charity."

"Charity ! Don't think to persuade me you would throw away half-a-crown for charity. In these times men do not give half-crowns to young women for nothing. Half-a-crown would have bought me a new set of ribbons for my bonnet. But it's no use talking ; I vow and protest I'm quite sick of it."

"And so am I."

In a few minutes my wife's spleen picked up fresn fuel

for conflagration. "Good heavens, Mr. Fitzmaurice, how fast you walk! Pray do move a little slower; I am tired to death already. There—there you are off again! Well, I declare I never—"

"Does this suit you?" I replied, altering my pace to a deliberate lounge.

"How uncommon aggravating you are, Mr. Fitzmaurice! Pray when do you think we shall get to our journey's end, if we keep on this snail's pace? I declare that Irish trollop has quite turned your head."

"Just turn yours, my dear, and you will find a black cloud behind us that—"

Before I could complete the sentence, one of those showers which are so apt to surprise the pedestrian in mountainous districts compelled us to run a few yards back to some umbrageous hedge-row elms which overhung the road. Here, while adjusting her bonnet, and nestling close up under the trees on tiptoe, my wife, in order to make the most of her time, again burst out with, "I told you we should want the umbrella, Mr. Fitzmaurice; but no, you would be so positive, and now you see the consequences. I shall catch my death of cold, I'm sure I shall. Aye, you may laugh as much as you please; but if I were you, I should have too much decency to make a jest of such things. But you haven't a spark of feeling;" and in this way she ran on, while I stood, with all the sullen fortitude of an Indian at the stake, beside her.

At length, the sky having cleared up, we were enabled to resume our walk, and soon reached the appointed spot, where we found almost the entire population of Llandwarrys drawn up on either side the Llandilo road. The captain, who had preceded us by but a few minutes, was the first to welcome our approach.

"Happy to see you, Mrs. Fitzmaurice; you look quite charmingly to-day."

"Ah! Captain Caustic," replied my wife, with a gracious simper, "you military gentlemen are so full of compliment, one never knows when you're speaking the truth."

"Except when we run down one lady in the presence of another. By the bye, Fitz, how did you leave Rupee? Croaking, I suppose, as usual. And Mr. Davis, too? How comes it that he is absent? But I suppose he thinks that one fool more or less is of no consequence, where there are so many of us."

My wife was just in the act of replying, when a loud shout of "The King! the King!" rose among the crowd; and presently two limbs of the law, followed by a squadron of Lord Dwarry's yeomanry, came galloping along the road, announcing the near approach of the royal *cortège*.

Just previous to this we had been standing apart from the throng; but on seeing these *avant couriers*, we rushed to take our places among the foremost group, in which, by dint of squeezing and elbowing, we succeeded; where we found the attorney, the auctioneer, and one or two others of the deputation drawn up in formal line.

"The awkward squad at drill!" whispered the captain to me; then turning to the auctioneer—"Well," said he, "what have you done with your address."

"The address is given up," replied the auctioneer sulkily.

"We're non-suited," added the attorney; "a messenger, whom we despatched for advice to Dwarrys Castle, informed us that his lordship considered the project too absurd to be thought of for an instant."

"As regards myself personally," rejoined the auctioneer, "it's a matter of perfect indifference whether the address be spoken or not. But as respects his Majesty, I must confess I do still think, notwithstanding Lord Dwarry's opinion, that he would have been pleased with it; especially as I had taken a hint or two from the celebrated one that was presented to him as Prince Regent, when he dined with the allied sovereigns at Guildhall, the same year that I was in London. However, it's given up, so there's an end of the matter."

"Hark!" exclaimed the captain abruptly, "is that the trampling of horses I hear? By Jove it is!" and, as he said so, the royal cavalcade came sweeping round an angle of the road, a few hundred yards beyond us. At this moment the utmost confusion reigned among the crowd, which kept heaving like the waters of an agitated sea; when the auctioneer with a stentorian voice cried out, "Hats off!" and presently the whole mighty mass stood uncovered, at the same time cheering and huzzaing till they made the welkin ring again.

His Majesty, beside whom sat a fat peer with a leek at his button-hole, was by this time right opposite us; and as he cast a glance at our group, in the centre of which stood the captain, upright as a ramrod, with the back of his hand to his hat, he turned with a smile to the nobleman at his elbow. The smile, I suspect, was called forth by Mrs. Fitzmaurice, who had dropped so profound a courtesy that it actually brought her head to within three feet of the ground!

No sooner had the cavalcade swept past us than away rushed the crowd after it, in the full conviction that it would make a halt at the Red Lion. But, alas! they were doomed to disappointment; for, on reaching that ambitious *auberge,* his Majesty evinced not the slightest desire to partake of the good cheer provided by the Llandwarrys' club. This so astounded the curate, who had been all the morning absorbed in culinary preparations, and who now stood at the door ready to receive his Majesty, that, in the impulse of the moment, heedless of all etiquette, he rushed after the royal carriage, with, "May it please your Majesty, the roast beef and"—all further expression of surprise and chagrin being cut short by the disappearance of the cavalcade, which shot up the main street like lightning.

The rest of the day passed off, as was to have been expected, amid general gloom and dejection. As a sample of the sort of feeling that pervaded the village, I subjoin a conversation that took place between two labouring-men, and which I chanced to overhear.

" Well, David, did you see the King?"

" Yes, sure."

" And what was he like ?"

" Like !" replied the other, with evident disappointment, " why, just like any other man. I saw nothing in him. Squire Gryffyths was dressed twice as fine."

But by far the most chapfallen individual in all Lland-warrys was the landlady of the Red Lion, whose malicious rival, for at least a fortnight after, made a point of daily sending to inquire at what hour his Majesty might be expected back at the Red Lion ; greatly to the delight of the attorney, who carefully fostered the quarrel, in the hope that, by good nursing, it might be made to fructify into a lusty lawsuit.

CHAPTER VII.

A RECIPE FOR THE BLUES.

NEITHER the club at the Red Lion nor its landlord and landlady were the only folks in the valley who had reason to remember his Majesty's visit with regret. To higher and more influential individuals it was the source of equal annoyance. A Mr. Gryffyths, of Gryffyths, a Welsh squire of ancient descent, who resided within a mile or so of the nabob, in his zeal to commemorate the great event, had exercised his hospitality on so extensive a scale, and set such a loyal example of conviviality, that before the week's end the rheumatic-gout had chained him fast down by both legs to his arm-chair.

In this predicament, the good squire bethought himself of his usual medical adviser, Mr. Davis ; but, as my brother happened to be from home when the summons for his immediate attendance at Gryffyths arrived, I caught at such a favourable opportunity of making myself known to the *élite* of the district, and volunteered to go in his stead.

As my road lay by Rupee Lodge, I called in just to pay

a passing visit to the nabob, whom I found airing a damp newspaper by a fire that might have roasted an ox.

As usual, he was in great affliction. "I have been reading 'Buchan's Domestic Medicine,'" he began, "since I last saw you; and, strange to say, there is scarcely a single disorder mentioned in it that I have not got some symptoms of. Very hard, but nothing seems to do me good. Thickskull was here yesterday, and advised me to try the blue-pill. He begins now to think that the seat of my complaint is the liver, and that the affection at the chest is merely a secondary symptom. Well, well, be this as it may, I can assure you, Mr. Fitzmaurice, I've long since shaken hands with the world, and shall be far from sorry to bid it good-night. I made the very same remark to Caustic, when he was pestering me about making a will. It's very odd, how persevering that man is! Because I once accidentally let drop some intention of the sort, he has never let me have a moment's peace since. I wonder he can like to talk on such a subject; but he is a sad croaker—and such an egotist!"

The old hypochondriac was running on in this dismal fashion, when his attention, most opportunely for me, was called off by the yelping of his dog Venus, the only creature on earth in which he ever seemed to take the slightest interest. On hastening to the door to see who or what it was that was thus wounding the sensibilities of his pet, he discovered that the offender was no less a personage than Roger—his "treasure" Roger! who, having forced the cur up into a corner in the passage, was belabouring it with a bamboo-cane, and cursing it between whiles with an energy that might have created a sensation at Portsmouth Point.

The nabob seemed quite thunderstruck at this unaccountable behaviour of his "treasure." "I am astonished, Roger," he said, "at your conduct! What do you mean by your cruelty to that harmless animal?"

"What do I mean?" replied the fellow, who chanced to be in one of those surly humours with which men with

12

only half a liver are apt to be visited ; "why, I mean to thrash her—that's what I mean. She's almost bit my thumb off, the b—h !" and forgetting, in the rage of the moment, his usual respect for his master, he aimed another blow at the animal, which, instead of reaching her, took an oblique direction, and alighted upon Mr. Rupee's shin-bone.

The unexpected impudence of this reply, and still more the assault by which it was accompanied, set the nabob trembling from head to foot.   I never saw him in such a state of excitement.   He turned white ; he turned red ; he turned yellow ; he absolutely foamed with rage ; and at length, with incredible difficulty, while he kept standing on one leg, like a stork, and giving sharp jerks with the other, by way of easing the pain, he stammered out, "Quit my service instantly, sir.   D'ye hear ?   Quit it this instant."

Roger, whose blood was quite as much up as his master's, was about making another saucy answer, which would infallibly have ended in his being knocked down either by myself or the nabob, when I stopped him by placing my hands on his shoulders, and driving him before me to the back-door ; after which, having seen him fairly ejected from the premises, I returned into the parlour, where I found Mr. Rupee taking quick, frenzied strides up and down the room, like a man who has just read his banker's name in the *Gazette*.

For a few minutes, indignation was the one predominant feeling in his mind ; but when I had prevailed on him to resume his seat, and take a full glass of madeira, a bottle of which was lying, together with his tiffin, on the table, he remained silent for a time, and then, tossing off a second bumper, he flung himself back in his arm-chair, and, to my inconceivable surprise, burst into a violent fit of laughter.   "Well," said he, "this is, without exception, the most ridiculous piece of business I ever was engaged in.   I could not have believed it possible that anything would have power to rouse me so.   It has actually made me feel quite strong again."

"And no wonder," said I; "depend on it, there is nothing like a good honest passion to brace the nerves, and set the blood in motion. In Ireland, whenever we are low-spirited, we make a point of pitching into our next neighbour, and it is astonishing the good it does both parties. Take another glass, Mr. Rupee. Bravo! I protest you look quite hearty."

"Hearty!" replied the nabob, rubbing his hands with ecstasy; "why, sir, I'm full twenty years younger. Haven't I a fine colour in my face? Egad, I feel strong enough to do any thing. I'll get up by candle-light to-morrow, and go fox-hunting with the squire! I'll poke the fire out, and sit without one! I'll give up my barley-water, and take to brandy! I'll toss my physic out of the window, and—"

"For God's sake, Mr. Rupee, don't do anything so rash. It may be your death. No doubt your late excitement has done you good; but the relapse, sir, that is what we have most to dread in a case of this sort. If you will be advised by me, you will double your usual dose to-night, and early in the morning I will send up a few tonics, which, with one or two composing draughts, a box of pills, and a mild blister, will set you all to rights. Physic, Mr. Rupee, physic, sir—after all, there is nothing like physic."

At this moment the door gently opened, and in walked the penitent Roger, who, halting a few paces off the table, where his master was seated, was commencing a most submissive and elaborate apology for what he called his "little indiscretion," when the nabob cut him short with, "Go your ways, Roger, go your ways, and think no more about it. If you were hasty, so was I;" and then turning to me, he added, "As you were saying, Mr. Fitzmaurice, we must take care to guard against a relapse. But surely you have no apprehensions on this score?"

"Oh, dear, no, sir. A little physic, judiciously applied, will prevent anything of the sort, particularly as you're just now in such a fine train for recovery."

"That is, if I don't fall back," replied the nabob, whose

ecstasies were by this time beginning to get a little moderated.

"And if you should," said I, with a waggish and most unprofessional smile, which, however, I could not for the life of me resist, "you have your remedy in your own hands."

"And what is that?"

"Thrash Roger!" and so saying, I made a precipitate retreat, and hurried on to Gryffyths.

————

CHAPTER VIII.

A SKETCH OF A WELSH SQUIRE OF THE OLD SCHOOL.

THE family-seat of the Gryffyths was a low, spacious mansion, portions of whose architecture dated as far back as the reign of Henry the Eighth, while others had been renewed within the last century, presenting as many quaint samples of building as there are patterns in a tailor's show-book. Everything seemed to be just in its wrong place; while the whole structure—more especially the windows, some of which were boarded, and others bricked up, with a view no doubt to save taxes—was so crazy and dilapidated, that nothing short of a large outlay could have sufficed to put it into proper repair; but as Mr. Gryffyths was unable to make this outlay, he was fain to content himself with botching up, every now and then, those portions which stood most in need of restoration.

Fronting the building was a large lawn; in the centre of which, right before the parlour-windows, stood a solitary majestic oak, bowed down by years and infirmities; its larger branches carefully propped up, and its trunk fenced round with strong wooden stakes, to protect it from the assaults of cattle. Surrounding this lawn, and wholly shutting out a view of the high-road, was a thick belt of magnificent forest-trees, one clump of which formed a rookery, while another consisted merely of stumps, the rest of the trunk and branches having, from the same motives that had suggested the blocking up the windows, been cut down and sold for timber.

At the hall-door of this unique mansion stood the housekeeper, with a strip of brown paper wrapped round each wrist, and one hand held up before her eyes, to shade them from the sun, while ever and anon she cast an inquisitive glance along the footway.

As soon as she saw me she said, "I suppose you're the doctor. The squire's been expecting you a long while since." At this instant the parlour-bell rung with prodigious violence. "That's the squire's summons," exclaimed the old lady; and, bustling forward, threw open the door, and ushered me into her master's presence, with the brief and blunt introduction of "Here's the doctor."

On hearing this announcement, the squire turned slightly round in his easy elbow-chair; and, seeing a strange face instead of the one he expected to see, gave vent to his surprise by a "Whew!" or low whistle; whereupon I explained the reason of Mr. Davis' non-attendance, but was stopped half-way by, "No matter; one's just as good as another; so, sit down, sir, sit down; but stay, there's no chair. Lewis, place a seat for the doctor."

This was said to a meek, sedate young man, in whom, at the very first glance, I detected that miserable animal, a dependent relative. The next bad thing to being a poor poet is to be a poor relation. There is no mistaking either.

When I had taken my seat, and cast a hurried glance about the room, which was lofty and spacious, with a bow-window looking out upon the lawn, and a branching pair of antlers fixed against the wall, I inquired into all the particulars of the squire's illness; and, having been duly enlightened thereon, I observed, "You have a picturesque view, sir, from this window."

"Yes," replied the squire, "it's a capital sporting country,"

"And a fine day like this brings out the landscape in all its beauty."

"Not so fine neither; the scent won't lie, there is too much frost in the air."

A pause of a few minutes ensued, after which the conversation turned on his Majesty's late visit to Dwarrys Castle; when the squire, who had been formally presented to him there, pronounced him to be a king, every inch of him, "And such a capital judge of horseflesh, too ! Why, sir, he no sooner set eyes on my bay mare than he said she was one of the finest bits of blood he had ever seen. I assure you I felt quite flattered by the compliment."

"You were more fortunate, Mr. Gryffyths," I observed, "in being honoured with his Majesty's notice than we were at Llandwarrys," and then proceeded to acquaint the squire with all the details of the late grand doings at the Red Lion; at which he laughed heartily, adding, "I heard something of that, but could not believe that people would make such asses of themselves. Invite his Majesty to dine in a pothouse ! Never heard of such a thing ! But it's all that Radical auctioneer's doings ; I hate such fellows—they're a perfect nuisance."

"You should not blame them, sir," I replied ; "they are but labouring in their vocation—serving an 'apprenticeship' to the gallows, as your neighbour What's-his-name would say."

This sneer was purposely made in allusion to a wealthy Humbug merchant, who had just purchased some tracts of land in the neighbourhood, which adjoined the squire's. To this person it was well known that Mr. Gryffyths bore an inveterate animosity. He envied him for his wealth— he despised him for his occupation—he detested him for the injury he bade fair to do to his own hereditary influence in the neighbourhood. "Do you know anything of this Mr. What's-his-name ?" he inquired.

"Nothing ; but he's a sad, vulgar fellow, I'm told—the tradesman all over."

"Yet he has the assurance to give himself airs, just as

if he were one of us;" and the squire drew himself up with much hauteur. "When the family," he added, "first came to reside here, as they seemed a harmless sort of people, I felt it my duty to act in a neighbourly way towards them; but so ungrateful were they for my civilities, that old What's-his-name had actually the impudence one day to order my gamekeeper off a dirty bit of moorland which he swears is his, though the man had gone there by my express command. Monstrous, wasn't it, Lewis?"

"That was the old man's doing, sir; the sons have always expressed the greatest respect for you."

"Old or young, I'll have no such freedoms taken with me. Pretty business, if a family like mine can't do as they please in their own neighbourhood. That's what the Radicals call liberty, I suppose. Hang all such liberty, say I! And to talk of law, too! A low, pettifogging—"

"Mr. Jointstock is just what you describe him," replied Lewis; "but his eldest son John is really a very clever, well-disposed young fellow."

"Clever!" retorted the squire, "why, yes, I suppose he knows better than to beat for a black cock in a parsley-bed; but since you think the son so clever, what would you think of the father, if you were to see him, as I saw him the other day, riding to cover with an umbrella over his head. Such a turn-out! Why don't you laugh, Lewis?"

"He! he!" replied the young man, but the mode in which he gave vent to this faint apology for cachinnation convinced me that there are few things in life more full of pathos than the laugh of a poor relation.

"Commercial men," continued Lewis, when his countenance had recovered its usual meek expression, "seldom exhibit to advantage in field—"

"Be quiet, Lewis; you're always so fond of hearing yourself talk, I can't get in a word edgewise. O Doctor! what a twinge!"

"Permit me, Mr. Gryffyths," said I, moving my chair towards him, "just to feel your pulse."

"Keep off, sir, keep off; oh, my knee!"

"If you will be ruled by me, sir, you will retire early to rest. Nature, Mr. Gryffyths, is a better physician than art."

"That's just what I say, when Davis advises me to give up my second bottle. I take to it so naturally, I tell him, that I'm sure I can't be wrong. Besides, my family have always been proverbial for their hospitality, and it's my duty to show myself worthy of them."

"I can fully sympathise with your feelings, sir," I observed; "for I am myself the descendant of an old Milesian family, though a long series of misfortunes—'

"Aye, aye," rejoined the squire briskly, "I can feel, no man more so, for the misfortunes of a gentleman of birth. I have known what it is to suffer them myself. To say nothing of this gout, it is not a month since I lost my bitch pointer, the best sporting-dog I ever bred."

"That is her portrait, I presume," said I, pointing to a painting at the far end of the room.

"What! are you fond of paintings?"

"Very; I have seen some of the finest in the world at the Louvre, and in the Florence Gallery."

"No doubt, no doubt—travelling is all the fashion now-a-days. Well, I thank my stars that, except on one occasion, when I went to London on some law-business, I was never a hundred miles from home in my life. But I think you said you were fond of paintings? I can show you some of the finest you have ever seen;" with which words he directed Lewis to throw open the door of an adjacent apartment, and wheel him into it.

The room in question was dark and lofty, with walls of black polished oak hung with portraits, not a few of which, from want of adequate space, leaned against the floor.

"There, sir," said the squire, looking round him with much complacency, "there you see all the Gryffyths at one *coup d'œil*—as his Majesty observed, when speaking of the view from Dwarrys Castle. They deserve a better stall than this ; but the truth is, the workmen are busy just now with the picture-gallery, the floor of which gave way last week, when the young folks were dancing there. Mark that portrait to the left of you. The original was my great-grandfather. Very handsome, isn't he ? And how clean in the fetlock ! They say I'm just like him."

I affected to be much struck by the painting ; and, after an attentive survey of one or two stout old cavaliers in full-bottomed wigs and armour, directed Mr. Gryffyths' notice to a small picture which had been thrust, as if on purpose, into an obscure part of the room. The portrait was that of a beautiful girl, young, and fair, and gentle, but with a look of profound melancholy.

"Ahem ! ahem !" said the squire, "that picture, you mean ; oh, it's a mere nothing, not worth looking at—the likeness of a relation—that is, of a sort of distant connexion of the Gryffyths."

I inferred from this that the portrait was one of a poor girl, who, by marrying beneath her, or some such heterodox means, had brought dishonour on the family scutcheon ; so, averting my gaze, I fixed it on a fat old man attired in a full court suit.

The squire's countenance brightened up as he saw my attention thus diverted, and he entered into a prosing history of the original. "He was a great man, sir ; the finest made man in all Wales, and had the honour of presenting the first county address to his late Majesty—God bless him !—on the birth of our present most gracious Sovereign. On that occasion, the good old King said, turning with a sly glance to the Queen—for her Majesty, I should tell you, was always an admirer of well-made men, and indeed so, for the matter of that, are most women—'Mr. Gryffyths,' said his Majesty— Oh, murder, another twinge !" and cutting short his story, the squire absolutely roared with pain.

"The air of this room is too damp for you, sir," said I ; "permit me to wheel you back."

"Egad, I believe you're right," replied the squire; then suddenly, in a loud voice of spleen and impatience, as I pushed the chair somewhat too forcibly over one or two rough knots in the oaken floor, "Halloo, sir! halloo! you drive on as if you were driving at a five-barred gate! There, that will do, that will do; now shut the door, if you please, and take your chair."

"I am sorry I must be on the move; it's getting late, and I have yet some patients to visit at Llandwarrys."

"Well, well, I press no man to stop against his inclination. This is Liberty Hall; you come when you please, and go when you please. I shall see you again in a day or two, I suppose? Good night, sir. Take care of the dogs."

"Bravo!" said I, as I returned home to Llandwarrys, "I have made as decided a hit here as with the nabob, but must take care to improve my advantage by studying the squire's character. No doubt, with a little management, I shall find him as good a patron as a patient. To be sure, he has no great fancy for physic. But what of that? Advice swells up an apothecary's bill quite as well as medicine. So, vive Humbug! And myself, too; for, had I not been the most modest and meritorious of quacks, I should have insisted on the merits of my elixir, both with the nabob and the squire. Pray Heaven I don't suffer by such excessive diffidence!"

CHAPTER IX.

AN INVALID SPORTSMAN.

MR. GRYFFYTHS of Gryffyths was one of those frank, jolly fellows whose character may be read at a glance. He had a round rosy face, presenting about as much of a profile as a turnip; a beard as black as a shoe-brush; and a spacious mouth, calculated sadly to perplex a round of beef. His arms, of which he was not a little proud, were miracles of muscle, and his nails were always bitten to the quick.

In his attire he was the old English sportsman all over. He wore a faded epigrammatic green coat, with huge pockets at the side; drab breeches; waxy top-boots, as full of wrinkles as one's grandmother; and a huge gold watch, with figures on the dial-plate almost large enough for a kitchen-clock, and to which were attached an enormous chain and seals, that reached half-way down to his knees.

In early life he had been notorious for his rustic gallantries; and even now was fond of chucking a pretty girl under the chin, and styling her "my dear." People called him handsome; but this the captain always contended was a gross calumny. "Look at his legs, sir," he would say, when any one praised Mr. Gryffyths' good looks in his hearing; "how can a man with such millposts be handsome?" and then he would cast a sidelong, complacent glance at his own shapely leg and foot. I think nothing of this, however; for wherever women were concerned, Caustic made a point of recognising no claims but his own. He had the bad taste to condemn *even* my exterior!

Among the squire's most marked peculiarities was an inveterate addiction to family customs. That a habit or prejudice was ancient was with him sufficient warranty of its excellence. Though on the whole a good-natured man, yet scarcely a day passed but something or other occurred to ruffle his temper. In the first place, he was never free from pecuniary embarrassments; secondly, he had seldom less than one lawsuit on hand, but frequently more, which, however harassing to his mind and trying to his pocket, he yet seemed perversely to cherish as among the necessary adjuncts of an ancient pedigree; and thirdly, he lived in a neighbourhood where, with all the passion for the undivided empire of a despot, he found himself compelled to "bear a brother near the throne" in the person of Mr. Jointstock.

The consequence of this was, that for some time past

he had been gradually contracting the circle of his society, and dividing it between those few among the squirearchy who held the same opinions as himself, and the strolling players, when they happened to be in the neighbourhood, whose fun, anecdote, and general recklessness of character jumped with his own peculiar humour. To these last, together with the poachers, with whom he held many sporting tenets in common, he knew he might play the great man with impunity.

But though Mr. Gryffyths (who, I should have observed, had been a childless widower for many years) was thus comparatively withdrawn from the world, yet there were certain times and seasons when he came publicly forth, like a "giant refreshed," in all his feudal glory. The eighth of September was one of these epochs. On that memorable day, some sixty or seventy years since, his grandfather, after a protracted course of litigation, had succeeded in wresting his patrimonial property from a usurping kinsman, and the family had ever since celebrated the anniversary.

When I next saw the squire, he was full of the subject. The eighth of September was approaching, and he would not, for the value of his whole estate, be the means of delaying its celebration. But how was the thing to be accomplished? This confounded gout would not let him stir. What would Mr. Fitzmaurice advise?

My advice, of course, was that he should keep his mind free from excitement, and live upon slops, when, as it still wanted nearly a fortnight of the eighth, I had little doubt he would recover in time enough to take the field as well as ever.

As I said this, the squire shook his head, with an air of distrust and despondency. He might or he might not recover, God only knew! For himself, he was far from confident, for he had had a warning only the night before, which had never yet been known to fail.

"Warning!" said I, much astonished; "to whom or to what do you allude?"

Mr. Gryffyths made no reply; on which Lewis, who was sitting next me, whispered in my ear that the warning to which his uncle alluded was the fall of one of the branches of the oak in the centre of the lawn, which was generally supposed to be the forerunner of some calamity to the family.

There is scarcely an ancient family in all South Wales that does not boast its warning oak. In one district of Caermarthenshire alone, there are not less than six families thus endowed. The legend is a truly national one.

On being made acquainted with this curious ancestral superstition, I proceeded to administer consolation to Mr. Gryffyths by turning the whole affair into ridicule. But the task was more difficult than I had anticipated, and had only the effect of unsettling his temper more than ever; for, though far from sorry to be promised a quick recovery, yet he was shocked at the idea of having an old family legend ridiculed and falsified.

Seeing this, I altered my tone, and, admitting that the fall of the branch could scarcely be looked on in any other light than as a warning, I yet added that there was not the slightest reason to suppose that it had any reference to himself personally.

The squire caught eagerly at my suggestion. "A good idea," said he; "the warning is, as you say, a warning; still there can be no reason why it should apply to me. Why shouldn't it? Ah! a lucky thought. Lewis, run down to the stables and see if all's right there. But no, I think you had better take a peep at the kennel; poor Madoc was off his meat yesterday."

Lewis, with whom I exchanged smiles at this proposition, which was made by the squire with the most edifying gravity, left the room to fulfil his uncle's directions; and returned in a few minutes with intelligence that one of his best harriers, Don, was missing.

"I thought so," said Mr. Gryffyths, with a whimsical mixture of chagrin and satisfaction; "didn't I tell you, Fitzmaurice, that the oak's warning had never been known

to fail? Yet to lose such a treasure as Don! I would
not have taken fifty pounds for him. However, it's well
it's no worse."

On further inquiries among the household, it appeared
that a beggar had been seen loitering near the premises
that morning, and shortly afterwards to make a precipitate retreat, with Don hard at his heels. But this part
of the story the squire indignantly rebutted. "What!"
said he, "Don hunt vermin! No, no; he's been spirited
away by the vagabond; but I'll ferret him out;" and,
ringing the bell, he gave orders to his groom to post off
to Llandwarrys, and mention the circumstances of the
theft to the constable there, with Mr. Gryffyths' orders
that he should stop all suspicious persons.

These points settled, the squire returned to his favourite
subject of the oak. His ancestors had always regarded
it with veneration; for there was an old tradition current
in the neighbourhood that, when the oak fell, the dynasty
of the Gryffyths would fall, too. But Lewis could tell all
about it, for he had written some verses on the subject,
which he (the squire) had read, and which were exceedingly clever; though, for his own part, he was not much
of a judge of such matters: anything in the shape of
rhyme always puzzled his poor brain.

His nephew here took up the subject, and was busily
expatiating upon it, when the housekeeper entered the
room with a basin of water-gruel in her hand, which she
placed deliberately under the poor squire's nose. His
countenance fell as he began to stir up this "slip-slop."
He looked first at me, then at Lewis, with an indescribably
diverting air of sheepishness; and then, forcing a laugh
at his own weakness, began to apologise in such terms as,
'Well, it can't be helped, so I suppose I must put a
good face on the matter, and swallow this vile water—
      ter—"
wa"Gruel," said Lewis, helping out his recollection.

"I know that as well as you can tell me, so you needn't
be so officious. You'll please to remember, Mr. Fitz-

maurice, that it's by your express order, and no wish of mine, that I swallow this villanous mess. By the bye, don't you think a glass of brandy would improve it? Well, well," said he, seeing that I shook my head, "it can't be helped, so here goes; but, then, how Jointstock would crow if he could see me in this pickle!" And in this way he kept on sipping and grumbling, while his nephew and myself had the greatest difficulty in subduing our muscles to the proper decorous gravity.

At length, when the draught was finished, the squire by my advice retired for the night, and I followed. On reaching home, I found my wife engaged in an animated altercation with her submissive brother, touching the compound fracture of a pickle-jar, which was "all owing to his abominable carelessness," so I left the amiable pair to settle their disputes themselves, and hastened to the Red Lion to while away an hour with the club.

CHAPTER X.

A WOLF IN SHEEP'S CLOTHING.

THE eighth of September had now arrived; and crutch, flannels, and water-gruel, thrown aside, the squire was "a man again." Agreeably to the directions I had received from him on the preceding day, I made my appearance at Gryffyths shortly after eight o'clock, where I found some ten or a dozen farmers, together with a small sprinkling of the neighbouring gentry, among whom were Lewis and the parson, seated at a well-laden breakfast-table. Not the slightest order of precedence was observed among the guests; for the squire's anniversaries were a species of saturnalia at which all distinctions of rank were for the time dispensed with.

Mr. Gryffyths welcomed me with a hearty slap on the back. "Fine day, doctor," said he; "glorious day. I was in a sad fidget, though, all last night; up at least a dozen times, looking out to see what chance there was for us. Ah! captain," he continued, addressing Caustic, who just then entered the room, "glad to see you. How's that old ass Rupee. Sit down, man, sit down; we've no time to spare." And without more ado he took his place next me, and, tackling to some cold roast-beef, said, "Good stuff this, doctor; better than all your drugs, hey, you dog?" and then, by way of giving point to his sarcasm, he kept pegging me in the ribs till he made me roar again. During the repast, the squire gave us directions as to what were to be the "orders of the day." We were to meet, he told us, beside the Talleen lakes, but not later than three o'clock, where we should find everything prepared for our accommodation; for which purpose he had despatched a whole waggon-load of *sutlers* at daybreak.

After breakfast, during which I could not extract a word from either the curate or the captain, both of whom informed me by signs that their time was too precious to be so wasted, we all set out on our excursion. The squire and some few others led the way on horseback, the rest trudged afoot, while Lewis and myself brought up the rear; but as neither of us was very ambitious of figuring among the Nimrods of the day, we soon lost sight of the rest of the party, and made a short cut across some fields for the purpose of mounting a hill, whence, as Lewis assured me, we should have a view of all the "classic ground" of South Wales.

Having seen all that was to be seen, we returned into the high-road; but scarcely had we proceeded a few hundred yards, when we observed, at a slight distance before us, a crowd standing on a bridge that spanned the little river Cothy.

"Halloo," said I, "what is the meaning of all this gathering? Is there another George the Fourth being exhibited?"

"Oh! a preacher, I suppose," replied Lewis; "we have hundreds of them in South Wales;" and he led the way across a broad swampy meadow, which soon brought us

out on the high-road; when, on nearing the crowd, we
found, as Lewis had surmised, that it was collected to
hear an itinerant expounder of "the Word." Not a few
of our own party figured among the congregation, whom
the curate, in his zeal for orthodoxy, was endeavouring to
drive onward; but in vain, for the preacher's eloquence
prevailed over all his intreaties.

At length a circumstance occurred which created a re-
action in his favour. A shepherd's boy came running along
the banks of the river, and, when he arrived close under
the bridge, shouted out, "An otter! an otter!" whereupon
the whole congregation scampered off in the direction
whence the lad preceded them.

I remained behind, attracted by a certain something in
the preacher's voice and gestures, which I fancied were
familiar to me; and on looking steadily at his features,
half-concealed as they were by a huge slouch hat, whom
should I recognise but my philosophic friend Mr. Justinian
Stubbs, looking, if possible, more sleek, smooth, and oily
than ever!

The sly fox saw that I remembered him, and that it
was of no use, therefore, to deny his identity; so, after a
moment or two's hesitation as to whether he should be
candid or not, cant carried the day, and he began indulging me with a full and particular account of the circumstances attending what he called his miraculous
conversion.

"Ah, my friend!" he drawled out, in the true twang of
the conventicle, "it was, indeed, a blessed change, and
wrought in me just at the fitting season. Heaven only
knows what would have become of me, surrounded as I
was in Humbug by implacable enemies, and living in
constant fear of detection by the profane, had I not one
night, as I lay sleepless on my pallet, devising divers
schemes for the future, heard a voice cry, 'Justinian
Stubbs, whose name is henceforth Habakkuk Holdforth,
arise, and flee into Wales. The Lord hath need of thee
there.'"

13

" Truly, as you say, Mr. Stubbs, the summons came just in the nick of time. I think I never heard of so discreet and convenient a conversion. However, what will be, will be, as your philosophy teaches."

" Philosophy! Mention not the profane term! Thank Heaven, I have eschewed it for ever, and become, albeit at the eleventh hour, an humble labourer in the Lord's vineyard."

" Ah, Mr. Stubbs—Holdforth, I should say—it was in a far different vineyard you were labouring, when you disembarrassed me of my pocket-book, on the night of the conflagration at Humbug."

The accomplished hypocrite indulged in a faint smile as I reminded him of this small backsliding; but instantly correcting himself, he observed, " That was the Lord's doing, who permitted me to fall, like David, in order that I might rise again regenerated, like Nicodemus. 'All men,' as the great Helvetius"—(here I buttoned up my pockets)—" I mean, as the pious John Huntingdon says, ' have their time to sin, and their time to repent ;'" with which words he thrust his hand into his coat-pocket, and, drawing out a tract, placed it in my hands, adding, " Would to Heaven, my friend, that your day of grace were arrived, and that I could see you, by the aid of this precious work, cleansed and sweetened by the waters of life, even as I now am. Oh! you know not the bliss that is reserved for those who hold fast by the faith, and fear not. Faith can remove mountains."

" Yes, and pocket-books too. Doubtless, Mr. Stubbs, your new faith has proved as profitable to you in a temporal as in a spiritual sense ?"

" Temporal considerations," he replied, casting his eyes devoutly upward, " weigh no longer with one who has put off the old Adam, and clothed himself in the white garment of regeneration, though it is but just and fitting that, as I expound the Word, I should live by the Word. I have called many to repentance, and, thanks be to Him who feedeth the young ravens, I have found no lack of food or raiment during my sojourn in this country."

He was proceeding in this fashion, when a sudden idea suggested itself to me ; and, resolved on having a jest at his expense, I interrupted him with, "I am sorry, Mr. Stubbs, you should have selected this part of Wales as the theatre of your exploits, for the ordinary of the Humbug jail—you remember the ordinary, of course ?—happens to be just now on a visit to some friends at Talleen."

"Indeed!" replied Justinian, turning quite pale with apprehension.

"Fact. I have met him twice already, but luckily he did not recognise me. I hope you may be equally— Bless me, is it possible ! Why, here comes the very man himself;" and I pointed to an elderly person in black, who was walking slowly along the road towards us.

"D—n it, you don't say so!" exclaimed Justinian, dropping, in the alarm of the moment, all his assumed sanctity ; and then, without stopping to look behind him, or even wishing me adieu, he waddled off with a grotesque and ungodly speed, worthy of the most flagitious son of Belial.

When I had recovered from the laughter which the success of this ingenious stratagem had occasioned, I rejoined the crowd, whom I found prepared to move on again to Talleen, with the body of the slain otter borne triumphantly before them on a pole.

CHAPTER XI.

THE ANNIVERSARY.

When we reached the village, we found a large party in readiness to receive us, who no sooner caught sight of our trophy than they set up a lusty halloo, which brought about us the whole village-school, to whom, at the squire's particular request, the pedagogue had granted a holiday, and who now followed in our wake towards the place of rendezvous.

This was on an isthmus that divided the two Talleen lakes, and once formed the site of a monastery, within whose ruins—the rank grass and weeds having with some difficulty been cleared away—a huge tent was erected, capable of containing at least thirty persons, in the centre of which was placed a long table, or rather a collection of tables.

About this tent, cooks and servants were now humming, busy as bees; hampers, too, of wine, ale, and spirits, baskets of all sorts of provender, were strewed about in every direction ; together with boxes full of hay, in which glasses, crockery, plate, &c., were packed up ; while just at the edge of the land, where it jutted upon the water, a whole sheep was roasting before a fire that hissed and roared, and threw out a broad red glare, like a blacksmith's furnace.

If one of the old monks, thought I, could now pop his head out of the grave, how he would stare at the scene here presented to his eyes ! Yet why so ? It can be no novelty to him. These walls, though they have been silent for centuries, must have witnessed many a jolly carousal in their time. Yes, yes, the ghostly fathers, no doubt, made hay while the sun shone, and drained the cup of enjoyment to the dregs. But they are all gone now. Possibly, at this very moment, I am treading on the grave of my lord abbot.

Lewis, who seemed to divine my thoughts, said, " I see you are surprised at my uncle's choice of site, and no wonder. To me it appears little short of an insult to the *genius loci*. However, it's no use to argue the matter. The snugly-sheltered site of the monastery has prevailed with Mr. Gryffyths over every other consideration."

At this moment the squire, who had been busy replying to the congratulations of the villagers, joined us, with some half-dozen chubby boys and girls pulling away at his jacket, to each of whom he gave a large lump of gingerbread, which he had bought in the village for that purpose. Immediately on entering the ruins, he summoned the whole party about him, and told us that each man might employ himself as he pleased, for that we had yet three good hours before us.

This had the effect of dispersing the company. Some seized a gun, others embarked on the lake in a coracle, while others, among whom were the squire and Caustic, contented themselves with fitting a huge artificial fly to a whipcord line, and trying their piscatory skill along the banks. I did the same; but, meeting with my usual luck, soon threw aside my rod, and scrambled up the side of a mountain that rose somewhat precipitously from the lake. From this height I commanded a fine panoramic view. The dwindled lakes, with the coracles flitting like fairy shallops across their surface, lay glittering in the sunshine at my feet; while from the heart of the old monastic ruin came up the rude sounds of laughter, strangely at variance with its venerable, melancholy aspect. A few yards beyond, at the extremity of the first lake, stood the village of Talleen, the smoke from whose chimneys ascended like an incense to heaven; and, far as the eye could discern, the horizon was bounded, to the north by the Cardigan crags, and to the east by the long billowy range of the Black Mountains, with Llynn-y-van towering high above them all, like a Titan petrified.

Having satisfied my gaze, I was just preparing to ramble off in the direction of Edwinsford, when my ear caught the well-known "halloo" of the squire; and, descending in the direction whence the sound proceeded, I saw him darting to and fro along the banks of the lake, and manœuvring so vigorously with a fish of nearly equal strength that it seemed a moot point whether he should pull the creature *out* of, or it should pull him *into* the water.

"A fine fellow," observed the squire, as I congratulated him on the chances of victory. "A noble fellow—weighs upwards of fourteen pounds, if he weighs an ounce. Davis, bear a hand here with the landing-net. Ah! there he goes—by Jove, I shall lose him!" and the brute, who for a few seconds had been lying quite sulky, made a sudden plunge that set the waters in a foam around him. In an instant he rose again, and darted off among the weeds, from which sprung out a frightened wild-duck,

which was instantly brought down by Lewis' gun, much
to the delight and astonishment of his uncle, who observed
that, notwithstanding his "verses and such-like," he had
always entertained a good opinion of the lad's abilities.

The fish, snugly couched among the weeds, was now again
quiet; but, on Mr. Gryffyths proceeding to wind up the
reel, he made another dart, drawing after him the whole
length of the line, so that the squire was actually compelled to wade knee-deep among the rushes; and, to my
remonstrating with him on the danger he was running of
a relapse, bluntly replied, "Curse the gout! do you think
I will lose the fish?"

But there was not the slightest prospect of such a loss,
for the creature was, by this time, quite spent; and after
rolling about heavily, like a black log on the water, turned
upward on his back, his head sinking in the stream, and
was thus drawn to land. Just after this came up the rest of
our party, bearing with them a fine show of wild-fowl;
so that, what with one thing, and what with another, the
day, as the squire significantly remarked, was one of the
best-spent he had ever known.

We now prepared for our return to the monastery,
attracted thither by a huntsman's horn, which was the
signal that all was ready for our accommodation. And
a glorious sight awaited us within its old walls! The
tables groaned beneath the weight of a thousand dainties.
Rich venison pasties, game of every description, hares,
fowls, tongues, and hams, the stately sirloin, and the
irresistible haunch, embellished the upper table; while
at the lower smoked an entire sheep, right before which
stood the squire's bailiff, with his coat-sleeves tucked up,
his elbows rounded, and a gravity in his countenance that
indicated a becoming consciousness of the importance of
his vocation.

Dinner over, a full glass of choice port was handed
round, not only to every guest at table, but also to every
one who thought it worth while to attend; and, from
time to time, nearly the whole village poured in on us,

the squire's anniversaries being well known and appreciated throughout the district; after which, on a given
signal from the parson, our host's health was proposed,
and drunk with enthusiasm.

Mr. Gryffyths' reply was brief, and to the point, and
even Caustic was pleased to declare that, considering all
things, it was not so much amiss; "but," he added, "of
all the speakers I ever heard, commend me to my old
friend Major Tipple."

"What!" replied the parson, "have we got that old
major again? This is the third time I have heard his
name to-day."

By the splenetic tug he gave at his shirt-collar, I could
perceive that the captain was bristling up for a wrathful
repartee, so I interposed to preserve peace by saying, "It
is a long time, Caustic, since the old monastery has known
such a jolly day as this."

"Well thought of," said the squire; "let us drink to
the memory of the monks and their abbot. Doubtless,
doctor, you are surprised at my choosing a site like this.
I used to keep the day at Gryffyths, but there were always
such strange goings on in the course of the evening between some of my young guests and the maid-servants—
for you can't put old heads on young shoulders, you know
—that my poor wife made me promise never to hold
another within doors. But, gentlemen, I see you're
waiting; so here's to the memory of the monks, and my
lord abbot. Ah! he was a hearty old cock, I'll warrant.
Took his wine like a gentleman. But so, for that matter,
do most Churchmen. Hey, parson? No offence, I hope?"

"None in the least," responded the divine, with a sly
affectation of demureness; "no man, to be discreet, has
a greater relish for the innocent enjoyments of life than
I have; though Heaven forbid I should ever be tempted
to exceed the bounds of modest vivacity."

"No! no!" said the captain sneeringly, "that you
never will, while that old-seasoned cask of yours can hold
its two or three bottles on an emergency."

"So much the better ; glad to hear it," said the squire ; "all honest fellows are fond of their bottle. I like a moderate glass myself. Parson, a song. Come, let's have 'The Storm ;' it's an old favourite of mine."

But there was no occasion to call for a storm, for one was already brewing. An allusion having been made, by one of the farmers at the lower table, to his Majesty's visit, an angry political discussion took place, which at length reached such a height that an appeal was made by some of the more moderate to the squire, who no sooner understood the cause of the quarrel than his hot Welsh blood was up in an instant ; and, giving the table a thump with his brawny fist that set all the glasses clattering, he said, "Harkee, gentlemen, this is Liberty Hall, where every man is free to do or say just what he pleases. Nevertheless, I'll have no politics talked here. The very next man who offends in that way shall swallow a bumper of salt and water ; so strike up, parson, and let us have no more interruption."

Thus requested, the curate commenced his bravura ; but scarcely had he got through the first verse, when Mr. Gryffyths, turning round, said, "Halloo ! where's Lewis ? Stole away ?"

"Your nephew," I replied, "left us about an hour since. The wine, I fear, disagreed with him, for I saw him change countenance as he rose from table."

"Just what I suspected. I'm afraid I shall never make anything of that lad. It's a thousand pities, for his intentions are good—but—such a head ! However, to do the boy justice, he brought down that bird very cleverly this morning. Gone off ! Well, well, no matter, provided he has not taken the punch-bowl along with him. Thomas, bring in the punch-bowl."

This was the signal for the introduction of a huge flowered china bowl, which the bailiff, preceded by two servants, brought up with infinite pomp, and placed before the squire, who, while helping us to its contents, took care to let us know that it was a bowl of vast antiquity, and such a favourite with his father that he had bequeathed it to him by a separate codicil in his will.

"A noble bowl, no doubt," said the captain; "if one could but see it."

"See it! I see two," hiccupped a voice from the lower table.

"A good hint, captain," said the squire; "ho! lights there;" and in a few minutes a profusion of torches brought from the village blazed up in all parts of the monastery, throwing a wild, ghastly aspect on the ruins; while lamps and lanterns were lit within the tent, the whole forming one of the most singular and impressive spectacles I ever witnessed.

When the squire had helped those within his own immediate neighbourhood, room was made for the bowl to take its rounds, which it did with a rapidity that soon produced very visible effects. The curate began to indulge us with a variety of sporting anecdotes; the captain to recapitulate the virtues of Major Tipple and his East India madeira; and the squire to enforce the still more expeditious circulation of the bowl, in such terms as "Push her along, captain! parson, she's at anchor alongside you; shove her off, man, shove her off; that's right; there she goes; huzza! blessings on her sweet face. I remember my poor father—"

Before he could finish his anecdote, he was interrupted by a second squabble, which was not appeased without difficulty; because all kept shouting away, each at the very top of his lungs, and not a soul among them all knew or cared what it was he was wrangling about. Even the squire's stentorian voice was unheard among the din; and it became necessary, therefore, to disperse the assembly, which could only be done by the *élite* of the company resolving on instant departure.

This, at the curate's instigation, was accomplished; and the squire, much against his will, was prevailed on to make the first move; but not before he had left injunctions with his major domo to take especial care of the punch-bowl, of which he was as proud as ever was Magnus Troil of the "Jolly Mariner of Canton."

As he rose from his seat, I could perceive that his convivial exertions had made him a little unsteady; so I offered him my arm, which he accepted, muttering, as we kept *tacking* on towards the village, "Singular, how weak that gout has left me. Steady, doctor, steady; keep to the right, or I shall have to fish you out of a horsepond;" and he made a lurch to windward, which very nearly threw me on my beam-ends.

At length, after encountering various perils by land and water, that guardian angel which never fails to befriend virtue in extremity enabled us to reach the village in safety, where we found the crazy old rumbling family coach waiting at the inn the squire's arrival; who, after making inquiries respecting Lewis, was informed by the compassionate landlady that the "poor young man was ill abed, with a sort of a nervous headache like."

"A what?" said Mr. Gryffyths, with huge contempt; "a nervous headache? Never heard of such a thing in all my life! If it had been the gout, indeed—but nerves! What will he have next, I wonder?" and, thus speculating, the squire took his place in the carriage, and offered me a place beside him; while the rest of the party followed shortly afterwards in waggons, which had been duly matted and fitted up with benches for their accommodation.

CHAPTER XII.

AN UNEXPECTED DENOUEMENT—A SUDDEN FLIGHT.

My time was now, for the first time since my entrance into South Wales, beginning to pass very much to my satisfaction. I was here, there, and everywhere; now sentimentalising with the nabob, now waxing convivial with the squire, and now discussing local politics with

Caustic and my brother-in-law at the Red Lion. I must confess I should have preferred a more enlarged sphere of action ; but this being just now wholly out of the question, I had nothing left for it but to make the most of my situation.

But prosperity, like adversity, is not without its drawbacks. If it was fortunate for me in one sense that I extended my connexions among the more respectable circles, in another it was far otherwise ; for it called forth the jealousy of the narrow-minded coterie at the Red Lion, who could not understand upon what principle of justice or common-sense it was that I was more looked up to than themselves. Much of my luck was attributed, as a matter of course, to my profession ; still the club, with the exceptions of Caustic and Mr. Davis, could not, or would not, be brought to acknowledge that a man who but the other day came among them as an adventurer, with scarce a penny in his pocket, had now any right to affect the superior.

For some few weeks, however, their feelings were confined to sneering insinuations and significant shrugs of the shoulders, whenever my name happened to be mentioned ; but by degrees they assumed a more offensive character. First it was hinted that I gave myself unwarrantable airs ; and secondly, that there was something mysterious about me : whereupon the gossips would revert to my first appearance, without any ostensible motive, among them, and hope that all would be right "this time next year."

Unfortunately, so far from endeavouring to soften this hostile disposition, as any rational being in my peculiar situation would have done, I only increased its acerbity by my show of utter indifference—an act of suicidal folly which was very soon brought home to me in a way that I could never have anticipated.

It ahppened one day when I dined with Mr. Gryffyths he was so delighted with my queer, broad stories that in the exuberance of his satisfaction, he promised that when

Lord Dwarrys returned to the castle he would take an opportunity of introducing me to him. This was the very thing I most coveted, for I knew that, if I could but once gain such an influential patron, there was nothing in the way of professional advancement that I might not calculate on during my stay in South Wales; so hurrying home in high glee, I just stopped to communicate the news to my wife, and then stepped over the way to the Red Lion.

Never was I in better condition—never fuller of anecdote and vivacity than on this disastrous evening. Not a remark was thrown off—as Mr. Gryffyths would say —but I followed in full cry at its heels with some opposite pun or joke; and this with so little effort, and such invincible good-nature, that, despite their late prejudices, the coterie again began to look on me, if not with positive good-will, at least with something not very far removed from it.

But one among the assembled party—ominous unit !— was silent amid the general mirth. Where others affected the conciliatory, he merely sneered, at the same time keeping his eyes fixed on mine with a marked pertinacity that attracted the attention of the whole room, and at length so annoyed me that, thrown off my guard, I said cavalierly, " Are my face and figure to your liking, sir ?"

" Less, perhaps, than you may suppose," replied the fellow; " for I have seen both before, and that not very long since, under circumstances which—"

" Circumstances !" exclaimed one and all in a breath ; " what circumstances ?"

"Oh, no matter. Mr. Fitz—What-d'ye-call-'em" (with a sneer), " I dare say, will understand me."

My nerves, always delicate, misgave me at this trying moment, and I began to run over in my mind what the fellow could possibly allude to. Had he met me on the Continent ? Had he known me as an actor at Mollymoreen, or as an editor in London ? Had he been engaged with me in the election-scenes at Humbug ? Had he been an eye-witness of my flight from prison ? Impossible, for surely I should have recollected him ! Still, despite this conviction, I felt far from comfortable, and would gladly have beaten a retreat ; but for the life of me, I could not summon up a plausible excuse, so there I sat, nailed to my chair, while not less than a dozen pair of eyes, opened to their widest extent, kept glaring on me like so many burning-glasses.

The suspicions of the company being once roused, they insisted on following up the conversation, notwithstanding I made repeated attempts to divert it; till, driven to desperation, like a stag at bay, I fixed a menacing look on the stranger, and said, "Who or what you may be, sir, that thus claim an acquaintance—"

"Acquaintance, sir ? God forbid !"

"Why, what is the meaning of all this?" said Caustic peevishly; "if you have anything to say against Fitzmaurice, sir, out with it. No friend of mine shall have his character sneered away in this manner. Fair play's a jewel ; so on with your story, man, and be—"

"Aye, on with it," cried out a dozen voices at once.

I was so much struck with Caustic's generous bluntness, that for a few minutes I was wholly unable to say a word ; at length, deriving confidence from the reflection that I had at least one friend in the room, I resumed my address to the stranger as follows :—"Who, or what you may be, sir, that thus affect a recollection of me, I know not ; I have mixed much with the world in my time, especially in the metropolis ; and my friend the auctioneer here, who has done the same, knows well that under such circumstances a man meets with strange acquaintances. No offence to you, sir."

I threw out this flattering insinuation for the purpose of conciliating the auctioneer, who, however, took no notice of it further than by a surly " Humph !" on which I continued my address : "It is not unlikely, therefore, sir, that I may have met with you before ; but most assuredly, wherever it was that this rencounter took place, there can be no circumstances attending it which I should wish to forget."

The stranger was stung with the determined coolness of my manner, which was not without its effect on the company, and, being moreover somewhat touched by frequent libations of brandy and water, he replied, "Since you say that you have no wish to forget the circumstances under which I last met you, I can have no hesitation in publicly bringing them to your recollection. But first of all, I should tell you that I am traveller for the firm of Hoax and Co., wholesale chemists in Humbug."

The club pricked up their ears at this exordium. The attorney was particularly attentive, and no sooner heard the word "Humbug" mentioned, than he stole quietly out of the room—a movement which filled me with dismay.

"Humbug! Humbug!" said I; "true, I passed through it some months since on my road to South Wales; and, now I think of it, I do remember having had the good fortune to spend an evening with you at the White Lion. I am glad you bring the matter to my recollection. Your health—I hope you left your family well at home?"

I could see that the company were disappointed at this simple solution of what had appeared to them a most important mystery; the auctioneer especially muttered half-audibly between his teeth, "Pshaw! is that all?" but, together with the others, he was soon relieved from his disappointment by the stranger replying, "You're mistaken, sir; I have no family, nor am I married!"

"Bless me, how forgetful I am! I recollect you told me you were a bachelor, and amused me uncommonly, too, by your quizzical allusions to the married state. What a capital joke that was of yours about the fat widow of Clifton!" I added; for necessity is the mother of invention, and I felt the importance of putting the fellow into good-humour.

The man stared at me as if I had been a ghost.

"Fat widow! Clifton! White Lion, sir! I never

spent an evening with you at the White Lion. I never told you a story about a fat widow. I never joked with you about the married state. I am a plain, blunt man of business, and detest joking. I never cracked a joke in all my life, and never meant it."

"Well, well, my good sir, there's no occasion to put yourself into such a passion. I might have known from your face you were no joker."

"And from yours I might have known, what I'll take care the company shall know, too, that you are a—swindler. There, sir, what do you think of that for a joke?"

My face burned like scarlet at this insult. "Sir," I replied, "you are a scoundrel, but your condition protects you. It is clear to me, as it must be to every one else in the room, that you are drunk—shocking drunk. I might have told you so before, but a false delicacy prevented me."

"And no false delicacy shall prevent my exposing you as you deserve." The fellow then, with the most tedious circumlocution, went through the history of my connexion with Alderman Snodgrass; of my conduct during the election, where he first saw me on the hustings; of the proceedings that had been instituted against me, in consequence of my "deliberate frauds on one who had proved himself my best friend;" of my arrest, imprisonment, flight—in a word, of the whole of my political career during my residence in that most villanous of all towns.

"But his name?" inquired the attorney, who had re-entered the room while the man was in the midst of his statement; "you have forgotten to tell us that."

"His name is O'Blarney; though, it seems, he now calls himself Fitzmaurice."

"So I thought," replied the man of law, "and"—winking sagaciously at the company—"I have had my suspicions a long time on the subject, though I said nothing about it; but now, in order to be quite sure of my man, I have brought with me an old number of the Humbug paper, wherein this same Mr. O'B——, *alias* Mr. F——, is described as not only having been guilty of all that this gentleman has alleged against him, but as having been seen on the night of the conflagration in company with a convicted felon who assisted to rob the ordinary of the jail."

The parson here fairly groaned aloud. "What, rob a clergyman? Oh, the sacrilegious villain! Hanging is too good for him."

"I am sorry for you, Mr. Fitz—O'Blarney—or whatever else may be your name," said Caustic. "Your pecuniary difficulties I could have sympathised with, for all gentlemen are liable to accidents of this sort; but your ingratitude to your friend and benefactor—this is what no man of honour can overlook; so the sooner you vanish the better."

"Right, captain," said the auctioneer, "I never half liked the fellow's looks. If he had been one of the allied sovereigns, he could not have given himself greater airs."

"And he's my brother-in-law!" gasped forth Mr. Davis.

Before I could reply to these flattering innuendoes, the attorney had pulled out the Humbug journal from his pocket, and, putting on his spectacles, commenced reading it aloud; but scarcely had he got through the first sentence, when I snatched it from his hands, tore it into a thousand fragments, and, flinging them in his face, said, "This is a monstrous conspiracy, got up for the sole purpose of ruining an innocent man; but, sir," turning fiercely towards the traveller, "rely on it, you shall pay dearly for your outrageous calumnies, and *this* before another week is over your head;" and so saying, I rushed towards the door, taking the company so completely by surprise that not a soul attempted to stop me.

When I reached the street, I stood for a moment like one bewildered, so sudden had been the blow, and with such stunning severity had it fallen on me. Nevertheless an immediate decision was necessary. Ruin stared me in the face. By the morrow the stranger's calumnies would be in general circulation throughout the valley; and not only would my prospects be for ever blasted in South Wales, but intelligence also of the place of my retreat would reach Humbug.

The last consideration decided me, and remembering luckily that the Milford-Haven coach would in a few minutes pass the end of the street, and halt at the Towy-bridge Inn, I resolved on taking my departure by it—but whither, I was not just then sufficient master of myself to determine.

Having come to this decision, I rushed full-speed home. My wife met me at the door. "Good news—glorious news, my dear," said I, rubbing my hands with affected ecstasy; "I have just heard from a friend at the Red Lion, by the merest accident in the world, that my old uncle at Pembroke—you must remember my often speaking of him—now lies at the point of death, and desires to see me instantly, with the view, no doubt, of making me heir to his vast property."

"Well, I declare," replied Mrs. Fitzmaurice, "this is just what I expected. I said only at breakfast-time, some luck would befall us, for I dreamed last night—"

"Quick, quick, my dear, I have no time to listen to dreams now. The mail will pass the end of Llandwarrys within ten minutes; so give me twenty pounds for my travelling-expenses, as I may perhaps be detained some little time at Pembroke."

"Twenty pounds, Fitzmaurice! That is a large sum; I should think ten would do."

"No, no; nothing under twenty, and do pray be quick. There is not a moment to lose."

Grumbling, yet still with more alacrity than she ever before evinced on such occasions, Mrs. Fitzmaurice hastened to her secret escritoire, and in a few minutes returned with the requisite sum, just as I heard the coach clattering along the end of the street, and the well-known footstep of Mr. Davis hastening across the road from the Red Lion.

"There, Fitzmaurice," said my wife, thrusting the money into my hands, "there's twenty pounds for you. Now, mind you husband it carefully. You'll have no need to stop on the road, and with respect to the coachman—"

"Good-bye, my dear, I—"

"You'll be sure to write and let me know how your uncle is."

"Yes, yes."

"And with respect to the coachman—"

"I can't wait, God bless you;" and with these words I hurried off to the Towy-bridge, my wife calling after me, "Be sure you only give the coachman sixpence; some folks, I know, give a shilling; but you will go outside, of course, so sixpence will be quite enough."

And thus abruptly terminated my rustication in a Welsh village, to the great vexation of the undertaker, who had been induced, on the strength of it, to set up his one-horse chaise.

BOOK IV.

THE PATRIOT.

CHAPTER I.

A SUDDEN RESOLUTION—A MEETING WITH AN OLD ACQUAINTANCE.

" HAIL, land of my earliest and best affections! Long, too long have I been a reluctant wanderer from thy shores; but now I return, friendless indeed, but in manhood's prime, to associate thine interests with mine, to attach myself to thine injured sons, to live with them—to plead for them—to suffer for them—and, if necessary, to die for them. Oh! what are the enjoyments of wealth, rank, or intellect, compared with those which visit the pilgrim's heart, when, after many wanderings by sea and land; after many misfortunes, aggravated haply by his own indiscretions, or, what is oftener the case, by the ingratitude of others, he once more treads the green turf of his native land! Oh, never till now did I feel the full magic of that little word—country. Now, indeed, I am at home. Every face I see wears a friendly and familiar smile; every tongue is tipped with a brogue that is more than music to my ear!"

Such were my reflections as I sat alone in my lodgings in Dublin, gazing from an open window at the crowds that passed below. Soon, however, my reverie was cut short by a tremendous chorus of voices raised in every conceiv able variety of intonation. Looking up the street to see what occasioned such dissonance, I beheld, slowly advancing along the pavement, a tall, burly gentleman, followed closely by a pretty considerable sprinkling of the seven millions.

As the stranger drew near the spot over which I was stationed, I had ample leisure to scrutinise him. Apparently he was between forty and fifty years of age; cheerful and comely in face, with an eye slightly puckered up to the angles, and expressing infinite shrewdness and humour. His build was atlantean, particularly about the shoulders, which looked as though they were capable of sustaining the weight of the two fattest Protestant bishops of the most oppressed country on earth.

And who was this Patagonian peripatetic, who walked and talked as though he should say, " I am Sir Oracle, let no dog bark when I do speak!" Who but the mighty Agitator—O'Cromwell!

On what trifles do the leading events of life at times depend! The fall of an apple made Newton a philosopher! The sight of O'Cromwell confirmed me a—patriot! My wandering resolves—my undecided speculations—were called home and fixed at once. I felt the soul of Brutus stir within me. "Yes," said I, in a sudden transport of enthusiasm, " I too will devote myself, body and soul, like a Hannibal or a Plunket, on the altar of my country. I have got the best of all patriotic requisites, an empty pocket." It is astonishing what a fierce, outrageous love of country throbs in the bosom of him who has scarcely a sixpence in the world. Oh, to be as powerful as O'Cromwell! To be followed, like him, by the shouts of admiring thousands; to have the pulses of a nation beat as those of an individual, at one's slightest word and action; to be the barometer by which the funds are regulated, and the movements of troops decided; to be the bugbear of cabinets, freedom's bulwark and despotism's scourge; idolised on the banks of the St. Lawrence, execrated beside the Danube and the Neva: oh for but one day, one hour, to wield the sceptre of this mighty demagogue!

Such were the ambitious aspirations of my newly awakened patriotism. Virtuous wishes! How have they been repaid!

Next day a grand Catholic meeting was held at the Corn Exchange. I went, and lo, the Agitator! He was seated in smiling dignity at the upper end of the room, listening to a thin, sallow, acetous orator, who looked as if he had been begotten of a crab-apple on a vinegar-cruet; and who was pouring forth hot words of spleen and passion, while his every feature appeared convulsed, like the Delphic priestess under the influence of oracular inspiration.

No sooner had this atrabilarious Demosthenes resumed his seat, than silence for a few minutes ensued; and then a loud, unanimous call for O'Cromwell, which that illustrious individual was by no means slow to obey.

He commenced in dulcet accents; but when fairly launched into his theme—the enormous injuries inflicted on Erin by the sister-country—he recapitulated those injuries in a style and with a spirit that absolutely electrified his audience, whose attention he kept on the stretch for full four hours; when, the business of the day being at an end, he sailed away like some triumphant seventy-four, with a tumultuous mob in his wake; and next day six columns of his "winged words" were on their way to every nook and corner of the three kingdoms.

"Here's fame!" said I, as I slowly and thoughtfully quitted the place of meeting, "here's power! Here's all that man can desire! No wonder that the weaver quits his loom—the smith his forge—the labourer his plough—the clerk his desk—the apprentice his counter—that all professions, all trades, are at a stand-still throughout Ireland—when expert enthusiastic patriots like these ply hourly the wholesome task of agitation."

On turning down Sackville-street, on my road back to my lodgings, I heard a familiar voice pronounce my name; and looking round, beheld my old colleague Donovan, with whom, it may be recollected, I had had a little dispute in London, touching a certain libel for which he wished to make me responsible. He was now engaged as a reporter on a Dublin journal, and filled up his leisure hours by occasionally holding forth at the Corn Exchange.

To meet Donovan, and to ask him to dinner, were the acts of one and the same moment. I had long since forgiven his behaviour to me, and as he seemed equally disposed to be conciliatory, we agreed to adjourn to a neighbouring tavern and pass a social evening together.

There are few greater pleasures in life—few that more actively call forth our dormant sympathies—than sudden meetings of this sort; more especially after time, absence, and continual commerce with the world have wrought their usual blighting effects on our feelings, They are like sunny glimpses of spring bursting forth in the midst of winter; we feel that they are born and will die with the day, and relish them for their very evanescence.

In the course of the evening, when the good cheer had opened our hearts, Donovan gave me the history of that "cursed libel," which, it seems, had not only been the means of subjecting him to fine and imprisonment, but had saddled him besides with a host of legal expenses, which he was only enabled to liquidate by the sale, at a heavy loss, of his Sunday journal. "However," he added with vivacity, when he had brought his narrative to a close, "these things are all done with now; I have quitted London for ever, and am here a fixed resident in Dublin, where I have been upwards of three months. But what brings you over the water? A truant disposition, or a pressing necessity?"

"Oh, the old story, necessity," I replied. And without entering too minutely into the history of my adventures since we last parted (for I am naturally delicate in alluding to my own private affairs), I contented myself with a brief rambling sketch, and then proceeded to ask advice as to the best and readiest means of putting my new resolves into execution.

"My good fellow," answered Donovan, "your intentions are every way worthy of you; but here, in Dublin, they will be found, I fear, impracticable. The Liberal press is already overstocked."

"Then what am I to do?—where betake myself?"

"Those are questions more easily asked than answered."

"But surely your tact and experience can help me to some suggestion?"

"No indeed, I can't. All I know is, that in Dublin you have not the slightest chance. Why, even I have made no great hit as yet, whatever I may do hereafter; how then can you? But I hate comparisons: let's talk of something else."

But this was not what I wanted; so, in a few minutes, I returned to the charge by announcing my intention of offering my services to the editors of the Dublin journals: whereupon Donovan, jealous, no doubt, of such a competitor, said,—

"A good idea has just struck me. Why not try the provincial press? A county newspaper, in a Catholic district, will be the very thing for you. You will find no rivals there; and, by exerting due tact, may make yourself as popular as you please."

"But the arena is so circumscribed."

"Stuff! How can you tell till you try? But suppose it is, you can enlarge it."

"Yes; but to fall back again, after all one's efforts to emerge from it, to the condition of a village Hampden—"

"Better that than nothing."

"Oh, of course; but I am by no means sure that my case is yet so desperate. However, let us drop the subject for the present; to-morrow evening I will call and acquaint you with my decision."

We separated shortly afterwards; and the next day, without hinting a syllable of my intentions to Donovan, I made the round of the Dublin morning and evening papers, with an offer of my services; but meeting with equal discouragement at every office I visited, and seeing, moreover, that there was not a moment to be lost, I resolved on adopting Donovan's suggestion.

"I congratulate you," said he, when we met pursuant to agreement, "on your decision. In what way do you propose to proceed?"

"By advertising. I know of no other method."

"Humph! Precarious, to say the least of it. Far better to work through the agency of private connection."

"But I have no private connection, unless, indeed, you can assist me."

"Maybe I can. What say you to a trip, by way of experiment, to Ballinabrogue?"

"Why do you ask?"

"For five good reasons. First, because the district is the most decidedly Catholic in all Ireland. Secondly, because it affords a fine opening for constitutional agitation. Thirdly, because the inhabitants are wealthy. Fourthly, because an important Catholic meeting is to be held there within the month, at which you may exhibit your eloquence to advantage. And, lastly, because the editor and proprietor of the leading Ballinabrogue journal is my very particular friend. Here is a goodly show of reasons for you!"

"And equally unanswerable."

"Then you will think seriously of my proposal?"

"I accede to it at once."

"Good; and I will pave the way for you by a letter of introduction to the proprietor in question, who, as my friend, will put you in the way of acquiring a connection, which you may extend or not as you please; and, possibly, should the editorial chair be vacant, enthrone you in that seat of honour."

"My dear fellow," said I, grasping him warmly by the hand, "I am eternally your debtor."

"Just what my confounded tailor says of me, whenever I chance to meet him."

"What is the name of the gentleman to whom you are going to introduce me?"

"Flannaghan; and you'll find him as able and willing to assist you as any man that ever breathed."

"Thank God for that; for I never was in more need of a friend:" with which words we parted; and early on the following day, having received testimonials, letters of introduction, and so forth, I mounted his majesty's mail, and made the best of my way to Ballinabrogue.

Nothing of the slightest importance occurred during the journey, except that the coach was stopped on the road, the guard robbed of the mail bags, and the coachman twice shot at from behind a hedge.

CHAPTER II.

ECCE ITERUM CRISPINUS!—ONCE MORE AN EDITOR!

THE first thing I did on reaching Ballinabrogue was to ensconce myself in a suitable lodging; the second, to find out the proprietor of the county journal, by whom, as an old acquaintance of Donovan, I calculated on being favourably received.

Mr. Flannaghan, however, happened to be out when I called, engaged as witness on a trial at the quarter sessions; whereupon, leaving my credentials enclosed in an explanatory note, I placed it in the clerk's hands, with a special request that he would tell his master, the instant he came back, that the person who left the letter would, himself call for an answer in the course of the day.

In the evening, accordingly, I presented myself again at the office, and was ushered into the proprietor's private room. I found him just as Donovan had described him, a frank, jovial, good-natured Irishman—one of that class of beings with whom one is at home in an instant. Yet, though social in temperament, Mr. Flannaghan was not without strong political feelings, being a staunch Catholic and an equally staunch O'Cromwellite. I know not that I have anything further to observe of him, than that he was held in general esteem among his neighbours; moved in excellent circles (for he was a gentleman by birth as well as by feeling), and, in point of fortune, was in what may be called "easy circumstances;" and this, independently of the emoluments he derived from his journal, which, being the oldest and the most liberal, enjoyed by far the greatest circulation of any newspaper in that quarter of Ireland.

Such a connection was quite a god-send to an embryo patriot like myself, and more especially was it of value, because from the fact of his being a man of substance, and by no means a chick in age, Mr. Flannaghan had of late begun to entertain certain convivial predilections, which at times, when politics were fiercer than usual—and such was the case when I made my appearance at Ballina-brogue—rendered the conduct of his journal not a little irksome to him.

Under these circumstances, he naturally looked on me as an angel sent from heaven to his deliverance; so the question of writing, and upon what terms, was broached, even on our first interview; in the course of which I took care to let drop cursorily, and as if the details were drawn from me, a discreet sketch of the rise, progress, and termination of my connection with the London press, to which Mr. Flannaghan listened with marked attention; but taking for granted that, like a man of the world, he would believe only one-half of what I said, I was resolved that one-half should be such as to ensure me a favourable verdict.

It was not till a late hour, after an agreeable and, considering the circumstances, quite a confidential tête-à-tête, that I took leave of my hospitable host. The best part of the next day I spent in drawing up a political communication in the form of a "letter from a correspondent," with a view to keep alive public interest in favour of the approaching Catholic meeting. As this article was penned *con amore*, I am willing to suppose that it was skilfully executed ; at any rate, it answered its purpose ; for, being peppery and personal, it drew from Mr. Flannaghan the *naive* acknowledgment that he could not have done it better himself. I should think not. But I did not say so.

This communication was followed up by some five or six rampant leading articles, which I had the good fortune to find favourably noticed by the *quidnuncs* in the neighbourhood—so favourably, indeed, and so opportunely, as to induce Mr. Flannaghan, without further hesitation, to make over to me his editorial functions, to which he attached a weekly stipend, just sufficient to enable me to keep my head above water.

But this was not the only kindness I received at the hands of this estimable individual. As our acquaintance strengthened, he introduced me to many respectable Catholics, who, fascinated by my modest demeanour, by the consummate knowledge I appeared to possess of the state of parties in Ireland, and above all, by the freshness and enthusiasm which I brought to the stale question of emancipation, treated me with signal respect and courtesy.

CHAPTER III.

HOW TO TALK POLITICS.

THE day appointed for the Catholic meeting was now fast approaching. For some time previous, it had been the theme of general discussion throughout the country, arraying the two parties of Papists and Protestants against each other more violently than ever.

On the evening preceding it I paid a visit to Mr.

Flannaghan, who, since his retirement, had taken up his residence in a cottage just outside the town. As it was late when I called, I found him seated over his "nightcap," with a Protestant friend and neighbour, one Kelly,—a lean, pompous attorney, with a short body and long legs, like a pair of tongs,—whom I had seen in his company once or twice before, and who, in common with many other persons of the same persuasion, bore with Mr. Flannaghan's politics in consideration of his excellent qualities as a man. The curtains were drawn, a cheerful blaze went roaring up the chimney, a box of Havana cigars was on the table, and both gentlemen seemed imbued with a befitting sense of the comforts of their condition.

Mr. Flannaghan had evidently been just delivered of one of his smartest anecdotes; for when I entered, a dying grin still lingered on his guest's countenance.

"I can guess, O'Blarney," said the former, "what brings you here at this late hour. It is about to-morrow's meeting."

"Yes; I am anxious to know whether you will attend or not."

"That will depend on the weather. You'll speak, of course?"

"I can't avoid it, for the committee have placed in my hands one of the most important resolutions. But surely, sir, you'll say something, as well as the rest of us?"

"No, no," replied Mr. Flannaghan; "at my age men begin to sicken of public life."

"I wish to fortune, Flannaghan," said Mr. Kelly, "that all Catholics were as sensible as yourself."

"Why, I—certainly—*do*—flatter—myself," drawled out mine host, stroking his chin with an air of much self-complacency, "I do flatter myself that if I have one redeeming quality beyond another, it is just a sufficient stock of common sense to enable me to steer clear of all extremes. I detest your bigoted partisans who look only to their own side of a question."

"That's precisely my way of thinking," rejoined Mr.

Kelly, "and therefore it is that I feel such pleasure in chatting with you. Though we sometimes differ, (as who do not?) yet we always do so with temper."

"I wish I could say as much for some other friends of ours. Do you remember Hourgan last Sunday at the news-room? What an ass he made of himself about your Attorney-general Saurin! I never saw a man so violent."

"Come, come," rejoined Mr. Kelly, with a good-humoured smile; "you are too severe Flannaghan. The fellow was warm, certainly; but then, consider, he had the best of the argument."

"The worst, you mean; men in the right never lose their temper."

"Why, surely, my good fellow, you won't pretend to deny that William Saurin is a man of first-rate powers of mind? Even his bitterest enemies allow that."

"If for 'mind' you will substitute 'brass,' I will agree with you with all my heart."

"Hah! hah! I love a joke in season as well as any one, but this trifling is a little mistimed; for if there be one man distinguished beyond all his compeers by his learning, his sagacity, his boldness, his stern, straightforward integrity, Saurin is that man."

"I acknowledge him," replied Mr. Flanaghan, "to be a shrewd, bold, active—"

"Come, now, that's handsome; that's just what I should have expected from you. Ah, Flannaghan, if all Catholics thought as you do, Ireland would not be what she is now—a hot-bed of sedition."

"And if she be so, Kelly, who but your Ascendancy-men are to blame?"

"You are hasty, my dear sir; take time and digest your thoughts. Come, suppose we replenish;" and to saying, Mr. Kelly filled his glass, and handed over the ladle to mine host.

By this time the punch was beginning to *tell;* seeing which, I turned the conversation, by inquiring of Mr.

Kelly whether he had seen the king during his late stay in Dublin. But my efforts were fruitless. The demon of politics had taken full possession of both gentlemen, who, though usually shy of discussing public matters, yet seemed resolved, on this occasion, to make up for past reserves by an inordinate exhibition of candour.

My allusion, therefore, to the royal visit, so far from being productive of good, only brought matters to a speedier crisis; for Mr. Flannaghan, enlarging on the question, said, " See, Kelly, what your party have reduced Ireland to! Before the king landed on these shores, we were, comparatively speaking, tranquil. If we had no great cause for hope, neither had we any for despair. But you took care that even this negative state of things should not continue; for no sooner had his majesty made his appearance among us, than night and day you beset him, until you finally succeeded in confirming your old monopoly, while for us you procured—what? The barren honour—say, rather, the insulting mockery—of a royal letter, comprising a royal blessing, and as much bad grammar as is usually to be met with in a king's sheep. Can you wonder that we are indignant at such conduct."

" My dear Flannaghan," said Mr. Kelly, with assumed calmness, " this may be all very fine; but, to say the truth, I prefer your punch to your principles. However, every man has a right to his own opinion."

" Bravo! I see we shall make a convert of you at last."

" Never, Mr. Flannaghan; never, sir. If I thought that—"

" My good fellow, don't think at all. Of what use is reflection, if it tends only to confirm prejudice?"

" No man can entertain a greater horror of prejudice than myself, as I think I have sufficiently proved by saying nothing against your frantic meeting of to-morrow."

" Frantic meeting! Rely on it, Kelly, no public

meeting at which O'Cromwell's spirit presides can be otherwise than rational."

Up to this period the attorney had kept his feelings under tolerable restraint, but the name "O'Cromwell" now caused them to boil over.

"O'Cromwell!" said he, with vehemence, "pray don't mention that man's name again. Nothing but the respect I bear you, can make me sit still while he is made the subject of praise. He has done more injury to Ireland than all the Rapparees or Rockites that ever robbed—burned—or cut a throat."

"Fine words, Mr. Kelly; nevertheless I think you will be puzzled to prove them. Did you read O'Cromwell's last—"

"O'Cromwell again!"

"Yes; and why not? Once—twice—thrice—or a dozen times if I choose it! I say, Mr. Kelly—I say, sir, did you read his last speech at the Corn Exchange?"

"Not I, indeed."

"Why, surely you are not apprehensive of being too speedily convinced?"

"This is poor trifling, Mr. Flannaghan; but since you talk of reading, I wish I could persuade you to read Saurin's Address to the Protestants of Londonderry; it would help you to a much sounder vein of thinking than you at present possess."

"What! I read Saurin! I thank God I never yet perused a line of the bigot's nonsense."

"Don't abuse a better man than yourself."

"Better, Mr. Kelly!"

"Yes, better, Mr. Flannaghan. I speak plain English, don't I? How would you have me speak? Like O'Cromwell?"

"Egad, it will be news to me indeed, when I hear, that you speak like him."

"Sir," retorted the attorney, fiercely, "give me leave to tell you, that you are, without exception, the—"

I here attempted a second time to interfere. "For

Heaven's sake, gentlemen, cease these personalities! They're unworthy of friends, who, in their cooler moments mutually respect each other."

"Respect!" thundered Mr. Kelly, "what respect can I have for one who has the assurance to condemn a man of whose writings he confesses to know nothing."

"That is to say, I know as much about Saurin as you know about O'Cromwell."

"Granted; but, pray consider the difference—"

"Consider! I'll consider nothing."

"Oh, very well; I see there's no contending with ignorance and bigotry."

"This to me, in my own house!" exclaimed mine host, starting up, and thrusting his chair behind him; "there's the door, sir!"

Mr. Kelly rose at the same moment, and with equal heat, while I, by endeavouring to appease him, only drew down his wrath on myself.

"What business is it of yours?" he said; "who asked you for your opinion, sir?" then, before I could reply, he continued, " as for you, Mr. Flannaghan, from this time forward, I shall take care that we never exchange another syllable together;" and he rushed from the house, banging the street door after him like a whirlwind.

No sooner was he gone, than "I'm astonished, O'Blarney," said Mr. Flannaghan, "at the strange—the absurd—the unaccountable prejudices which *some* fools entertain."

"True; but *we*, who are above such prejudices, should learn to make allowances for them in others."

"Just so. I see you read my character to a T Throughout life, it has always been my grand aim to keep my mind clear of prejudice of any sort, which, no doubt, has contributed to give me that advantage in argument of which you have just now seen a proof. Poor Kelly! Upon my soul, I can't help pitying him, notwithstanding his insolence. Did you observe how foolish he looked when I asked him if he had read O'Cromwell's last speech?

Egad, I pressed him home there. He had not a word to say for himself—the hot, spluttering potato!"

I did not tell Mr. Flannaghan that he was in precisely the same predicament as regarded Saurin's address; but contented myself with passing a variety of delicate encomiums on his singular candour and magnanimity, which I could see gave me a wonderful lift in his good opinion.

Omnipotent Flattery! Let them say what they will of their Alexanders, and Cæsars, and Napoleons, but thou art the only true conqueror.

CHAPTER IV.

A CATHOLIC MEETING, AND ITS CONSEQUENCES.

THE important day at length arrived, and all was excitement in Ballinabrogue and throughout the neighbourhood, for the meeting was the first provincial one of consequence that had taken place since his majesty's departure. I spare my readers any detailed account of it; enough to state, that it was attended by full fifty thousand individuals, scarcely one of whom but was convinced, before he quitted the hustings, that he was the most miserable wretch that ever crawled on the surface of the earth.

I have said that I shall be brief in my details of this great meeting. But this brevity I do not intend to apply to my own speech, which deserves a somewhat minute analysis, if only for the consummate ability which all allowed that it displayed.

People talk of the modesty of the young maiden when she first reveals the secret of her heart to the man she loves; but commend me to the modesty of the young Irish patriot when he makes his first oratorical appeal to his countrymen. With what a shrinking, bashful air he

15

stands before them! In what meek, faltering, reluctant accents he addresses them! There is no swagger—no outrageous gesticulation—no Boabdilism or buffoonery about him. He is humbled—overpowered by a sense of his own unworthiness; and to more than woman's grace adds more than woman's timidity. And then his brogue! What syren sweetness in its melody, calculated to electrify Almack's! And then his language! How full of unsophisticated beauties, borrowed neither from Demosthenes nor Cicero! Did you mark that brilliant metaphor, proudly disdainful of sense, and scorning the ignoble trammels of syntax? Again: Jupiter! what a flight was there! Our young orator has just perched an eagle on the chimney-tops of Derrinane, and peopled an English cabinet with crocodiles.

Thus I spoke—looked—blushed—and gesticulated, on this my first occasion of holding forth in public. I commenced with a graceful apology for my intrusion on the time and patience of the meeting; but observed, that when I bethought me of the wrongs of unhappy Erin, which the stranger and the Saxon polluted with their vile hoof, my sensibilities would not be repressed. I then alluded to the atrocious system of corruption by which the ascendancy faction strove to perpetuate its power. I insisted that while there was freedom for all else in Ireland—while the breeze blew free over the mountain, the stream wandered free through the valley, the cattle pastured free on the moor (except when they happened to be *pounded* for tithe), while even the humblest Orangeman exercised the rights and privileges of a freeman—the Catholic alone, the legitimate inheritor of the soil, grovelled, prostrate in the dust, bedaubed from head to foot with the mud flung off from the whirling chariot-wheels of Protestantism, as it traversed Erin, like a pestilence, from sea to sea. Quitting this part of my theme, I reverted, with characteristic modesty, to my own sufferings in the cause of freedom, which I stated had been severe, protracted, indeed, almost without parallel; and concluded amidst a tempest of acclamation that shook all the bogs about Ballinabrogue.

This able philippic, being fully reported in my own journal, soon found its way to the Dublin Press, by which it was praised or blamed, as it squared with the politics of those who took it up. The Catholic papers applauded it to the skies; the Protestant ones denounced it with equal energy. By the former I was dubbed a patriot; by the latter a shoot from the stock of Antichrist.

Such lavish praise and abuse re-acted, of course, on Ballinabrogue; and, joined with my own personal activity, the zealous patronage of Mr. Flannaghan, and, above all, with the apt, combustible diatribes which I thundered forth unceasingly in my journal, had the effect of raising me into considerable notoriety.

Even the haughty Protestants now thought me worthy of their special animosity; and well indeed they might, for such was the effect that my hebdomadal apostrophes to freedom had upon the Catholic peasantry, that Mr. Kelly was honoured by a shower of Papist brick-bats at midday, in the streets of Ballinabrogue; and a Protestant magistrate, whose conduct on some particular occasion I found it expedient to call in question, was tied to a tree, and soundly flogged by two enormous Terry Alts.

As a still further proof of my popularity, I may mention, that on the day following the meeting, when I happened to drop in accidentally at the theatre, I was recognised by the gallery, and honoured with nine distinct rounds of applause. Another recognition, also, took place on this occasion, which, trivial as it appeared at the time, was yet fraught with the most disastrous effect on my after-fortunes. The play chanced to be Hamlet, and who should come forward as the representative of the moody Dane but my old Galway friend—that friend who was the means of introducing me to the stage at Molly-moreen, and assisting me in my first matrimonial speculation!

As I was seated in a box right over the orchestra,

there could be no mistaking the man's identity. He was something changed by time, which had ploughed two deep ruts down either side of his face; something more by tipple, which had coppered his nose, and encircled his eyes with a red watery rim; still there was the same reckless assumption of manner about him, which had so impressed my unsophisticated fancy in the little wayside public-house.

While I sat pondering, half in sadness, half in pride, on the strange fatality that had thus brought us again together, under circumstances of so opposite a nature, he happened to look up, when I could see, by his sudden, electrical start, that the recognition had been mutual. I took no further notice of him at the time, but early the next day called at the theatre, with a view of finding out his address, when I learned, to my regret, that having been engaged only three nights, he had quitted Ballina-brogue by daylight, but where he was gone the manager could not inform me. Fatal miss! But I will not anticipate.

When I look back on this period of provincial excitement, I reflect with pride on the share I had in promoting it. Yes, I it was who mainly contributed to raise the thunder storm which was to clear the labouring atmosphere; and who put the peasantry through a wholesome, stirring course of arson, burglary, and abduction, in order that they might thereby qualify themselves for the great part they were afterwards destined to play as freemen.

True it is, that some "boys" were transported, and others hanged, for these lively outbreaks of public virtue; still this was in strict accordance with the "fitness of things," which from time immemorial has prescribed that the interests of the few should succumb to those of the many. It is true also, that while exhorting others to wrestle for their liberty, I myself made a point of keeping out of harm's way; but God knows this was from no pusillanimous motive, but simply because it is the duty of a good patriot, like that of a good general, not to act himself, but to teach others how to act.

Meantime weeks rolled on, and the millennium of freedom seemed hourly drawing near. Its spirit blazed up from every farm-house—its voice spoke in every bullet that whistled past a tithe-proctor. The agitation became at length so general, that it was no uncommon thing for an Orangeman, in accepting a neighbour's invitation to dinner, to insert a P.S. in his note, to the effect that he would come, " provided he was not shot by the way." It was evident from all this that the peasantry were ripe for independence, and that nothing was wanting but the presence of a few Dublin *pacificators* to bid them rise *en masse* in arms.

But as no substance is without its shadow, so no good but has its alloy. It is to be lamented that the peasantry were at times more indiscriminate in the exercise of their energies than they should have been. Not unfrequently it happened, that, in the hurry and confusion of business, they would shoot the wrong man, and set fire to the wrong house. One instance of such unpardonable blundering I will here specify :—Mr. Flannaghan's cottage was situated next to a tithe-proctor's, who had contrived to render himself odious by his indecent legal officiousness. Late one night, when I was passing by my worthy friend's house, I was astonished to find it in flames, and a vast mob hemming it on all sides, so as to cut off from the inmates every chance of escape.

" Halloo, boys ! " said I, rushing into the midst of them, " do you know whose house you're burning ? "

" Arrah, sure now, it's the tithe-proctor's," said the man who stood next me.

" Tithe-proctor's ! It's your friend Mr. Flannaghan's, the best friend you ever had."

" Oh, murder ! " replied the fellow, wringing his hands ; " what'll we do now ? "

" Aisy, Pat," said his neighbour, who was evidently a

philosopher of the Justinian Stubbs school; "sure one house is jist as good as another."

Just at this moment Mr. Flannaghan rushed out of the house, with the tail of his shirt streaming like a fiery comet to the wind. No sooner was he recognised than the penitent mob overwhelmed him with apologies, caught him up in their arms, and, in spite of his shouts, protestations, and even menaces, passed him twice through his own fish-pond, in order that one element might neutralise the injuries inflicted by another.

But this was not the only whimsical incident that diversified this period of agitation. The tithe-hunts were equally ridiculous. From the very first moment of my connection with the press at Ballinabrogue, I had advocated the abolition of these imposts; for I could not but see that pay-day, which, under any circumstances, is the day least respected in the Irish calendar, is, as regards tithes, held in absolute detestation. Frequent, therefore, and furious were my philippics on this subject; and so well did they accord with the temper of those to whom I addressed myself, that not individuals merely, but whole parishes began to be numbered among the defaulters.

Under these circumstances it became necessary to have recourse to the military; who, however, were no sooner drawn out in marching order, than intelligence of their movements would be circulated far and wide by sentinels duly posted for that purpose at every convenient point; so that by the time the troops reached the offending district, the devil a cow, horse, ass, pig, scarcely even an article of furniture, was to be found in it; all were carried off to the neighbouring bogs, whither, if the soldiers followed, they were pretty sure to get ingulfed and disappear—like ghosts through a theatrical trap-door —amid the shouts and caperings of the "boys," and the encouraging melody of a dozen pipes and fiddles. Your Irish bog is no respecter of persons. Major, captain, cornet, corporal—no matter; his " great revenge hath stomach for them all." I have known him to swallow even a K.C.B!

CHAPTER V.

THE MAN OF FEELING—BUT NOT MACKENZIE'S.

WHILE Mr. Flannaghan's cottage was being rebuilt, the ex-editor took up his abode at the house of a Catholic relation, by name Mahon; a quiet, amiable, single-minded recluse, who lived about three miles from Ballinabrogue, at the head of a narrow glen, well known as one of the most romantic spots in the county. To this gentleman Mr. Flannaghan made a point of introducing me; and, backed by his recommendation, to say nothing of my own deserts, I experienced a flattering reception.

Mr. Mahon was a widower in easy circumstances, with one only child, to whom he was devotedly attached. With this young lady, whose lightest word was law at Bellevue (the name of her father's residence), I of course did my best to ingratiate myself, in which I so far succeeded that my visits were generally looked forward to with satisfaction; for Mr. Mahon, whose mind the untimely death of his wife had touched, but not soured, with gloom, had been for some time gradually withdrawing himself from society; and all the world knows how cheering, under such circumstances, is the casual dropping in of a sprightly accommodating visitor, who has all the gossip of the neighbourhood at his fingers' ends, and is ever ready to be merry or grave, silent or talkative, as suits his host's humour.

The departure of Mr. Flannaghan, which took place the instant his own cottage was again ready for his reception, did not at all diminish my influence at Bellevue; indeed, it served rather to strengthen it, for it made the inmates—especially Ellen, with whom solitude had not yet become a source of enjoyment—more dependent on me for the resources of an agreeable companionship. Accordingly, an intimacy soon sprung up between us, which at length increased to such a height, that whenever my official duties were closed for the week, I invariably hastened over to the enchanting solitude of Bellevue.

The spot was indeed a paradise, and Ellen was its Eve. This young creature, just emerging from girlhood, was exquisitely beautiful in face and figure ; full of gentle life as a summer wind ; of a fond confiding disposition ; artless and playful as a lamb—a being, in fact, wholly made up of sensibility. Oh, how different were her good sense and simplicity from the inordinate vanity of my first wife, or the stern cold avarice of my second ! Neither of these had ever engaged my affections ; the connection on both sides originated solely in interested motives ; but Ellen was all disinterestedness. She loved me for myself alone. And no wonder, for I am a handsome fellow, and I care not who knows it.

Miss Mahon and I were much together, yet, strange to tell, notwithstanding such favourable opportunities, I could not bring myself to turn them to account. Passion and principle kept perpetually clutching at my heartstrings ; while, to aggravate my sufferings, in stepped modesty, bepainting my cheek with blushes, whenever any thing like an avowal of love rose to my lips.

Between these conflicting interests, I had for some weeks a precious time of it, till one night, as I lay twisting and turning on a pillow which seemed stuffed with thorns, a bright idea struck me :—" Eureka ! " said I, starting up, " I have found it. I will enter into a compromise with my conscience, by avoiding extremes, and pursuing the mean path of discretion and safety."

When once I had resolved on this virtuous line of conduct, it is astonishing how complete was my tranquillity. There is nothing like a good conscience to set a man at ease with himself and others.

Meantime, scarce a day elapsed but I found some excuse or other for making my appearance at Bellevue. I had always a new book to lend or to borrow, a new political topic to discuss with Mr. Mahon, or a new speech of O'Cromwell to read over to him, and to eulogise. On these occasions, a bed was always at my service, and after dinner, when papa dropped asleep in his arm-chair, Ellen and I would indulge in a commonplace *tête-à-tête*, or a more expressive silence; for, as my conscience would not allow me to betray myself by my tongue, I had nothing left for it but to discourse with my eyes.

Sometimes, when the weather permitted, we would take a stroll together along the glen, or round by some romantic rocks; and there, while pausing to rest herself on the projecting fragment of a crag, twilight dropping like a silver veil round us, Ellen would open her budget of legendary gossip, and affect a charming displeasure when she found that I was not so full of faith as herself. In the evening the music-room was our usual place of resort, for Ellen's harp was always at hand, and there was a certain something in the act of singing and listening that accorded wondrously well with the inclinations of both parties.

Fathers and mothers, ye whose pretty daughters may happen also to be Philomels, bear this in mind—*wherever there is a Philomel, there will be a Tereus!* Look sharp, then, after the youth who stands close behind your child, drinking in the intoxicating spirit of her melody. Watch his every glance, sit in judgment on his every respiration. Take care that his eye rests not too fondly on the alabaster bosom that heaves and swells like a soft summer sea beneath him; that in stooping to turn over the music-leaves—oh, dangerous position, that might thaw the icy virtue of an anchorite!—his sighs disturb not the ringlets of the blushing girl whose face is half-turned towards him, and (for such sighs possess a strange power of transmigration) pass into her own heart, and amalgamate with her own being;—fathers and mothers, take heed, I beseech you, to these things, or peradventure some fine morning you may find that your Philomel has flown from the parental nest, to chirp in one constructed for her by Tereus.

When the summons to tea hurried us from the music-room, Mr. Mahon, invigorated by his brief snatch of sleep, would join us, and then politics would usurp the place of sentiment; and the night would be wound up by a game at chess, or backgammon, in both of which mine host delighted, the more so, as I invariably made a point of being beaten, with a flattering show of reluctance; or should Mr. Flannaghan, which he frequently did, drop in, we would engage in a sober rubber at whist, till it was time to retire to bed.

I have made the above confession of sentiment at the hazard of looking, like Falstaff, an "exceeding ass," for whose ears are so long as those of a lover? But no matter. I glory in my weakness. Besides, I have lots of precedents to keep me in countenance. We may be singular in our wisdom, but there is no fear of our standing alone in our folly. Even the philosophic Gibbon bent the knee to love; why then should I hesitate to plead guilty to the delicate indictment.

In this delicious state of intoxication, then passed the only happy fortnight I have ever known—a fortnight of such full, rare sunshine, that it brought all my dormant virtues into blossom. But, alas! the halcyon season was not destined to endure. My sun had attained its meridian, and was already journeying westward.

CHAPTER VI.

DISCRETION *versus* PATRIOTISM.

" WELL, O'Blarney," said Mr. Flannaghan, calling unexpectedly one morning at my lodgings, while I was busy making additions to my private journal, "any news to day? What say the Dublin papers?"

"Nothing of moment, except indeed that the Protestants in the north are beginning to get a little uneasy at our late 'insurrectionary movements,' as the Mail styles them."

"And the Catholics too, if I may judge of others by myself."

"Ay, indeed!" said I, staring at him with astonishment, "how is this?"

"Oh, I merely mean to say," replied Mr. Flannaghan, "that I have always entertained a dislike to extremes, which recent circumstances have not a little contributed to strengthen. I have no objection to our struggling for our rights in a constitutional manner, but really, when one comes to have one's house burned over one's head, the thing becomes too serious and personal to be tolerated."

"Yet, in struggles of this nature, occasional irregularities on the part of the peasantry must be looked for."

"True, but why is my house to be burned down?"

This was logic to which there was no reply; so I contented myself with saying, "We must make allowances for slaves madly contending to recover their freedom."

"Very fine, no doubt," replied Mr. Flannaghan, impatiently, "but why the devil am I, of all men in the world, to be sacrificed to this same freedom? Why am I to be ducked in a fish-pond, and without my own consent? The truth is, O'Blarney, I don't half like these inflammatory articles of yours. Depend on it they will bring us into serious trouble with the government. There's that mischief-making Kelly is already talking about the necessity of proclaiming the district."

"Why, you have cooled down of late, Mr. Flannaghan," said I, with an arch smile.

"When you have been passed twice at night through a fish-pond, you will cool down too. But jesting apart, I have no longer a taste for patriotic martyrdom. With a man at my time of life, such distinction loses all its relish. Besides, Kelly, who is not without influence here, is so enraged with me on account of that foolish quarrel the other night—"

"Depend on it, Mr. Flannaghan," said I, "Kelly's quarrel is with me, not you. It is here the shoe pinches. I am a sort of provincial O'Cromwell in his estimation, and you remember the scorn and loathing with which he spoke of that illustrious patriot?"

"To be sure, he was the main cause of our dispute."

"Well, then, if Kelly still cherishes anger towards you, it is solely because you were the means of making me known here. I am the more convinced of this, because he has already been heard publicly to declare, that he will not rest till has reduced me to what he calls my level."

"Well, no matter; so long as you keep within the limits of discretion, you may set him, or a thousand such, at defiance. I do not ask you to cry peccavi; but simply to take care that you do not get my house burned down a second time. It is extremely embarrassing, and induces painful reflections, to awake and find one's bed-curtains in a state of conflagration. But I am forgetting the object of my visit, which was to ask you, as I suppose you have pretty well finished your labour for the week, to accompany me over to Bellevue. I have been promising the Mahons a visit for some days past."

"Nothing will give me greater pleasure," I replied.

"Then let us be off at once; we have no time to spare, for the weather at this season of the year is not to be depended on from one moment to another;" and with these words he hurried me from the room, with such extreme impatience, that in the haste and confusion of the moment I left my MS. journal open in my desk at the table.

When we reached Bellevue, we found Mr. Mahon hard at work in his garden, and Ellen with her bonnet on, just preparing to go out. Of course I did not hesitate an instant to which of the party I should devote my attention; so, leaving the two gentlemen together, I offered my services as an escort to Miss Mahon, which she readily accepted, and we wandered away for two or three hours, occasionally halting to rest at some of the cottages of Mr. Mahon's tenants.

In the course of the evening Mr. Flannaghan and his host sat down to their wonted game of backgammon; while Ellen and myself flew off to the piano, where we busied ourselves in turning over a new number of the Irish Melodies.

Among the airs, "Has Sorrow thy young Days shaded?" particularly caught my fancy; whereupon Ellen sung it for me with a sweetness and simplicity that I have never heard surpassed—rarely equalled. Her voice was scarcely more than a gentle flute-like breathing; but there was such a clearness, such a rich mellowness in its tones, that it was impossible to resist their magic. Oh Music!—but I resist the temptation of a commonplace.

When she had finished singing, "Miss Mahon," said I, "you are fast spoiling me for my duties as an Irishman, by bidding me lose all sense of public injury in that of private happiness. Indeed, indeed, you have much to answer for."

"Oh," she replied, laughingly, "if you are to be diverted from your path by every will-o'-the-wisp that may happen to flit across it, there is little left in you for me to spoil. But, tell me, what do you think of this last ballad of Moore's? Is it equal to his 'Love's Young Dream?'"

"Certainly not; though tender and plaintive, it is too monotonous. I am loath to speak against Moore; yet you must allow, Miss Mahon, that, as a national poet, he has defects, and great ones too?"

"Indeed; but I will allow no such thing."

"So I should have thought; yet his lyrics, however much they may soften and captivate, seldom stir the soul to action like those of Burns. The majority are made to be sung at a lady's piano, in white kid gloves; but who would think of singing 'Scots wha hae' in such dandy trim?"

"Now don't say a word more against Moore. It's high treason here, I can assure you."

"Happy poet, to call forth such praises, and from such lips!"

"What is all this you are talking about?" said Mr. Flannaghan, rising up from the game which he had just finished, and advancing towards us.

"Oh, nothing of consequence, sir," replied Ellen; "we were merely chatting about Moore."

"So I could have sworn. Whenever two or three young folks are clustered together about a piano, Moore is always sure to be the theme of their discourse. But a word with you, Ellen. You would scarcely credit the difficulty I had in persuading this refractory fellow to accompany me here. He kept me in his room, Heaven knows how long, while he conned over a pack of trumpery manuscripts, just as if he were some old bachelor busied with his week's accounts. You must take him in hand, and teach him better manners."

"He is incorrigible, I fear," retorted Ellen; "I have given him up ever since I heard him speak irreverently of our Irish melodies."

"Can five minutes, then, have sufficed to sink me so low in your estimation, Miss Mahon? Oh, that I were but ten minutes younger!"

"Five minutes, man!" said Mr. Flannaghan; "why, that is a century, when spent in pulling down a lady's idol before her face. But come, we must be going, O'Blarney; it's later than I supposed;" and accordingly we took leave of our hosts, and returned together to Ballina-brogue.

When I reached my lodgings, the first thing I learned from the servant who sat up to let me in was, that a lady had called who refused to give her name; but, mentioning that she was an old acquaintance, had requested to be shown up-stairs, where she remained full half an hour, till finding that I did not return, she departed, leaving word that she would take an early opportunity of repeating her visit.

Concluding, from the servant's description of the strange female, that she was Mr. Flannagan's maiden sister, who now and then did me the honour of a visit, but whom my informant had not yet seen, I took no further notice of the circumstance, but hurried to bed, to dream of Ellen and Bellevue.

CHAPTER VII.

AN EVENING WALK.—AN UNEXPECTED SHOCK.

ONE fine evening, after an early dinner, Mr. Mahon, who chanced to be in better spirits than usual, accompanied Ellen and myself in one of our favourite strolls. Our road, selected by him, lay through a narrow rocky pass, which opened, at the distance of about a quarter of a mile, upon a tolerably expansive valley, which was closed in on every side by ranges of sloping hills, except in the direction of Ballinabrogue, where the landscape gradually rose into downs, or rather, wide, uncultivated moors, and sunk again into level land, just at the outskirts of the town.

The pass was one that would have done credit even to the Highlands. It was narrow, deep sunk, and walled in on both sides by a rampart of rocks, piled confusedly one upon the other. Half-way up, and just at that spot where the pass opened on the valley, the rocks projected so far, that they nearly formed an arch over the road, which, with the lichens and wild shrubs that clung thickly about them, partially excluded day-light; so that when one looked through this natural tunnel, as it were, into the open valley beyond, the effect was singularly picturesque, from the bold contrasts of light and shade that at one and the same moment flashed upon the eye.

When we reached this romantic spot, which was rendered still more impressive by the fitful shadows of evening, Mr. Mahon halted, and turning round to me (for I was close behind him, with Ellen leaning on my arm), said, " I never pass this place but my heart does homage to the *genius loci*, by the seriousness, amounting almost to melancholy, that creeps over me.   Ellen, however, will tell you that it is a dull, unsocial spot, fit only to inspire abhorrence."

" And indeed so it is, papa," replied the lively girl ; " I always feel as if a load were off my mind when I have passed it.   What a gloom these frowning rocks fling down upon us !   No bird ever sings here, for the poor thing would be startled at the sound of its own voice.   Pray let us hasten on to the valley.   I can breathe freely there, but this horrid place quite stifles me."

" Had Orpheus been a native of Ireland," I observed, " I should at once have accounted for the odd configuration of these rocks, by supposing that they had been suddenly petrified while dancing a jig to the music of his lyre. Look, for instance, at that overhanging granite giant above us.   One might almost swear he had been transfixed while in the act of bowing to his partner over the way. But listen, Miss Ellen, your old friend the night-owl is beginning his song again."

" My friend !   No, no, he is too dismal a songster for me.   Owls are fit only to be listened to by grave philosophers, or crabbed politicians, or gentlemen who have no ear for the melody of Moore's verses.   Now, don't look so cross ; you know it is quite impossible I can mean you."

" Cross !" said I, in a whisper : " oh ! Miss Mahon, if you knew what was passing in my mind at this moment !"

" Something very dreadful, I make no doubt, if I may judge from your terribly wise countenance ; so I am glad papa has not heard you, for he is but too apt to sympathise with the forlorn.   Poor man, how I pity you ! What can we do for you ?"

Mr. Mahon just caught these last words, and, misapprehending their import, said, " What, are you indisposed, O'Blarney ?"

"Oh no," I replied, laughing, "but Miss Mahon has been renewing her attack on me for my late unfortunate criticism on Moore. I saw you were absorbed in reverie, or I should have summoned you to my aid. But we loiter; let us hasten on to the valley, for, see, the sun's disk is just dipping behind the hills yonder, and your daughter seems anxious to escape from this comfortless glen."

Thus chatting, we mended our pace, and soon reached the extremity of the pass, which brought us out again beneath the red, unobstructed light of day. After about half an hour's stroll, during which Ellen had diligently insisted on my admiring the various beauties of the valley from I know not how many points of view, had told me every legend connected with it, and lured me on to the exact spot where the last assembly of "good people" had been seen, and put to flight by a belated peasant; Mr. Mahon proposed a return home, for the sun was just touching the horizon's edge, and a brisk wind springing up, hurried before it such heavy masses of clouds as betokened an inclement night.

Accordingly, I drew Ellen's arm closer within mine, while her father preceded us by a few yards; and, led on by the enchanting frankness and familiarity of her manner, which had been gradually assuming a more flattering character towards me—forgetting, also, in the impulse of the moment, all my virtuous resolves—I seized the favourable opportunity, at once avowed my love, and— but why dwell on the painful topic? Suffice it to say, that the trembling arm of the gentle listener—the half-averted face, and low, deprecating voice, struggling to conceal what the heart too strongly felt, convinced me that I had not pleaded in vain.

Oh, moment of irrepressible ecstacy! Am I awake? Is Ellen really mine? Down—down, thou busy, bewildering fancy, that lurest me on to hope, even while despair is tightening her folds round me.

No sooner had my declaration escaped me, and Ellen

16

murmured some indistinct words of reply, than, as if suddenly awakened to the embarrassment of her position, she insisted on my joining her father. Accordingly, we made the best of our way back towards the pass, where Mr. Mahon stood waiting for us, when, just as we had reached its dark rocky portal, we were startled by the sound of footsteps, and at the same instant a female figure, of most forbidding aspect, started up right before our path.

I know not why it was, but my spirits sunk as I beheld this intruder, who, fixing her eyes full on me, as if she would have blasted me with their lightning glance, disclosed the countenance of my first wife, Catharine—that wife whom I had quarrelled with, and quitted, at Naples!

CHAPTER VIII.

A MATRIMONIAL EXPLANATION.

FROM the expression of my wife's countenance, I saw at once that I was recognised; nothing, therefore, I felt persuaded, was to be done, but to make up my mind for a scene; so, summoning my utmost presence of mind, I addressed myself to Mr. Mahon:—"I think we had better hasten on, the sky looks threatening, and if we stay loitering here, we may be caught in a storm."

"You are right; but stay, let us hear what this stranger has got to say for herself. She appears to eye you steadfastly, and not with the most amiable expression."

"Oh! yes, she is a poor maniac," I replied, catching at the first wild random idea that crossed my brain, as a drowning man catches at a straw, "whom I have met occasionally in my walks from Ballinabrogue to Bellevue, and who, because I have relieved her once or twice, and thereby established a sort of claim on her attention; imagines, unhappy creature! that we are bound together *vinculo matrimonii*, as the lawyers call it. Would you believe it, sir!" I added, in the same under-tone, " she has actually got a strange whim into her head that I am her husband! Very ridiculous, isn't it? Nevertheless, I should not wonder if she were to occasion me some annoyance. These mad folks are often exceedingly tenacious of what they conceive to be their rights."

" Nonsense, you are too sensitive ; but let us be going."

But my wife, who had hitherto stood at a slight distance, with all her jealous feelings roused into action by the sight of Ellen's youthful countenance and figure, was resolved I should not escape exposure; so, planting herself right before Mr. Mahon, she exclaimed, " But one word, sir—but one word, as you value your own character and peace of mind."

" Poor thing!" said Mr. Mahon, waving her from the path, and at the same time preparing to move on.

" I do not ask your pity, sir," she replied, scornfully, " I ask only your justice. Hear me, Mr. Mahon; not one inch will I stir from this spot until I have exposed the real character of that man who stands beside you."

" Catharine," said I, letting go Ellen's arm, and advancing close up to my wife, " if you have been wronged, rely on it *I* will see you righted," laying all due stress on " I."

" Righted! yes, when disgrace and ruin—"

" Hush! Catharine, not so loud. Why should we expose our domestic differences to strangers? Forgive but the past, and anything—every thing you may demand, I will at once agree to. Come, let us be friends. Has Juliet so soon forgotten Romeo?"

" Friends!" she replied, with a loud voice and flashing eye, " yes, when ruin stares you in the face, then from very apprehension you will do me justice. But mark me, sir! I seek far other justice than you can afford to bestow. Mr. Mahon," she added, turning to that gentleman, whose suspicions began to be roused by the low tones in which this brief colloquy had been carried on, " that man whom you have so prematurely called your friend, was—nay, is still, my husband !"

Ellen here earnestly besought her father to proceed, which drew down on her a cutting reproach from my wife ; till, finding that Mr. Mahon seemed disposed to lend a favourable ear to whatever explanation she might have to offer, she somewhat softened her tone, and proceeded to detail the history of her first acquaintance with me—with which the reader is already conversant—of our subsequent marriage and departure for the Continent; of the frequent altercations that had taken place between us at Naples—in every one of which I, of course, was represented as the sole party in fault; of my abandonment of her, and her own consequent return to Mollymoreen, where she found Mr. O'Brien at the last gasp ; and of the solemn vow she had made to apply what sums remained to her from the wreck of his fortune in exploring every quarter of Ireland, for the purpose of discovering and denouncing me.

Bearing in mind (she went on to state) the profession to which I originally belonged, and thinking it far from unlikely that necessity might have compelled me to resume it, she made a point, at every town she visited, of first directing her attention to the theatre. But all her inquiries were fruitless; not a single manager, of the number to whom she applied, could give her the slightest information of my " whereabouts."

Vexed at her ill luck, she returned to Mollymoreen, where she lived for some time secluded, a prey to chagrin; when one day, as she was passing by the theatre, she suddenly encountered an individual, whose features, she imagined, were not altogether unknown to her. The stranger seemed equally surprised at so unexpected a rencounter, and addressing her by the name of Fitzgerald, made himself known to her as the actor who had been the main instrument in forwarding her marriage with me,

This led to further inquiries, when the fellow — of course unacquainted with all the circumstances of our subsequent estrangement—frankly informed her that he had seen her husband, but a short time before, in one of the boxes of the theatre at Ballinabrogue!

The start I gave at this part of my wife's explanation was too visible to escape so attentive an observer as Mr. Mahon: he, however, took no notice of it, but encouraged my wife to continue her narrative, which she did in the following terms, breaking out occasionally into such fits of rage and jealousy, when she mentioned my name and the circumstances of my second marriage, that I thought she would be suffocated:—

"From this moment," said she, "I felt inspired with new life; the certainty that I had at length revenge within my grasp gave me the first sensation of joy that I had known since I quitted Naples; and, hurrying without an hour's delay to Ballinabrogue, I laid my whole case before a magistrate, by name Kelly, with whom, I believe, you have some slight acquaintance—"

"Kelly!" said I, unable longer to control my agitation.

"Yes, Kelly," resumed my wife; "and at his express instigation—for though at first incredulous, yet he soon became convinced of my sincerity—I took the opportunity of this wretch's absence to call a few days since at his lodgings, and there make such inquiries as I thought might tend to substantiate my case; nay, even to possess myself of certain documents, which proved, not only that he was my husband, but the husband also of another woman in South Wales;" and, as she mentioned the word "woman," she darted a glance at me, symptomatic of an immediate assault and battery.

"So, then, you have dared to rob me!" said I, crimson with suppressed rage. "Where are those papers?"

"They are safe, monster! and you know it; not one has been carried away. I have merely availed myself of their contents."

By this time I could not but see that all was over.

My wife, it was clear, had perused my journal, which it was my usual practice to keep fast under lock and key, but which on that disastrous morning, in my hurry to accompany Mr. Flannaghan to Bellevue, I had indeed left open in my desk.

Catharine watched the changes in my countenance with an expression of malignant satisfaction.

"Mark me, sir," she went on to say, "your hour is come! What! you discredit what I say? 'Tis well; but hear me out. A letter has been despatched to South Wales; ay, and an answer returned too, which proves your guilt beyond all question. Moreover," she added—waving her hand to some figures, who now, for the first time, I perceived had been watching all our movements in the distance—"here come those who will conduct you back to Ballinabrogue, as such a wretch deserves to be conducted."

It was but too true. To the astonishment of Mr. Mahon, his daughter's affright, and my extreme disgust, three policemen, who must have been purposely concealed in the neighbourhood, no sooner saw the concerted signal, than, before I had time to arrange my thoughts, they rushed up and secured me without opposition. What a situation for a patriot!

My wife had by this time quitted the scene; so, taking advantage of her absence, I resolved to venture on one final appeal to Mr. Mahon. But that gentleman was far too indignant to hear a word; and, drawing his daughter's arm, who was nearly fainting, poor girl, hastily through his, left me to the custody of the policemen; who, on our road back to Ballinabrogue, informed me, at my particular request, of all the circumstances attending my detection, which fully bore out my wife's statements. They further acquainted me with what they had heard relative to the substance of Mrs. Fitzmaurice's letter; who, it seemed, expressed no unwillingness to bear evidence against me, provided she could be assured of reimbursement for travelling expenses, &c.

As I listened to this statement, a gleam of hope shot athwart my soul. If my wife, thought I, refuse to come over, the main link of evidence will be wanting. But, alas! my hopes proved to have been built upon the sand; for, in addition to the charges allowed by government, which I was not lawyer enough to take into calculation at the moment, Mr. Kelly, on hearing the motives of my second wife's reluctance to stir from home, volunteered to satisfy her demands, "if only," said he, "to mark my detestation of a fellow who has been the means of disseminating such abominable political principles."

CHAPTER IX.

THE TRIAL.—AN IRISH ASSIZE COURT.

A MONTH had now elapsed since the events detailed in the last chapter, during which time scarce a day passed but I was busy in consultation with my attorney respecting the mode in which my defence should be conducted. As this person entered into my case with remarkable zeal, in the hope of gaining eclat by my acquittal, and had, moreover, engaged the services of the illustrious O'Cromwell, who happened to be retained on some important tithe question in the Civil Court, I was not without hopes of a favourite result; "in which case," said I, "so far from doing me injury, my trial may actually be productive of good; for my countrymen, who cannot but see that political motives have been at the bottom of it—for why otherwise should Mr. Kelly have taken such a deep personal interest in it! why; otherwise, gone the length of insisting on the co-operation, and even arranging the plan of it, of both my wives?—my countrymen, who cannot but see through all this, will no doubt bear in mind that I am a sufferer in their cause, and recompense me for my sufferings by a handsome public subscription."

The consideration of this idea enabled me to keep up my spirits during the protracted term of my imprisonment.

Meantime the period fixed for the Assizes drew on, and the town was filled with visitors flocking in from all parts of the county; such a carnival is that season considered in Ireland as well as England, which dooms the unfortunate and the criminal to exile, and perhaps to death.

The second day was the one appointed for my trial, the particulars of which (as it is far from my desire to make any parade of egotism, or excite pity by any highly wrought description), I shall take simply as I find them reported in the columns of my own journal. Strange that the very paper which had so long borne testimony to my patriotism, should be the very one to chronicle my disgrace!

" BALLINABROGUE ASSIZES.

"CRIMINAL COURT.—BEFORE LORD NORVERY.— IMPORTANT TRIAL FOR BIGAMY.

" FITZMAURICE *v.* O'BLARNEY.—This long expected trial came on this morning. From an early hour the court was crowded to excess; all ranks and ages partook of the same curiosity; and in one corner of the court, close behind the jury-box, we ourselves counted not less than six individuals, whose united ages amounted to upwards of four hundred and fifteen years!

"The learned judge took his seat on the bench precisely at eleven o'clock, when the prisoner, O'Blarney, was ordered to be placed at the bar. The appearance of this young man is remarkably prepossessing. He is of middle size, and well proportioned, with a face full of intelligence and sensibility, and which created an impression in his favour, especially among the female portion of the audience. There is nothing in his look or manner to denote the criminal; indeed, there is an air of bashfulness about him, quite different to what we should have expected to see in a man charged with the diabolical crime of bigamy. He was dressed in deep mourning, with a small shamrock sprig in his waistcoat button-hole, just above his heart—a modest and unassuming trait of patriotism, which seemed to produce quite a pathetic effect on Mr. O'Cromwell.

"The names of the jury having been called over, and each duly sworn, Mr. Sheilly opened the case in the following energetic speech, which was delivered with such extreme rapidity that our reporter has been able to give only a brief and hasty sketch of it, which, however, he trusts will be found correct in the main:—

"'May it please your lordship,—Gentlemen of the jury,—Never in the discharge of my professional avocations did I rise with such painful feelings of embarrassment as oppress me on the present awful occasion. The crimes I have to expose are so colossal, and the criminal so satanic, that my mind shrinks aghast from the overwhelming diabolism of the subject. Gentlemen, I have heard that no noxious insect can thrive in the consecrated soil of Erin. Alas! the sweltering reptile at the bar proves the fact a fiction. With these few remarks, wrung from me in the agony of my spirit, I proceed to lay before you the particulars of this heart-rending case. The plaintiff is a young lady of Mollymoreen, who resided, up to the period of her inauspicious nuptials, with a venerable and universally adored uncle. The name of this estimable individual was O'Brien, and his niece bore the same patronymic. She was a lady of the highest accomplishments—the most consummate beauty—simple, unsophisticated, and twenty-six—slim, susceptible, and a spinster. In an evil hour, however, when her guardian genius slumbered at his post, it was her fate to descry, through an opera-glass from the dress-boxes of the Mollymoreen theatre, the unparalleled prisoner at the bar. His person filled her with admiration, and he reciprocated the sentiment. But, alas! his love was not the inspiration of Cupid, but of Mammon. He fixed a fond gaze, not on the plaintiff's person, but on her purse. His attachment was not the holy and lambent flame which burned of old on the altars of Vesta; but an illusory, phosphoretic radiance, like that which shoots from out the electric back of grimalkin, when stroked backward by the hand of scientific curiosity. The plaintiff's guardian, with the wary sagacity of age, soon fathomed the nature of the defendant's attachment. But his discovery was made too late. The land was ploughed—the seed was soon—and ready at the first opportune season to produce a copious crop of tribulation. Finding this to be the case, Mr. O'Brien had no other alternative left, than to sob forth a reluctant consent to the nuptials. Disastrous concession! Frightful alternative! Within one brief year from their consummation my unfortunate client was bedded, beggared, and betrayed! I can image her distraction when the tidings of her husband's flight first reached her; when, in reply to her agonizing interrogatory, "Where's your master?" the horror-struck footman, in the familiar, but expressive language of his tribe, stammered forth, "Master's bolted!"'

"[The learned gentleman was here interrupted by violent screams, which were found to proceed from an elderly lady, who, overpowered by her emotions, had fallen into the kicking hysterics, in which state she was carried out of court.]

"'Gentlemen,' continued Mr. Sheilly, 'I perceive my appeal has struck home. I shall therefore proceed, without further comment, to the details of the prisoner's second marriage. This took place at Llandwarrys, in South Wales. The unoffending victim, for whose afflictions even the crags of Snowdon might shed tears, and the peaks of Cader-Idris veil their sympathetic summits, was a lovely, intelligent widow, universally respected by all who had the honour of her acquaintance. Five-and-forty times had Phœbus made his annual circuit of the globe, since this Cambrian floweret was ushered into being. Oh, that the sirocco of sorrow should have spared the infant bud, only to blight the full-blown blossom! Gentlemen, of the prisoner's two victims, I scarce know which most deserves your commiseration. The one was the green and sportive spring; the other, the mellow and voluptuous autumn. But the defendant gave the preference to neither. He was the personification of perfidious impartiality; and, like the raging Boreas, blasted with equal alacrity the opening buds of spring and the ripe efflorescence of autumn.

"'Gentlemen of the jury, you are fathers—you are husbands—you are men—you are Christians—above all, you are Irishmen—and, by these sacred titles, I implore you to mark your sense of the prisoner's attrocity by a verdict which shall brand him, like Cain, with the stamp of imperishable infamy. Erin blushes for his birth—earth travails at his presence—heaven cries aloud for his condemnation! He is a monster of moral deformity, compared to whom, Cacus was a Cupid, Sycorax a Sylph, and Caliban an Adonis.'

"The learned gentleman sat down amid the most vociferous acclamations from all parts of the court, which were so long continued as to awaken the venerable judge, who, rubbing his eyes, and looking angrily about him, in the direction of the jury-box, exclaimed, ' Officer of the court, wake the foreman of the jury!' after which the certificates of both marriages were put in, and Mr. Sheilly proceeded to call witnesses in corroboration of his statement, who were subjected to a rigid cross-examination by Mr. O'Cromwell; but nothing occurred to invalidate their testimony.

"When the case for the prosecution had closed, Mr. O'Cromwell rose for the defence. The following is as correct a report as we could give of the learned gentleman's speech, considering that he was inaudible at times, owing to the great confusion that prevailed throughout the court :—

"'May it please your lordship,—Gentlemen of the jury,—I am well aware that to a certain extent judgment must pass against my client. I mean not to deny the fact of his first, nor yet of his second, marriage; but this I will maintain, that notwithstanding the eloquent vituperation of my learned friend, the evidence you have this day heard proves that defendant has been far "more sinned against than sinning." In considering your verdict, gentlemen, I trust you will take this fact into your consideration. Besides, do not let it escape your attention, that this prosecution has at least as much to do with politics as justice. The Protestant magistrate Kelly, who takes such extraordinary pains to promote it, does so for the sole reason that the defendant is a Catholic and a Radical. But this is nothing new here, for Irish justice is notoriously of the Orange faction. Oh, my beloved countrymen, when shall we be free from this galling Ascendancy chain? Where is there a lovelier climate? Where a finer peasantry? Oh, it galls me to the quick, to think that where God has been so bountiful, man has been so base! We were designed to be a nation—we are a province. We were designed to be happy—we are miserable. But we have one consolation—WE ARE SEVEN MILLIONS!'

"Mr. Sheilly.—'I beg my learned friend's pardon. We were seven millions a month ago. We are eight now.'

"Lord Norvery.—'Mr. O'Cromwell, you are travelling wholly from the record.'

"Mr. O'Cromwell.—'My lord, justice to my client compels me to show that this prosecution is for the most part of a political—'

"Lord Norvery.—'Sir, we know nothing of politics here.'

"Mr. O'Cromwell.—'I should have thought otherwise, from your lordship's extreme hurry to—'

"Lord Norvery (in a loud voice).—'Sir, I will have respect paid to the Bench. I insist on it.'

"Mr. O'Cromwell.—'Really, my lord, this interruption is most—'

"Lord Norvery.—'Oh, very well, sir; I understand

your meaning. If you fancy yourself aggrieved, you know how to apply for your remedy.'

"Mr. O'Cromwell (solemnly).—'My lord, I have a vow —a sacred vow!'

"Lord Norvery.—'Enough, sir. Go on.'

"Mr. O'Cromwell.—'Gentlemen, my client's case is only another proof of the necessity that exists for cleansing the fountain-heads of justice in this most afflicted country.'

"His lordship here again interrupted Mr. O'Cromwell, and the two parties continued addressing each other with inflamed gestures, at the very top of their voices, for fully ten minutes, while the court roared with laughter. At length, after a vehement altercation, Mr. O'Cromwell's superior wind prevailed, and he proceeded as follows :—

"'Gentlemen, I repeat my former statement, this prosecution is almost wholly political. But thus has it ever been—thus will it ever be, until Irishmen have learned to know and vindicate their rights.

'Hereditary bondsmen! know you not,
Who would be free, themselves must strike the blow?'

Yes, we are indeed a nation of bondsmen, and England is our task-master. We are hewers of wood and drawers of water, and the Saxon is our overseer. Yet nature designed us for freedom. (A sort of running duet here took place between Mr. O'Cromwell and his lordship.) Our every hill is a fortress—'

"Lord Norvery.—'Mr. O'Cromwell, this is no Corn Exchange meeting.'

"Mr. O'Cromwell.—'Our every road a defile—'

"Lord Norvery.—'Sir, I insist—'

"Mr. O'Cromwell.—'Our every field a redoubt—'

"Lord Norvery.—'This conduct is really—'

"Mr. O'Cromwell.—'Up, then, countrymen, and be stirring! (Here his lordship sank back exhausted with his vehemence.) Up with your weapons; but let them be those of constitutional agitation! Strike; but let it be in theory! Fight; but let it be in a contest of obedience to the laws—to those laws which, were they but once thoroughly reformed, would make Ireland again, what she once was,

"Great, glorious, and free,
First flower of the earth, and first gem of the sea!"

"When the learned gentleman had concluded, the venerable judge commenced summing up the evidence; after which, the jury returned a verdict of 'guilty:' whereupon his lordship sentenced the prisoner to transportation for life.

"The trial excited the most intense interest throughout; indeed, the oldest inhabitant in Ballinabrogue never remembers any thing equal to it."

CHAPTER X. AND LAST.

THE EXILE OF ERIN.

My narrative now draws to a close. After my trial I was conveyed back to prison, no longer buoyed up with that hope which had sustained my spirits, even up to the moment when the jury delivered in their verdict. All prospect of ever regaining character was lost; for the sentence of the court had placed a bar between me and society for ever. The Mahons had blotted me out of their recollection, and even Mr. Flannaghan had abandoned me to my fate. Both these were liberal, high-minded, intelligent Irishmen, yet both abandoned the poor patriot to his fate without a sigh! The very peasantry, of whom I had so lately been the idol, treated me with equal indifference. A slight sensation, indeed, was occasioned by my sentence; threats were made use of, and a hint thrown out of a rescue: but in a few days all this show of spirit evaporated; the peasantry returned to their usual duties, the town to its usual tranquillity; and the poor imprisoned patriot was as completely forgotten as if he had never existed. Such is mob popularity!

I mean not to deny that I was guilty; still, when I came seriously to reflect on my situation, I could not but feel that I was in a considerable degree a martyr to my principles. Hundreds had committed the same offence, but not being politically obnoxious, they had incurred only half the penalty. In one respect, therefore, my sentence was a compliment to the sense entertained of my public influence; but this was a poor consolation.

On the evening of the second day after my trial, as I was seated in my cell, companioned only by my cheerless thoughts, a letter was delivered to me by the turnkey. On looking closely at the superscription, I saw that it was in the handwriting of my first wife; and concluding, after what had taken place between us, that it might be of a forgiving, if not a penitential character, I hastily broke it open; but judge of my astonishment when I found that it consisted of only this one sentence!—

"You once called me old; you were right, I am old—far too old ever to hope to live long enough to welcome your return from transportation!

"CATHARINE."

"Insulting cockatrice!" said I, tearing the letter into a thousand fragments; "what an index to character is here! If this be not revenge in its subtlest, most malignant, and most feminine form, I know not the meaning of the term. Oh woman, woman! what a mystery is that heart of thine! I thought I knew you. Alas, I might just as well have flattered myself that I had fathomed the mysteries of eternity. You were born to be our curse. *One* was enough to set all Troy in flames; can I wonder, then, that *two* have been my ruin? Yet, gracious God! who could have believed it possible that a sneer, thrown out in a hasty, thoughtless moment, should be so long remembered, and lead to such disastrous results? It is plain now, that wounded vanity, not blighted affection, has been at the bottom of my wife's recent conduct towards me. She never loved me, or she would not, when I so solemnly promised to make her every reparation in my power, have offered me up a sacrifice to an ill-timed truth. Well, never again will I venture to call a woman old. Henceforth she shall bloom an evergreen in my speech."

Scarcely had I recovered from the astonishment into which the perusal of this vindictive communication had thrown me, when the door of my cell was again unlocked, and the turnkey entered, with the information that a lady was waiting without, who expressed a wish to be admitted into my presence. " Lady !" said I, peevishly ; " I will see no lady. I have had enough of ladies to last me my lifetime. I am a martyr of a too generous admiration of the sex. But stay," I added after a moment's pause ; I can guess who is the applicant, so show her in ; she cannot possibly treat me worse than her predecessor."

The man accordingly quitted the room, and in a few minutes returned, leading in my second wife, Mrs. Fitz-maurice, who was closely muffled up, as if labouring under the embarrassing consciousness of an *alias.* I rose to greet her ; but as I did so, there was something in the repulsive coldness of her manner that induced me to stop short and say, " You have come, madam, I see, to exult over the unfortunate."

" Unfortunate ! Oh, Mr. Fitz—O'Blarney, is that the sort of language to be applied to you? I am the unfortunate. How could you have the heart to use me so ? Such a wife as I always was to you ! I am sure I thought I should have dropped when I found that you had run away and left me with a horrid Irish name that does not belong to either of us."

" If you felt so much for me as you say, why did you appear against me ?"

" Because my brother and all Llandwarrys insisted on it. I was told that it was the only way I could clear my character in the eyes of the world. Even the squire himself—"

" What, did Mr. Gryffyths take part in the conspiracy ?"

" Yes; he told us that though he saw through you from
the first, he was determined to say nothing till the proper time
arrived.   The attorney, too, kept constantly telling me that
if I did not come over, the law would compel me to do so ;
then there was Mr. Rupee, he sent expressly for my
brother, to say that he was convinced that you would be his
death, for he had never had a day's health since he called
you in, and that, therefore, it was a duty we owed
society to prosecute you. In fact the whole town cried shame
on you, with the exception of the undertaker, who always
stood your friend.   But I think I can partly guess the
reason of that."

" Pray come to the point, and tell me the object of this
visit."

" Well, then," rejoined my wife, drawing a small Bible
from her pocket, and placing it in my hands, " though I
know you think I have come to upbraid you—and, indeed,
it is natural you should think so—yet, believe me, I came
here with the kindest intentions,—merely to present you
with this volume, in the hope that it may be the means of
bringing you to a proper sense of your condition.   I would
have written my own name in it, as a proof that I forgive
you ; but, alas !—for shame, for shame, sir ; I wonder you
can laugh at such things !"

" Do not grudge me one poor smile ; it is the last I shall
ever know."

" Yes, and you have taken good care that I shall never
smile again.   But I saw from the first how matters would
end.   You will do me the justice to remember that I
always prophesied your ruin.   Oh dear ! oh, dear ! what
a sad business is this !   To think that a woman at my
time of life should be so situated as scarcely even to know
her own name !   Was the like ever heard of ?"   In this
lachrymose strain, Mrs. Fitzmaurice continued for the best
part of half an hour, when our conference was terminated
by the ringing of the prison-bell, which was the signal for
the departure of all visitors, and the locking-up of the

17

jail. Almost instantly afterwards the turnkey entered, and told my wife that her time was expired, and she must quit the prison.

This abrupt announcement had a strange effect on the poor lady's feelings. She moved towards me for the purpose of bidding me farewell; but as she did so I could see her hand shake, and her countenance visibly alter. For a minute or two she struggled to conceal her feelings; but the effort was beyond her power: and just as I had seized her hand, and was faltering forth a "God bless you," I saw tears—real tears—rolling down her cheeks. A sight like this, so wholly unexpected, quite unmanned me. I tried to speak, but could not; so there I stood, rooted to the floor, with my wife's cold hand fast locked in mine.

"Come, come," said the turnkey, "this will never do. I am sorry for the poor gentlewoman, but she must turn out. It's as good as my place is worth, to let her remain here after lock-up hours."

"Good-by, then," said my wife, "God bless you, I forgive you from the very bottom of my heart;" and so saying, she hurried towards the door; but just as she reached it, stopped, turned once more round, then tore herself away, and the door closed on her for ever.

It was on a charming summer morning, in the year 1822, that the most aggrieved patriot that ever quitted the Irish shores stepped on board the vessel that was to waft him to a new world. Who shall say what emotions were mine at this trying moment! Yet it was not for myself I grieved. No, it was the ingratitude of the land of my nativity that pierced my soul with anguish. "Oh, Erin!" I exclaimed, "ungenerous Erin! Like Aristides, I have sacrificed my all in your behalf; and, like him, I am rewarded with banishment. Though, conjointly with abler but not more disinterested spirits, I taught you the secret of your strength; lit up the beacon-fires of freedom in your farm-houses; and roused you from the state of base, contented tranquillity in which I found you but too willing to indulge. How have you repaid me? By thrusting me from your presence with contempt and obloquy! Had I acquired titles, or heaped up riches, you might justly have distrusted my zeal; but I have neither pension nor peerage; nay, I quit your service poorer than when I entered on it. Such was ever the patriot's lot. Belisarius begged his bread, and I am driven forth to herd with the kangaroos of Australia! Oh, that I had never been born, or, being born, that my face, like the statue of Achilles, had been cased in triple brass! But bashfulness first sowed the seeds of that ruin, of which patriotism has since reaped the harvest. What but the one withheld me from returning a penitent to Naples, and kept me in a state of vacillation when, by a prompt decision, I might have secured the hand of Ellen Mahon, and in some remote corner of Ireland have lived to this hour in respectability? What, but the other, made me court notoriety, whereby I hurried on my own downfall? But complaint is idle now. Henceforth all hope is dead within me. Ye whom I may perchance have wronged, be content; ye have now an ample revenge. Ye who have unquestionably wronged me, be content also; from my inmost soul I forgive you."

Just as I concluded this touching soliloquy, I cast my eyes toward the shores of my native land. The last faint glimpse of its iron-bound coast was still discernible in the distance; an instant, and it had disappeared, and I felt that I had seen green Erin for the last time.

GENTLE READER,

The tale of the "Bashful Irishman" is concluded; and the autobiographer himself, his task accomplished, vanishes, like other phantoms, into thin air. The narrative was intended to be a sort of ironical commentary on the old adage, "Know Thyself"—the most difficult to be acquired of all knowledge; for how often do we find, in real life, men like O'Blarney, piquing themselves on the possession of that one faculty or acquirement in which they are the most deficient,—some coarse, business-like John Bull, for instance, on his refined and lofty gentility; or some chattering monsieur, on his philosophic depth of thought. In the selection of his hero, the author, some of whose oldest and most respected friends are Irishmen, has studiously confined himself to that class of low, impudent adventurers who are to be met with in all countries, as Mateo Aleman has done in his "Spanish Adventurer," and our own immortal Fielding in his English one. Perhaps, also, gentle reader, the author may have had another object in view—your amusement; but here, though he would fain hope the best, he dare hardly flatter himself that he has succeeded. No critic can be more sensible of the deficiencies of the tale than himself; nevertheless, he has done his best; and, having penned it throughout (or at least endeavoured so to do) in a spirit of cordial and unaffected good humour, he trusts that you will take these mitigating circumstances into consideration, and, adopting Portia's advice to Shylock, temper justice with mercy in your verdict.

END OF ADVENTURES OF A BASHFUL IRISHMAN.

MAGIC OF LOVE.

THE groundwork of this tale is founded on fact, though the circumstances of the journey are in some degree fictitious. Of the three parties interested, one only survives. A slight sketch of the narrative has already been given in print. It is here materially enlarged.

IT was at the commencement of the summer of the year 1819, that I quitted Cambridge for the Continent. For some months previous I had been in what is called an ailing state, the result of incessant application to my literary pursuits at the University; on perceiving which, my father insisted that I should throw aside my books and accompany him home to Gwynnevay, in the hope that the mild air of my native Welsh valley might work a healing effect on my constitution; but finding that the change was of no avail, as I still persevered in my old system of study and seclusion, he called in a physician from Caermarthen, by whose express injunctions I was interdicted from all but light reading, until my health should be sufficiently re-established to enable me to resume my favourite pursuits with safety; and finally I was despatched to pass the long vacation in Italy.

It was a sad day for me when the carriage that was to convey me to London, on my road to the Continent, drove away from the old monastic halls of Gwynnevay. Though I had everything that could render a residence abroad desirable—ample pecuniary resources (for I was my father's only son, and, I believe I may add, his favourite child), and letters of introduction to some of the most distinguished families in Rome—still I felt a sense of discomfort and dissatisfaction at the idea of quitting home, which can only be appreciated by those who, like myself, have been torn suddenly, and, as they fancy at the time, wantonly, from those pursuits from which alone they derive the slightest gratification.

At this period—I was then just entering on my twentieth year—literature was with me, not a mere pastime, but a continuous, all-absorbing passion. I breathed but the air of books. My mind fed but on the past. As for the world, I knew as much, and cared as much about it as an infant, my society being for the most part restricted to those who cultivated the same tastes.

My father, a disciplined man of the world, who, from the concurring circumstances of birth, fortune, and connection, was entitled to move in a highly respectable sphere, made many attempts to polish off what he termed "the rough edges" of my character, by compelling me to mix with him in the gay circles of the metropolis; my sisters, too, were perpetually endeavouring to laugh me out of my "old-fashioned bookish notions;" but their efforts were fruitless; I felt that I was out of place in modern society, being wholly made up of odd crotchets, and that high-toned but visionary sort of feeling which is one of the inevitable results of a studious solitude.

Mr. Wordsworth has well observed—

> "Books are a substantial world,
> Round which, with tendrils strong as flesh and blood,
> Our pastime and our happiness may grow."

This truth was never more fully realised than in my case; and it was with a listlessness amounting almost to apathy, that I took leave of this "substantial world," to enter upon another which had nothing but its bustle and novelty to recommend it.

In such a frame of mind I reached Rome. My father had previously made me promise to avail myself of all my letters of introduction, foreseeing that otherwise I should fall back on my old habits; but I was in no great hurry to redeem my pledge, contenting myself, instead, with solitary visits to those spots over which the historians, and poet·, and orators of old Rome, have thrown an unfading halo. I sought the Tusculum, and thought of Cicero; I fixed my eyes on the summit of the distant Soracte, and Horace's social ode flashed on my recollection; I bent my steps towards the Aventine, and my ear caught the sound, and my eye the spectacle, of the triumphal rejoicings of the Republic.

So passed a month, at the expiration of which time letters arrived from Gwynnevay, in reply to one I had sent announcing my arrival at Rome. My father particularly requested me to inform him whether I had made myself known to the friends about whom he had spoken to me; for it was to the diversion afforded by society that he looked chiefly for my recovery.

The receipt of this letter reminded me of duties that I had too long neglected towards the fondest and most munificent of parents; and I determined on the following day punctually to obey his directions,—a resolution which was not a little assisted by the circumstance I am now about to relate, and which had the effect of materially influencing all my after fortunes.

I had gone to pay a visit one evening to the Palatine, and was standing among its crumbling masses of brickwork, in that fixed, thoughtful mood which such a scene is so calculated to inspire, when the sound of voices diverted my attention; and looking in the direction of the Circus Maximus, I saw a party, consisting of two ladies and a gentleman, advancing from that quarter to the spot where I stood.

As they came slowly on, pausing every now and then to look about them, I had ample leisure to observe them. Two were of middle age; but the third was a lady, who, judging from appearances, I should say had scarcely completed her eighteenth year. I never saw so lovely a creature. There are some faces which, once beheld, though but for a moment, take ever after an imperishable hold on the memory. Such was hers. Her large black eyes were full of deep and earnest expression; her mouth was small and exquisitely shaped; her rosy lips, on which a thousand meanings seemed to vibrate, indicated extreme sensibility; her complexion was pale, but clear; the contour of her countenance of a Grecian, rather than a Roman, character; and her slender figure, replete with that natural, easy grace which we associate with a Juliet or a Miranda. Just such a vision, so youthful—so ethereal —so full of all that we admire and dote upon in woman— burst on the sight of the Indian Bacchus among the woods of Crete.

But it was not so much the beauty of the stranger that riveted my attention, as the profound melancholy that characterised her every look and movement. There was no mistaking the expression that spoke in her eloquent eye, and quivered on her restless lip. So young—so attractive—what could render her thus wretched? Could it be the influence breathed out, like a mildew, from the ruins that surrounded her? Possibly; for there is indeed a sad solemnity—a majestic desolation in their aspect; and we behold them with something of the same sympathy with which we should behold a noble mind in decay.

The party had by this time reached the place where I was standing, and, as they passed, the young girl just turned a glance towards me; but, hasty as was that glance, it was quite enough to overturn all my speculations. 'Twas not the melancholy akin to pleasure, that is called forth in refined minds by contemplating the solemn ruins of the past, that threw its touching shadow over her countenance; but a deep, silent, corroding anguish, that was gnawing at the very roots of life. Oh, how I longed to address her! But could I even have mustered courage enough to break through that conventional etiquette which perpetually, in spite of himself, clings about an Englishman, the opportunity would have been wanting; for in an instant, before I could call home my wandering thoughts, the strangers had disappeared, and left me once again to solitude, in the cold gray evening, among the ruins of the Palatine.

The whole of that night—that memorable night—I could think—dream—speculate on nothing but the fair Unknown, and the cause of the melancholy that threw—not a cloud, but—a dim, softening veil over her brilliant loveliness. No doubt, the romantic circumstances under which I had encountered her had much to do with the matter; for my age—my inexperience—and more especially my course of study, rendered me peculiarly sensitive to such an influence; still, independently of these adventitious helps to the imagination, there was quite enough in the face—the figure—the air of the stranger, to justify the enthusiasm of a far more worldly man than I am, or shall ever be.

My favourite metaphysician has accounted for a sudden infatuation like this, by attributing it to the realising of some image of female loveliness, of which all men, unconsciously to themselves, have entertained a previous conception. Such was not my case. I had formed no previous theory of beauty. If I had ever thought of woman at all, it was only in connection with a waltz, a ball-room, and a knot of lisping dandies; the present, therefore, was, in every respect, the dawn of a new existence within me; whose first immediate effect was, to render me as active, impassioned, and full of hope, as before I was listless and reserved.

Under the influence of these new feelings, I haunted day and night the majestic ruins of the Palatine. I saw them under every varying aspect of light and shade—of sunshine and moonshine; sometimes I was there alone; sometimes I stood among them in the presence of beauty; but she, the most beautiful of her sex, came there no more.

Still I would not despond. First love, though timid, is skilful, and fertile in expedients, with ever a redeeming spirit about it ; so, finding that my excursions to the Palatine were fruitless, I extended them to all the grand and classic scenery in which the neighbourhood of Rome abounds,—to the heights of Frescati—the pictur-esque Alban Hill—the groves, the grottoes, the cascades, and temples of Tivoli,—to every spot, in short, which I thought was likely to attract the attention of youth and beauty ; and then, as a last resource, resolved on availing myself of my letters of introduction, in the hope that in society at least, if not among the *chef-d'œuvres* of art and nature, I might stand a chance of meeting with the Unknown.

Fraught with this idea, I permitted not a moment to elapse, but made my appearance at the house of the Countess C——, to whom my father had specially recom-mended me; and whose hobby it was to collect once a week, in her saloon, all the literature, and philosophy, and science, and even fashion of the capital.

By this lady, who was in high repute with the English at Rome, I was received with a world of urbanity, and introduced into several delightful circles; but, wherever I went, the same disappointment awaited me ; I could see —hear nothing of the Unknown.

At length, one day when I was sauntering along the Corso with the Baron de G——, whom I had previously met at the countess's *conversazione,* and who was well known in Rome for his classic taste and erudition, and— what was with me of far more consequence just now-- for the extent and variety of his acquaintance, a carriage halted close to the spot where we were walking; for the street being thronged with equipages, like Hyde Park on a spring Sunday, it became a matter of difficulty for any vehicle to proceed beyond a snail's pace.

At once, as if by instinct, my eyes were riveted on this carriage, in which were seated two females ; in the younger of whom I recognised—oh, moment of triumph, that even now, at the distance of eighteen years, I recall with transport!—my fair Unknown of the Palatine! She, too, seemed as if she remembered me; for, as the coach drove on, she threw on me a furtive glance of recognition, (or did my vanity deceive me?) stamped, however, with all her former melancholy.

I cannot say what my feelings were at this instant; excited, however, as they were, I yet managed to repress them; and, with assumed tranquillity, inquired of the baron if he knew who those ladies were in the carriage that had just passed us.

"In the dark-green one, you mean? Oh, they are the wife and sister of the French minister. Pleasant women enough, but too loquacious."

"No, no; in the carriage immediately preceding them. See, it is just now turning the corner."

"What, you are interested in them?" he replied archly, struck with the involuntary eagerness of my manner.

"Not so. But I think I have met with them before— the youngest, at least—and have the curiosity natural to all of us to know the name of, if not to become acquainted with, a pretty woman. Who are they—or rather, who is she?" and I felt my heart leap within me as I put this direct inquiry.

The reply was all that the most sanguine enthusiast could desire; for not only did the baron make me acquainted with the names of the strangers, but, finding that I took an interest in his communication, proceeded also to acquaint me with the details of their history.

They were, it seems, mother and daughter, and of the distinguished family of Di V——. The younger, whose name was Hortense, had been affianced from an early age to a young Italian *élève* of Napoleon, who held a high military command in the capital. The match received the full sanction of the mother—a widow, with this only child—but, unfortunately, before it could take place, one of those sudden political changes which were of such frequent occurrence among the emperor's adherents when he him-

self had been hurled from power—and which, in this
instance, was supposed to have been hastened by the
intrigues of the Austrian nuncio, to whom the young
soldier had contrived to render himself obnoxious—not
only deprived him of his military situation, but was the
cause also of his banishment from the papal territories;
and this but a month before he was to have espoused
Hortense di V——.

When the news of her intended son-in-law's disgrace
reached the ears of Madame di V—— —a stern, cold,
haughty woman, whose one engrossing passion was ambition—she insisted on her daughter's breaking off all
communication with the young soldier; and though the
poor girl implored her on bended knees to recall this harsh
mandate, her mother was deaf to her appeal, and kept her
under a state of the most rigid surveillance, until assured that
her affianced husband had taken his departure from Rome.

For full six months Hortense had remained in this
state of "durance vile;" but latterly her mother had been
induced to relax a little in her vigilance, finding that her
child's health was slowly wasting away under the cruel
shock; and allow her occasionally to make her appearance
at the *soirées* of some of their friends, and, among others, at
that of the Countess C——; in the hope, no doubt, as my
informant added, that her daughter, by her beauty, her
accomplishments, and the rank of her family, might form
such an alliance as might do credit to her mother's ambition.

There was nothing in this communication that, strictly
speaking, should cause me any despondency; for what
was I to Hortense? nevertheless, it produced an extraordinary effect on my mind; and when I quitted the baron
to return home, the tumult of my feelings was such as it
is far more easy to ridicule than remedy. I had been
flung with a rude stunning shock to earth, from the seventh
heaven of imagination. Hope's silver chord was loosed;
her golden bowl was broken; and the glittering fragments
lay shattered at my feet. In vain I called common sense
to my aid· in vain I turned to study for consolation; in

vain I resumed acquaintance with my favourite classic and Italian poets. My feelings rejected all attempts at discipline; my thoughts were perpetually wandering to the Palatine, and brooding over the vision that had there first taught me I had a fancy to be fired and a heart to be touched.

This was a wretched state of mind to be in—amounting, in fact, to a species of monomania. I determined, therefore, to make one resolute effort to shake it off; and the baron happening to look in on me one morning with an invitation to a *soirée* at the countess's, where he told me I should be sure to meet " all the world," I gladly embraced the opportunity, if not of restoring my mind to a healthy tone, at least of reducing it to something like subordination.

But, alas! in my eagerness to fly from self, I found that I was only rushing from Scylla uopn Charybdis; for, on entering the saloon, among the earliest visitors, whom should I see, seated on a sofa in an obscure quiet corner, but—Hortense herself! Yes, there she was—lovely, interesting, irresistible as ever! Next her was a middle-aged lady, in whom, from the strong resemblance she bore to her daughter, I was at no loss to recognise Madame di V——. Both had the same full dark eye, the same hair the same exquisitely chiselled outline of countenance; but the *hauteur* and stately dignity of the one were tempered into softness and sweetness in the other. The one seemed born to command ; the other, to love and be loved.

Of course, as the most *distingué* females in the room, they soon gathered about them a crowd of those lively coxcombs who, in Rome as with us, are always to be seen humming and buzzing about the ear of beauty. One in particular, a handsome but intolerably conceited fop, paid Hortense the most marked attention; from which, however, she shrunk with an eagerness that not a little displeased her mother, and convinced me that the coxcomb in question was considered of sufficient rank and fortune to be encouraged as a son-in-law.

It was with mixed feelings of pleasure and jealousy that I watched at a distance this little scene ; but when I saw Madame di V—— rise from her seat, for the purpose of addressing the lady of an English attaché, drawing after her a crowd of beaux, who felt their self-conceit wounded by her daughter's unaccountable reserve, a strange courage came over me ; and hastening toward her, at the same time mentioning the name of our mutual friend the baron, I introduced and placed myself by her side. By *her* side! What a world of bliss is contained in these few words !

How I looked—what I said—I cannot at this distance of time pretend to recall ; my manner, however, must have convinced Hortense of the deep—the intense interest I took in the circumstances of her story, for she repaid me with gentle words and grateful looks ; in fact, I so far contrived to interest her feelings, by talking with her in an earnest and impassioned style, which suited the temper of her mind, about the various scenes I had visited in the capital, and the associations they called up—not forgetting, be sure, the Palatine, where I had first seen her—that her usual reserve gave way, and something like an animated conversation took place, in French, between us ; but when I happened accidentally to mention that I should quit Rome for Naples in a few days, she gave an involuntary start, her countenance assumed an expression of the utmost eagerness, and, after looking timidly and anxiously about the room, she said, in a low voice, with a forced effort at composure, " We go to-morrow to Cardinal F——'s. You know him, I believe ?"

" Yes ; I was introduced to him a few days since."

" Possibly, then, we shall see you there ?"

I had only just time to reply in the affirmative, when Hortense abruptly changed the conversation ; and with good reason,—for, on looking up, I saw Madame di V—— returning, on which I quitted her side, and mixing with the gay throng which now filled the room, was soon lost to the eyes of both.

On returning to my hotel, I occupied myself for some hours in thinking over all the circumstances of my conversation with Hortense. Her hint about the cardinal's *soirée*, which I could not but remember had been put in the earnest and pleading tone of a request that I would be there, especially engaged my attention. "What could be her motive," said I, "in asking me such a question, and in such an anxious manner? Was it merely that she was pleased with my conversation,—flattered by my respect and evident sympathy? or was it a deeper feeling? But no, no; 'tis sheer madness to cherish such a hope! However, be the cause what it may, at least by to-morrow night I shall know enough to regulate my future conduct."

On my arrival next night at the cardinal's I looked in vain for Madame di V——— and her daughter; they were not there; and after waiting some time, I was sullenly preparing to move away, when the baron stopped me at the door, and engaged me in conversation for a few minutes—most fortunately, for while I was talking with him, Hortense and her mother entered, accompanied by the same young fop who had so excited my aversion the previous evening.

As the party drew near us, Madame di V——— halted an instant to speak to the baron; and just at that instant Hortense, catching my eye, thrust a letter into my hand; which she had scarcely done, when her mother hurried her forward. All this occurred in less time than I have taken to describe it; and my curiosity, and perhaps a more flattering feeling, being excited beyond all restraint—the more especially when, from a distant quarter of the room, I saw Hortense's eyes turned frequently towards me—I hurried home, unfolded the precious document, and read the following lines :—

" You told me last night you were on the eve of quitting Rome for Naples; you saw, too, that the intelligence affected me; but you knew not—you could not know—the deep cause I had for emotion. At Muro, within three days' journey of the city you propose to visit, *he* lives whom I hold most dear on earth. But a week since, a letter was conveyed to me in secret from him; and in that letter he implores me, by the memory of our past and the hope of our future happiness, at all hazards, to fly this hated place and rejoin him.   When I say *him*, you know to whom I allude, for your manner last night convinced me that my story was not unknown to, or unlamented by, you.   Pity me then, and do not misinterpret my motives, when I supplicate your aid in escaping from a home which has become my dungeon.   You start at this application from one to whom you are comparatively a stranger! You are astonished at the boldness that could have suggested it!   Alas! it is not boldness, but the frenzy of despair. Long and severe were my struggles before I could bring myself to address you.   I thought of the censures of the world ; of the indignation of my mother ; of the scorn that *even you* might entertain for me ; but I thought, too, of him, and for his sake I am resolved to brave everything. Should I remain here a week longer, my doom is sealed ; for my mother has insisted on my accepting, without further hesitation, the hand of a man I detest.   Do not, then, reject my supplication, but aid me to rejoin him ; and two hearts that you have saved from breaking shall bless your name for ever.   I will intrust myself unhesitatingly to you.   You are manly—you are generous—you have sisters, you told me, whom you love, and by whom you are loved ; imagine, then, that I am one of them, and be to me a brother.   Oh! if you did but know the agony I have endured, the long dreary days and sleepless nights that have been my portion since he quitted me, you would not hesitate to grant my request.   I have no friend to advise me ; no hope, but in you : (though I have numbered few years, yet my heart is already wrinkled) ; the accents of kindness are unfamiliar to my ear ; and when they fell from you last night, I could have wept from the strange delight they gave."

The letter then went on to state that Madame di V——

intended setting out immediately to visit a relation who resided near the Alban Hill; and that on the following morning, the writer, availing herself of this only opportunity of escape, would meet me by daybreak, at a spot which she specified near the Aventine; and concluded in the following words, penned evidently under feelings of the strongest agitation, and so blotted with tears that I had the greatest difficulty in deciphering them. "Forgive me, if I have been too bold or too rashly confident: my brain is wandering; I scarce know what I have written; but still, even amidst my darkest apprehensions, a something assures me that you will not betray or desert me. Hark! a voice—my mother's voice. I must break off.

"HORTENSE."

My emotions, on reading this letter, were of a strangely complex character, made up of surprise, admiration, and bitter disappointment. First, I was struck with the simplicity—the confidingness—the strength and purity of affection—the mixture of timidity and resolution—of gentleness and desperation—that it developed in every line; secondly, I felt but too painfully convinced that it crushed out the last faint spark of hope, which even up to this moment I had unconsciously nourished. For a time this last feeling predominated; but soon a worthier spirit prevailed. I felt it impossible to refuse a request thus urged; so I resolved, at whatever risk to my own peace of mind, to show Hortense that I was not unworthy of the noble confidence she had reposed in me.

No sooner had I formed this resolution than, without allowing myself a minute's pause, I proceeded to make preparations for carrying it into execution; the hurry and bustle of which, luckily allowed me no time for those discreet, but in many instances erroneous, reflections, which are usually styled "second thoughts."

How slowly passed the night that was to usher in the eventful morning! Vainly I strove to compose myself to sleep; the excitement of my nerves would not be allayed;

18

and hour after hour I lay listening to the slow ticking of my watch, vexed—maddened with its monotonous click, click; and then vexed with myself for being such a slave to impulse.   At last—oh, joyful sight!—a few faint streaks of day came trembling in at the window; on which I leaped from bed, dressed, arranged what few conveniences I had to carry with me, and then hurried off to the place of rendezvous.

On reaching the spot, where I found my carriage and horses in waiting, all was still and solitary. I took out my watch.   It wanted but ten minutes of the hour at which Hortense had appointed to meet me, Yet she came not. What could be the reason?   My first idea was that her flight had been detected; my next, that her timidity had taken the alarm, and she had repented of her desperate enterprise; but I did injustice to her firmness of character; for, just as St. Peter's Basilic struck six, I could discern a figure wrapped up in a mantle advancing towards me. As it drew nearer, there was no mistaking the shrinking, bending form of Hortense. She trembled from head to foot, as if she apprehended the worst; whereupon I said, " Courage, lady! remember I am your friend, your sworn brother and guardian."

" My generous benefactor !" she replied, looking up timidly and beseechingly in my face, " you will save me, then, from this detested marriage ?   Speak; let me know my fate at once."

" I will; and more than this, I will restore you, at all hazards, to the arms of him"—(I could not bring myself to pronounce the word 'Eugene')—" from whom you ought never to have been separated;" and so saying, without allowing her time to pour forth her thanks, I hurried her into the vehicle, which soon left the Eternal City many long miles behind.

For the first three or four hours, Hortense was in a con- stant flutter of alarm. At every sound of wheels she started, turned pale, and flung herself back in the carriage; and not a horseman passed, but her fears instantly suggested that he had been despatched in pursuit by her mother. How harsh—how ungenerous—how cruel—must have been the conduct of that mother, the very mention of whose name thus acted on her daughter like a spell of horror!

By sunset, however, my young fellow-traveller had so far regained her composure, that she readily closed with my proposal of resting for the night at a little town, or village, which we reached just as darkness was gathering round us: and at an early hour on the following morning we resumed our route; which we continued, without intermission, until we arrived at Venafro, where we made our second night's halt, and thence struck at once into the heart of the Apennines.

From this period our course became one of difficulty, if not of danger; for though, generally speaking, the Apennines present no such formidable appearances as the Alps or the Pyrenees, yet they are not without their steep declivities and narrow rocky defiles—and unfortunately it was among the worst of these that our course lay— in winding along which the traveller has need of all his caution. Nor are these the only hazards to which he is subjected; for among the secluded recesses of the mountains, lurk hosts of ferocious brigands.

The evening of the third day was drawing on, when we came to one of the wildest and most secluded passes to be found in the whole Apennine range. It ran along the edge of a black, thunder-splintered cliff, and here, for the first time, the landscape assumed an aspect of imposing, not to say terrible, grandeur. Above us rose a vast wall of loose toppling crags, which seemed ever ready to fall on our heads; and before us a stormy sea of mountains, some lifting, "sheer, abrupt," their sharp naked summits to the sky, with deep channels worn into their sides by the action of the wintry torrents; and some swelling up more gradually from the valleys, their huge foreheads frowning with the eternal gloom of pine and fir.

Our progress here was necessarily slow, for the road was broken, craggy, and narrow—in fact, little better than a footpath, and so full of sharp turns and angles, that more than once I was compelled to leave Hortense in the carriage, and go forward and assist our driver in guiding the mules' heads.

Night, meanwhile, came striding forward at a giant's pace, and the unsettled aspect of the west betokened an approaching storm. To increase our embarrassment, we found that we had mistaken our way; and as to go back was now quite as useless as to go forward, we had nothing left for it but to push on, in the hope that we might reach some convent or osteria before the storm should burst on the mountains.

We had maintained our course for upwards of half an hour along a pass which seemed interminable, when a brisk wind sprung up; a broad, red, and dusky light gathered for an instant round the horizon, then faded into a dull glimmer; the trees rocked and groaned; and the sultriness, which had prevailed more or less throughout the day, began to be succeeded by a damp, oppressive chill. Almost immediately afterwards—so quick is the transition from calm to storm in these elevated regions— we could hear the hurricane uplifting its voice among the pines, and whistling shrilly through the clefts in the precipice above us.

At this moment we were winding round a projecting crag, beyond which, as well as we could perceive by the faint light that was left, our road began to slope a little; when suddenly, without any other warning than one vivid flash of lightning, the whole fury of the tempest was let loose on us. The thunder burst in stunning crash upon crash right above our heads, till the disjointed masses of cliff and crag seemed rocking to their very foundation; and the rain fell in such a deluge, that the little streams which we had constantly heard trickling across our path now swelled to the size of torrents, and dashed in cataracts into the ravine beneath.

Fortunately, just previous to this, I had prevailed on my companion to quit the carriage, and walk forward with me—my mantle being closely folded round her, so as to shield her as much as possible from the rain—while our postillion followed, guiding the mules, which had become quite restive from fright, and kept plunging towards the edge of the cliff. I say fortunately,—for scarcely had we advanced a hundred paces, when a second thunder-clap, louder than any that had yet preceded it, detached a fragment of rock which overhung the road we had passed but a few minutes before. Down fell the enormous mass, crushing and bearing down all before it, right into the very middle of the path; and hardly had the postillion time to let go his hold and make a desperate bound towards us, when it came in contact with the carriage, and hurled it over the edge of the pass into the glen; from whence, heard far above the roar of the hurricane, came up the piercing yell of the mules, as they bounded from crag to crag and then plunged into the black abyss.

"What cry was that?" exclaimed Hortense, in great terror.

"'Tis the mules," said the driver; they're gone right over the cliff, and are dashed to atoms by this time."

"Gone!" murmured Hortense, with a shudder that shook her whole frame, "gone! it will be our turn next."

It seemed, indeed, but too probable; for night was around us in all its gloom, and by the lightning only were we enabled to track our progress. Under these circumstances, I felt it was madness to proceed; so, seating my companion on a bit of broken rock that projected into the path, I proposed to go forward alone, and see if I could discover any cave or recess where we might find shelter till the storm had subsided.

But she was too much terrified to hear of my proposition. "Don't leave me," she whispered; "I am sure you will be lost if you do. If we die, let us die together."

The postillion, who was close behind us, here volunteered to go himself and look out for a place of shelter, which enabled me to direct my whole attention to Hortense; so, taking my seat beside her, I wrung the wet from her mantle, chafed her cold hands, and endeavoured to inspire her with confidence.

In a few minutes our guide returned, with intelligence that he had discovered a recess hard by, whither we instantly proceeded to support Hortense. 'Twas a damp, forlorn spot, and the wind moaned through it like the low wailing of a ghost: but I heeded not its gloom; I felt only that *she* was by my side; that it was her head that reclined on my shoulder; her small white hand that gently clasped mine; her sweet voice that in low fervent tones acknowledged me as her friend and brother. In her presence all was cheerfulness. It was desolation only when she was absent.

We remained in the cave upwards of half an hour; when, the rain having abated, and my young companion having recovered from her first alarms, we ventured to pursue our journey; and were soon rewarded for our perseverance by finding the path become less irregular and precipitous as we descended, and hearing, in the pauses of the wind, the distant ringing of a convent-bell.

A few minutes' more toilsome walking brought us on level ground, whence we could distinctly see through the darkness, apparently but a few yards ahead, the glimmering of a light. "Thank God, we are safe now!" said I, pointing out this welcome ray to Hortense.

"I trust so," was her faint reply; "but what a night has this been for us all!" and as she spoke, I could feel her arm quivering like an aspen-leaf within mine.

The rage of the tempest was by this time greatly abated; but the lightning was still vivid, and, by its frequent coruscations, I could see that we were indeed approaching the habitations of men. The bark of a dog confirmed me in this opinion; the light, too, which we had before noticed, became every moment more distinct; and, following its direction, we at length arrived under the walls of one of those small convents which are so frequent among the Abruzzi, and the more inland branch of the Apennines.

The monks had just quitted the chapel, and were about retiring to their cells for the night, when our ringing brought them to the portal. There was no need of words, for the dismal plight we were in sufficiently told the nature of our wants; so, ushering us into a kind of hall or refectory, the good fathers instantly got ready a cheerful fire, together with the best repast their scanty means would allow.

Spent with the day's toil, Hortense declined any further refreshment than a single cup of wine; and after waiting till her room was prepared for her reception, retired to the only convenient chamber the convent had to boast, which was devoted to the use of benighted travellers like ourselves; while I remained up, drying my clothes by the fire, and conversing between whiles with the superior, who invited me to occupy his cell; but on my expressing a desire to remain where I was, he quitted me at a late hour, after trimming the lamp and throwing fresh logs on the hearth.

All was now silent within the convent, though without I could still hear the wind whistling about its old walls. 'Twas an hour for meditation, and I felt its power. I thought of the events of the last few days; of the sudden transformation they had effected in my character; and of the strange magic of that passion which had compelled me, as it were, to minister to my own despair. "Yes," said I, aloud, while at the same time, to drown the sense of loneliness that crept over me, I kept quaffing cup after cup of wine, "she whose very presence is sunshine, without whom all is sterile and cheerless in nature and my own heart, this divine being—so loved, so reverenced, so worshipped—I have become the means of resigning to another! And can he prize her as I do? Can he make the sacrifice to her that I am doing? Why, even amidst the wildest fury of the tempest, when death spoke in the thunder, and glared on me in the lightning, I felt a tumultuous thrill of rapture, such as I never felt before, while I clasped this treasure in my arms, felt her breath upon my cheek, and heard her whisper, 'We will die together.' Die together! Yet we may not live together!"

At this instant the convent clock struck twelve. I rose and went to the casement. The storm had rolled away in distance. The sky was without a cloud. "All is still," I continued, gazing abroad on the night; " *she* too sleeps ; and, perhaps, at this very moment, while I keep lonely watch, is dreaming of Eugene. See! they have just met! How she welcomes him—hangs about his neck—feeds, stifles him with kisses, and calls him—— I shall go mad!" and rushing to the table, I quaffed another full cup of wine, in the hope of driving away the phantoms that a too vivid fancy had conjured up.

By this time it was past midnight; and, finding that slumber, despite all my efforts, was gradually stealing over me, I took up my mantle, which I had stretched out before the hearth to dry, and wrapping it round me, threw myself along the floor in front of the fire, and, in a few minutes, sunk into a profound sleep, from which I was only awakened by the morning sun glancing in at the window.

My first sensations on rising were merely those of chill and numbness ; but soon other and more unfavourable symptoms, aggravated by my late state of health, began to develop themselves ; and by the time my sister—for as such she was considered by the monks—made her appearance at the breakfast-table, I had become so seriously indisposed that the superior, who was a bit of a leech in his way, insisted on my retiring to his pallet—a proposal, however, which Hortense would not hear of; so, at her earnest entreaties, I was supported to her own room, where she and Padre Battista volunteered to play between them the parts of nurse and physician.

But the former was my chief attendant. For four days, during which my state was really critical, she counted the long dull hours beside my couch. When I awoke at midnight from dreams of horror, it was to see her angel form bending over me ; when I started from a feverish doze, to see the midday sun streaming in through the closed windows, or its declining ray giving place to the brown shades of evening—still, there she was ; and though I would fain have released her from such irksome attendance, and even the superior insisted on taking her place, she would not be denied ; but if she ever quitted the room, it was but to return in a few minutes, prepared for fresh offices of kindness. She it was whose hands administered my medicine, wiped the damps from my brow, and freshened my glued and clammy lips. She seemed to feel no weariness—no disappointment at the temporary frustration of her hopes ; but wore ever an encouraging smile on her countenance, speaking in accents that fell like music on my ear, and moving about with the light noiseless tread of a fairy.

The fourth night was the crisis of my disorder, and, during the whole time, I lay in a state of almost constant delirium. My ears rung with strange noises, my veins seemed charged with fire, and all those spectral illusions which fever is so apt to conjure up were let loose on me in dreams. First, I thought that I was pacing alone, at sunset, over an Arabian desert, when suddenly I heard a strange hurtling in the air, and gazing far into the distance, beheld, on the horizon's verge, a gigantic column, whose head was hidden among the clouds, rushing towards me. On—onward came the tornado, filling my mouth, my eyes, every pore of my skin, with dust, and crushing me to a mummy beneath its weight. A sound, as of the rush of mighty waters, roused me from this state of torture, and, lifting up my feeble eyes, I descried, first, the indistinct heavings of a surge, then the long, unbroken swell of billows, till at length a whole ocean burst in thunder on the desert, sweeping me far away on its bosom, now tossed high up in the air, now plunged into an abyss, amid the roar of the winds, the bellowing of the waves, and the shouts of a thousand unknown monsters.

A change ensued. The scene was Gwynnevay. It was a summer daybreak; the air was brisk and elastic, the hedges were alive with music, and the dewdrops hung half-melted on the thistle's beard. Before me, at no great distance, lay the sea, darkened here and there by the shadow of a passing sail; and behind, my native village put forth its glad beauty in the sunshine. But hark! whose is that fairy step that comes gliding down the lane? She hastens towards me. Ah! 'tis Hortense! But the maiden's cheek was wan, the spirit of a premature decay lent a fatal lustre to her eye, and her voice seemed to have caught its tones from the grave. While I was yet rambling with her among the woods of Gwynnevay, a cloud rolled between us, the landscape assumed an altered character, and I stood solitary in the churchyard, low down in the lane, where the elms, meeting overhead, cast ever a cold shadow on the earth. But where was Hortense? Gone; and in her place stood my rival Eugene, glaring on me like a demon. A sword was in his hand; but what of that? I rushed on him; the steel snapped like glass in my grasp; and, burying the fragment in his breast, I bore him to the ground—spit—trampled on him, and—" Ha, ha, the fiend is dead!"—" Dead?" repeated a mocking voice in my ear. 'Twas his. An icy hand grasped mine. 'Twas his. A glassy, freezing eye fixed its horrid glance on me. Still, 'twas his—and I awoke with a shudder that convulsed my whole frame.

It was some minutes before I regained my recollection; but when I did, the first object on which my eyes settled was Hortense, who was seated by my side, pale with watching. The instant I recognised her I exclaimed, " Speak to me, lady; let the last music I shall hear on earth be your voice;" and I sank back again in a swoon; from which I recovered only to hear the stifled sobs of my young nurse, who was watching each change in my countenance with eyes dimmed with tears.

When she perceived that I was again conscious of her presence, she whispered, with a forced smile, that belied her words, "You are better now; I am sure you are;" and was rising to shade the lamp from my eyes, when, mistaking the object of her movement, I said, "Do not leave me; I have had frightful dreams; *he* was with me; if you go, he will return."

She saw that my thoughts were wandering; so, placing her hand gently on my mouth, she said, "Hush! you must not speak; the superior has enjoined silence on us both."

Padre Battiste here entered the room, and had no sooner taken my hand, on which a refreshing moisture was beginning to break out, than he pronounced the crisis of the fever to be past.

"Thank God!" cried Hortense, clasping her hands. "My friend—my brother!—if you had—but no, no; the worst is past! Come, let me smooth your pillow. See, father, how much brighter his eye is! How calm he lies! He can breathe freely now."

The superior made a sign to her to be silent, and was preparing to administer an opiate, when, with the wayward feeling of an invalid, I made a sign that Hortense should give it; and receiving it accordingly from her hands, I soon dropped off into a long, dreamless slumber.

In a few days my strength was so far recruited that I was able to take short walks in the convent garden with Hortense, occasionally accompanied by some of the monks; and the pure mountain breezes that blew about me, the quiet in which I lived, and, above all, the constant presence of my young fellow-traveller, completed the work of restoration; so that at the end of a fortnight I felt strong enough to pursue my journey. I had proposed to go even earlier; but my gentle nurse, with that disinterestedness which formed so prominent a feature in her character, would not hear of my proposal. Even the claims of love were, to her lofty mind, inferior, under the circumstances, to those of gratitude.

Early on the morning of the fifteenth day, we took leave of our hospitable entertainers; and as no better means of conveyance were to be had—our carriage having been found dashed to atoms at the bottom of a ravine—we hired a couple of mules, and under the direction of an active young peasant, whom the superior had engaged for a guide, and provisioned with all things needful, we set forward for the little town of Muro, the place of Eugene's abode.

Our journey throughout this day was delightful, especially to Hortense, who, feeling for the first time since her flight, a tolerable sense of security, began to develop a thousand sprightly traits of character. Her disposition, indeed, was naturally cheerful; and there was a buoyancy in her every movement, a sunniness in her smile, a laughing witchery in the tones of her voice, that had all the effect of intoxication on my mind. I had already experienced the kindness of her nature; I was now to become acquainted with other and rarer qualities. Though her manner was soft and deferential, still there was a conscious dignity—a uniform sense of propriety about her—a proud, but not austere, reliance on her own innate rectitude of intention, and an unvarying confidence in the integrity of mine, that, had I been inclined to presume on my situation, would have awed me into shame. She had taste, too, and fancy, and a mind fertile in intellectual resources; and the various grand and lovely scenes over which we passed, drew forth all these refined qualities.

Sometimes our road would lead us along a narrow strip of valley, shut out from the world by huge mountains, among whose recesses were perched the rude summer cabins of the Apennine peasantry; and at others, into the heart of a dark glen, where the sun looked in on us through woods of cork and chestnut, over giant crags unscaled by human foot.

One landscape, in particular, struck us with such involuntary admiration that we both halted by tacit consent to enjoy it. We had been toiling for some time up an ascent of almost mountain elevation, when, on reaching the summit, we saw crag, valley, and meadow, and waving woods, and villages hanging on the sides of hills, robed in the rich green drapery of summer, with here and there the towers of a convent gleaming through the trees, basking in the meridian sunlight at our feet; while in the far perspective, where sky and land seemed peacefully commingling, we could catch a glimpse of a town, which Hortense's ardent imagination instantly suggested to her as Muro.

It was a scene to feel, not to describe; and I was reluctantly preparing to quit it, when our guide approached, and suggested that, as many a long mile yet lay between us and the place where we were to make our night's halt, we should seat ourselves and take some refreshment; and, without waiting for a reply, he produced from his wallet a bag of boiled chestnuts, the remains of a fine ham, a loaf of bread, and a small flagon of wine. It was a homely repast, but mountaineers are seldom fastidious; and as I sat beside Hortense, listening to her sprightly talk, and gazing on the vast landscape around, which was hushed into a Sabbath stillness, except when now and then the piping of a shepherd's reed, or the tinkling of a mule's bell came sounding up from the valley below us, I would not have exchanged my situation for that of the proudest monarch in Europe.

Our guide's tongue was not idle during this mountain bivouac, and he indulged us with various anecdotes of the brigands, in which all the Apennine peasantry abound; till, finding that Hortense began to be alarmed, he stopped short, and, rising from his seat, said, "We have delayed so long here, that we have not a moment to lose; for if night should surprise us before we reach that village"— pointing to a small cluster of cottages which, though they seemed close beneath us, were in reality many miles distant—"we might be exposed to some hazard."

This decided us; and, remounting our mules, we resumed our journey: but we had not advanced farther than a hundred yards, when we heard the shrill tones of a bugle, and presently a small troop of Austrian cavalry appeared, winding round the base of a low broad hill before us.

Hortense was the first to see them; and, pointing them out to my notice, exclaimed, exultingly, while her whole countenance was lit up with animation, "Eugene, too, is a soldier!" Never had I seen her look so lovely as at this moment. Expression had given the last magic touch to her beauty. When I had first met her among the ruins of the Palatine, she reminded me of some soft sylvan landscape, seen on a day when winds are still, and skies are clouded; she was now like that same landscape, when laughing breezes play about it, and all its graceful features are drawn forth, and live, and glow, and sparkle beneath the inspiring influence of a cloudless sun.

"Eugene is a soldier!" said I, repeating her words; "are all manly excellences, then, summed up in the word 'soldier?'"

"You mistake me," she replied; "I meant not that; how should I, when I bear in mind what you have braved in my behalf? But Eugene was the friend of my childhood; we grew up together, and my heart was wholly his before I knew I had one to bestow."

"Well, lady, well, I meant not reproach; though feelings that I could not—but no matter; you are my sister."

"I am, I am," she replied eagerly, with all the charming vivacity of her nation; "and no sister ever loved a brother dearer than I will love you."

By this time the sun had wheeled towards the west, and long pensile streaks of gold and silver edged the clouds, which lay piled up in fantastic masses on each other, while a warm purple glow hung like a glory over the landscape.

"What a divine sunset!" said I, addressing Hortense. "Of all the sources of enjoyment which nature unfolds for our use, I know few equal to those we feel when gazing on a scene like this. There is something in this hour, so tender—so holy—so fraught with simple yet sublime associations, that it seems to partake rather of heaven than earth. The day, with all its selfish commonplace interests, has gone by, and the season of intelligence—of imagination—of spirituality, is dawning. Yes; twilight does indeed unlock the Blandusian fountain of fancy: there, as in a mirror, reflecting all things in added loveliness, the heart surveys the past; the dead—the absent—the estranged—come thronging back on our minds; and thus, lady, will it be with me, when you are no longer by my side. Never, at this hour, shall I recall the past, but fancy will bring you to my mind."

"Such was the way," replied Hortense, "that Eugene used to speak, when it was no crime in me to listen to him; and it was the remembrance of his last conversation with me, on an evening like this at Tivoli, that pressed so heavily on my mind, when you met me with my uncle and my mother on the Palatine."

"Happy Eugene! to be able to call forth such feelings! Would to God that his lot were—" then suddenly checking myself, I added, in a more equable tone, "See, Hortense, how the cold evening is saddening over those rocks, that but a few minutes since blushed with the red light of the setting sun. Just such a change, so sudden, so cheerless, will take place in my feelings, ere another day goes down on the Apennines. You now shed light and warmth on them; but when once your enlivening presence is withdrawn, they will be as dull and lonely as before."

"Not so," returned Hortense, kindly; "it cannot be as you say. But you talked of quitting us?"

"Even so."

"This must not be. You must stay with us, and share in the happiness you have yourself created."

All further conversation was here put an end to by the guide, who informed us, not a little to our surprise and dismay, that it would now be wholly impossible to reach the village before darkness overtook us, unless, indeed, we were prepared to lose our way in a wild district infested by brigands.   He added, however, that there was a little ruined chapel hard-by, within which, as the night was warm, and dry, and clear, we might perhaps make shift to rest till daybreak.

To this Hortense was by no means willing to accede; but seeing that I pressed it, apprehensive of the hazards to which we might otherwise be exposed—for our little party was wholly unarmed—she gave up the point; and in a few minutes we reached the chapel, which was erected close beside the road.   The walls alone were standing; and within, right under what must have once been the main window, was fixed a plain crucifix, which no sooner caught Hortense's eyes, than, alighting from her mule, she threw herself on her knees before it.

How touching is female piety!   How sweetly fall its accents from the lips of the young and the beautiful!   I had heard the solemn choirs beneath the majestic roof of St. Peter, where religion puts on her most imposing form; but never was my heart so touched, so purified, as when I saw Hortense kneeling in that lone chapel, among the dim silent mountains, looking the very incarnation of peace and piety.

When she had risen from her knees, we proceeded together into the heart of the ruins, where, after a diligent scrutiny, I discovered a small nook, which had apparently once formed the oratory, but was now detached from the main building.   As this wing or angle was the most sheltered part of the chapel, being surrounded on all sides but one by low walls, just outside of which rose a thick grove of firs, I proposed to Hortense to make it her resting-place; and having collected some dry moss and leaves, to form a sort of couch, and spread my mantle over them by way of coverlet, I quitted her for a short time, while I arranged with the guide to stay and take charge of the mules in the wood, which ran sloping down a small mound into a meadow below.

I was absent but half an hour, looking about in all directions to see that no one was observing us, yet when I came back I found Hortense buried in deep sleep. There she lay, beneath the light of the now risen moon, which never watched over the slumbers of a purer being; with one snowy arm half-hidden beneath her head, and the other pressed on a bosom that just lightly heaved with a serene swell, like ocean on a breezeless summer day. How lovely she looked! A warmer flush than usual glowed on her cheek; a faint smile that might have become the sleeping Psyche, played around her lips; her long silken lashes drooped over her eyes, which were shut up, like sweet flowers at twilight; her delicate swan-like neck, on whose alabaster surface lay one or two straggling ringlets was partially revealed; and beneath the mantle that concealed the rest of her figure, peeped out one small slender foot.

I was dazzled—bewildered by this image of transcendent beauty, and stooping down, I imprinted one kiss—the first, the last—on the peach-like down of the young sleeper's cheek. But hark! she moves — she smiles—a name escapes her lips! Is it mine? Am I the subject of her dream? Have I called forth that smile? Mad, conceited fool! 'Tis Eugene's name she murmurs. With a sickening feeling of despair, I started from the ground as I heard this word; and, stifling a groan that struggled to my throat, I rushed from the chapel into the thick dark grove that frowned beside it.

It was now night. All was hushed around—below—above—while I, restless and desponding, moved alone amid the solitudes of earth. Alone on earth! What a dreary hopeless feeling do these few words convey! Yet this, I said, must be my destiny. A few hours, and the form that now gilds my path will have passed away, leaving but the memory of what has been. Well, better it should be so. To walk with her—to listen to her—to banquet on her smiles—to draw in love from the liquid lustre of her eyes—to share her thoughts, yet be compelled

19

to restrain my own—to be devoted to her, yet not dare to tell her that I love—to be studiously reserved, when my heart is at my lips—I should sink beneath the struggle, were it to endure but another day.

In vain I strove to shake off the gloom with which these feelings inspired me. The very hour served to enhance it, What—I continued, looking up to the blue, quiet sky—-what is there in the holy stillness of a night like this, that should thus cast a deeper shade over my mind? The stars that send down their tranquil radiance on earth; the moon that walks the stedfast floor of heaven in the spirit of peace and benignity; the breeze that brings the various harmonies of creation to my ear, till the very soul of sacred melody seems breathing in them; surely, these are sights and sounds to elevate, not depress me. Where then lies the secret of the dark spell which night holds over my feelings? In the power with which it enforces meditation, and, by consequence, melancholy—for with me, at least, reflection has become but another word for sadness.

Thus, restless and moody, I was slowly making my way back into the chapel, when my attention was called off by the sound of footsteps, and presently I could hear voices at the bottom of the slope. I listened; the strangers evidently drew nearer; so, concealing myself behind one of the thickest of the trees, I watched their movements, and could see, by the pistols in their belts, and the relics at their breasts, that they were brigands,—a discovery that was confirmed by the imperfect fragments of their conversation which I overheard. and which related to some enterprise in which they had lately failed, on the road between Muro and Naples.

What a state of intense anxiety was mine at this moment! What should I do? How protect the young sleeper in the chapel? I was unarmed. My guide was at some distance. He might wake. The mules might stir; in which case inevitable destruction awaited our whole party.

The brigands were by this time right underneath me; but as the nature of my hiding-place screened me from observation, I endeavoured, with extreme caution, to steal back into the chapel, if not to awaken Hortense—for I feared the effects of alarm on her mind—at least to keep watch beside her.

But the practised ear of the robbers had caught the sound of my tread. "Hark!" said one, "some one is stirring here. I heard a footstep."

"Nonsense," replied his companion, "'tis only the wind among the trees."

Both then halted an instant, and the first speaker, unslinging his carbine, and bringing it to the ground with a heavy clang, stood leaning on it, and darting his eyes right towards that part of the grove where I was stationed. 'Twas a moment of unutterable agony; for from the keen suspicious glance of the ruffian I made sure we were discovered, and in an instant I should have sunk to the ground, had not the fellow, apparently satisfied that he was mistaken, relaxed his scrutiny, and said, " It is of no use loitering longer in this neighbourhood; we had far better return to the pass above Venafro; for the travellers whose broken carriage Jacopo saw in the glen must have reached Naples by this time;" and so saying, I could hear them slowly retiring, on which, after thanking God for our timely deliverance, I quitted my hiding-place, and went in search of the guide, whom I found fast asleep a few paces from me in the grove, with the mules tethered to a tree beside him.

I waited until convinced the brigands were out of hearing, and then woke the guide; and having acquainted him with the dangers we had all just escaped, I bade him keep watch outside the chapel, so that, should any more of the troop come up, we might be better prepared to make resistance; and then entered the little nook, where I found Hortense just waking from her sleep, and I remained by her side till daybreak summoned us to depart.

Brightly broke the morning—the last morning that I was to meet, face to face, on the Apennines with Hortense. The mists were fast rolling off, like smoke, from the mountains' sides; earth was steeped in dewy freshness; and my young fellow traveller, refreshed by sleep, and anticipating, ere the day should be many hours older, her reunion with Eugene, partook of the cheering influence of the season.

How different were my sensations! Every mile that brought her nearer to happiness was bearing me farther from it. I made several efforts to rouse myself, or, at least, to conceal my depression; but it was of no avail; and I rode for miles beside Hortense, scarce able to make any reply to her apt remarks, when any bend of our road brought out some more than ordinary picturesque feature in the scenery.

Seeing this, she prevailed on me to alight from my mule, and ramble on with her on foot; and on one particular occasion, when I had made no answer to some sprightly question she had put, she began bantering me with that arch yet delicate familiarity which is so irresistible a weapon in the hands of beauty.

" See what it is to be a philosopher !" she said; " I have asked you a simple question three times, but your thoughts have been wandering with the sages of old, in the clouds, and you have not yet made me a reply."

" Forgive my rudeness, but I was thinking at the time—"

" I know you were, you looked so grave. But why are you so? Are you not well?" she asked, in a more softened tone.

" No, my mind is weighed down with—"

" Come, come, you must not give way to dark thoughts. Remember, you are still bound to adopt whatever regimen I shall prescribe. So let me see you smile. Good. Upon my word, you do wonders for an invalid! Oh, if you did but know how much more a smile becomes you than a frown! Now don't shake your head so gravely at me. I am silly—I know it; but it is your fault—you have made me so—so happy!" and flinging back her sunny tresses, she held out her hand to me with a smile that went to my heart like a sunburst.

In this way we kept chatting on, Hortense doing all she could to raise my flagging spirits, until we reached the village, which we had missed the night before. Here we halted to breakfast at a small osteria, and then set out again on our journey, and, in less than two hours, reached the last chain of hills that alone divided us from Muro.

'Twas a lovely landscape that now spread itself out at our feet, but looked on by me with feelings far different from those of Hortense. I saw nothing in the broad elevated valley, at one end of which the town is situated, in the classic ruins that adorn it, and in the clear chattering stream that winds through it, but objects calculated to impress me with bitter regret; she, naught but what was enlivening and beautiful. She looked on the prospect with the bright eyes of hope; I, with those only of clouded disappointment.

On, on we went; and now we have passed the hills, have reached the level ground, and are halting within a mile—yes, within one short mile—of Muro! This halt was made at my request. I had resolved on no account to see Eugene; indeed, the sight of his happiness would have roused feelings in me that I would not, for the world, have betrayed; so, hastily furbishing up the first pretext that presented itself, I said, "'Tis the last favour I shall ask of you, lady; but, as it is just possible you may have erred in Eugene's abode, or he may have been discovered and compelled to fly, let us send forward our guide, and here await his return."

To this request Hortense, wondering, no doubt, at its singularity, acceded, though not without reluctance; and, accordingly, we despatched the young muleteer into the town, who returned within the hour with a note, written in evident haste by Eugene, and to the effect that he had been expecting his mistress' arrival for some days; but that, having been discovered, he dared no longer remain within the States of the Church, and had, therefore, set out for Cagliari, where some friends were staying, through whose influence at the court of Turin he was not without hopes of obtaining employment in the army. The letter concluded by imploring her to lose not an instant in rejoining him, and was clearly written under the sanguine idea that Madame di V—— might have relented, and allowed her daughter's departure.

The receipt of this letter was a sad blow to Hortense; all the enthusiasm which she had evinced during the morning was at once put an end to; and I could only restore her to composure by acceding to her request that I would not lose a moment in setting out for Cagliari.

In fulfilment, accordingly, of this promise, we hastened on to Muro, where we discharged our guide—the difficulties of our journey being now nearly at an end—and, travelling at the utmost speed that circumstances would admit of, reached Naples at the end of the third day.

Fain would I have detained Hortense at this superb city, but she was in agony to depart; seeing which, I interposed no further delay; but finding on inquiry that a vessel was lying in the harbour which was about to sail for the Sardinian coast, I engaged for a passage in it, and embarked the very morning after our arrival at Naples.

Had either of us been in the mood, we might have lingered with admiration on the magnificent scene that presented itself, as we floated over the waters of this unrivalled bay. We might have marked the heights of Pausilippo—the little isle of Ischia—the frowning Vesuvius —and, above all, the splendid appearance that the city we were leaving behind us made from the sea; but other thoughts engrossed our attention, and we cast but an idle look at this most beautiful of landscapes, in a region teeming with beauties.

Our voyage was brisk and prosperous; no sooner had we lost sight of Naples, and were abroad on the open sea, than Hortense's usual cheerfulness began to return; and she would sit for hours upon deck, listening to the mysterious sounds that ever and anon came wafted towards us; and bending a lively, inquisitive glance over the waters, in the hope, as she laughingly observed, that she might be the first to catch a glimpse of the Sardinian shores.

We had been about three days at sea, when, on the morning of the fourth, the cry of " Land " was raised by a sailor at the mast-head; and soon afterwards we discovered the distant island-coast, hanging like a cloud in the horizon. Hortense, of course, was among the first to greet this welcome object; and, after gazing on it for some time in silence, she turned to me, and said, " How slowly the vessel moves! See, the land seems to recede as we advance !"

" Slow !" I replied, " I was just now wondering at the rapid progress we are making," and bade her mark the swelling outline of the coast, which was gradually becoming more broadly and distinctly traced on the horizon.

Towards evening we came within sight of Cagliari, and by sunset had approached it so closely that we could hear the convent-bells ringing for vespers, and perceive the vessels in the offing, and even the palaces, churches, and streets rising up, like the work of enchantment, from the sea. A few minutes more, and we had cast anchor within bowshot of the town, from which several boats instantly put off, for the purpose of assisting us to land.

At this instant, Hortense and myself were standing alone at one end of the vessel. I seized the favourable opportunity, and, in a voice half choked with emotion, which I strove in vain to subdue, thus, for the last time, addressed her : " Lady, De Grey has kept his word, and the time has arrived when you and he must part. I anticipate your reply—I respect its motive—but my resolution is unalterable."

She looked at me, as I said this, with unfeigned astonishment. " Part !" she exclaimed ; " surely you will see Eugene ? You have been my saviour—you must become his friend. Oh, if you did but know him !"

"Too well I know him, and too well, but too late, I know myself. You, lady, have taught me that knowledge. When I first met you, I was a cold, shy recluse, living alone in a world of abstraction; but you breathed warmth into me; you brought all my better thoughts into leaf; you taught me that I could love, and perhaps even that I was worthy to be loved. If I now confess thus much, it is only because my motives can no longer be misinterpreted; and because, in spite of myself, my feelings at this hour, when we are about to be separated, will find a voice. Lady—Hortense, from the first moment I beheld you, your image filled the void which I had so long felt in my heart. Asleep or awake, absent or present, it has never left me for an instant. You start. Surely my words cannot take you by surprise! 'Twere not in human nature to feel otherwise than I feel. How could I be insensible to your beauty? How forget the forbearance—the tenderness—the devotion—the noble disregard of self you showed me at the convent? or that rare magnanimity of soul which, judging of others by itself, selected me as the object of its confidence? If these are things to be forgotten, what is there that deserves to be remembered?"

"My kind—my noble benefactor—"

"No thanks, lady; I deserve none. I have but done my duty, and it is the consciousness of this, joined with the respect—the reverence I entertain, and must ever entertain, towards you, that sustains me at this parting hour, and has enabled me to repress my feelings, even when my heart was bursting. 'Twas not when I was most reserved that I was least sensible of the magic of your presence. Often, during this memorable journey, have I longed to tell you of the deep, the impassioned feelings with which you inspired me; that my existence was bound up in yours; that I had no other use of being than to devote it to you; no sense of suffering, but when you suffered; of enjoyment, but when you were happy; that I loved you with a passion, fervent, exalted, disinterested as ever yet beat within man's bosom;—often, lady, have I longed to tell you this, but I respected your situation; I felt, too, that you had placed confidence in my honour, and that I was bound, by all the ties that can bind an honourable man, to prove myself worthy of it."

"How shall I thank you? What shall I say?"

"Nothing, lady: yet stay; when to-morrow's sun sets, look at it, and think of me. I shall be gazing at it too, and 'twill be some little consolation for me to feel that both of us, at that moment, are dwelling on the same object. 'Twill be no treason to love, that you should bestow a passing thought on friendship."

"I will—I will—but you must not give way to this melancholy. You must return home—mix with the world—and, in the love of some other woman, learn to regard me as a sister."

"Never. None can again be to me what you have been, but must be no longer. You were the first woman I ever loved; and to your name, fancy, and sentiment, and memory, will cling henceforth for ever. When I am sad, I will think of you; when I am cheerful, I will think of you; you shall be a pure, holy talisman, to wean me from ignoble thoughts, and prompt to generous actions; and when I die, yours shall be the last name that shall escape my lips, and be found graven on my heart's core. And now, dearest Hortense—sister—idol of my soul—in parting with whom I seem to part with hope, and even life itself—farewell; be happy, be prosperous; but do not forget De Grey, or the hours passed with him among the Apennines."

By this time the boat was close under the vessel's bows, and Hortense and myself embarking, we were speedily conveyed to land. Not a word was spoken on either side. The thoughts of both were too deep for utterance. When we reached the quay, we instantly proceeded to the house whither Eugene had directed us in his letter. It was easily found, being situated within a few yards of the castle. A light was burning in the passage. Hortense rushed in. A stranger advanced to meet her, and I just heard the words "dearest Hortense," when, before she could turn round to bid me farewell, I tore myself away, and quitted her sight for ever.

On returning to the vessel I sat down, like one stupified, on deck. "But a few minutes ago," I said, "and Hortense was here beside me. She is now gone—gone, with her angel smiles—her voice so full of music—her countenance so radiant with beauty—gone, never to come back!" and, fairly overcome by my feelings, for I knew not the bitterness of my bereavement till now, I wept and sobbed like a child. Still, while even the slightest trace of day remained, I kept my eyes fixed on the shore, striving through the mist to catch the last glimpse of Cagliari. Suddenly I saw two figures moving along the quay. "'Tis Hortense and Eugene," I said; "they have come to look for their benefactor;" and watched them as they proceeded slowly back into the town, till the sea-fog shut them out from my sight.

Within a few days I again reached Naples, and thence set out for Rome, by way of Muro and the Apennines, anxiously retracing every scene over which I had so lately travelled with Hortense. 'Twas a sickly feeling to pamper, but I could not help it. The chapel where I had watched her sleeping, the hill from which I had pointed out to her the first view of Muro; but, above all, the little mountain convent, where she had shown me such unwearied kindness in my illness;—oh, who shall say with what emotion I again beheld these objects. Yet, forlorn as they all appeared, they were still sacred, for they were indissolubly linked with the memory of Hortense. "Here," I exclaimed, "she sang her evening Ave Maria; and here, from the spot where I now stand, she bade me mark the distant Mediterranean. Perhaps she is gazing on it still; but she thinks not of me; oh, no! far happier thoughts engross her mind, and De Grey, like a dream, is forgotten."

This bitter, perhaps ungenerous, reflection continued to haunt me for years; and often, in the midst of crowds, when a fairer form than usual flitted across my path, I turned with a sigh to the recollection of Hortense. I thought of that sweet pale face which had so often bent over me in sickness, of those rosy lips which mine had once pressed, of that smile which used to greet me in the morning, and all those endearing graces by which, unconsciously as it were, a beautiful girl winds herself into the affections of man. Even to this day, her image blooms green in memory. Every spot that I visit brings her to my mind. She is beside me in my father's halls; she walks with me at sunset among the woods of Gwynnevay; her voice speaks in the summer wind; and ever, when in dreams the Apennines rise before me, I see her gliding like a spirit among their solitudes. But years have passed, and they are gathered to their kindred dust, Eugene and his devoted Hortense; their very names have long since perished, and all that is now known of them is—that they once existed.

THE END.

"If the steamboat and the railway have abridged time and space, and made a large addition to the available length of human existence, why may not our intellectual journey be also accelerated, our knowledge more cheaply and quickly acquired, its records rendered more accessible and portable, its cultivators increased in number, and its blessings more cheaply and widely diffused."—QUARTERLY REVIEW.

LONDON : FARRINGDON STREET.

ROUTLEDGE, WARNE, & ROUTLEDGE'S
NEW AND CHEAP EDITIONS
OF
Standard and Popular Works
IN

NATURAL HISTORY & SCIENCE.	POETRY AND THE DRAMA.
BOTANY AND GARDENING.	DRAWING ROOM TABLE BOOKS.
AGRICULTURE AND FARMING.	PRESENT AND GIFT BOOKS.
SPORTING AT HOME OR ABROAD.	PASTIMES.
THE RIFLE.	HOUSEHOLD ECONOMY AND COOKERY.
HISTORY.	
BIOGRAPHY.	DICTIONARIES AND BOOKS OF REFERENCE.
FOREIGN COUNTRIES.	
GENERAL LITERATURE.	LAW.
RELIGIOUS AND HYMN BOOKS.	FICTION.
EDUCATION, LANGUAGES, &c.	

WITH A GENERAL INDEX.

TO BE OBTAINED BY ORDER OF ALL BOOKSELLERS, HOME OR COLONIAL.

In ordering, specially mention "ROUTLEDGE'S EDITIONS."

NATURAL HISTORY, SCIENCE, &c.

In post 8vo, price **6s.** cloth gilt, or **6s. 6d.** gilt edges.

A NATURAL HISTORY. By the Rev. J. G. WOOD. A New Edition, with many additions. Containing nearly 500 Illustrations, from original designs by WILLIAM HARVEY, engraved by the Brothers DALZIEL. Its principal features are :—

1st. Its Accuracy. 2nd. Its Systematic Arrangement. 3rd. Illustrations executed expressly for the Work. And 4th. New and Authentic Anecdotes.

"One of the best of Messrs. Routledge and Co.'s publications."—*Times.*

B

In royal 8vo, handsomely bound in cloth, price **18s.**

THE ILLUSTRATED NATURAL HISTORY.   First
Volume—MAMMALIA.   By the Rev. J. G. WOOD, M.A., F.L.S.
With 480 Illustrations by WOLF, ZWECKER, HARRISON WEIR, HARVEY,
COLEMAN, &c. ; engraved by the Brothers DALZIEL.

This superb Volume, containing no less than 803 pages, beautifully
printed, and embellished with a profusion of admirable representations of
animal life by the most eminent artists of the day, completes the important
class of Mammalia.   The Publishers refer with much satisfaction to the
success of this great undertaking already achieved, and they trust that the
execution of the work as far as it has now progressed, will be accepted by
the subscribers as a sufficient guarantee for its adequate treatment until it
be completed.

*** *The Illustrated Natural History—Birds—This Volume is now
progressing in Monthly Parts, price One Shilling each.   It will be
completed in October, 1861, and will form a Volume, price 18s., uniform
with that of Mammalia.*

In small post 8vo (nearly ready),

NATURAL HISTORY NOTES.   With Reflections on Reason
and Instinct by the Rev. J. C. ATKINSON, Author of "Play Hours
and Half Holidays."   With 100 Illustrations by COLEMAN.

In cloth gilt, price **3s. 6d.**, or with gilt edges, **4s.**,

THE COMMON OBJECTS OF THE COUNTRY.   By the
Rev. J. G. WOOD.   With Illustrations by COLEMAN, containing 150
of the "Objects," beautifully printed in Colours.

This book gives short and simple descriptions of the numerous objects
that are to be found in our fields, woods, and waters.

Also, a Cheap Edition, price **1s.**, in Fancy Boards, with plain Plates.

In fcap. 8vo, price **3s. 6d.** cloth lettered,

THE COMMON OBJECTS OF THE SEA-SHORE.   With
Hints for the Aquarium.   By the Rev. J. G. WOOD.   The Fine
Edition with the Illustrations by G. B. SOWERBY, beautifully printed in
colours.

Also, price **1s.**, a Cheap Edition, with the Plates plain.

"This little work is of low price, but of high value, and is just the book to
be put into the hands of persons (and there are many such), whether young or
old, who 'having eyes,' have hitherto 'seen not' those 'common objects'
which bear within themselves whole cabinets of wonders.—*Globe.*

Price **3s. 6d.** cloth gilt, or **4s.** gilt edges,

SKETCHES AND ANECDOTES OF ANIMAL LIFE.
By the Rev. J. G. WOOD, M.A., F.L.S., &c.   With Eight Illustrations
by HARRISON WEIR.

"A fresh spirit pervades the book, as well in the narratives as the descriptive account of the nature and habits of the animals."—*Spectator.*
"Is replete with interest and information, and will be a valuable work to
the rising generation."—*News of the World.*

Price 3s. 6d. cloth boards, or 4s. gilt edges,

A NIMAL TRAITS AND CHARACTERISTICS. Comprising Anecdotes of Animals not included in the "Sketches and Anecdotes." By the Rev. J. G. WOOD, M.A., F.L.S., &c. With Illustrations by HARRISON WEIR.

"Young people will spend their time pleasantly and well who should be found engaged over its pages, aud those very wise people, their elders, if they took it up, would certainly be instructed."—*Examiner.*

Price 3s. 6d. each, cloth gilt, or 4s. gilt edges,

M Y FEATHERED FRIENDS. Containing Anecdotes of Bird-life, more especially Eagles, Vultures, Hawks, Magpies, Rooks, Crows, Ravens, Parrots, Humming Birds, Ostriches, &c. &c. By the Rev. J. G. WOOD. With Illustrations by HARRISON WEIR.

"The author's endeavour has been to show *the life* and *the character* of the creatures described rather than their outward shape, the *strictly scientific* part of the subject having been treated of elsewhere. He has avoided the use of harsh scientific terms, and has, in every case where it has been practicable, exchanged Greek and Latin words for simple English. An attempt has also been made to show how the nature of the lower auimals is raised and modified, their reason developed, and their instinct brought nuder subjection, when they come in familiar contact with man—the highest of the animal creation."

Fcap. 8vo, price 3s. 6d. cloth, or 4s. gilt edges,

W HITE'S NATURAL HISTORY OF SELBORNE. A New Edition. Edited by the Rev. J. G. WOOD, and illustrated with above 200 Illustrations by W. HARVEY. Finely printed.

"A very superior edition of this most popular work."—*Times.*
"Is a pleasant-looking volume, liberally illustrated with excellent pictures of nearly every animal or tree therein mentioned."—*Examiner.*

Foolscap, price 3s. 6d. cloth gilt, or 4s. gilt edges,

B RITISH BUTTERFLIES. Figures and Descriptions of every native species, with an Account of Butterfly Development, Structure, Habits, Localities, Mode of Capture, and Preservation, &c. With 71 Coloured Figures of Butterflies, all of exact life-size, and 67 Figures of Caterpillars, Chrysalides, Eggs, Scales, &c. By W. S. COLEMAN, Member of the Entomological Society of London.

** A Cheap Edition, with plain plates, fancy boards, price 1s.

"This pretty and complete little manual of British Butterflies is another valuable contribution to popular scientific literature, and may be safely recommended to all who have a hobby for collecting that beautiful class of insects."—*Critic.*

Cloth limp, price 1s.

C AGE AND SINGING BIRDS: how to Catch, Keep, Breed, and Rear them ; with Full Directions as to their Nature, Food, Diseases, &c. By H. G. ADAMS. With 22 Illustrations.

Fcap., price 1s. 6d. cloth limp.

THE RAT: its History and destructive character, with nume- rous Anecdotes, and Instructions for the EXTIRPATION of Rats from Houses and Farms. By JAMES RODWELL (Uncle James).

"This is one of the most interesting books upon a subject, more or less repulsive, we have ever had the good fortune to meet with. It is one of the most charming episodes in natural history possible to conceive. The author has a ' Vendetta ' against the Rat."—*Despatch.*

LOVELL REEVE'S POPULAR SERIES.

NATURAL HISTORY DIVISION.

Square, cloth gilt, price 7s. 6d. each.

BRITISH ORNITHOLOGY; containing a Familiar and Technical Description of the Birds of the British Isles. By P. H. GOSSE. With 19 Pages of Coloured Plates, embracing 100 subjects.

HISTORY OF BIRDS; comprising a Familiar Account of their Classification and Habits. By ADAM WHITE, F.L.S. With 20 Pages of Coloured Plates, embracing 110 subjects.

BRITISH BIRDS' EGGS. By RICHARD LAISHLEY. With 20 Pages of Coloured Plates, embracing 100 subjects.

BRITISH ENTOMOLOGY; containing a Familiar and Tech- nical Description of the INSECTS most common to the localities of the British Isles. By MARIA E. CATLOW. With 16 Pages of Coloured Plates.

BRITISH CONCHOLOGY. A Familiar History of the MOLLUSCS inhabiting the British Isles. By G. B. SOWERBY, F.L.S. With 20 Pages of Coloured Plates, embracing 150 subjects.

BRITISH CRUSTACEA; comprising a Familiar Account of their Classification and Habits. By ADAM WHITE, F.L.S. With 20 Pages of Coloured Plates, embracing 120 subjects.

MOLLUSCA; comprising a Familiar Account of their Classification, Instincts, and Habits, and of the Growth and dis- tinguishing Characters of their Shells. By MARY ROBERTS. With 20 Pages of Coloured Plates, embracing 120 subjects.

[*Continued.*

LOVELL REEVE'S POPULAR SERIES—*continued.*

BRITISH ZOOPHYTES, or CORALLINES. By the Rev. Dr. Landsborough. With 20 Pages of Coloured Plates, embracing 120 subjects.

THE AQUARIUM, of Marine and Fresh Water Animals and Plants. By G. B. Sowerby, F.L.S. With 20 Pages of Coloured Plates, embracing 120 subjects.

HISTORY OF MAMMALIA; comprising a Familiar Account of their Classification and Habits. By Adam White, F.L.S. With 16 Pages of Coloured Plates, embracing 120 subjects.

SCRIPTURE ZOOLOGY; containing a Familiar History of the Animals mentioned in the Bible. By Maria E. Catlow. With 16 Pages of Coloured Plates, embracing 120 subjects.

PHYSICAL GEOLOGY. By J. Bate Jukes, M.A., F.R.S. With 20 Pages of Coloured Plates by Mr. G. V. Dunoyer.

MINERALOGY; comprising a Familiar Account of Minerals and their Uses. By Henry Sowerby. With 20 Pages of Coloured Plates, embracing 120 subjects.

DR. BUCKLAND'S BRIDGEWATER TREATISE.

In 2 vols. demy 8vo., price **24s.**, cloth extra,

GEOLOGY AND MINERALOGY, considered with reference to Natural Theology. By the late Very Rev. William Buckland, D.D., F.R.S. A New Edition, with additions by Professor Owen, F.R.S., Professor Phillips, M.A., M.D., Mr. Robert Brown, F.R.S., &c. Edited by Francis T. Buckland, M.A. With a Memoir of the Author, Steel Portrait, and 90 Full-Page Engravings.

"A work as much distinguished for the industry and research which it indicates, as for its scientific principles and philosophical views. The extraordinary and inestimable facts which he has brought under the grasp of the general reader, have been illustrated by numerous and splendid embellishments; and, while his descriptions of them are clothed in simple and perspicuous language, the general views to which they lead have been presented to us in the highest tone of a lofty and impressive eloquence. We have ourselves never perused a work more truly fascinating, or more deeply calculated to leave abiding impressions on the heart; and if this shall be the general opinion, we are sure that it will be the source of higher gratification to the author than the more desired, though on his part equally deserved, meed of literary renown."—*Edinburgh Review.*

Fcap. cloth, boards, price **2s.**, or in cloth gilt, **2s. 6d.**,

THE MARVELS OF SCIENCE, and their Testimony to Holy Writ. A Popular System of the Sciences. By W. S. Fullom. Twelfth Edition, revised. 12 Illustrations.

In fcap. 8vo, cloth, price 2s. 6d.,

GEOLOGICAL GOSSIP; or, Stray Chapters on Earth and Ocean. By Professor ANSTED, M.A., F.R.S. With Illustrations.

CONTENTS.

Rivers and Water-Floods.	Origin of Rocks and Metamorphism.
The Surface of the Atlantic.	New Discoveries in Iron Ores.
The Great Deep and its Inhabitants.	Coal-Fields and Coal Extraction.
Statistics of Earthquakes.	Gold Deposits.
Origin of Volcanoes.	Water-Glass and Artificial Stone.
Antiquity of the Human Race.	Preservation of Stones.

&c. &c.

Post 8vo (in the press),

MINES, MINERALS, AND METALS. A Popular Description of them and their Uses. By J. H. PEPPER, late Lecturer at the Polytechnic Institution. With 300 Practical Illustrations.

In square royal, price 5s., cloth extra,

BEACH RAMBLES, in Search of Sea-Side Pebbles and Crystals, with Observations on the Origin of the Diamond and other Precious Stones. By J. G. FRANCIS, B.A. With 14 Illustrations, designed by Coleman, and printed in Colours by Evans.

"What Mr. GOSSE's books are to marine objects this volume is to the pebbles and crystals with which our shores are strewn. It is an indispensable companion to every sea-side stroller."—*Bell's Messenger.*

Price 2s. 6d. cloth gilt, or 3s. gilt edges.

THE ORBS OF HEAVEN; or, The Planetary and Stellar Worlds. A Popular Exposition of the great Discoveries and Theories of Modern Astronomy. By O. M. MITCHELL. Eleventh Edition, with many Illustrations.

"This volume contains a graphic and popular exposition of the great discoveries of astronomical science, including those made by Lord Rosse (illustrated by several engravings), Leverrier, and Maedler. The Cincinnati Observatory owes its origin to the remarkable interest excited by the delivery of these Lectures to a succession of crowded audiences."

Fcap. 8vo, price 5s., cloth gilt, with Coloured Illustrations,

THE LAWS OF CONTRAST OF COLOUR, and their application to the Fine Arts of Painting, Decoration of Buildings, Mosaic Work, Tapestry and Carpet Weaving, Calico Printing, Dress, Paper Staining, Printing, Illumination, Landscape and Flower Gardening. By M. E. CHEVREUL, Director of the Dye Works of the Gobelins. Translated by JOHN SPANTON.

A Cheap Edition, without the Coloured Plates, price 2s. cloth.

"Every one whose business has anything to do with the arrangement of colours should possess this book. Its value has been universally acknowledged, having been translated into various languages, although but recently into our own."

Crown 8vo, price 2s. 6d. cloth, or 3s. gilt edges,

POPULAR ASTRONOMY. A Concise Elementary Treatise on the Sun, Planets, Satellites, and Comets. With an Appendix, containing very complete Tables of the Elements of the Planets and Comets, and of the 33 Asteroids. By O. M. MITCHELL, LL.D., Author of "The Orbs of Heaven." 12 Illustrations. Revised and Edited by the Rev. L. Tomlinson, M.A.

Fcap. 8vo, price 2s. cloth extra,

ARAGO'S POPULAR ASTRONOMY: Revised and Edited by the Rev. L. TOMLINSON. With numerous Illustrations and Diagrams. A valuable Chapter in this book is devoted exclusively to Comets, and was expressly compiled by Arago to dissipate the great apprehension of danger to the earth by the movement of these heavenly bodies.

Post 8vo, price 6s. cloth gilt,

THE MICROSCOPE: its History, Construction, and Application. New Edition, with numerous Additions. By JABEZ HOGG, Author of "Elements of Natural Philosophy," &c., Assistant-Surgeon to the Royal Ophthalmic Hospital, Charing Cross.

"This book is intended for the uninitiated, to whom we cordially recommend it as a useful and trustworthy guide. It well deserves the popularity to which it has already attained."—*British and Foreign Medico-Chirurgical Review.*

Fcap. 8vo, price 6s. half bound,

A DICTIONARY OF TRADE PRODUCTS: Commercial, Manufacturing, and Technical Terms. With a definition of the Moneys, Weights, and Measures of all Countries, reduced to the British standard.

"Is a work of reference, such as is needed in every industrial establishment."—*The Times.*

Fcap. 8vo, price 1s. 6d. boards, or cloth, 2s.

NOVELTIES, INVENTIONS, AND CURIOSITIES IN ARTS AND MANUFACTURES. By GEORGE DODD, Author of "Curiosities of Industry," &c.

"Every novelty, invention, or curiosity that modern science has brought to light is here explained in an easy and natural style."

In post 8vo, cloth, price 6s.,

THE BOY'S PLAYBOOK OF SCIENCE. By JOHN HENRY PEPPER, late Chemical Lecturer at the Royal Polytechnic Institution. With 300 Illustrations by HINE, includes the Manipulations and Arrangements of Apparatus required for the performance of experiments, illustrating the various branches of natural philosophy.

Fcap. 8vo, price **6d.**, limp cloth,

THE VILLAGE MUSEUM; or, How we gathered Profit with Pleasure. By the Rev. G. T. HOARE, of Taudridge, Surrey. General Contents :—What is a Museum ?—A First Visit—The Shark— The Microscope—Antiquities—Works of Art— Hieroglyphics — China— Pictures—Models—Needlework—Zoological Gardens—The Use of Arms— Air Pump—Cotton and Manufactures—Precious Stones, &c. &c.

In 13 vols., demy 8vo, price **42s.**, cloth ; or in half-calf extra (13 vols. iu 7), **63s.** ; or the 13 vols. in 7, half russia, **70s.**,

KNIGHT'S NATIONAL CYCLOPÆDIA OF USEFUL KNOWLEDGE; founded on the Penny Cyclopædia, but brought down to the present state of information.

Demy 8vo, cloth, price **5s.**,

SUPPLEMENT TO THE NATIONAL CYCLOPÆDIA OF USEFUL KNOWLEDGE. By P. AUSTIN NUTTALL, LL.D. This Volume (Vol. 13) comprises under a distinct alphabetical arrangement all the accumulated information of the last 12 years. Many articles, entirely new, have been written : and all the leading subjects of the twelve preceding volumes have been carefully written up to the present time ; it comprehends nearly 2700 articles replete with varied and useful information.

In 2 vols., royal 8vo, 1100 pages in each vol., price **£2 2s.**, cloth lettered, or half-bound in russia or calf, **£2 10s.**

CRAIG'S DICTIONARY, founded on WEBSTER'S. Being an Etymological, Technological, and Pronouncing Dictionary of the English Language, including all terms used in Literature, Science, and Art.

To show the value of the Work, the General Contents are given :—

IN LAW — All the Terms and Phrases used and defined by the highest legal authorities.

IN MEDICAL SCIENCE — All the Terms used in Great Britain and other Countries in Europe.

IN BOTANY—All the Genera in Don's great work, and Loudon's Encyclopædia, and the Orders as given by Lindley in his Vegetable Kingdom.

IN ZOOLOGY — All the Classes, Orders, and Genera, as given by Cuvier, Swainson, Gray, Blainville, Lamarck, Agassiz, &c.

IN GEOLOGY, MINERALOGY, CONCHOLOGY, ICHTHYOLOGY, MAMMOLOGY—All the terms employed are carefully described.

IN MECHANICS AND COMMERCE— It contains a complete Encyclopædia of everything eminently useful to every class of society, and in general use.

IN QUOTATIONS—There are above 3000 Quotations from standard old authors, illustrating obsolete words.

IN DERIVATIONS AND PRONUNCIATION—All English known words are fully expressed.

Price **6d.**, sewed wrapper,

THE EARTH: Past, Present, and Future. A Lecture delivered by the Rev. GEORGE H. SUMNER, M.A., Rector of Old Alresford, Hants, and Chaplain to his Grace the Archbishop of Canterbury.

Post 8vo, price **9s.**, cloth extra,

SEAMANSHIP AND NAVAL DUTIES. By A. H. ALSTON, Lieut. Royal Navy. Comprising in detail the Fitting out of a Man-of-War; Her Management under all Circumstances at Sea; and the Employment of her Resources in all Cases of General Service. With a Treatise on NAUTICAL SURVEYING. With 200 Practical Illustrations.

BOTANY AND GARDENING.

REEVE'S

POPULAR NATURAL HISTORIES.

(BOTANICAL DIVISION).

Price **7s. 6d.** each, cloth gilt, with Coloured Illustrations.

" A popular series of scientific treatises, which, from the simplicity of their style, and the artistic excellence and correctness of their numerous illustrations, has acquired a celebrity beyond that of any other series of modern cheap works."—*Standard.*

GARDEN BOTANY; containing a Familiar and Scientific Description of most of the Hardy and Half-hardy Plants introduced into the Flower Garden. By AGNES CATLOW. With 20 Pages of Coloured Illustrations, embracing 67 Plates.

GREENHOUSE BOTANY; containing a Familiar and Technical Description of the Exotic Plants introduced into the Greenhouse. By AGNES CATLOW. With 20 Pages of Coloured Illustrations.

FIELD BOTANY; containing a Description of the Plants common to the British Isles. By AGNES CATLOW. With 20 Pages of Coloured Illustrations, embracing 80 Plates.

ECONOMIC BOTANY; a Description of the Botanical and Commercial Characters of the principal articles of Vegetable origin, used for Food, Clothing, Tanning, Dyeing, Building, Medicine, Perfumery, &c. By THOMAS C. ARCHER, Collector for the Department of Applied Botany in the Crystal Palace, Sydenham. With 20 Pages of Coloured Illustrations, embracing 106 Plates.

[*Continued.*

REEVE'S POPULAR NATURAL HISTORIES—*continued.*
Price 7s. 6d. each, cloth gilt, with Coloured Illustrations.

THE WOODLANDS : a Description of Forest Trees, Ferns, Mosses, and Lichens.   By MARY ROBERTS.   With 20 Pages of Coloured Plates.

GEOGRAPHY OF PLANTS ; or, a Botanical Excursion round the World.   By E. M. C.   Edited by CHARLES DAUBENY, M.D., F.R.S., &c.   With 20 Pages of Coloured Plates of Scenery.

PALMS AND THEIR ALLIES ; containing a Familiar Account of their Structure, Distribution, History, Properties, and Uses ; and a complete List of all the Species introduced into our Gardens. By BERTHOLD SEEMANN, Ph.D., M.A., F.L.S.   With 20 Pages of Coloured Illustrations, embracing many varieties.

BRITISH FERNS AND THE ALLIED PLANTS ; comprising the Club-Mosses, Pepperworts, and Horsetails.   By THOMAS MOORE, F.L.S.   With 20 Pages of Coloured Illustrations, embracing 51 subjects.

BRITISH MOSSES ; comprising a General Account of their Structure, Fructification, Arrangement, and Distribution.   By ROBERT M. STARK, F.R.S.E.   With 20 Pages of Coloured Illustrations, embracing 80 subjects.

BRITISH LICHENS ; comprising an Account of their Structure, Reproduction, Uses, Distribution, and Classification.   By W. LAUDER LINDSAY, M.D.   With 22 Pages of Coloured Plates, embracing 400 subjects.

BRITISH SEAWEEDS ; comprising their Structure, Fructification, Specific Characters, Arrangement, and General Distribution, with Notices of some of the Fresh-water ALGÆ.   By the Rev. D. LANDSBOROUGH, A.L.S.   With 20 Pages of Coloured Illustrations, embracing 80 subjects.

Cloth limp, price 1s.,

FAVOURITE FLOWERS: How to Grow them ; being a Complete Treatise on the Cultivation of the Principal Flowers, with Descriptive Lists of all the best varieties in cultivation.   By ALFRED GILLETT SUTTON, F.H.S., Editor of "The Midland Florist."

In small post 8vo, price 5s. cloth, or 5s. 6d. gilt edges ; or in illuminated cover, bevelled boards, and gilt edges, 6s.,

A TOUR ROUND MY GARDEN.   By ALPHONSE KARR. Revised and Edited by the Rev. J. G. WOOD.   The Third Edition, finely printed.   With upwards of 117 Illustrations by W. Harvey.

Fcap., cloth gilt, price 2s. 6d.,

THE KITCHEN AND FLOWER GARDEN; or, the Culture in the open ground of Roots, Vegetables, Herbs, and Fruits, and of Bulbous, Tuberous, Fibrous, Rooted, and Shrubby Flowers. By EUGENE SEBASTIAN DELAMER.

Also, sold separately, each 1s.,

THE KITCHEN GARDEN. | THE FLOWER GARDEN.

In fcap. 8vo, price 3s. 6d. cloth gilt, or with gilt edges, 4s.,

WANDERINGS AMONG THE WILD FLOWERS: How to See and how to Gather them. With Remarks on the Economical and Medicinal Uses of our Native Plants. By SPENCER THOMSON, M.D. A New Edition, entirely revised, with 171 Woodcuts, and Eight large Coloured Illustrations by Noel Humphreys.

Also, price 2s., in boards, a Cheap Edition, with Plain Plates.

Fcap., price 3s. 6d. cloth gilt, or 4s. gilt edges,

OUR WOODLANDS, HEATHS, AND HEDGES; a Popular Description of Trees, Shrubs, Wild Fruits, &c., with Notices of their Insect Inhabitants. By W. S. COLEMAN, M.E.S.L. With 41 Illustrations printed in Colours on 8 Plates.

₊ A Cheap Edition, with Plain Plates, fancy boards, price 1s.

Fancy boards, price 1s.,

BRITISH FERNS AND THEIR ALLIES; comprising also the Club-Mosses, Pepperworts, and Horsetails. By THOMAS MOORE, F.L.S., &c. With 40 Illustrations by W. S. Coleman.

In square 16mo, price 2s. 6d., cloth limp,

FIRST STEPS TO ECONOMIC BOTANY; a Description of the Botanical and Commercial Characters of the Chief Articles of Vegetable Origin used for Food, Clothing, Tanning, Dyeing, Building, Medicine, Perfumery, &c. For the Use of Schools. By THOMAS C. ARCHER. With 20 Pages of Plates, embracing 106 Figures.

"An admirable and cheap little volume, abounding in good illustrations of the plants that afford articles of food or applicable to purposes of manufacture. This should be on the table of every family, and its contents familiar with all rising minds."—*Atlas.*

Fcap., cloth limp, price 1s.,

FLAX AND HEMP: Their Culture and Manipulation. By E. SEBASTIAN DELAMER. With Illustrations.

"We may, if we choose, grow our own hemp to quite an indefinite extent, and hold ourselves independent of foreign supply. The soil of Ireland alone is capable of sending forth an enormous export."—*Preface.*

AGRICULTURE AND FARMING.

———♦———

MECHI'S SYSTEM OF FARMING.
Price 3s. boards, or 3s. 6d. half-bound,

HOW TO FARM PROFITABLY; or, the Sayings and Doings of Mr. Alderman Mechi. With a Portrait and three other Illustrations, from Photographs by Mayall. New Edition, with additions.

The above work contains : Mr. Mechi's account of the Agricultural improvements carried on at the Tiptree Estate—His Lectures, Speeches, Correspondence, and Balance Sheets—and is a faithful history of his Agricultural career during the last fifteen years.

₊ In this Edition is incorporated Mr. Mechi's valuable Pamphlets on TOWN SEWAGE and STEAM PLOUGHING.

———

In 1 vol. price 5s. half-bound,

RHAM'S DICTIONARY OF THE FARM. A New Edition, entirely Revised and Re-edited, with Supplementary Matter, by W. and HUGH RAYNBIRD. With numerous Illustrations.

This book, which has always been looked up to as a useful and general one for reference on all subjects connected with country life and rural economy, has undergone an entire revision by its present editors, and many new articles on agricultural implements, artificial manures, bones, draining, guano, labour, and a practical paper upon the subject of animal, bird, and insect vermin inserted, which at once renders it an invaluable work for all who take pleasure in, or make a business of, rural pursuits.

———

Limp cloth, price 1s.,

SMALL FARMS. A Practical Treatise intended for Persons inexperienced in Husbandry, but desirous of employing time and capital in the cultivation of the soil. By MARTIN DOYLE.

———

In fcap. 8vo, price 2s. cloth boards, or 1s. 6d. cloth limp,

AGRICULTURAL CHEMISTRY. Comprising Chemistry of the Atmosphere, Chemistry of the Soil, Water, Plants—Means of Restoring the impaired Fertility of Land exhausted by the growth of Cultivated Crops, and of improving Land naturally Infertile—Vegetable and Animal Produce of the Farm. By ALFRED SIBSON (Royal Agricultural College, Cirencester), with a Preface by Dr. Augustus Voelcker, Consulting Chemist of the Royal Agricultural Society. With Illustrations.

" This is an excellent treatise—comprehensive, full of most useful, and, to the agriculturist, necessary information. It enters fully into the composition and various physical conditions of soil, atmosphere, and other agents which contribute to agricultural results. It should be in the possession of every agriculturist in the kingdom."—Weekly Times.

In post 8vo, price 5s. half-bound,

BRITISH TIMBER TREES. By JOHN BLENKARN, C.E.
The work is essentially practical—the result of long experience and observation, and will be found of especial service to Landed Proprietors, Land Agents, Solicitors, Landscape Gardeners, Nurserymen, Timber Merchants, Timber Valuers, Architects, Auctioneers, Civil Engineers, and all persons having the management of, or in any way connected with, the improvement of Landed Estates.

In post 8vo, price 5s. half-bound,

THE PIG. By WILLIAM YOUATT, V.S. Its History, Breeding, Feeding, and Management in Health and Disease. Enlarged and re-written by Samuel Sidney, Member of the Central Farmers' Club, and Author of "The Illustrated Rarey's Horse-Taming." With numerous original Illustrations.

"This work, although nominally a new edition, is substantially a new book, describing the breeds, and giving directions for breeding and feeding English Pigs. All those portions of Mr. Youatt's book which had become obsolete or of no value have been omitted, and information judiciously brought together is substituted, which, so to speak, brings our knowledge of the subject treated of down to the present moment, and shows the present practice and opinions of our most successful and intelligent breeders."—*Mid Counties Herald, Birmingham.*

Cloth limp, price 1s.,

THE PIG. How to Choose, how to Breed, how to Feed, how to Cut-up, how to Cure. By W. C. L. MARTIN. Revised and Improved by Samuel Sidney.

"I have condensed from the principal agricultural periodicals the pith of many capital contributions, and consulted my Pig-breeding friends in six counties. The chapters 'Will a Pig pay?' 'How to choose a Pig,' 'The Chemistry of Pig-feeding,' and 'Pigs for Workhouses,' are new, and I believe, valuable additions to the volume."—*Editor's Preface.*

Cloth limp, price 1s. 6d.,

CATTLE: their Breeds, Management, and Diseases. To which is added THE DAIRY. By W. C. L. MARTIN. Revised and Improved by William and Hugh Raynbird.

Fcap., price 2s. 6d. half-bound,

THE HORSE: its History, Varieties, Conformation, Management in Health and Disease. With 8 Illustrations. By WILLIAM YOUATT. A New Edition by CECIL, with Observations on Breeding CAVALRY HORSES.

** A Cheap Edition, thin paper and limp cloth, price 1s.

Cloth limp, price 1s.,

B EES : their Habits, Management, and Treatment. By the Rev. J. G. Wood, Author of the "Illustrated Natural History."

Crown 8vo, price 5s. half-bound,

I LLUSTRATED BOOK OF DOMESTIC POULTRY. Edited by Martin Doyle. With 20 Illustrations, printed in Colours, from Designs by Weigall.

Cloth limp, price 1s.,

T HE POULTRY YARD. Comprising the Management of Fowls for Use and Exhibition. By W. C. L. Martin. Revised by Miss E. Watts. With 12 Illustrations.

Cloth limp, price 1s.,

S HEEP : their Domestic Breeds and Treatment. With 8 Illustrations. By W. C. L. Martin.

In post 8vo, price 2s. 6d., cloth extra,

S CIENTIFIC FARMING MADE EASY. By Thomas C. Fletcher, Agricultural and Analytical Chemist.

GENERAL CONTENTS OF THIS VOLUME, VIZ.:—

Habits and Food of Plants.
Carbonic Acid.
Constituents of Water.
Ammonia.
What Plants derive from Carbon.

Inorganic Constituents of Plants.
Manures. Artificial ditto.
Chemistry of the Dung-hill.
Gas Refuse, Lime, Bones, etc.
Cattle Feeding, Appendix, etc.

SPORTING AT HOME AND ABROAD.

In 1 thick vol. fcap. 8vo, price 10s. 6d. half-bound, 11th Thousand,

BRITISH RURAL SPORTS : comprising Shooting, Hunting, Coursing, Fishing, Hawking, Racing, Boating, Pedestrianism, and the various Rural Games and Amusements of Great Britain. By STONE-HENGE, Author of "The Greyhound." Illustrated by numerous Engravings, from designs by WELLS, HARVEY, and HIND.

"Invaluable to all Sportsmen."—*Bell's Life.*
"The very best and most instructive work on British Rural Sports."—*Sporting Review.*
"The English Sportsman's vade mecum."—*Illustrated News.*
"A complete, readable, and instructive book."—*The Field.*

Post 8vo, 10s. 6d., half-bound,

THE SHOT-GUN AND SPORTING RIFLE ; By STONE-HENGE. With full descriptions of the Dogs, Ponies, Ferrets, &c., used in all kinds of Shooting and Trapping. Illustrated with 20 large page Engravings, and 100 Woodcuts, finely printed.

The comprehensive nature of the "Shot-Gun and Sporting Rifle" will be best shown by a General Summary of its Contents, viz. :—

THE GAME-KEEPER'S ASSISTANT.

Choice of Preserve, or Shooting—The Game-keeper and his Duties—Rearing of Game—Trapping Vermin—Poachers—The Game-Laws.

SHOOTING DOGS, PONIES, FERRETS, &c.

Pointers and Setters—Spaniels—Retrievers—Rabbit Dogs and Ferrets—General Management of Shooting Dogs—Shooting Ponies.

THE SHOT-GUN.

Principles of Construction—Varieties in Common Use—Muzzle or Breech-loaders—Choice of Guns—Gun-makers, and Prices—Gun Trials—Powder, Shot, Caps, &c.—Management of Shot-guns.

THE SPORTING RIFLE.

Principles of Construction—Varieties suited to the Sportsman—The Muzzle and Breech-loader—The Revolver—Choice of the Rifle—Makers and Price —Rifle Trials—Powder, Balls, &c.—Management of the Rifle.

SHOOTING IN ALL ITS VARIETIES.

Preparatory Shooting—First Lessons in Shooting—Hedge Popping—Rook Shooting—Pigeon and Sparrow Trap Shooting—Laws and Practice of ditto —Grouse and Partridge Shooting—Snipe Shooting—Covert Shooting—Wild Fowl Shooting—Ditto Inland—Ditto Marine—Rifle Shooting—Target Practice—Rook and Rabbit Shooting—The Use of the Rifle in Stalking Deer and Large Game, &c., &c., &c.

"This is one of the most useful and practical manuals that has ever appeared, and proves that the writer is thoroughly conversant with the subject upon which he treats. No Sportsman or country gentleman should be without this work, which will prove a standard volume for generations to come."—*Sporting Magazine,* Oct. 1, 1859